The
FABRIC
of
NIGHT

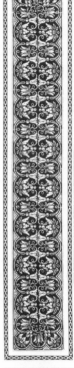

The
FABRIC
of
NIGHT

CHRISTOPH PETERS

TRANSLATED FROM THE GERMAN BY

JOHN CULLEN

Nan A. Talese · Doubleday

New York   London   Toronto   Sydney   Auckland

PUBLISHED BY NAN A. TALESE
AN IMPRINT OF DOUBLEDAY

Published in the United States by Nan A. Talese, an imprint of
The Doubleday Broadway Publishing Group, a division
of Random House, Inc., New York.
www.nanatalese.com

DOUBLEDAY is a registered trademark of Random House, Inc.

The Fabric of Night was first published in 2003 under the title *Das Tuch
aus Nacht* by btb, an imprint of Wilhelm Goldmann Verlag, Munich.

Book design by Michael Collica

Library of Congress Cataloging-in-Publication Data
Peters, Christoph, 1966–
[Tuch aus Nacht. English]
The fabric of night / Christoph Peters ; translated from the German by
John Cullen.
p. cm.
I. Cullen, John, 1942– II. Title.
PT2676.E7719T8313 2007
833'.92—dc22
2006045551

ISBN-13: 978-0-385-51447-7
ISBN-10: 0-385-51447-6

1 3 5 7 9 10 8 6 4 2

First Edition

Thou shalt not make unto thee any graven image, or any likeness of any thing that is in heaven above, or that is in the earth beneath, or that is in the water under the earth: Thou shalt not bow down thyself to them, nor serve them.

EXODUS 20:4-5

The honor paid to the image passes to its prototype.

BASIL THE GREAT

Truth is an image, but there is no image of truth.

MARIE-JOSÉ MONDZAIN

We all know that art isn't the truth. Art is a lie that teaches us to grasp the truth.

PABLO PICASSO

Art is art, and everything else is everything else.

AD REINHARDT

What is truth?

PONTIUS PILATE

The
FABRIC
of
NIGHT

1.

"Take care of you, baby."

I wonder how Albin came up with this ridiculous expression. It seems highly unlikely that he could have actually heard it. Maybe if there had been a very strong offshore wind, but not otherwise. Under ordinary circumstances, if you're here, you can't hear anything that's being said over there; the Otelo Sultan and the Duke's Palace are much too far apart. And besides, it should be, "Take care of *yourself,* baby."

Later, when Livia and I were alone, she described what happened, but she didn't say anything about wind. It was a cold morning, she said. The yellow sun was shining through dark, lowering clouds, and there was no way of telling what the weather would be like. Maybe the day will turn out fine, she thought, or maybe it'll rain again, like yesterday and the day before that. The morning light was quite pleasant—filtered, but still bright. Although they hadn't quarreled, Albin remained silent. He looked pale as he sat there, mechanically chewing a sesame ring and drinking pots of coffee. A beautiful man, Livia thought, in spite of everything; beautiful like a chalk cliff. She'd woken up hungry and loaded her plate at the buffet with olives, sheep's milk cheese, sausage, ham, and eggs, the kind of breakfast Albin always found nauseating. On this occasion, however, he diverged from his usual practice and kept his opinions to himself. They'd known each other long enough to be untroubled by silence, so Livia saw no reason to break it, either. Nevertheless, it was a silence that Albin had clearly started, all on his own. For her part, Livia would have been glad to discuss their plans for the day, analyze the puzzling acne epidemic among the waiters, or speculate about Miller's business deals. After a while, for no discernible reason and with his mouth full, Albin said, "The minarets stick up into the sky like acupuncture needles, diverting energy into the right channels."

He did not, however, expect a reply. The image appealed to her. Lost in thought, still warm from sleep, she turned in her chair, shifting her eyes from the view she was facing—narrow, sloping streets, and beyond them the sea—to share Albin's view: the city, with its countless mosques and its covered Grand Bazaar. And then, suddenly, there was this ship. She hadn't noticed it earlier— maybe Albin's remark made her look more closely—but there on the horizon, which seemed to have slid strangely to the left and moved much closer, she suddenly saw a burning ship. It was already listing badly, about to sink into the water at any moment. Thin black plumes of smoke drifted away toward the southwest. She was expecting a soundless explosion or, at the very least, a flare-up, an eruption of flames. The thought that people might be in danger, or even that there were people on the ship, never occurred to her, nor did she feel any impulse to point out the sinking vessel to Albin. For a few moments, she considered going inside and getting her camera out of their room, but not because disasters are always big sellers and the burning ship offered the prospect of some highly marketable shots. No, Livia wanted her camera because—and here she stopped, shrugged her shoulders, and lit a cigarette—because something was bothering her, something didn't seem right. At the time she was telling me this, she still didn't know what exactly it was that had caused her uneasiness, but in any case the camera stayed in the room, because after a few minutes, she realized she wasn't looking at the horizon at all, nor was there any blazing ship, just an immensely long harbor warehouse that kept appearing between blocks of houses. It was venting ordinary smoke from its heating system through a red-and-white striped chimney. Livia laughed—or rather, she tried to laugh—but found she couldn't and shook her head. Discovering the true nature of her vision had done nothing to alleviate her discomfort; on the contrary, she was left with a sinking, anchorless feeling, as if she'd stopped being able to read her watch all of a sudden or had accidentally tried to unlock some stranger's door.

After Albin had eaten three quarters of his sesame ring, he went out onto the roof terrace to throw the rest to the hotel's two resident seagulls. He knew they'd fight over the bread. As soon as the crumbs hit the tiles, the birds would spread their wings and start hopping around each other, making evil hissing sounds and flashing their narrow tongues like little knives. From where she was sitting, Livia had a good view of this scene, but then Albin disappeared in the direction of the artificial sunbathing lawn, probably because he was hoping to peer through the windows across the way and catch a glimpse of something interesting, a woman getting dressed, say, or a father striking his daughter. Up to this point, Livia said, she hadn't noticed anything unusual about Albin; she was certainly accustomed to his silences.

For this time period, Livia's account is all I have to rely on, because at that moment the rest of us were on an InterCity train, the Markgräfler Land, somewhere between Mannheim and Frankfurt. Mona was sitting at my side. For the last ten minutes, she'd been holding a sharpened pencil in one hand and staring at her brand-new Istanbul city map, searching in vain for the street where our hotel was supposed to be. According to the index, the Duke's Palace Hotel was to be found in quadrant F5, but Tiyatro Caddesi, the street the hotel was on, wasn't marked on the map. The Ramada, the Baron, the Prestige, and the Sultan were also allegedly in F5. However, there were only four blue *H*'s in this square, all of them so haphazardly placed that they could have been on any one of two or three different streets. With the help of a list of addresses, she'd managed to identify the Ramada, the Baron, and the Prestige, but she still had to choose between one of the remaining two hotels.

"I really want to know where we're going to spend the next ten days," Mona said.

"Forget about it," I said. "They can't be more than fifty meters apart, so it doesn't matter."

"All the same, I want to know."

"As soon as we're on the street—"

"I want to know *now*, Olaf, not later!"

Although Istanbul lies on practically the same latitude as Naples, cold air sweeping in from Siberia had already made the temperature quite chilly. Albin was shivering as he leaned over the balustrade. Because the Duke's Palace stands farther down the slope (which of course Mona had no way of knowing about, as her map didn't show topography), the Otelo Sultan towered above Albin. He noticed that two of the Sultan's guests, Mr. Miller and his girlfriend, Ireen, were finishing their breakfast, which had been served not in the designated breakfast room but in their suite, with champagne as well as coffee, and ham and eggs freshly cooked in a skillet instead of warmed in a metal steam tray. Albin watched Miller light a long cigarillo. The blue smoke hovered festively over the remains of the meal, and while Mona was sitting in the train, penciling a circle around the last *H* without knowing that it actually stood for the Duke's Palace, Livia went back to the hotel room to take a shower. Ireen leaned away from the table, binding her hair in a loose knot. In a room on the floor below, the wrinkled back of an older woman emerged from the darkness as she awkwardly tried to fasten her brassiere. Albin grimaced, first in disparagement of aging flesh, second because he found his interest in other people's lives banal, and third because he had heartburn. The seagulls perched on the railing and ogled the guests in their rooms. Later, Mona tried to draw the gulls, even going so far as to get special permission from the hotel to stay on the terrace after breakfast was over, but at about ten-thirty, when the buffet was being cleared away, the birds sprang into the air and glided toward the harbor. It didn't matter, because she could never have captured the suspicion in their eyes. Mona's drawing skills are limited; that's why she's in such demand as a model.

It was very quiet on the terrace, Albin told me, so he went out there for half an hour every morning after breakfast. According to him, Istanbul consists of pure cacophony, and that terrace was the only quiet place he ever found. He thought of the endless tumult as the binding material that held the city together: if the noise stopped, the whole place would fly apart. This last observation was an example of Albin's fondness for dramatic phrases. However, as far as the quiet on the roof terrace of the Duke's Palace Hotel is concerned, he was right. The all-enveloping uproar—the noise of engines, horns, fan belts, brakes; the shouts of infuriated drivers, eager tradesmen, worried mothers, ill-bred children—stops halfway up the façade of the building. Up there, on the terrace, all you can hear is a distant murmuring, scarcely louder than the sea, and now and then the howl of a ship's siren.

Albin said that Miller's balcony door was wide open. He heard Ireen laughing, a long, melodious laugh, slightly forced, and then

Miller leaned over her and whispered something. He spoke too softly for Albin to hear, but Ireen suddenly looked terrified, and then—Albin said he didn't care whether I believed this or not—Miller said, "Take care of you, baby." This sentence struck Albin as rather fatuous, even coming from an American, but a split second later a sound sizzled over the rooftops, a short, sharp sound like rubber bursting or the cork coming out of a wine bottle, and Miller fell forward, still holding the cigarillo pressed between his lips. He didn't writhe, nor did any look of pain distort his face. His forehead struck his plate first, and then the glass tabletop. Miller was a giant, at least six foot three and well over three hundred pounds. With his puffy eyes and slicked-down hair, Albin said, Miller looked like Marlon Brando in old age.

2.

Now that it's dark, you can really hear how old the engines sound. I'd have to shout over them if I wanted anyone to understand me. From time to time they perform a brief variation, three or four beats in another key, marginally quieter. Actually, the volume is of secondary importance. Any noise that goes on long enough and keeps to a primitive rhythm generates silence. Conversely, in a soundproof room the rustling of your own shirt can frighten you, and a fair amount of time will pass before fear relaxes its grip on your chest. There's a mild breeze.

With this burning cigarette in my mouth, I'd make a good target.

Snatches of American hit tunes filter through the swinging doors. Their glass panes are etched with strange decorations: cables, propellers, anchors, exotic flowers, and leafy branches coiling through a traditional network of rays. If there's a system to all this, it's not readily apparent. At home, we call all passenger ships Dampfer, "steamers." If I should lean farther out over the railing, I'd lose my balance, or at the very least I'd be in danger. My disappearance wouldn't be noticed before we docked—unless Livia should suddenly decide there's something she absolutely must tell me. But that doesn't seem likely.

Meanwhile, the Bosporus is black and viscous and reacts fairly sluggishly to the movement of the ship. Maybe it just seems sluggish because you can't hear the waves striking the hull—in fact, you can't hear them at all. It's as if we were floating on a sea of oil. Early this morning, the water was a shimmering blue, like scratched steel, and the sunlight was refracted in the scratches. The last clouds were moving out, headed west. They didn't look like rain, they looked like ornaments.

There's no moon. It rises around midnight, wanders around until late morning, and then falls apart. Not counting the crew, there are maybe thirty people on board. That's why they haven't even switched on the string lights.

Pain again. Somewhat worse than usual at the moment, but not too bad. It could be in the stomach, the gallbladder, the intestine, the liver. It hurts more since we've been here, but the anxiety's gone.

The reflections of the shore lights are cut into narrow yellow strips. The yellowing photographs that show passengers how to put on a life jacket are hard to see now. Professor Nager's lying below the photographs, sleeping off this afternoon's mild carouse. He's a fairly well known sculptor in his mid-forties. In the light of the neon tubes, his face looks like it belongs to an unembellished corpse. The dead man plainly had too much to drink. Rust spots discolor the planks here and there. The wooden benches are worn smooth and covered with a mix of messages from the last several decades. Turkish words with exclamation points. A phallus spraying out "Fuck the U.S." "Jon was here 7/3/71." Not many little hearts. Miller's name was Jon, too, Jonathan, to be exact, but Ireen called him Jon. I don't know when he came to Istanbul for the first time, but I doubt that he cut his name into a bench. I think about this other Jon for a while, so his carving was not in vain.

In the summer of '71, my father bought the vacation home, a thatched-roof cottage near Marienhafe. I collected crabs and starfish and put them in plastic bowls, where they died within a few hours. Sundays were car-free days, even though we had enough money to pay any price for gasoline. Xaver had to repeat a school year, and Mother cried a lot, but not because of that. Claes tried to operate on Charlotte, his guinea pig.

The pain goes away, dully, without any peaks; it belongs to someone else. It's as though an ichneumon wasp injected an egg into my bloodstream. Years ago, maybe. The larva found me a rich source of nourishment, and now it's a fat, slime-secreting worm, working itself around my vital organs with great care as well as an instinctive knowledge of human anatomy. I can't die, however, not yet; until the pupation process is over, I can't die. But now, the end is approaching, the signs are multiplying: sweating episodes, racing pulse. Street dogs scent something, draw in their tails, and give me a wide berth. At night, as sleep flees away, I lie on my back, able to distinguish clearly between my own heartbeat and the pounding of the alien blood. The air conditioner hums along monotonously; there's no gurgling or bubbling, not even the flapping of a rope in the ventilation shaft. Livia lies next to me. Her breathing seems a touch too quick.

Now Nager and I are the only two still out here. His girls got cold and withdrew belowdecks. Livia did the same. A brief interval ensued, and then the boys followed, slowly, one at a time, so it wouldn't seem as though they were chasing after the ladies. Jan went first, and now he's sitting up with her, I'd bet on it. Livia's talking and snapping pictures. I wonder what she sees in him. Then Hagen left, followed by Scherf, ostensibly to get some beers. That was half an hour ago, and the bar's about twenty meters away. A little later, Fritz suddenly discovered that he was cold, too. No one likes to sleep alone. Next went Olaf Rademacher, mumbling a few words that included "sketch something." I believe he's the only one who wasn't making up an excuse. His nostrils twitched as though he'd picked up a scent. Now he's perched somewhere out of the way, drawing cubes on graph paper.

Livia wanted to go to Istanbul, although or because she'd heard a thousand clichés about the city. Now she's decided to photograph these art students, who are as clueless about why they're here as we are. I can't imagine any magazine would be interested in such shots, but that's her affair.

On the east bank, behind the residences of the sultans and the viziers and the generals, they're shooting off fireworks. The sky is making an effort to look festive. I was twelve in 1978, the year our business burned down, together with all the trucks, backhoes, cranes, and Caterpillars. Four weeks later, a telegram came from Buenos Aires. Father wrote that we had nothing to worry about. He said he'd taken care of everything, but he didn't want to go into details. At the time, Uncle Gerald's chicken farm was turning a good profit, despite the occasional organized protests; his remittances arrived punctually on the first of every month. A few months after Father's disappearance, Uncle Gerald began ordering new cages and building expanded facilities. Claes hated Uncle Gerald. It was a while before I dared to go out onto the streets on New Year's Eve again.

Apparently, somebody with money and influence is giving his daughter a wedding the guests will still be talking about twenty years from now. A burning warehouse filled with heavy farm equipment makes a deafening noise, especially when the fuel tanks explode. The Big Dipper, the only constellation I'm sure of, is shining above the fireworks. Nager's snoring, competing with the engines. The drunker he gets, the more obvious his designs on Mona become, despite the fact that he's got a wife in Cologne, significantly younger than he is, and two little girls, for whom he's been buying souvenirs everywhere. He calls his wife a "top-notch girl." According to him, she doesn't look bad—looks quite good, in fact. He says that men who have reached a certain age are chiefly interested in propagation. In his view, love and sex are secondary considerations; it's the end result that counts. She was the secretary of the gallery owner who got him into the Documenta, the big contemporary art exhibition in Kassel. Among the also-rans, but still . . . Now she devotes all her attention to their progeny. He never refers to her by name. Of course, his real name isn't Nager, either, it's Walter Schaub-Scheffelbock. Livia found this out from Jan, who saw his passport when they came through customs. He and I could be friends.

I'm certain that Livia's sleeping with Jan. Let them do what they want. It doesn't interest me.

An ache spreads out from my chest into my arms. I drank raki with the prawns I had for lunch, which were very fresh indeed. I stare at the black water, trying to see my reflection, cut into strips like the lights on the shore.

Very soon, it will stop. The whole thing was futile. Right from the beginning, something didn't fit. I failed to establish a connection. I slid between people and places, gliding on a smooth, sloping surface, every action a sham, performed because one must do something, one can't do nothing; there's too much outside pressure. And then you look back, and that's what your life was made of.

The Big Dipper's empty, an old pot rusted through and through. I would have liked to learn how to find my way by the stars, like a caravan leader or an old sea captain. Then I could have sought out Father's grave in Bahía Blanca and spat on his stone image. But with the exception of Claes, there's no one in our family who can even identify birdcalls, to say nothing of constellations, and Claes taught himself, with the help of some phonograph records. I'd really like to know why Jonathan Miller was shot. I saw him die—that forms a bond. Dying is an intimate matter; one doesn't often get the chance to watch people doing it. Why did Messut Yeter deny so vehemently that Miller had a room in the Sultan? And where has Ireen disappeared to? If I knew the answers to those questions, nothing would change . . .

Bit by bit, I've become part of an alien organism. By now, I'm nothing but the thin shell around a being that consists entirely of me. It's transformed my complex primate structure into the simple configuration of a prehistoric insect. I can feel it moving, struggling to burst out of its cocoon.

The cigarettes will last until we get ashore. If I have to, I can borrow tobacco from Olaf. I'm dizzy. I feel as though I've climbed up a steep flight of stairs, drunk. My cigarette lighter's flame shivers as a freighter with a heavy cargo passes close to us. The point of light is right before my eyes. It flares up, goes out. A blow tears my chest apart. Then warmth pours over me. Soundlessness. The smoke tastes like iron. Why don't I feel any pain?

Ethereal tickling, buzzing capillaries. My blood vessels groan like an obsolescent steamer, stoked by a madman bent on setting a record. With every breath, my pulse throbs harder. In my groin, in my temples, in my neck. The steam turbines hiss as they drive the ship onward, but it's slowing down instead of going faster. It's as though an invisible hand were resting on the paddle wheel. For a slow motion shot, Livia says, the camera exposes a minimum of fifty frames per second, twice as many as usual. Maybe a sudden rush of adrenaline flooding the brain makes it capable of processing considerably greater amounts of information, so that all movement, for a second, comes to a standstill.

3.

Ireen didn't scream. Her vocal cords shirked their duty. She stumbled across the room, turned the key in the door, opened it, stepped out cautiously into the hall, sank briefly to her knees, and then pulled herself together, intercepting her faint at the last moment like someone catching an expensive cup knocked off its shelf by a careless elbow. But she didn't look relieved. Miller was wearing a thick jacket, cut in the English country-house style, and it had fallen in such a way that Albin could see neither wound nor blood. The material of the jacket had stood up to the shards of glass from the tabletop. Ireen started looking for the elevator, but she couldn't remember which way to go. Her breathing was shallow and very rapid. She pressed herself against the wall, dug her nails into the rough plaster, felt no pain when they broke, and slid to the floor. Her hair caught on the plaster and spread out above her head. Miller's upper body ground deeper into the glass. The strange sound made her flinch—it must have been quiet in the room. Death perched on the arm of a chair, laying his forefinger on his puckered lips. Now, at last, she cried out—or at least her lips moved—calling for someone to help her. Maybe Miller was still alive, maybe he could be saved. But the few people who occupied rooms on that floor were either at breakfast or already fanning out for sightseeing or business transactions. The housecleaning staff had begun its daily dawdling.

Later, Albin told me that he'd stood there like an idiot for a few seconds or a few minutes, he couldn't be sure, shifting his gaze back and forth between Miller's dead body at the table and Ireen in a heap on the floor. He said the hall outside the room was brightly lit, so he was able to see Ireen quite well, at least in silhouette. Miller's corpse, wedged among fragments of broken glass, put Albin in mind of Jacques Cousteau's ship *Calypso,* trapped in the pack ice. Albin freely admitted he'd had a hangover that morning but couldn't see how it might have made any difference. On the contrary, he said, "Every time I visit a museum after boozing all night without sleep, I realize I see things more clearly in that condition. My perceptions are sharp as a blade." Albin went so far as to describe the cloud formations over the Sultan: white, chaotic-looking cirrus clouds very high up, and below them dark gray cumuli. The wind was tearing strips off their edges and whirling them into the blue. According to Albin, the gusts sweeping the terrace were sometimes quite strong.

Ireen's decision to move down the hall to the left, looking for the elevator, freed Albin from his paralysis. He began to run around, ten steps this way, ten steps that, spinning in a circle and agonizing over what to do. After a little thought, he started peering at the surrounding roofs and windows, looking for the shooter, who at that very moment was probably either dismantling his weapon or packing it into an inconspicuous suitcase or disappearing down the nearest fire escape, smartly but without haste. Like a scene in a bad movie. It's crucial to know where he fired from, Albin thought. Had any residents in the other buildings noticed anything unusual? Had someone merely made a bedroom available, preferring not to speculate about the wad of money he received in return? The police investigators could answer some questions by using computer simulations and other means of determining the line of fire. Albin saw no one who looked suspicious, and no curtain made a false move. He would have been well advised to procure another witness, a waiter or guest with stable nerves, if only to be certain he wasn't imagining things, and because four eyes see more than two. Instead of doing this, however, he shook his head for a long time and then went away without looking back. Before leaving the terrace, he kicked at the gulls, shooing them off for no apparent reason—maybe it was just a reflex, the one that causes you to kick a can into the gutter. No one on the hotel staff and none of the last coffee drinkers paid any attention to him. Afterward, no one could swear to having seen Albin make his way across the dining room, and no one had noticed how perturbed and nervous he was, how he kept yanking at his earlobes.

He took the elevator down to the third floor, where their room was, and where Livia was standing under the shower. The elevator took him there directly, without any intermediate stops. He found the soapy music villainous. Livia was enjoying the warm water and imagining the hands of a good hairdresser massaging her scalp. When Albin shouted, "Miller's been shot!" into the bathroom, she could barely understand him, and after he repeated himself she thought he was staging one of his usual farces.

"In retrospect," Livia says, "it was probably a mistake not to believe him. But you've seen him like that, Olaf, you know what condition he was in. Would you have believed him?"

"No."

"But your man Nager, he believed him."

"Nevertheless."

Whether out of contempt or because of his sheer delight in the game, Albin would make up stories to confuse and test his opponents. At such times, his face took on an earnestness that made people who didn't know him believe the most improbable things:

that NASA had recruited him because of his special genetic qualifications and very soon would send him up in the space shuttle to orbit the earth for ten days; that his father owned a gold mine in the Amazon forest, thus exempting him, Albin, from the necessity of holding down a job. Then he would immediately burst out laughing.

"One shot. About twenty minutes ago. At breakfast."

Livia asked him if he needed a doctor and went on to suggest, quite casually, that perhaps it was time for him to stop drinking so much.

"But Miller said, 'Take care of you, baby.' "

At this point, even though she hadn't finished rinsing the shampoo out of her hair, Livia turned off the shower, reached for the towel, wrapped it around her head, and stood before him like a marble beauty from ancient Greece, tall, graceful, and not too heavy in the hips.

"So what was he supposed to say? He's probably the godfather of the New York Cosa Nostra, and he told his girlfriend—what's her name again?"

"Ireen."

"He guessed what was coming, and he told Ireen all his secrets."

"I saw it happen."

Livia says there was a pleading, almost imploring undertone in his voice that irritated her at first; Albin never sounded like that. Now she's sure that tone was there, but at the time she decided she'd simply misheard or imagined it. All the same, something was obviously wrong; she could tell, because he didn't give her the usual once-over, examining her naked body to see whether he still liked it. Instead, he looked past her, playing with the lighter in his left hand while striving with his right to extract a cigarette from the pack in his jacket pocket without damaging the cigarette or removing the pack. He stared at the soap suds running down the tiles.

Albin didn't even stay to watch her dry herself off. She heard him flop on the bed and switch on the television. He did that only when he came home drunk or decided to drink himself senseless in the room.

During the course of the last night we wasted together in the hotel bar, Albin told me he hated television on principle, but engaging in the trouble-free operation of a technological product gave him back his confidence in his ability to take action. He could get the same feeling from driving a car, but then Livia wouldn't talk to him for two days.

A buxom, garishly made up woman was singing interminable melodies to imaginary lovers, then dancing with tinkling bells and rattling sabers. Commercials: for tea, featuring a childish song; for insect control, a cheap-looking animation in which the cockroaches made a favorable impression; for tea cakes, for bathroom tile, for scouring cleanser, *da dee don don*.

Albin clicked off the television and opened the window in hopes of hearing police or ambulance sirens. All he heard, however, was the usual honking and shouting. He thought his testimony might be important; in any case, he thought, he should report what he'd seen to the police—it was possible that he and Ireen were the only witnesses. Moreover, the Otelo Sultan had a bar that was open twenty-four hours a day.

Livia was standing in front of the washbasin and rubbing cream into her face. She saw her reflection in the mirror as a question, which, after some hesitation, she answered: she looked as though she had possibilities. Five years of Albin lay behind her.

They had often been horrible, but not always. She would never marry him. She would never marry anyone at all. Basically, she could leave whenever she wanted to.

Just before we got to the central station in Frankfurt, Mona, in a fit of nerves, broke off her futile search for the hotel. She grew visibly, increasingly furious, gnawing a pencil she would have preferred to jam into someone's back: into Corinna, perhaps, or Swantje, or Scherf, or Scherf's smarmy retainer, Hagen. Those last two had picked Istanbul as our destination and pushed everyone to agree, Mona said, "just because the rest of us were too dumb, too lazy, too *lame* to come up with any alternatives. Or did you want to go there, Olaf? Can you tell me the name of a single Turkish artist?"

"The geometrical ornamentation is interesting."

"To you, maybe. All the same, you two could have said something, you and Jan. As a rule, Jan never passes up an opportunity to quarrel with Hagen."

"Just wait a while."

"I'll bet Jan gets here at the last minute again."

Jan and Mona weren't a couple, even though the news that they were got passed around the academy at regular intervals, and even though she posed nude for him and him alone. If there had been anything between Jan and Mona, I would have known about it. Jan and I had gone to the same school since we were kids; we started college in the same semester, and we lived together until a short time ago. Be that as it may, however, Mona took off her clothes only when the door to his room was shut.

4.

What if everything goes backward after the standstill?

For the past few minutes, a pale green will-o'-the-wisp has been shimmering on the water where my reflection should be. All the same, and even though the city is moving closer, blackness envelops me like a sheet soaked in pitch. The green shimmer spreads itself on the sea, like an air cushion being inflated, then shrinks, then fills again, calmly and regularly. A buoyant jellyfish, almost floating through the air. If I stare at the pale glow, it doesn't disintegrate, it withstands my gaze. That's unusual. I can make out five fissurelike orifices—breathing holes or sense organs or stigmata—one in each corner, and one that looks a little bigger in the center. Puts me in mind of a playing card: the ace of spades.

The roar of the motors sounds far away now, as though the wind were carrying it here from the opposite bank. A movement like falling, wrapped in the fabric of night.

When we walk across the rickety landing stage in Düşünülen Yer and go back on board, it's four-thirty in the afternoon. The bloated body of a dog, covered with pink festering wounds, is floating between the quay wall and the ship's hull. The dog's eyes are gone and its side has burst open. Its mustard yellow coat combines with the capsized sky to produce a color scheme that reminds me of the enameled-tile friezes of Babylon. Lions, gazelles, stags, and mythical creatures against a background of overturned blue. A school of little fish, hungry or playful, surges into the dog's belly from below. "Tomorrow they'll be on someone's plate," I say to Livia, who's walking right behind me. "Pan-fried whole, with dog flesh in their guts."

And she groans loudly. Her face is so white that for a moment I'm afraid she's going to throw up. She swallows hard, but she doesn't turn away. While she stares at the spectacle, what strikes her most, overcoming even her nausea, is the utter defenselessness of the dog's carcass. Once she's on deck, she quickly digs her camera out of her bag, changes the wide-angle lens for a telescopic lens, leans over the rail so far it scares me, and shoots a whole roll of film in two minutes. I keep my hand on her unbearably lovely behind, now only a memory; I can barely hold her.

The sound is muffled but not dull. It's clearer than that, a silvery, whirring din, and it doesn't come from the sea. It's made up of a million sonic points, from the highest to the lowest, every imaginable note, and each one sharply defined against the menacing silence behind it. If my eyes could hear, a mountain lake in the full moon, between the glaciers and the icy cliffs, would sound like that.

Messut Yeter called our conclusions "provisional." I didn't know what he meant, so I asked him to give me an example of a "definitive" conclusion. He just laughed.

"I'm sure those are the first good pictures I've taken since we've been here," Livia says, even though she hasn't seen any pictures yet, just a dead dog's carcass, close up. "And totally unsellable, I might add." She seems particularly pleased about this lack of commercial value, and yet two weeks ago she proudly announced that this year she was finally going to earn a proper amount of money with her photographs.

There can hardly be a photographic subject less commercial than dead dogs, unless they're used to stir up some righteous public outrage.

Hagen, who's still onshore, throws a stone at the carrion and misses it; Scherf bawls, "You idiot!" The school of fish, acting as a single organism, dives for deeper waters. The contempt on Livia's face is meant to kill Hagen, who throws a few more stones, searches the quay, finds an empty soft drink bottle, and hits his mark. The clump of guts bobs away on the water. The tension goes out of Livia like air out of a balloon. Suddenly she's weak and vulnerable. I've always thought she was at her most beautiful like this. Ever since she's started being successful, she seldom shows anyone her soft side. When I stroke her back, she steps away and says, "You're drunk," glad to have found a reason to reject me so quickly. She's paying her good-bye in installments. A few feet away from us, Jan, who's engaged in a conversation with Olaf, meets her empty eyes and grimaces disdainfully in my direction. Livia answers him with a smile that goes awry. Then again, maybe I'm wrong, maybe Jan's actually making a face at Nager, who's stepping gingerly over the landing stage with outstretched arms, uncertain whether his swaying is due to rotten planks, waves, or liquor. He bellows, "This is all junk, this stuff! Scrap metal! The only thing left to do with it is to make art out of it. Where's Swantje? She should pack this up and have it sent home. That'd be a good way for her to get high marks on her midterm exam."

Without a word, Livia picks up her camera bag, walks slowly to the covered benches, drops down onto one, and sits there, leaning forward and staring at the deck as she wraps strands of her hair around her fingers.

That attitude, and nothing else, in Carrara marble.

Jan ends his conversation with Olaf, ambles over to her, and sits down at her side, as though that's his regular place. Asks no question, *utters no thought, has no particular thing to say, nothing for her ears only. No pretext necessary. He just holds out his pack of cigarettes, followed by the flaring lighter. From the outset, all distances are correctly judged, as naturally as if they've had years of practice. Although he knows I'm watching. Under other circumstances, I'd like him. I look back at the dog. Now it's nothing but mute, ugly wretchedness, and once again the fish are scrapping over bits of its flesh. Either Livia's photo snapping or Hagen's direct hit has robbed the carcass of its expression. Or maybe the triad of skin, wounds, and water loses its cohesion in the gathering dusk. A light that enkindles minarets is unsuitable for carcasses.*

Livia shakes her head. Jan seems to have thought of a few words to say, after all. He must have said them very softly, so only she could hear. In any case, she doesn't share his opinion. Their knees are touching, or so it appears from my vantage point. Maybe Jan has shoved his hand under her thigh. Like every sort of illumination, evening becomes her hair, and now it's surrounding her face with a coppery gleam.

Livia's probably been unhappy with me. I'm good for a little while, but not for life. Who is?

The neon lights have been turned on belowdecks—milky balls of light from the portholes fall onto the water. In this luminescence, the dog suddenly looks transparent, lit from within, as though he'd eaten phosphorus, but no one sees this except me. I think, he's not dead, he's just shamming so as not to be recognized. I wonder, what would be the advantage of that for an animal? Perhaps none at all. Messut Yeter talked about djinns and how they sometimes like to play with us. He gave me an urgent warning: Even the good ones are dangerous, he said, because they have no idea how weak men are in comparison with themselves.

While I'm leaning out over the railing, Jan takes Livia's hand, or she takes his, or each takes the other's, as intimately as before, when he held out the cigarette lighter and she knew exactly how close to get to the flame. Our love was never like that.

Cursing loudly, Nager stumbles through the swinging door, and I turn around. Jan and Livia have already let each other go. Nager misses Mona. Not for private reasons, exceptionally enough, but because the ship is going to cast off in a few minutes. He's afraid that one of the sheep entrusted to him may be lost. He counts on his fingers, burns himself on his own cigarette, and tries to put a name to every face, desperate to reach ten by any means possible. He reaches ten, but Mona's still missing, because while it's obvious that Livia belongs to Jan, she doesn't belong to his class. "Let's get this straight," Nager says. "Next time you're walking in double file, and I'm going in front of you with an umbrella. Like the Japanese!" Large, oily drops of perspiration dot his forehead. He tears his tie loose, rips the top button off his shirt, and grabs the first sailor or steward who comes along. Nager explains to him that the departure absolutely must be delayed, at least for a few minutes, because he's missing a girl, she can hardly spend the whole night here alone, Turkey is much too dangerous. He's a professor, he says in English— "German university of fine arts, you know"—on a class trip with students, for whom he bears the entire responsibility, doctor, academia, Allemania. "Ship no go. Must wait. Understand?" he says. The man performs a series of obsequious nods but obviously understands nothing. Nager pokes around in his money purse, comes up with a hundred-mark note, and whispers, "Deutschmark." The bill has just disappeared into the threadbare uniform jacket when Mona appears on the shore. She shouts something unintelligible, waves her sketch pad, and runs a few steps toward the quay. She's completely out of breath. Nager, unnerved and relieved, rolls his eyes. The sight of Mona immediately makes him stop thinking of her as the foolish little student who almost gave him a heart attack. He's so exhausted that he hasn't got enough strength for *further ranting and raving. He wails that he's supposed to be a university professor, but instead he's running a kindergarten, as though his daughters aren't too much for him already. He runs his hand through his greased hair with a gesture midway between pulling and scratching. He finally grows still and looks like a wet hamster.*

When Mona comes on board, Jan stands up and moves a few steps away from Livia. This coincidence doesn't seem to annoy or confuse Livia in the slightest; she probably doesn't see the connection yet. For a moment I consider asking her whether she knows what kind of a relationship Jan and Mona have (*Maybe he explained it to you last night, I could say, wherever you were*) or whether she doesn't think she's too good for half a man.

(*Counterquestion: Do you know how many women you've slept with in the last five years, Albin?*)

The ship slowly turns away from the quay. Mona smiles at Jan, deputizing him to excuse her for getting everyone upset; she was drawing, and she forgot the time. He knows how that is. There was this butcher shop, and in the window were two stuffed goats, a she-goat and a kid, preserved so badly, so touchingly, she had to laugh, although she thinks it's disgusting to slaughter a kid just for decoration. A thick blue glass heart was hung around the kid's neck. An artificial eye stared out from the center of the glass heart, while one of the kid's own eyes dangled a little, like a loose curl. I myself noticed that window, and Fritz was sitting on the quay earlier, making a cartoon sketch of the shop on one of the innumerable postcards he sends to women and friends. I'm sure Livia photographed the butcher's window, too. A fine subject for people with elevated touristic tastes: "Want to see some pictures from the trip?"

Jan does, or at least he tells Mona he does; puts a fascinated expression on his face and leafs through her sketchbook, slowly and meticulously, praising where he can and camouflaging criticism as stimulation.

He tries hard to keep Mona from noticing how much pain her amateur-ish efforts cause him. She's the only one whose complete lack of talent he doesn't take as a personal affront. As far as the rest are concerned, except for Olaf and maybe Fritz, he'd prefer that they be forbidden to do so much as buy drawing pencils.

Livia's busy with her hair again. After looking through various lenses and deciding that it's too dark for picture taking, she lets everything—the ship, the city, the sky, the water, the people—disappear behind a blond veil. Mona and Jan don't interest her. I'd gladly go over to her, but I can't think of anything I might actually say. Not even anything mean.

I meet Nager again at the bar. He's leaning on the counter with his chin in his hand, watching the barmaid as she counts her change. Black hairs grow out of three warts, arranged in a triangle on her face: on the left side of the bridge of her nose, her right cheekbone, and the middle of her chin. She apparently attaches no importance to the prospect of selling anything. Or maybe her ugliness has embittered her, and so she's abusing her monopoly in order to humiliate us. Under ordinary circumstances, Nager would sort her out at top volume. When she finally serves us, he pays for my beer, too.

He wants to know: have I found out anything more about this Miller person?

I dodge this question, telling him something about various detailed pieces of information that I haven't managed to put together yet. The thing is complicated, I tell him.

While I'm talking, he sucks in his cheeks deeply and then suddenly releases them, producing a loud smacking sound. I can see from his expression that he's making a serious effort to think, and also that it's difficult for him to think in silence. He needs almost the entire bottle of beer to produce a single sentence: "Basically," he says, "it doesn't make any difference whether your story is true or you made it up."

I can't hold on to my cigarette; it slips through my fingers and falls, tumbling over itself several times before striking the deck, where it bounces once before rolling a couple of feet away. The burning tip breaks off and bursts into glowing fragments that lie on the planking like the remains of a meteorite. I want to tread them out, but my foot is already too far away to obey any further orders from my brain.

5.

It's hard to reconstruct exactly what happened that morning, and in what sequence.

When Livia came out of the bathroom, her hair newly blown dry, her eyes and lips made up—very important to Albin—she found a note on the table: "I'm in the Sultan to see about Miller, A."

She'd heard nothing when he left the room, no good-bye, no steps, no door, no door lock. Albin had apparently been at pains to disappear surreptitiously. From this, Livia at once concluded that the whole story had been nothing but a diversionary tactic designed to allow him to drown the day in alcohol, unmolested and unreproached.

She saw the imprint of his body on the bedspread and the remote control on the pillow. A narrow column of smoke rose up from the ashtray, and the room smelled like a scorched filter. Moreover, she noticed that her camera bag was open and that an empty film package lay on the table where Albin's Minox had been.

Livia tried to remember if he'd had the shakes; it would have been a clue, she thought, but he hadn't, not at breakfast. She considered going to see some sight by herself, perhaps a mosque or a cemetery, or just letting herself drift through the city, ready for pictures that might impose themselves on her but not lying in wait. Pictures, Livia thought, are shyer than wild animals.

Then she remembered the distant look on his face—his eyes hadn't even grazed her—and the pleading undertone in his voice. And suddenly she was filled with doubt; she no longer thought Albin had been lying or playing one of his games. She was convinced that he'd really witnessed something. In two hours he'll be back, she thought, and maybe he'll bring me a mysterious tale. He'll want to tell it, and I want to hear it. If he doesn't find me here, he'll start drinking, and by morning he'll have either forgotten half of what he saw or developed a dozen different versions in the course of the night, one for each bar companion, and one for the woman who'll take him home just before dawn.

And so Livia decided to wait for him. She flipped through the set of postcards—photographs of Byzantine mosaics—that she'd bought from a street vendor a few days previously. She hesitated between the peacock, which was tearing the young shoots off a dried-up branch, and the head of Christ from Hagia Sophia, looking at her so sadly she was almost willing to believe him. There were other eyes in the picture, too. Livia chose the peacock.

Dear Thea,

 I'm afraid Albin may have finally gone crazy, but I'm not completely sure. In any case, after this trip, if not before, we'll probably—no, definitely—break up.

 It would be great if I could take refuge with you for a while—I hope this card reaches you before I do. I'll give a call.

Fondly, Livia

Tiyatro Caddesi, a steep, narrow street, still lay in shadow when Albin stepped out of the hotel. It was cold, so the fruit and vegetable

remains and the bones and the scraps of meat and fish in the rubbish piles in front of every building had not yet begun to stink. Albin inhaled the aromas of fresh flat bread and sweet pastries
wafting over from the nearby bake shop.

Out of old darkness a battered image, Sunday in Staudt, rose
before his mind's eye; he heard Mrs. Francke's droning voice, asking for the hundredth time, "Will there be anything else?" as his
mother's bony hand hauled him away from the big glass candy
jars, and he felt faint, he felt a hatred that shone as brightly as polished silverware, even though she was the most beautiful mother
in the world.

Albin says there wasn't a single police car outside the Otelo
Sultan, and inside everything was quite relaxed. He had expected
to see managers and chambermaids and businessmen running
around and gesticulating while a few people collapsed sobbing into
armchairs and a black-bearded police inspector searched, strenu-
ously and fruitlessly, for clues. But the clerk was standing behind
the reception counter alone, filling out a form. Albin took up a position a few feet away from him, cleared his throat meaningfully,
and said, "I . . . ," and only then did the man raise his head.

"Welcome, sir, what can I do for you? Are you looking for a
room?" asked the clerk in flawless German.

"Thanks, I don't need a room. The reason why I'm here is, I'm
staying in the Duke's Palace . . ."

"Also a very fine hotel, sir, an excellent choice."

"My wife and I are quite satisfied with it. But what I wanted to
say was that a little while ago, less than an hour, I was up on the
roof terrace . . ."

"The air is splendid this morning, a fresh breeze from the
Bosporus, no smog. Believe me, you've picked the best time of year
for your visit to Istanbul."

"Listen: an hour ago, a man was shot in your hotel, Mr. Miller, I watched it happen from up there, I saw it with my own eyes. How can you not know about this? His girlfriend, Ireen, was with him. She's probably hiding somewhere. Someone should go up and see about her. Will you do that, please? The name is Miller, sixth or seventh floor, M-I-L-L-E-R, and when the police come, tell them to talk to me. I'm an important witness. The shooter must have been on one of the surrounding roofs . . ."

"I'm sorry, sir, but there's no Mr. Miller registered in this hotel."

"I—"

"We haven't had a Mr. Miller for at least the last month, and I don't believe we're expecting anybody by that name during the next several days. If anyone in the hotel had this information, it would be myself."

"I was sitting at a table with Mr. Miller last night, and this morning I saw him shot dead in his room in this hotel. I'd like you—"

"There's no Mr. Miller registered here."

"If you don't have someone go up to the sixth or seventh floor and take a look around, I'm going to call the police."

"Young man, if your desire is to cause trouble, I can assure you that those very police will throw you out of here immediately."

And at this point, the stone sculptor Albin Kranz, twenty-eight years old, whose powerful back muscles enabled him to handle 220-pound granite blocks with no difficulty, surrendered to a slight, shady-looking Turkish hotel clerk. Albin's shoulders collapsed, he shrank several inches, and he felt the way a wax figure must feel when its cabinet burns: held together by heavy clothes, supported by a couple of wires in its center, and standing in a puddle of itself.

"You know, I didn't want to go to Istanbul. My wife talked me into it. Even after she talked me into it, I still didn't want to go, but . . . Are you married?"

"I've been married for twenty-three years, and I have five children, four boys and a girl."

"Then you know how women are."

"Do you also have children?"

"No."

"I'm sorry. But you are still young."

"Where's the bar?"

"This way, to the left, then straight down the hall, and at the end left again. But before you go there, if you wish, you can go up to our roof terrace and take a look around. The university, the Suleyman Mosque. All very charming."

"Thanks, that won't be necessary."

Albin followed the signs. The drinking establishment in the Otelo Sultan—the Irish Pub by name—was one of those structural inanities that are unavoidable in international hotels. An oval mahogany bar occupied the left side of the room. Plaques with Guinness labels were everywhere, but you could also drink Stella or Heineken. Floor-to-ceiling mirrors, stamped with advertisements for whiskey, separated the individual tables from one another, so that every table had its own space, which extended itself outward in infinitely multiplying rows filled with confusing lines. Many an anxious European found it easy to imagine that someone had put a drug in his drink. The stools, chairs, and benches were covered with red leather upholstery. The interior decorator had hung thin nets from the ceiling, nets that couldn't have stood up to a sardine, holding plastic fish, lobsters, crabs, and sea stars. Inexpensively framed posters showing flourishing meadows, crystal streams, and foam-flecked seas hung on the mahogany-paneled walls. The pictures were called *Tullamore, Kilkenny,* or *Carrick on Shannon.* Another one bore the title *Cornwall.* The bartender seemed to be trying to remove the previous night's beer rings from the bar, but he was primarily interested in the gold-pierced navel of the black queen whose large mouth was moving silently on the muted television set that overlooked his workplace. A maid pushed a loud vacuum cleaner over the brown carpet.

Albin sat at the bar and, in memory of Miller, ordered a double bourbon. He tossed it down in a single swallow, lit a cigarette, and asked for the same again.

"Do you know an American in his mid-sixties, a big fat guy with a pretty young girlfriend?"

"Of course. You mean—wait, it's on the tip of my tongue—you mean Marlon Brando."

Albin was amazed to hear himself replying, "Right, exactly, Marlon Brando," as naturally as if he'd been trying to come up with this name for days.

"A large man. Large and tragic. We Turks love Marlon Brando, especially *The Godfather.*"

"He was shot dead this morning. Here in Istanbul. He was here making a film."

"Impossible!"

"Absolutely true. In this hotel. I saw it happen. He was supposed to play the role of the jewel dealer Jonathan Miller in a film about smuggling, a B-movie, if you know what I mean."

"No, I don't. And now I have no more time. Excuse me."

"Give me another whiskey."

While this was going on, our train arrived in the underground station at Frankfurt airport. Sabine was on crutches, the result of a compound ankle fracture, and the conductor helped her off. No one had forgotten anything, not even Swantje. We stood there and looked around. None of us had a clue which way we should go. Scherf, who supposedly knew Nepal, Colombia, and Morocco like the back of his hand, had never flown out of the airport in Frankfurt. Hagen acted intimidated. Even the question of whether we should take the escalator to Hall A, B, or C had to be debated at length. Adel said that flights to Beirut always left from Departure Hall C. Corinna's stomach was upset, and at first she wanted to find a bathroom, but then she was afraid she'd lose us. Sabine, unable to carry her suitcase, was looking around for an elevator. The few signs whose meaning we could understand indicated several directions for every conceivable need. Swantje suggested that we draw straws, but none of us had matches or toothpicks ready to hand. Surrounded by skycaps, flight attendants, vacationers, and business travelers, seven art students waited for something to happen. But nothing happened, until Mona had a screaming fit. We were all completely nuts, she said, and then she proved to us with mathematical precision that the most logical thing to do was to take the escalator to Hall B, because Hall B must necessarily be in the middle of the terminal building. Should our check-in counter turn out to be in A or C, then either one would be equidistant from B, but if we went up to C or A and found out that we had to go to A or C, then we'd have to go twice as far. Had we followed her, she wanted to know, or should she draw us a map? In any case, she didn't acknowledge any statistical probabilities in favor of any particular hall: Istanbul was not Beirut, there were bathrooms all over the airport, she didn't see an elevator anywhere, and apart from that, it didn't make any difference, because we had more than two hours' time before our flight.

No one dared to say anything. Adel silently picked up Sabine's suitcase, Corinna said she didn't have to go that bad, Scherf felt rebuffed. Hagen asked Mona why she was so upset. Mona found this question unworthy of a reply. As we were going up the escalator, she suddenly began to laugh.

6.

While the night sky becomes transparent, the glow at my feet dulls. We're approaching the city, which lies under a bell jar of light, the reflection of countless streetlamps and neon signs. Now the engines are running more calmly. I lean out over the side of the ship and think about the stars, moving away from one another since they came into existence, getting farther and farther away until the day there's no more day. Then (or there), they come to a stop for a fraction of a moment, which is completely still, and in that split second the reverse movement begins.

It's nearly noon when the ship puts into the harbor at Düşünülen Yer. The lengthy flight of a seagull ends when it carefully folds its wings and alights on an orange buoy, not far from some cutters, rocking on the water. Livia looks around as though she's searching for someone but can't find him anywhere. I watch her through the crack between the two swinging doors. Mona riffles the pages of her guidebook and reads aloud: "In Byzantine times, the Bosporus could be closed to ships by a chain that ran from this place to the opposite shore." This information interests no one. Beside the mooring stands a hotel, apparently never completely built and now a collapsing ruin inhabited by cats and pigeons. I feel, spreading out from inside, the kind of warmth for whose sake a man will drink himself to death. Livia asks Olaf, "Have you seen Albin?" He hasn't seen me. I listen closely to her voice, trying to detect *an undertone of anxiety. Jan says, "He's inside." She replies, "He needs a drink." Not anxiety, contempt.*

I gaze back out. The sun seems weaker, as though dimmed by the exhalations of the city. The silhouettes of hills, apartment buildings, and mosques are backlit, luminous as English watercolors. The two young Turkish women beside me are more nearly ugly than beautiful, but the certainty that their lives will be successful makes them radiant. I open the swinging doors too forcefully. Livia turns around. Our eyes meet, and in hers is a question: Has he been drinking? Not: Have you been drinking? That's the difference. An employee of the shipping company in a gold-embroidered fantasy uniform says goodbye individually to each passenger, briefly touching his cap with his fingertips.

Why do I believe Messut, an insignificant clerk in one of Istanbul's innumerable hotels, a man who barely manages to feed his family? Why, for almost a week now, have I been doing what he says, even when it makes no sense?

Nager's hungry. "Düşünülen Yer is famed for its seafood restaurants," Mona says, without even opening her guidebook. "I'm not going with you," I say. Livia hesitates, uncertain which company to choose. She wrinkles her forehead as though weighing different reasons against one another. Naturally, she wants to be with Jan. As soon as you fall in love, every separation becomes unbearable, even though you've felt exactly like this more often than you can tell, and your bliss has always dwindled into nothing more than the shared experience of a period of time, which one day became part of the past. I lift the burden of decision from her shoulders: "Stay with the others. You can't help me. I'll see you on the dock for the return trip."

For a moment, she loses control over her face, which briefly shows how relieved she is. She says, "I don't like this idea of yours, going off to conduct an investigation all on your own."

"I'm not conducting an investigation, there's just something I've got to find out."

I try to cover the streets systematically, but it's a hard thing to do. They look so much alike I mix them up. There are the same wooden pushcarts with displays of fish and other seafood in front of every restaurant, the same overflowing fruit and vegetable stands, the butcher shops with lambs and haunches of beef hanging from the ceiling, the carpet merchants, the display windows with cheap leather goods and assorted arts and crafts. The café patrons are exclusively male. All the streets seem to circle around a center, but the center remains hidden. There's no square anywhere, nor any outstanding building. For no good reason, I trust Messut, I'm relaxed. I amble down the streets, staring at people like an escaped mental case. It's cold. To keep my hands under control, I dig them into my coat pockets. You have to suppress the shakes, the really hard shakes that spread out from the middle of your back, or else people will think you're sick. A glass display case on wheels, pushed by a teenage boy, comes toward me. The case is filled with green vegetables and cooked sheep's heads. Cheek meat. I've never seen anyone gnawing on a skull. I'd rather not be exposed to the look in those dead eyes.

Does Messut have an informant who wants to give me some important information? Is that the reason he sent me here? If so, should I draw attention to myself, or should I behave inconspicuously so as not to arouse suspicion in the wrong people? Why didn't anyone arrange to meet me somewhere, or set a time, or propose some kind of signal? I'm weary. I need to lie down like an old dog in the entrance to the next house and sleep for twenty hours straight. I'll drink something. Maybe eat something, too, on account of my stomach. Mona's right: the fish look good. The restaurant owner comes charging to the door, stands next to me, waves his arms. He speaks in English: "Come in, sir, come in, we have the best fish in Düşünülen Yer." I merely stopped for a second to look at his stuff. "What's your name?" he says. He grabs me by the shoulder, even though I'm a head taller than he is. "Albin," I tell him, but I pronounce it like an American. He says, "Albin, my friend." I shrug and flick my cigarette away. "Albin, believe me." I don't have the strength to defend myself. Maybe he's recognized me from the description Messut gave him on the telephone; maybe he'll bring me to someone who'll help me, who'll explain to me about Miller's murder and Ireen's disappearance, so I can disappear too, with or without Livia. Without her, if it's up to me. I won't stay any longer than necessary on her account. "Albin, you must try our fish."

The room dissolves. Colors peel off of the bright blue ceiling and flare in the corners. A neon tube hung on cables starts swinging back and forth as soon as the door is opened. There's a smell of burnt garlic and frying fat. I take a seat and look at the television set. There's a cheap-looking show on, where the men still wear fezzes and all the women are veiled. The other people in the restaurant are fishermen. They brought in their catch before dawn, and now they have nothing to do. They play backgammon or curse the government. On the table is a menu, written in Turkish, English, and German, shiny from being touched by greasy fingers. I order a beer and a raki, no water. The owner puts on some music: Oriental pop. I should have preferred the voices of the backgammon players and the politically dissatisfied. A young man comes in, looks around, sits at the table next to mine, opens a newspaper, but doesn't read it. Unlike the others, he's not personally acquainted with the owner. When my drinks arrive, I say, "I take the fried prawns," happy in the shelter of a foreign language. The man at the next table sizes up the other customers but avoids making eye contact with anyone. It's possible that he's been following me since I left the dock. Now he's just as fearful of our meeting as I am, or he's fearful of a third party who he thinks might be of some danger to us. A cuckoo comes out of the hand-carved Black Forest clock and announces the time: one-thirty. The man shakes his head, like someone pondering something inexplicable. When my food is served, I order another raki. I don't understand what my neighbor orders. Abruptly, he asks me, in German, "Where are you from?" I've been speaking English the whole time. Why does he assume I'm German? I say, "Are you talking to me?"

"Yes, you."

"Germany." I'm not giving up the name of the city.

"Germany's good. I was there too, for a long time."

"Where?"

"Rüsselsheim."

We could prolong this game endlessly, but I'm not in the mood. I say, "Do you know Messut?"

"Of course I know Messut. Everybody in Istanbul knows Messut."

"I'm Albin."

"Yilmaz."

A pimpled boy brings Yilmaz a bowl of white soup with rubbery bits of meat floating in it. Yilmaz says something in Turkish that sounds like a command. One minute later, the owner serves me another raki. "It's on me," Yilmaz says. He's apparently someone who needs to communicate. He spoons his soup and talks. He's on the run, he says: "A stupid affair." Although he worked in Germany for a long time, he didn't have enough money to get out of doing his military service. He was called up shortly after he returned home. Then, when he had only three months left to serve, three bloody months, his unit was slated for transfer to Kurdistan. Sooner or later, all Turkish soldiers have to go to Kurdistan and fight. This past fall, one of his cousins got sent there and was flown back to Istanbul in a plastic bag. With this in mind, instead of reporting back to his barracks last weekend, Yilmaz went AWOL. Six days ago. Mr. Miller was shot five days ago, but Yilmaz doesn't mention that. He's hiding out with an uncle here in Düşünülen Yer. He feels about half safe. If they catch him, he'll go to prison. Turkish prisons are no picnic, least of all for deserters. They're hell on earth. He's going to try to head east, go through a mountain pass, and reach the border. "In the Caucasus, if you don't want to be found, no one will find you." His uncle can help him; his uncle's a carpet dealer, and he has contacts in Armenia and Iran. After we've eaten, Yilmaz says, "You're my guest." Then he invites me to his uncle's for tea. "I don't like to spend too much time on the street." Miller also had business partners in the Caucasus.

Yilmaz goes to the counter and pays. "Come on, it's not far." When I stand up, my chair gets stuck in the join between two floor tiles and falls over. "When we're on the street, don't say a word about the army."

The cold clamps my throat. He says, "Are you interested in carpets?"

"My father collected carpets." "Collected" is an exaggeration, but he spent a lot of money on them. Nobody else in the family wanted them. They lay on the floor in the attic, in Xaver's room. My steps are a bit uncertain.

"We go left." Yilmaz pulls his black woolen cap down low over his forehead, turns up the collar of his leather jacket, and ducks his head down between his shoulders. The houses move closer to one another. Four stories up, colorful towels and bedspreads hang from clotheslines strung across the street. A woman's voice passes from shrieking to pleading to whimpering. Our way goes slightly uphill. Fumes from mutton roasts hang in the air like clouds. The streets are deserted, empty of both tourists and locals. "My uncle will be happy. He likes to have visitors." How can a carpet dealer make a living in this godforsaken backwater? "Right at the corner." Fifty meters farther on, the narrow street ends in a little square in front of a high wall, the kind formerly used for firing squad executions. "Here we are."

Yilmaz's uncle lives in a two-story wooden house painted bright green. Carved shutters and a recessed balcony arouse memories of summer trips to the Crimea that never took place. All the windows are hung with pink-flowered curtains. No one would take this for a place of business. A sheet-metal bell clanks as we enter. I stand still, blind in the sudden darkness. "Wait," Yilmaz says, and disappears. At the other end of the room, a door opens. A shadowy figure glides through it and pulls it shut, leaving me alone. My pupils slowly adjust. I begin to distinguish between the wall and the hip-high piles of carpets, with passageways between them. There's an audible silence, produced by billions of woolen fibers sucking up every sound. With rags from this storeroom, you could wipe away noises, even screams. I have a dim perception of colors: umber, crimson, vermilion, different brightness levels of spilled blood. Someone in the next room switches on a cheap chandelier over my head. In the same moment, the door opens again. Yilmaz returns, followed by laughter, which is coming from a short, fat man of around fifty, with a mustache that hangs down to his lower lip. I'm in no position to judge whether this laughter sounds friendly, malicious, or sly.

"This is Uncle Oktay," Yilmaz says. Then he speaks to his uncle in Turkish, saying my name several times. "Uncle Oktay considers himself fortunate to be able to welcome a German carpet connoisseur and friend of Messut to his shop." I say, "Selam," the way Mona taught me to. Several bulbs in the chandelier are flickering, making the carpet patterns move, as though they weren't fixed, but woven from steppe grass and poppy fields in a hot wind. "We hope that Messut is in good health." Roses growing in the patterns, and tulips and lilies and anemones. Shimmering turquoise beetles and butterflies of jade, mother-of-pearl, and rubies have lighted on their leaves. "Uncle Oktay would like to tell you a little about the history of carpets." There's a whirring in the air. Monsters lash out with their tails and spit fire. Panthers tear gazelles apart, tigers gobble up goats. In the branches of the trees, an ibis awakens, ruffles its feathers, and flies away. There's a taste of anise, of dust. "There are countless theories about the origins of the art of carpet weaving. All are right, and all are wrong." I try to follow Yilmaz. I want to know exactly what Uncle Oktay is saying, so I can recognize concealed hints, so I won't tumble into a trap.

"The earliest known pile carpet comes from Pazyryk in Russia, in the eastern Altai Mountains. It was found, frozen, in the grave of a Scythian prince. It's about twenty-five hundred years old." Uncle Oktay's sentences draw lines in the room, curved lines, soft, graceful, and completely clear. Incantations could be recited like this. Although I don't understand a word the uncle is saying, I find it hard to concentrate on Yilmaz. "It's got a decorative element in the center, a bright cross, that's still used to this day." Uncle Oktay's answering questions I haven't asked. Why? "In the time of the Mongol khan Tamerlane, carpets in the provincial cities represented the khan himself. They had the status of modern embassies. Fugitives who managed to reach the khan's carpet were safe from harm." We had a special comb just for the fringes. I used to comb fringes for hours—I wanted the strands to lie perfectly parallel. "Naturally, Uncle Oktay doesn't have such old pieces for sale." Father loved his carpets, at least for a few years. He treated them badly, like everything he loved. Several layers of carpets covered the terra-cotta floor tiles in our bedroom. "Uncle Oktay is asking whether you want to drink tea or mocha." He never changed his shoes, not even when he came in from the garden on rainy days. In summer, the carpets felt good under your bare feet. "Mocha." In the end, they interested him as little as they did Mother and Xaver and me. They were just there so he could boast about them to his business friends. "Uncle Oktay can show you a huge variety of different types, Persian, Caucasian, Egyptian, even some from China. Of course, the most valuable carpets in our stock come from Anatolia." Once, late at night, he and Mother did it on the carpet. I must have been seven or eight. I'd had a bad dream, and I went and stood outside the half-open door.

"This is a prayer rug from Konya, a wonderful piece, about a hundred and fifty years old." Faster than I can jerk it back, Uncle Oktay grabs my hand and pulls it over the nap. He's got a firm grip. I feel a rough, dry surface. "Don't be afraid, you can touch it." "I'm not afraid." A woman brings a brass tray with three little cups. "The central field represents a prayer niche, which is used to orient the rug toward Mecca. Here the niche is black, an extreme rarity." When he lets my wrist go, it hurts. "But black was the Prophet's favorite color, not green, as one might assume. It's the black of moonless desert nights, when the djinns make their mischief and men have no protection save in Allah. The Qur'an says, 'I seek refuge with the Lord of the Dawn / From the evil which he has created / And from the evil of the night, when darkness spreads.' " The tables in my favorite Dutch bar had thick runners on them, sticky with ketchup and beer. "The rug comes from Konya. It belonged to Sheikh Abdur-Rahman an-Nasağ, who spent many waking nights on it, contemplating the mysteries." I don't know how many times I fell off my bicycle when I was pedaling home drunk. I'd sleep where I fell, right out in the open, because I couldn't even walk anymore, much less pedal a bike. "See here, the pile is worn smooth, you can see the white weft thread. But don't think this is an accident or a sign of poor quality. By no means. For many years, every time the sheikh bowed in prayer, he dipped into this darkness. The fear of plunging into this bottomless blackness forever darkened his heart." Why is he telling me this? Mr. Miller dealt in precious stones. I don't know anything about carpets. "But on the Night of Destiny in the year 1271 after the Hegira, in the very earliest morning hour, when it was still too dark for his eyes to distinguish black threads *from white, the sheikh touched his forehead to the carpet for the many-thousandth time. And then, directly in front of his eyes, Sheikh an-Nasağ saw a small streak of light shining through from the other side. A gift! Masha'Allah, what a gift!" Give us three razor blades, and we can start a miracle rug factory.*

"It could be yours. It is very valuable." I should have known. "Valuable, not expensive. Practically free." After a week of Istanbul, I should have known a sales pitch follows every invitation. "Or don't you like it?" Yilmaz asks. I say, "If it flies well, I'll take it." Yilmaz looks deeply shocked and hands me the mocha cup. "You want to try it? It'll certainly carry you back to the harbor. It's downhill all the way." The mocha tastes vile. Uncle Oktay starts to laugh. "But be sure not to fly off the end of the quay. The water's icy cold." At first his laugh is a soft gurgle. He drops down onto the nearest stack of carpets and slaps his thighs as the laughter coming out of him grows to a roar that hurts my belly, and then the roar swells to a bellow that's going to burst my eardrums any second. I want to clap my hands over my ears, I want to shout, "Make him stop!" Uncle Oktay's laughter dies away. Without an echo. There's a second of utter soundlessness; then he stands up and comes very close to me. The tips of our shoes are touching. Although he's shorter than I am, he looks down on me. I'm condemned to immobility, held fast by his gaze, an iron bar that pins my head to a nonexistent wall. Then the bar changes into a shaft of blazing light, and my bones dissolve. I go into a gentle spin, tottering, my knees buckling. I drop into a chair, but even when I'm sitting down I can hardly hold myself upright. I want to believe it's because of the raki. I know it's not because of the raki. Uncle Oktay's mouth forms a sharp, painful sentence. Yilmaz bends down to me and whispers in my ear: "You've lost your game, my friend." The sentence belongs to me alone. Instead of taking Sheikh Abdur Rahman an-Nasağ's prayer rug, I take this sentence, and I struggle against the urge to repeat it, again *and again, with my eyes closed and my lips moving rhythmically, like grass on the steppe when the moon is waxing and the east wind blows.*

I say, "I want to know who shot Jonathan Miller and why. That's the reason I'm here . . ." My voice disintegrates.

The answer I get: "Go now. Otherwise, you'll miss your boat."

7.

More than four months have passed since the Istanbul trip. Since I didn't keep a journal, it may be that details have slipped my mind. And it's certainly true that what happened later in the trip altered my view of the beginning.

Jan was sitting off to one side in a low black leather chair and smoking. I saw him from far away but said nothing. Contrary to Mona's fears, he had arrived at the airport not at the last second but ahead of us all. The khaki-colored knapsack he never traveled without was lying on the floor at his feet. He was looking at the sky through the glass above the entryway. A strong wind was tearing at the cloud cover and opening up patches of cool blue. Dully gleaming cars pulled up to the entrance. For the most part, the people who climbed out of them, men and women, were wearing business suits, and they were in a hurry.

Jan had a gray shirt on under his wrinkled linen sport jacket and a dark red scarf around his neck. Over his head hung an airplane, a newly restored propeller-driven machine from the 1930s. The plane shone in the light of the autumn sun, which was reflected from the windows of the office building across the street. Jan ground out his cigarette, took a clasp knife out of his knapsack, and started cleaning his fingernails. His jeans were torn under both knees. He looked like an impoverished aristocrat of the British Empire, on his way back for an extensive tour of the colonies, without a clue about what he should do with his life now.

"London would have been a good choice, too," I said to Mona. "Were you ever in London?"

Instead of answering, she cried out, "That's Jan over there!" And ran off.

At the same time, Livia was pacing up and down in her hotel room and getting angry: because she hadn't believed Albin, because now she almost believed him, because she was waiting, because she found waiting humiliating. She loathed herself for her inability to make up her mind. And between anger and self-loathing, there were several layers of anxiety.

Recently, she said to me, "Anxiety overshadowed everything in those last six days. Whatever I did or thought, everything turned dark. I was anxious about making decisions, but I was also anxious about doing things I normally liked—going to strange places, eating, drinking, buying clothes, visiting museums. I imagine I felt something like the way a person feels after the doctor says, 'You have cancer. It's inoperable.' "

In the previous weeks, Livia said, Albin had been extremely irritable. He'd spoken rudely to waiters and salesgirls, insisted, for no good reason, that Livia was cheating on him, and called her a whore. He was suffering from sleep deprivation, he might break into a sweat while doing nothing but sitting down, and in the morning his hands trembled more and more. Livia was worried about him, but she kept it to herself. Shortly before their trip began, she looked up "alcoholism" in the encyclopedia. There she found Albin's symptoms described as the early stages of delirium tremens. In such cases, she learned, any drinking bout, including the next one, could cause a life-threatening circulatory collapse or end in madness. Sufferers experienced sudden apparitions of white mice or read secret messages off blank walls. In spite of this information, Livia didn't have the courage to cancel their reservations.

She stood at the window, staring into the poisonous green of the artificial turf mats that covered large sections of the inner courtyard, and wondered which explanation she was more afraid of: that Miller's murder was the first image sequence to come out of Albin's newly imploded interior world, or that the killing had been an actual event, occurring in an identifiable place at an identifiable time. Livia contemplated her plight. If the first explanation were true, she would have to stand by a man who had recently lost his reason and accompany him on his journey through the world of Turkish psychiatry. The second explanation, the only plausible alternative, was that Albin had indeed witnessed the commission of a crime that, according to his spare description of it, bore all the earmarks of a professional job. If this were the case, then he was in mortal danger, and it necessarily followed that she was, too. Livia noticed that from many of the rooms, it was possible to reach the different terrace-like levels of the courtyard, which were connected to one another by spiral staircases. There were a couple of extendable ladders, which the gardener moved around as he needed them. At this point, Livia would have preferred to leave Istanbul at once, even though she'd chosen it for their holiday herself. To tell the truth, she said, she'd insisted on the trip to Turkey against Albin's opposition. She leaned over the table and picked up the postcard she'd written to Thea, the one where she'd announced that she was going to break up with Albin. When Livia reread her words, their tone of finality frightened her. The minute anyone saw that postcard, it would be out in the world; she'd never be able to get rid of any of it, not even the comma between "no" and "definitely." Livia wondered whether she was really ready to do anything so drastic as to walk out. If not, it would be better to let such clear statements of purpose as this postcard remain unsent. She spoke out loud: "If I leave Albin, he'll give up completely, and the guilt will land on me. If I stay with him, *I'm* giving up, and of course I'm responsible for that."

Livia could hear how what she thought sounded, but that didn't help her. If they broke up, Albin would wreck their apartment, throw furniture out the windows, and deliberately drive the car to its death. She didn't suppose he'd use physical violence on her. She murmured, "Self-inspection," and turned away from the window. Her hands executed some peculiar movements that resembled East Asian morning calisthenics and helped her bring into sharp focus the blurred image of her idea: "Look at yourself through a stranger's eyes. Objectively."

I know Livia, and I believe that was really the only purpose behind what she proceeded to do. Livia doesn't consider herself particularly attractive, nor does she take herself excessively seriously. Had there been so much as a shred of vanity involved in her actions, she would never have mentioned them to me at all.

The first thing she did was to hang the *Do Not Disturb* sign on the door before locking it from the inside. Then she took her tripod out of her bag and screwed her camera onto the threaded shaft. She looked through the viewfinder, corrected a slight tilt with the help of the water level in the ball-and-socket joint, moved the tripod farther to the right, shoved it forward a bit, and extended the rod until she found a point from which she could shoot into the bathroom as it was reflected in the mirror on the wardrobe. Then she turned on the lights over both washbasins and removed all her makeup. Once her face was thoroughly washed, she went back to the tripod and slowly tipped the camera forward until the perpendicular lines of the mirror and the door frame ran parallel to one another. Finally, she panned left, millimeter by millimeter, in order to create some tension between the empty surfaces and the midpoint of the frame. She looked at a detail of the image, noting the relative positions of the toilet, the bidet, the towel rack, and the washbasins. She did all this calmly, with great concentration, as though she were preparing a ritual sacrifice. Secure in the knowledge that there would be no surprise irruptions into her room, she sat on the bed and took off her boots. She pulled her sweater and her undershirt over her head and took off her brassiere, whose cups left marks on her breasts. She unbuttoned her skirt, let it fall to the floor, and stepped out of it. Sitting down again, she stripped off her black tights, gave each of her thighs a brief pinch, and found them too fat. When she set the aperture and shutter speed, wearing only a pair of underpants, she felt cold but did nothing about it. Livia couldn't tell what sort of light would pass through the lens and throw her image onto the film, nor could she adjust light and shadow so that they corresponded to her aesthetic ideals. Now she was completely naked. The question of whether she was ugly or beautiful was of no importance. She set the delay timer on the shutter, ran into the bathroom, tossed back her hair, folded her hands behind her neck, and held her breath.

For this first shot, she stood with her back to the camera and exhaled only after she heard the click. All told, she made eighteen photographs of herself, using a total of four camera positions. Toward the end, she stopped going the roundabout way through the mirror and posed directly in front of the lens, producing an image that began under her chin and ended at midthigh, like a classical torso. As she got dressed again, she thought about nothing at all. She was putting her eyeliner back on when she noticed her wristwatch, which was lying next to her vanity kit. An hour and a quarter had passed.

Livia shrugged her shoulders and sat down at the desk. She slid her card to Thea into an envelope, which she sealed, addressed, and thrust into her purse.

Albin ordered a third whiskey and drank it in silence, smoking several cigarettes and wondering what sense it would make to ask any further questions in the Otelo Sultan when the personnel so flatly denied both the event he was asking about and the existence of the people who had participated in it. Since nothing occurred to him, he paid for his drinks, omitting a tip, and left without a word to the bartender. He had no intention of striking up a second conversation with the clerk at the reception desk. The barman's peculiar reaction had convinced him that everyone in this hotel was determined to make a fool of him. They wouldn't get any more opportunities to do that. On the way through the lobby, he began to suspect that the man he'd spoken to at the desk was not who he claimed to be, and furthermore was not the person who was supposed to be on duty. Maybe he was an accomplice of the killer, planted in the reception area by the outfit they both worked for. Albin resolved to get a good look at his face and to make a note of his name. The real clerk was probably tied up in some closet or lying dead in the boiler room. The Turkish authorities would start looking for witnesses as soon as the first body was found, perhaps even before that. When that happened, Albin didn't want to be accused of having neglected details or paid insufficient attention. Whatever the identity and position of the middle-aged man behind the reception counter may have been, when he saw Albin approaching, he immediately hung up the telephone and changed his facial expression from tense seriousness to perfect congeniality.

Albin gave his voice a hard edge: "Tell me your name so I'll know who I've spoken with about this matter."

"Messut. It's here on the nameplate: Messut Yeter. Do you want to write it down?"

"Thanks."

"And your name?"

"Albin Kranz. I'm staying in . . . but I've already told you that."

Albin realized, too late, that it was foolish to reveal his name to the clerk.

"If I can be of any help to you . . ."

"I'll be all right."

Five days later, Albin was already uncertain whether Messut had called out, "Be careful," as Albin walked away, or whether he'd heard these words in one of the conversations he'd had with himself since then. He was sure, however, that he hadn't replied to them.

Albin walked through the automatic revolving door, stepped outside, and wondered what he should do. Shaking his head, he walked in the direction of the main street. As a sort of sound track for his shredded thoughts, he began speaking aloud in rhythmic nonsense syllables. He turned right on the main street but did not take the turn into Tiyatro Caddesi two hundred meters farther on, because he didn't feel like listening to Livia. A child selling knock-off perfumes from a display box slung against his belly walked beside Albin for a little while. He decided to jump on the next tram or bus he could find and take it to the end of the line. There he would get off, pick a direction at random, and start walking. Since he didn't know where any of the bus and tram lines stopped, no meeting could be planned, and because he had no idea what the outlying parts of the city were like, he couldn't even build up any expectations that would be fulfilled or dashed. Whatever might happen would have no connection with him personally. It would be a product of pure chance.

The bus stop was in the middle of Yeni Çeriler Caddesi. The traffic was so thick that Albin looked around for a traffic light. At the same moment, bear trainers appeared on the other side of the street. Two men, one older and one young fellow, with Indian or Pakistani facial features. Each of them was holding a thick stick, and each of them had a bear attached by a chain to his belt.

His father had often told stories about Gypsies with dancing bears. When he was a boy, he said, the dark-skinned Gypsies went from house to house, offering their services as tinkers and knife grinders. They, too, had a bear, who danced for money or bread. Naturally, the bear didn't exactly dance; what it did was turn around a little, and bob up and down, and whack its paws together. One of the Gypsy men played a fiddle, and the kids believed the bear was really going to dance. Meanwhile, a woman with gold earrings read Grandmother's future in her palm. Many of her predictions came true, Grandmother declared. Every year in late summer, the Gypsy crew returned and camped for a few days in a field near Halm. After they left, Father said, the people in the village counted their chickens, and there were always some missing: "Just plain trash, those people." At the time, Albin had imagined a life like that for himself.

He pulled his Minox out of his coat pocket to take a picture. But before he could click the shutter, the men, together with their bears, were already on his side of the street. For them, the thousand honking automobiles did not exist. One of the men held out a red plastic plate, on which someone with a felt-tip pen had written a large number in bold black digits—the price Albin was to pay for the photograph he had not made. Albin displayed a smile, intended to convey to the men that he was their brother. It failed to accomplish this result. Albin shook his head, whereupon the younger Gypsy grew cross and pulled his bear quite close to him. The animal, which wore no muzzle, bared his teeth. When it was scarcely an arm's length away, the man ordered the bear to rear on its hind legs and snarl until Albin yanked a banknote out of his pocket and tossed it onto the plate. The attack lasted only a few seconds. As they moved away, the older Gypsy hissed at Albin through his gold-capped incisors. His words were unintelligible, but they sounded like a threat.

Albin looked at his watch. His legs felt unsteady. Miller had now been dead for two hours.

We were scheduled to take off at twelve-forty-five. We got to the check-in early, but there was already a long line. The only person missing was Professor Nager, who was traveling in from Cologne. Except for us, all the people in the line were Turks. Since they were carrying huge amounts of luggage—including not only bags and suitcases, but also refrigerators, bicycles, and automobile parts—the checking-in process took forever. While we were waiting, I noticed that one of the airline's older employees was staring at Jan as if he'd known him for a long time but couldn't place him. Jan said, "Maybe he's queer."

After receiving our boarding passes, we broke up into the usual subgroups: Corinna, Sabine, and Adel; Hagen and Scherf; Jan, Mona, and I. Swantje hunched her shoulders and moved from one set to another, undecided about which conversation she wanted to take part in. Fritz wandered aimlessly around the terminal. The prevailing mood was not eager anticipation but rather vague dejection. But maybe I'm just imagining that in hindsight. Mona was flushed with excitement, but she was the only one. She talked about a holiday on the Turkish Riviera with her family, years ago, described the colors of the water and the taste of the grilled fish, and declared that the sand on the beach was finer than the sand in Scheveningen but coarser than the sand on the Algarve Coast. Jan nodded, wanting her to believe that he was interested in what she was saying. Only the deep crease between his eyebrows betrayed the wretched humor he was in. I suspect that his bad mood stemmed from the attack of temporary insanity during which he had agreed, for Mona's sake, to spend a week with her and ten other people, the majority of whom he didn't like. Conversely, if he had pleaded insufficient funds and begged off, no one except Mona would have been angry.

Around ten minutes before twelve, Sabine came over and asked what we should do if Nager failed to show up on time. He should have been here long ago, she said. Mona had spoken to him on the telephone; did she know what was going on?

"So we fly without him," Jan said, looking past Sabine's head and speaking before Mona could answer. "We leave without the chief. What's the problem?"

Instead of replying, Sabine turned around and hurried back to Corinna and Adel. She was afraid of Jan. He fell silent again. I can still remember what I thought: *Jan's going to back out.* The whole time—though I didn't realize it—he was listening to Scherf, who was explaining to Hagen his idea for a big art project that he wanted to start working on after the trip. Suddenly, speaking in such a loud voice that the two Turkish women behind the counter gave us questioning looks, Jan said, "Scherf, you're talking a load of bullshit."

Mona rolled her eyes. She was generally quite in favor of quarreling with Scherf, but not now: passengers traveling on Turkish Airlines flight 318 were requested to go to Gate B 42. Sometimes airplanes fell out of the sky. Nager had still not shown up, and even if everything went perfectly smoothly, no one knew what would be waiting for us in Istanbul.

"Oh, yeah? What makes you say so?"

"Because the Iconoclastic Controversy didn't have a thing to do with art, and the Eastern Schism wasn't in the eighth century, it was in 1054."

"The Iconoclastic Controversy raised a hell of a lot of important questions that are more relevant than ever today. And it most certainly led to a schism."

Except for Jan and Scherf themselves, no one knew what they were talking about, but we were all amazed to discover that both of them had been reading up on Byzantine history in preparation for the trip.

At that moment, Professor Nager appeared on the escalator. As he walked past us on the way to pick up his boarding pass, he called out, "Have you been waiting long?"

Mona was furious. She restrained herself until we were through customs control, and then she burst out: "It says on the ticket, passengers are supposed to be here two hours before their flight is scheduled to take off, but you apparently overlooked that!"

"Mona, my pet," Nager said, putting his arm around her shoulders. "I don't give two seconds' thought to such nonsense. I'm too old for that sort of thing, and besides, I can hardly get any work done anymore as it is. I have to divide my time so that pieces of me can be distributed evenly: to art, to my family, to my beloved students, and last but not least, to my financial counselor. Believe me, it's difficult to accommodate everyone. In the worst-case scenario, you would simply have flown without me. I would have gotten over it. And I'm sure all of you would have, too."

8.

We're getting farther and farther from shore. Voices waft over to me from inside the ship. They belong to people whom I know more or less well. And to strangers. They're all talking at the same time. Sentence scraps, laid over one another like stone strata in the profile of a landscape. I can pick out individual levels and hear things not meant for my ears: Livia is glad she met Jan. Someone has known since this morning that his son Imre will not live to see next summer.

On an aging rust bucket between Europe and Asia, latitude forty-one degrees north and longitude twenty-nine degrees east, I think about the Southern Cross and Tierra del Fuego. Father was there. He sat on his moss-covered boulder and waved at us. Behind him, the gray sea, darker than the sky.

I come back to the room at five-thirty in the morning. The air smells of fried food, because the kitchen flue vents into the inner courtyard. Livia's side of the bed is as untouched as mine. I stumble over shoes and fall against the open wardrobe door—luckily, the mirror remains intact. A sudden memory: the special kind of pain caused by blows. Livia has never stayed out all night without telling me what she was doing. I've always believed her. The art print (Janissary warrior with shouldered musket; oil, French, nineteenth century) next to the television set hangs askew. He won't waste a bullet on me. I've never suspected Livia of cheating. Recently, she's been acting cold. In the past months, she's traveled a lot for magazines and book projects. A bitch in heat in a strange city—who knows what she met up with?

I should have skipped that last gin and tonic, but Olaf's words were coming out more slurred than mine. Why couldn't I stop talking? He was getting bored. Meanwhile, a handful of petals were falling off these roses, one by one. The window's wide open, so wide a full-grown person could pass through it. Livia's not one of those people who decide one day to take a headlong dive into the unknown. Livia doesn't give up; she believes battles can be won. In the past, that's been lucky for me. I must be careful, she says. Since last Monday, she's been afraid of a possible break-in. The mats of artificial grass gleam blue in the light of the neon signs. The palm trees look fake, even though they're standing in big tubs filled with soil. Nobody on earth waters plastic palm trees, not even in Istanbul, where they let bears tear stray dogs limb from limb at night. I've watched the gardener moving from tub to tub with a watering hose. Maybe someone climbed through the window and left traces. Someone who knew we wouldn't be here and wanted to seize his chance. At first glance, nothing seems changed. Both ladders are where they were yesterday and the day before.

I light my cigarette lighter and look under the bed, even though there's hardly enough room under there for a rat. I yank open the bathroom door, ready to kill with my bare hands. Someone's flicked ashes into the washbasin. These ashes aren't mine. Livia must have had a visitor before she went out without closing the window. Or the unknown person was convinced that nothing could happen to him. I don't know my way around Livia's cosmetics purse—I can't tell which lipstick tubes she traveled with and which she left at home. The strip with the pills is missing. She takes a pill every morning, before she brushes her teeth. Her toothbrush is dry: Livia spent the night somewhere else. She didn't get up before dawn to see something special, to take photographs of some unique ceremony that starts at the bloody crack of dawn and is over in an hour. She would have told me about that. And the sun wasn't even up then. Livia hates using flashbulbs. Besides, her camera case is under the table.

She sat with Jan for a long time in the darkest corner of the Orient Lounge. Then they disappeared. I didn't see whether they left together or alone. Either way, it wouldn't prove anything. She says she and Jan have good conversations: about her work, about art in general. Up to now, everything I've ever heard him say about photography was disparaging. He's probably counting on using Livia's contacts for possible shows of his own work, but at the same time thinks her stuff is no good. She knows a few gallery owners, none very important. One of them is interested in figurative painting. Jan's going to use Livia, have some fun with her, and that'll be that. On the other hand, maybe she's the love of his life. In that case, he'll father her children, walk the dogs she's wanted to get for so long, and live a pleasant life at her expense, among the objects I picked out for her five years ago, three years ago, when she had money from her rich, generous parents but no idea what a chair or a cupboard was worth. She called her bed "ours," a statement of intent: that bed had no past. My bed belonged to me. She didn't like sleeping in it.

Livia won't lie next to me anymore, staring at the ceiling because it relaxes her to look at nothing and talk and talk, telling me confused stories I don't remember the next day. Because while she speaks, a movement begins, a stirring, under a soft, uniform carpet of background noise whose origin I can't determine. It lays itself over her and me, over the furniture, the floor, capturing the heat our bodies give off, so that the walls soften and throw up bubbles like mud seething around geysers on a snow-covered plateau with shadowy mountains in the distance, until the pressure under the surface grows too great and the bubbles explode. Then a viscous color slowly flows down in streams from the ridges and cliffs. The closer it comes to level ground, the more shades become dis-

tinguishable. The rivulets form mottled lakes that melt in all directions and spread out over the ground, until finally there's a solid expanse of color, hardening to damp earth and grass and sand. Some rainwater that has neither dried up nor drained off since the last thunderstorm fills a valley right in front of me. Towering clouds are reflected in this water, clouds so high they break through the atmosphere and whirl about in the frontier zone between gravitation and weightlessness. In the puddles at my feet, they form a whirlpool. Branches appear in it, and fence posts and barbed wire. On the right side, there's a sluggish streamlet, a sea of swaying reeds and swamp lilies, and Livia's slender shape. Her step is resolute, a bit faster than mine. Gravel crunches under our feet. She hops and jumps around, spreads her arms out wide and turns in a circle. Runs backwards, facing me, picks up stones, throws the stones into the water, into the sky, so high they punch through the barrier at the end of space, pass into the unknown, and never fall back down. Livia laughs. Gentle gusts of wind tousle her hair, blow strands off her forehead, stroke her face and her throat, throw her dark outline onto the ruffled surface of the stream. The wind pushes rows of waves toward us, friendly waves that wrap themselves around individual stalks, while the warmth of the spring melts the snow in the mountains, swells the stream, turns it into a river. It overflows its banks, floods meadows and fields and fallow land, but we're not afraid, no harm can come to us, the ground under our feet is solid. We unleash our German shepherds. They chase the birds' shadows and snap at the stripes of light that break through thornbushes where poison berries grow, black and red. Even as we're walking past the hedges, they sink in the inexorably rising river and turn into an indistinct weave of branches; patches of greasy algae dance around them. Driftwood sails past us on the smooth current, and so do seed capsules and a feather. Trees grow high behind us. Their boughs shimmer in the sun. Before us, all the way to the horizon, a plain of hammered silver. Our dogs run

away over the plain. Their paws don't touch the ground. Farther off,
they look no bigger than dragonflies, two buzzing points rushing away
unstoppably. I call to them before they disappear in the wall, I call out
clearly and distinctly, without a sound, after they disappear, because my
voice is only the thought of a voice in the image of a landscape along-
side the idea of my side the word for woman her name

Instead of sleep with dreams: black.

"Good morning. This is your wake-up call. We wish you a pleasant day
in Istanbul." I say, for the third time, "Yes, ja, OK, Danke, thank you,"
but then I realize that I'm being talked to by a machine. I didn't ask for
a wake-up call. Seven-thirty. When it comes to organizing the course of
the day, you can count on Livia. She still hasn't come back. At nine
o'clock, they're all going to meet in the lobby before going down to the
harbor together—that's the plan Mona made for them. Why are we following this kindergarten around? I thought we wanted to find out
whether we were still a couple. Have I misinterpreted Livia's campaign,
carried on over several weeks, to persuade me to take a trip to a place
where everything's foreign and no one knows us? I wanted to thwart
this trip; I knew the answer we'd get would be "No." For years, all of
Livia's friends have been hoping she'd finally bring herself to say that
"No." The worse I treat her, the sooner she'll understand she has to go.
Livia will make a new life without me. I've got dirt from my shoes on the
sheet. The hotel maid will have to bring us a fresh one. I drank my last
gin and tonic three hours ago. By any realistic estimate, my hands
should start shaking around ten o'clock. This sweater stinks. There's a
ship's horn, blowing farewell. I wanted to close that window. Afterward,
I'll meet the informer whose knowledge will straighten out this whole affair. I hope. So I can leave for home on Monday. Up until then, I can't
have any withdrawal symptoms. I must maintain my proper level of

consumption. It seems hardly likely that Livia would have checked the contents of the minibar. Besides, how will she know what time I came back to the room? I might have treated myself to a nightcap at two o'clock. Others can do it without having to listen to accusations of alcoholism. Why do they keep vacuum-packed peanuts in the refrigerator? "Vodka doesn't smell," Kurt says. "No foreman can tell how crocked you are. Of course, you have to keep from falling off the scaffolding." I place the empty little bottle in the middle of the table. Livia will think I'm not hiding anything from her because there's nothing to hide. Or I could fill the bottle up with water and put it back in the fridge. Then it'll be up to me whether I want to pour it out for myself, just so she can watch me do it, or whether I want to rage about the dishonesty of the prior occupants of the room and then open the whiskey.

Ever since we met, I drink less, as far as Livia knows, than I actually drink: I hide hip flasks and suck peppermints until they make me sick. This is going to be one of those days when I give myself a thorough scrubbing before I go to breakfast, thus eliminating all fumes and exhalations; I shall also gargle mouthwash and chew chewing gum.

Livia hasn't used any of the towels.

. . . Black, as though I had fallen out of the world without ever having been there. Leave no trace behind, anywhere. Not even in your own memory. That would be the only possibility. And if losing a woman were the price of that, a man could pay it. If something is possible, it also exists.

At the breakfast buffet, I take some corn flakes and yogurt and sit down at Olaf's table. He looks at me inquisitively but says nothing. Wordlessly, he spreads honey, jelly, marmalade, nougat cream, and black syrup on one slice of white bread after another, chewing steadily and constantly. After he downs the last slice, he rolls himself a cigarette. Before he strikes the match to light it, he sweeps the fallen tobacco— Van Nelle Halfzware—back into the pouch.

At eight-twenty-five, Livia appears. Her eyes are restless. She's wearing the same clothes as yesterday, which is something she never does. She doesn't see me right away, but then again, she's not looking for me. She's by herself instead of with Jan—which could well be a little production they're putting on. Livia's earning enough money now. If she wants to go to bed with Jan, she can take a room in another hotel. They must make some agreement about who's going to come back when to the Duke's Palace. On the way, Jan stops for another mocha. She looks exhausted. I'm not surprised—none of us has slept much in the last few days. Her hair lies wet on her shoulders. It's not raining outside; therefore, she took a shower somewhere. She loads her plate, sits down on the empty seat next to Olaf, diagonally across from me, gives a brief nod, and starts talking to him about today's excursion. She sees no need for even the cheapest little lie. Olaf seems flustered. He stares at me as though he wants to apologize for something, anything at all. I doubt that it's Livia alone who's causing his embarrassment, even though, like most of the others, he's got a crush on her. In any case, she doesn't like him, she's not making the big brown eyes. He knows all about the awkwardness of the situation. Jan's his friend. Maybe Olaf feels partially responsible. Because he concealed something from me last night.

"Are you looking forward to the trip, too?" Livia asks, so innocently that I have to laugh. "It looks as though the weather's going to hold."

"I've wanted to be a sailor ever since I was a child," I say, looking at her face for some telltale sign, a red spot on her chin or her cheeks. Jan was clean-shaven yesterday. Do her lips look fuller than usual? Do they have a healthier color? I stir sugar into my coffee and try to recall the way she looks when she's been fucked. No picture comes to mind; all my images of Livia have been extinguished.

"Where were you?"

"Out."

"At five-thirty?"

"I wanted to watch the city wake up."

I could say, "You forgot to brush your teeth," or, "And you took your pills along for that?" Instead, I say, "So I take it you were studying the habits of Istanbul's working population? Doing ethnological field research?"

"That's about right," Livia lies. She knows I know she's lying, and she's not ashamed.

Jan comes in exactly fifteen minutes after her, as though he's got a stopwatch and he's sticking to the agreed-upon interval. His hair's wet, too. He can easily have used the same shower. Mona feeds the seagulls. Since she doesn't want any fighting, she makes sure they both get some. Nager's going on and on to Corinna. He decided to confine his drinking yesterday to mineral water and tea, and therefore he's feeling good today. The boat trip was his idea. These days, when he makes excursions like this with his daughters, he feels like a happy father, a family man.

When I step out on the roof terrace, Mona says, with a mixture of horror and respect, "It's a wonder you can stand upright again so soon. Wait, I know. You haven't slept at all?"

"Bull's-eye." She gets on my nerves. I have no desire to talk to her. When I'm still about fifteen feet away from her, at the risk of hurting her feelings, I stop and lean over the railing.

There are new guests in the suite where Miller was shot. Light shines through the narrow space between the curtains. Then the light's turned off. A few moments later, a young woman wearing a black pants suit and high-heeled shoes pushes the curtains apart. She looks like Ireen, except she's wearing a pair of large, tinted glasses. I'm convinced that Ireen's still in Istanbul, but I don't have the strength to run over to the Sultan right now and knock on her door until someone opens it or the lock comes apart. The woman turns right and walks past the balcony door to the dresser. She moves the same way Ireen did: like a fashion model at work. With one curved index finger on her chin, she bends over the fruit basket and takes her time deciding. At last, she takes an orange, looks out the window for a while, and then sits on the very chair Ireen was sitting on when Miller was shot. The table's been replaced. She turns her face toward me and starts peeling the orange, meticulously plucking the little white threads off every slice before putting it in her mouth. When she's finished, she walks over to the window again and stares in my direction. I'd really like to know what picture that is in the heavy frame behind her. She stands there, beautiful and completely motionless, as though offering herself. Nothing happens. I think, I'll go now. She waves at me.

9.

During the flight, Jan and Scherf have seats that are far apart, so they can't continue their debate. Below us, shredded clouds are getting pushed up the north flank of the Alps. I can also see mountain meadows, glaciers, rock formations. Mona leans over to me and asks, "Do you know anything about this sinister Iconoclastic Controversy?"

"Not that much."

"I thought you paid attention in school."

"The Byzantines were constantly fighting about things that nobody understands today."

No one in the class had yet heard how Emperor Leo III, by ordering the removal of an icon of Christ from above the main gateway of the imperial palace in 726, had caused a national crisis that was to last more than a century, during which time numerous people were tortured, maimed, and killed because their opinion of the theological significance of an image differed from the view prescribed by the current ruler. None of us would have believed it was possible that emperors of any period and any realm, no matter which, had ever occupied themselves with these kinds of questions. The very first victim of the long struggle was not a person guilty of high treason, but rather the officer who had carried out the emperor's command. As soon as the icon was removed, there was a popular uprising, and the officer was beaten to death by a mob of outraged women, who were called *saintly* and *praiseworthy* in later historiography.

I don't know when and where Scherf came across the Iconoclastic Controversy. He claimed he'd studied it for a long time, completely independently of the Istanbul trip. He already had a cycle of overpainted prints of icons in his application portfolio for the academy, he said. He's never stopped thinking about the subject since, and that early series merely represented a part of the whole idea. Besides, he said, back then he still lacked the artistic means for dealing with such complex material.

What Scherf now had in mind was an installation made up of several parts. He wanted to photograph two Byzantine icons, one of Christ and one of Mary, from some book. The photographs must be black-and-white and deliberately amateurish, in order to emphasize the characteristics of the reproduction and therefore the images' potential availability, which would stand in contrast to their uniqueness as devotional objects. The two negatives were to be exposed as platinum/palladium prints on seven pairs of thick old oaken boards, which Scherf would then destroy or severely damage in seven different ways. He intended to bury the first pair in his parents' garden for several months; the second would be thrown into the local pond and left there the entire summer; he was going to smash the third pair with a hammer, scratch and gouge the fourth with shards of broken glass, throw acid on the fifth, and burn the sixth, controlling the fire so that the remains were still recognizable. As for the last pair, he would attach them to the trailer hitch on his car and drag them along a track across some fields. Before coming to the academy, Scherf had trained as a carpenter, so he planned to build fourteen altarlike wooden bases, paint the tops of these pedestals gold, and set his badly damaged icon boards on them. The two rows of pedestals would be positioned facing each other, with just enough space between them for an observer to pass. Scherf hoped that this work would cause a scandal in churchly circles. Strictly speaking, he said, any form of indignant reaction would serve as the indispensable continuation of the installation. Only through a public outcry would it become clear that, despite all modern theories of art, the beliefs of the Byzantine image worshipers have persisted to the present day. In this connection, Scherf told the story of the death of Saint Stephen the Younger. During a dispute with some iconoclasts loyal to the emperor, Stephen took out a coin bearing the ruler's likeness, threw it to the ground, and stamped on it. Through this action— Scherf sees Stephen's act as an "action" in the modern, political sense—Stephen wanted to demonstrate to his opponents that reverence or irreverence paid to an *image* did indeed pass to its *prototype*. They were so enraged by this demonstration that they lynched Stephen on the spot for the crime of lèse-majesté, thereby involuntarily confirming his argument.

Jan was really only marginally interested in the Iconoclastic Controversy. He had come across icons because of his preoccupation with portrait painting, and upon further investigation he'd discovered that Byzantine history made fascinating reading.

To this day, it's not clear to me what made those two carry on their dispute almost as bitterly as the hostile parties in Constantinople twelve hundred years ago. Maybe they were simply delighted to find a subject that each of them could use to display his contempt for the other's views on art.

Mona said, "I still think Jan's right."

"Probably."

South of the Alps, we had crystal-clear visibility. The television sets that dropped down out of the ceiling of the cabin showed a map. The size of its details changed constantly as the focus zoomed in and out. Immediately after Venice, the red line of our flight left the green and entered the blue. The real sea looked bronze, with turquoise enameling. The flight attendants offered drinks, but alcoholic beverages required payment. Nager didn't want to drink alone, so he offered to buy a round of beers. To alleviate their fear of flying, even Corinna and Sabine accepted his invitation.

Down there, in the place where the red line would come to an end in about two hours, Albin was standing on the street, counting his money. He determined that he had tossed the equivalent of about a hundred marks into the Gypsies' plate in payment for an unmade photograph. Despite the cold, he was sweating. He stared after the well-rounded behind of a Turkish girl whose face had eluded him and thought about Livia's brown eyes. He still didn't want to talk to her, not about Miller's murder, not about the conversations he'd had with the clerk and the bartender, and certainly not about his encounter with the Gypsies. He saw her large, heavy breasts above him, her closed eyes, heard how she cried out, and wanted to go to bed with her. He wanted it simple, clear, without many words. The last time had been weeks ago—he could no longer remember when. Albin hesitated, then turned around and walked in the direction of the Duke's Palace, considering how he could get her to want him, too, right now. In days gone by, there were none of these complications. They did it at every hour of the day and night, in likely and unlikely places. Then the bond of naturalness broke and it was no longer a matter of course. One day, he realized he no longer knew how to get to Livia; he'd forgotten which looks, which caresses she couldn't resist. He decided he'd try saying, "I want to fuck you." She'd probably answer, "I don't want to fuck *you*," or possibly, "Maybe later." In which case, he'd go out again. He knew how to order beer or vodka in Turkish. Albin's sweat was evaporating now, making him cold. He started shivering. Shortly before he reached the hotel, he came to a stop and leaned on a wall, because the earth was spinning too fast. When he stepped into the entrance hall, he became sick. He rushed to the men's room, dropped to his knees in front of the toilet, and vomited until he was spitting bile. Afterward, he stared hard into the toilet bowl, trying to make sure he wasn't having a hallucination. Yellow-brown liquid, little chunks of pastry, sesame seeds. That matched what he'd eaten and drunk. It was something to go on. He staggered over to the washbasin, rinsed out his mouth, washed his hands. A pale face stared at him from the mirror. Ugly, watery blue eyes, rimmed in dark red. He looked like a man who'd just puked. He said, loud and clear, "Miller was shot."

It was unmistakably his voice, echoing around the high, white-tiled room.

Contrary to his intention, Albin didn't go to Livia then. At least, that's what he claimed. Maybe he was lying on this count, because the rejection had been too embarrassing, and Livia told me nothing about it in order to protect him. It seems to me to be pretty unlikely that Livia slept with him one last time. I have no idea where he was before he came back to the room around five in the afternoon and asked Livia if she wanted to have a drink with him at the hotel bar.

After making the photographs, putting her card to Thea in her bag, and standing around awhile, Livia lay down on the bed and stared at the ceiling. She would leave Albin, she thought. For a brief moment, a cloud of tobacco sweat, alcohol, and aftershave lotion from his pillow wafted over her side of the bed. In any case, that's how it seemed, and she took a few deep breaths. It wouldn't be simple to jump over the distance between herself and the woman who had looked at her out of the bathroom mirror. Albin was lost to her. Her body tensed, all the way down to her bowels. She shoved her hand under her sweater and shirt and slowly stroked her belly to ease the pressure. Livia had made a decision, but she had no idea how she should translate it into action. Her own warmth was pleasant. On the hips, too, and the thighs. Albin reached for sexual parts without consideration for anything else. Sometimes she liked that; frequently, she didn't. For the first time in weeks, Livia was aware of her skin, the skin of a strange woman with millions and millions of sensory cells she'd forgotten about. Inadvertently or purposely, she touched her nipples through her bra, and a painless arrow shot down her spine all the way to the bottom of her pelvis. Gently, she took hold of herself. She felt every touch echoing inside her. When she slipped her right hand into her panties, her labia were swollen and soft. With cautious fingers, she felt her way inside. It had been a long time since she'd done this. Circular movements, gentle at first, then a little harder. She scrutinized herself: no longing for a man. A lovely, sorrowful feeling spread through her body. Like the memory of sunshine on her naked back after the dark winters of her childhood.

Livia woke up shortly before four. She was hungry, but she didn't feel like going to the restaurant. She called room service and ordered salad with roasted chicken. Twenty minutes later, a pimply waiter knocked on her door. Though she took the tray from him and gave him a big tip, the sight of her so intimidated him that he could scarcely bring himself to look her in the eye.

Our plane landed right on time. As we walked down the gangway, the air had a strange smell and an unusual consistency. After searching the baggage carousel for ten minutes, Corinna asked where the lost luggage office was, bitched about cheap flights, and explained that she had no money to buy new things and so she would have to fly back to Frankfurt if her bag didn't come. But then it rolled in. Outside the airport stood an employee of some kind with a plastic sign. The top of the sign, printed in ornate lettering, read *The Duke's Palace International Hotel Group.* Below these words there were four stars, and then a handwritten card: *Deutsche Studentengruppe.* Speaking in German, the man said, "I am Nazim. During your stay with us, feel free to call on me to assist you in any matter whatsoever." This was followed by a speech of welcome, a set piece with allusions to Turkish hospitality and the Oriental consciousness, and then he led us to the hotel bus. During the drive into the city, he used a microphone to tell us some humorously packaged facts about Istanbul, its history, its inhabitants, and its economy, which I forgot a moment later. He pointed out the central location of the Duke's Palace, from which one could walk to see almost all the important sights of the city. At the hotel desk, he saw to all the formalities. Jan and I took a room together.

We agreed that we would all meet in an hour and a half in the bar at the Duke's Palace—the Orient Lounge—and have an aperitif before dinner. And it was there that we met Albin and Livia for the first time.

10.

How did it start? I have no idea how it started. It'll be over soon. I've got a little bug living in me, Olaf, a larva nourishing itself on my entrails, eating me alive from the inside out. Soon it's going to enter a pupal stage and pass through a metamorphosis, and then it'll hatch and burst my empty husk wide open.

Livia seems to be gone. You can see the door. Tell me the truth. I don't want any misplaced consideration. Clearly, she left with your friend Jan, right? Or maybe she left alone. Makes no difference, either way. I don't expect you to betray him. It's getting close to three—I'll stay a while longer.

We missed each other, Livia and I. Strictly speaking, I missed her. I've put her through more than anyone should be put through, for five long years, trying to find out if she loved me, and if she did, whether her love had limits. I would have left her if it had.

I hardly know you, Olaf, but you're a good guy. I know nothing about your relationships, your affairs, or your family. I'm ignorant of your entire past, and I've been telling you my life story for hours. Will you have another vodka? I'll have one last gin and tonic for today, or yesterday, depending on which day it is. Listen up.

This took place beside a river called the Fries, a narrow, shallow stream, no more than two and a half feet deep in the middle. It flowed very slowly. I was six weeks from my twelfth birthday. What happened wasn't anything that would justify giving up. It wasn't anything in com-

parison with Miller's shooting, for example. Or Mother's death. It was an accident that happened without anyone intending to cause it. A chain of various circumstances led to an incident that left an image behind, a brand as ineradicable as the scar on my chin. None of which excuses anything. Still, a good two-thirds of what happened had scarcely anything to do with me.

You don't know our part of the country. The Fries cuts Staudt in two, right through the middle. Beyond the town, it meanders through an open plain with meadows and paddocks under the crest of a hill pushed up by the Ice Age. It's the only elevation for miles around. Farther on, the stream disappears at the edge of the state forest. We were on one of the Sunday outings we used to go on sometimes, when my father wasn't hungover or otherwise feeling low. There was a bright sun glaring through the trees, dissolving our surroundings—the ground, the trunks, the branches—into countless ornaments made of light and shadow. Through my pair of children's sunglasses, the scenery appeared almost black-and-white. Everything looked like this old Japanese film whose name I can't remember. It takes place in the ruins of a monastery destroyed in the course of some war or other. It must be at least six years since I saw this movie. It was late one night and I was at home, drunk, so I might get some details wrong, but this is what it's about.

Four people go before a court and tell the story of an attack in a lonely forest. There's a woodcutter, who has found the body of a nobleman robbed and murdered; the nobleman's wife; the robber; and the nobleman himself, who gives his statement through a spirit medium. The plot is simple. After taking all the nobleman's valuables, the robber ties him up and rapes his wife. Then he murders him, and the riddles begin: Does the robber come to the woman's aid because her husband is beating her? Does the robber threaten the couple, shrieking, baring his teeth, until the coward surrenders? Or does the nobleman heroically defend himself until his defeat is inevitable? And the woman? When the *robber violates her, does she feel revulsion, secret pleasure, or nothing at all? How does the nobleman die? Does he fall after a bitter struggle? Is he tied up and his throat slashed without further ado? Or does the robber kill him in response to his wife's express wish? The three people involved give such completely different accounts of what took place that the judge is unable to reach a decision. The dead man's declaration is no more credible than the stories told by the three living witnesses. He has undergone no purification in his passage from this world to the next. In the monastery, the woodcutter—the only apparently neutral witness—recants the statement he made before the court. He didn't come upon the scene after everything was over, no, not at all. He heard screams, hid in the bushes, and saw portions of what was going on, all the while shaking with fear and chiefly concerned with remaining undiscovered. As soon as the others cleared off, he crept out of his hiding place and stole the murdered man's dagger, which was lying on the path. He had several children to feed, this woodcutter, and the dagger had a valuable ivory handle. None of the four is lying.*

I drank a bottle of fruit schnapps during the movie, and after it was over I fell asleep in my chair. It must have been the light that caused their confusion, a glaring, restless light, as though the air consisted of a million microscopically small flies in perpetual motion. This fly cloud laid itself over things and gave them a kind of haziness, like a fluttering veil hanging over everything visible, so that eyes couldn't be trusted anymore. The same light was shining that Sunday in the forest on the banks of the Fries. Before my father disappeared the following year, we sometimes made a classic family excursion to that area and ate in a typical tourist café. I don't know if it's still there—I never went back—but in those days it was always crowded. You had to be lucky to get a free table. There was a playground next to the restaurant, with slides, swings, seesaws, and a little ferryboat attached to steel cables, which were used to pull it back and forth across the river by hand. The ferryboat was the main attraction. The proprietors had also set up an aviary with pheasants, owls, and falcons, and an enclosure with goats and potbellied pigs; there were also large cages for several martens and a fox. Claes would have liked to set them all free. We found a table on the big terrace and ate Wiener schnitzel and French fries under the red-and-white umbrellas. Claes went on a butterfly hunt. He ran around carrying a giant net and jars full of cotton balls soaked in ether. When he put the butterflies he caught in the jars, they beat their wings a few times and then keeled over. Claes claimed that the creatures had to be killed; otherwise, he said, a precise scientific assessment wouldn't be possible.

At the time of that last family outing, my brother Xaver had turned fourteen, and he spent the entire afternoon in a shadowy corner where the playground met the forest, talking to three girls he knew from school, trying to impress them. He blew chewing gum bubbles, handed out cigarettes, flicked the shiny silver American lighter that my father was missing. When he smoked, Xaver held the cigarette between his thumb, his index finger, and his middle finger, so that his hand would be covering it in case someone came near. When he drew on the cigarette, he squinted like James Dean. He made me puke. But he was standing around with these girls, making them laugh. Their laughter already sounded almost like women's laughter. Some high school students from Staudt had occupied the ferry. They weren't letting anybody get on who wasn't one of them. I trotted around aimlessly, hoping someone would speak to me, but since such a thing had never happened on all the other boring Sundays before this one, the likelihood seemed small. When Xaver saw me, he called out, "Come here, little one!" and I hated how young I was. But I liked the girls he was with. "Get us something to drink," he said, handing me a twenty-mark bill folded in half lengthwise, in my father's style. What I really wanted to do was spit at his feet, but I went so I'd have an excuse for coming back. Maybe he'd offer me a cigarette, too. After I delivered four cans of Coke and his change,

Xaver said, "Go play. You won't understand what we're talking about." I couldn't think of a response. "Hurry up. The sandbox is over there."

I went and sat down with my parents and built a pyramid out of beer mats. I was a master in beer mat pyramid construction. The biggest one I ever built was four feet high. My father looked irritable. There were empty cognac glasses and a half-full beer glass on the table in front of him. Mother was sucking mineral water through a straw. She had on a new, expensive, gleaming white dress with dark blue spots. It looked great on her. On account of the heat, she'd pinned up her hair, exposing her long neck. I was sure that the people around us thought she was a movie star. My father's tongue was already heavy, and those dangerous lines were already tugging at his mouth. Mother stared at the table so he couldn't see her eyes. They were quarreling about the company, which was doing badly. Or better, they were using the company's disastrous situation as a reason to quarrel.

For months, my father had counted on getting the contract for the last section of the autobahn to Holland, but in the end Keuser Brothers, Ltd., which had four times as many trucks as we did, was hired to do the job. My parents couldn't hide the imminent crash of the company from us children. They hated each other too much to be able to conduct their arguments in lowered voices or behind closed doors. Claes came by with his poison jars and put a dozen dead butterflies into little cellophane envelopes, which he then carefully stacked in a plastic container. He gave me a concerned look, shrugged his shoulders, and vanished again. "I'll make it," my father said. "Just like I've always done before. You can't keep a Kranz down." I don't know why I stayed in my chair. I could easily have gotten up and made myself scarce—they probably would've even preferred it. "We've got independence in our blood, Gerald and I. If you knock us down, we always get up again." Maybe, even though I knew better, I believed he wouldn't lay a hand on her as long as I was there. "Tomorrow I'm going to show Dr. Hollmann the figures one more time. It'll be the last time. If he says no, he's asking for it." I could have done it, they wouldn't have noticed. I was experienced in becoming invisible, a master in the art of vanishing without a trace. The impenetrable forest was all around us, bathed in this glittering light I could have dived into with no effort. "If he won't give me any credit to tide us over, he can write off the whole loan. He'll never get another payment from me." It wouldn't have been much of a trick to stand up slowly and withdraw, easy does it, one step at a time. Before they would have even realized it, I could've escaped into the trees. "That would be a laugh!" My mother said, "We've got enough debts. I don't want to pay the bank every mark we earn for the rest of my life."

That sent him into a fury. But she was wearing this marvelous dress, which made her movements seem even more graceful than usual, and at the same time as shy as a wild animal's, and she was all alone with him, the most brutish man I ever knew. She was totally defenseless, and she looked so fragile. He yelled at her: "What do you know about business, Ina? What do you know about anything at all? You wouldn't even be able to control your putrid sons without me." I put my hands over my ears and ducked away. "Look at this little titty-baby. Doesn't know what to do with himself, so he makes faces." I was already too old for my father's insults to bother me. Mother kept her mouth shut. She never talked back to him when the subject was us. This Sunday, too, she let a long time pass without making any reply. But unlike my father, who was busy jabbering away, I looked at her closely, and I could see something building up behind her forehead. I also saw that she was afraid, but not of him. She was frightened by the remnants of courage or pride or self-esteem that were rising up in her from where they'd been forgotten. Her eyes twitched uncontrollably, the corners of her mouth did the same, the look on her face no longer reflected what he was saying. She'd stopped listening to him, unlike the people at the next table, who were already starting to whisper.

Then something I'd never seen before flashed in her eyes, and she said, "Walter, you're a total flop as an entrepreneur. Sell the company, once and for all, and get yourself hired somewhere before it's too late." For a fraction of a second, my father crumpled up, as though she'd really gotten to him. Maybe she did really get to him, and he was barely able to summon up his strength this one last time. Anyway, all of a sudden he got sober, and he slapped her in the face so hard he almost knocked her off her chair. He stood up, grabbed her by her thin forearms, yanked her to her feet, and pulled her away from the table, even though she was crying out, "You're hurting me!" He couldn't have cared less about that, just as he couldn't have cared less about the other people in the restaurant. He was her husband, and if he was disciplining her, he must have a good reason. After going a few meters, my father turned around again and said, "You stay here. Your mother and I have to talk about something." The petite woman with the flaming red left cheek and the soft, summer-blond hair, which had partly come loose from its clips, this defenseless thing, my mother, was stumbling behind a man who was six and a half feet tall and out of control. She had no chance of keeping up with him; he slung her around right and left, and there was nothing she could do about it. It didn't mean shit to him when she fell—he just dragged her across the forest floor, yelling, "Let's go, move it, cunt!" until she got back to her feet. She didn't say anything, and she didn't cry. I knew he was going to kill her. He'd threatened to do it a dozen times, he was going to be true to his word, and we weren't going to have a mother anymore. Xaver, Claes, and I were going to be half orphans and our murderer father would be in prison. I stood beside the table. My legs seemed crippled. My heart pounded in my temples. When they disappeared around the first turning, when his voice broke off, the crippled sensation left my legs, and I took off after them. I ran from one tree to another. I kept under cover, each time waiting to move until they were almost out of sight. I didn't dare let him see me following them. He kept pulling her along for a good while, but finally he felt her resistance break. He struck into a thicket off to the right, dragging her behind him and shouting, "I'll show you! I'll show you!"

It was a stand of pines, a federal tree plantation. The pines were thickly planted, but their trunks were so small I had to let the distance between me and my parents increase. She was impassively following him, only now and then her knees buckled or she tottered. The lower branches scratched her face. Suddenly we were in a beech forest, and sharp-edged rays of light broke through the tops of the trees, so bright that I was blinded and leaves blown by the wind reflected the gleaming sun. I'll throw myself between them, I thought, if he puts his hands on her throat, if he tries to crush her tiny Adam's apple with his big callused construction worker's thumbs. The fluttering leaves and the vibrating light blurred the boundaries between things and gave the eye nowhere to hold on to. The woman staggered along behind the man, out of her mind, certain she was going to die. Finally, in a bright green meadow filled with yellow wildflowers, he came to a stop and let her go. She collapsed and lay in the grass for a minute, catching her breath. I crouched behind the trunk of a huge tree and tried to breathe soundlessly. From there I was able to reach the next tree, and then the one after that. I was just a few meters away from them. The man stood with his back to me. The woman slowly raised herself to her knees and knelt in front of him, looking up at him without a word. Her face was deeply flushed and dripping sweat, but I couldn't make out any tears.

The man fumbled around with the front of his trousers, and in the same moment when the woman spotted me, he shoved his big, swollen prick into her mouth, grabbed her head with his two meaty hands, and started moving it slowly back and forth; while she was looking at me, he held her in an iron grip and forced her into a steady rhythm. I thought this was the worst humiliation possible on the planet, worse than if he had killed her. I told myself, She'll never be able to walk with her head *up again. And all the while she kept looking at me. Her look was nei-ther desperate nor imploring: her eyes seemed to be staring at me from someplace unknown. Her look was only this mechanical movement, backward, forward, apparently endless. An eternity later, my father's se-men—which was a complete mystery to me at the time; I thought, Now he's pissed in her mouth—ran down her chin and dripped onto her white dress with the blue spots, the one that looked so good on her, and she wiped her burning face, wiped away his juice and her spit, and she kept looking at me the whole time, but her look was so strange that for a second I believed she was another woman wearing Mother's dress. When he was stuffing his prick back into his pants, she said, "Your son Albin's over there, looking at you." The man who was my father said, "The filthy pig," pulled his belt out of his half-open trousers, and charged at me with the belt clutched in his fist. While she was smiling, either absently or deep in thought, I stood there, rooted to the spot, un-able to move or run away. It wouldn't have done any good anyway—he was always faster, bigger, stronger. That's why he could piss in my mother's mouth.*

When Claes and Xaver came back, she said, "Your brother ran into a tree." I was lying on a bench by the side of the parking lot, staring up into the cloudless sky. My shirt was covered with blood. Our first-aid kit was on the ground nearby. She was crouched down beside me, cutting a compress to size. "You're a daydreamer, too, Albin," she said. "You go around with your head in the clouds." My father was in the car, sitting in the passenger's seat, stupefied by drink. He tried to smoke, but his eyes kept closing, and the cigarette slipped out of his hand. When we got home, she unlocked the door and led him into the living room, speaking softly to him all the while, explaining that everything was all right, that there was no need for him to get excited. She showed him the sofa so he'd lie down on it; she didn't want him in the bed. Then we drove to the hospital, where a friendly young woman doctor put two stitches in my busted chin. Poor little blind boy, who couldn't see the forest for the trees. Because I was so good and stayed so still, Mother bought me ice cream on the way home, five scoops, my choice, the biggest ice cream treat of my childhood. Three hours later, my father was still sleeping, and he slept until the following morning.

"What'd you do to yourself?" he asked at breakfast, when he saw the bandage on my chin. "Ran into a tree," I replied. "How lovely to have a jackass for a son," my father said.

What do you say, Olaf? We can handle another round, right? Nobody's waiting up for us, and the others are enjoying themselves, too. Who knows if we'll ever sit together like this again? Have another vodka or whatever you want, it's on me.

"Not a pretty story," says Olaf.

"One of several million ugly stories."

11.

Jan and I walked into the Orient Lounge around six-thirty. Nager, Mona, and Fritz were sitting at the bar with half-empty glasses of beer. There were two free stools between them and a couple in their late twenties. Jan strolled up to the bar and spoke to one of the couple, the woman, in English: "Excuse me, can we take the chairs next to you?"

She stared at him as though the threads connecting her to the world had broken apart in that very instant. After a long pause, she replied in German, addressing both of us. Her voice was wobbly: "Please sit down."

Unable to interpret her reaction, Jan said, "Thanks, that's nice of you."

For the first time since the trip started, Jan smiled. Despite the sadness emanating from this woman, he found her attractive, and since he was determined to spare her embarrassment, he made a conscious effort to conceal his irritation. She blushed and stammered, "Excuse me. I was a million miles away."

Weeks later, still astonished, Livia said, "When Jan appeared at my side and spoke to me, my brain suddenly lost the ability to process him. He was the one element too much. Albin had been going on at me for an hour and a half, telling me about the shot fired at Miller, describing the people he'd met in the Otelo Sultan. He kept on spinning out one theory after another about the back-

ground of the murder, the motives behind it, the possible connections with organized crime. The fact that there was no proof for
anything like this was what really stimulated his imagination.

"That morning, after Albin came into the bathroom and repeated the ridiculous sentence he claimed he'd heard—'Take care
of you, baby'—I'd already started vacillating among various possible reactions. First, I was certain that Albin had really seen Miller
get shot, and I broke into a sweat at the idea. Then I wondered
whether his mind was sound, and that thought segued into panic.
And finally, I was convinced that he was playing one of his deliberately confusing games, trying to pull the ground out from under
my feet. I hated him for that. Then Jan's voice and his question in
a foreign language blew away the last semblance of order in my
head. When our eyes met, our surroundings dissolved. We looked
at each other for a long time—at least, that's the way it seems in
my memory. There was a determination in Jan's face that Albin had
never shown, starting from the first time we met. He'd given up a
long time before, but it took me five and a half years to understand
that. Jan radiated something that released a great feeling of relief in
me. But at the same time, I was frightened. I thought about the
card to Thea in my handbag. I clutched the bag tightly, afraid that
Albin would stick his hand in it, tear open the envelope, and read
what I'd written. And simultaneously, a voice in my head was repeating, *I love looking into these eyes*. The muddle of images and
feelings led me to forget where I was for a second or two, and I
didn't understand what the person in front of me wanted."

"Are you German, too?" Jan asked them. Livia nodded.

"Well? What's Istanbul like?"

"Insane!" she said. "Stark raving mad!"

Albin added, "You'd better be prepared. There are things going
on here that you wouldn't imagine in your wildest nightmares."

"You don't sound very enthusiastic."

Neither before nor since have I ever known Jan to engage utter strangers in conversation at a bar. At first, I thought the prospect of spending the next eight days with Nager and the class was so unbearable to him that he was looking for people who seemed more agreeable. It would never have entered my mind that, from the moment he saw Livia, all he cared about was getting to know her.

"Albin and I are both pretty baffled."

"What are you doing here?"

"We're on vacation," Albin said. "At least, I am. Livia's taking pictures, but she doesn't know for what."

"That's not true."

(Later that night, when we were sitting in our room and drinking beer from the minibar, Jan declared, "I want this woman. Don't bother to comment, Olaf, I wouldn't pay any attention to your misgivings. I've already thrown love away once, just because I had scruples about wounding other people. That was a mistake. I'll regret it for the rest of my life. But I won't repeat it."

I hadn't the least idea whose love Jan thought he'd thrown away. Although we've been friends for more than ten years, we seldom speak of such things.)

"Have you had some bad experiences?" Jan asked.

Livia tried in vain to assess what our reaction would be and looked at Albin helplessly. Albin dodged the question. He would decide, all by himself, whether he was going to tell his story, and how much of it. He pursed his lips, inhaled noisily, and stuck the tip of his tongue into first one cheek and then the other. Finally, he said, "I know this is going to sound crazy—my wife's even having doubts about my mental condition—but this morning I saw an American businessman shot to death in the hotel across the way, the Otelo Sultan. The name of the dead man was Jonathan Miller.

He was a dealer in precious stones from the states of the former Soviet Union. He was sitting with Ireen, his girlfriend, having breakfast, when a bullet hit him. It came through the open balcony door. The rifle must have been fitted with a good silencer, because the shot itself made no sound. Mr. Miller crashed into the table headfirst and broke a lot of dishes. I was surprised that the glass tabletop withstood the impact. He weighed at least three hundred pounds."

When Albin told me this story again later, he changed some details, but not this one. Livia says he'd been talking to her about Miller's unbroken tabletop right before we arrived. She also claims that Albin had already started to slur his words by then. I didn't notice that. Of course, it may be that she picked up nuances in his articulation that I took for his normal way of speaking. Albin was constantly pouring all manner of alcoholic beverages down his throat, but I heard him slurring his words on only one occasion: toward the end of the last night we spent together in the Orient Lounge. At our first meeting, I would never have suspected that he'd been drinking since that morning.

Jan and I ordered beers.

"Why would this be hard to believe?" Jan asked. "Your guy probably wasn't the only person murdered in Istanbul today. Besides, it's an easy thing to check on."

"Wait till you hear the rest," Livia said.

"I ran into the Sultan—"

"When you left off, you were in the room."

"Have it your way. After I looked into the bathroom where you were, standing naked in front of the mirror and plucking your eyebrows, I went downstairs and ran over to the Sultan, because I thought the police would be there, they'd be securing the evidence and all that sort of thing, and they'd be glad to hear my statement.

But nobody was there except for an older gentleman behind the reception desk, filling out forms as though nothing had happened. So I say to myself, Well, Ireen's probably lying unconscious in the corridor, and apparently no one has noticed anything. I go over to the clerk and I say, A few minutes ago, a guest in your hotel was shot, a Mr. Miller. I saw it happen from across the street, from the roof terrace of the Duke's Palace. You've got to call the police and an emergency doctor, the man may still be alive. But instead of reaching for the telephone, the clerk says, We don't have a guest named Miller, we haven't had a guest named Miller, and no Mr. Miller has made a reservation. Period. And he threatens to throw me out if I don't shut up."

"Sounds strange," Jan said.

"What would you do if someone was shot right before your eyes, someone you knew, and then you were told no such man exists? It's just crazy! I went directly to the bar and ordered a double bourbon."

I asked him, "What did the police say?"

"I haven't talked to the police, not yet. I may be a little tired of living, but I'm not so far gone that I want to get mixed up with the Russian mafia. I'm not anxious to get my nose or my ears or God knows what cut off before I die."

While he talked, Albin was flicking the little wheel of his cigarette lighter, making it give off sparks. In his left hand, he held an unbroken string of lighted filterless cigarettes. Nager, Mona, and Fritz had broken off their conversation. They were also listening to Albin, and Nager couldn't decide whether to contribute a few tales from his own experience or wait for the rest of Albin's story. A frown wrinkled Mona's forehead—something was meeting with her disapproval. Hagen and Scherf came through the door and waved, but they didn't step up to the bar; they sat in armchairs near the entrance.

"Two nights ago, Albin and this American businessman were here in the Orient Lounge, drinking until they were both ready to keel over," Livia said. "I went to bed long before they stopped. I'm amazed you were able to recall his name. I remember seeing a fat guy sitting in the corner over there with a much younger woman. Albin claims he looked like Marlon Brando. In any case, that must have been Miller. He and the woman were enjoying themselves."

"At the time, you said you thought he looked like Marlon Brando, too."

"I was incredibly tired."

Livia still looked helpless. Nevertheless, she seemed glad we were there. The tension in her face relaxed.

"We'd already seen Miller and Ireen in the street," Albin said. "The old part of Istanbul is small. You're constantly running into the same people."

Jan ordered cognac. He was pale. His eyes were shut, and he was breathing as though in pain.

"In any case, you have to go to the police," Mona said. "The hotel clerk knows you witnessed the murder. From the way he behaved, he surely had something to do with it. Or at least, he knows who did. Do you think these people are going to assume you'll keep quiet just because you're a tourist?"

Albin gave no answer.

"So what happened next?" Jan asked.

"So far, nothing's happened next. I don't know what I should do, but I clearly have to do something. There's no rush. If you sleep on something for just one night, everything will look different, or so my uncle always said."

"If you wait that long, your friend Miller's murderers will be miles away!" Mona said.

"Did I ask for your opinion? And Miller wasn't my friend. One morning, from three o'clock until five o'clock, we drank whiskey and exchanged a few sentences. When it was over, he paid for two bottles."

"Not bad," Nager said. "But it can be done if the whiskey is decent. These old scotches are quite digestible, even in large quantities."

"Miller insisted on bourbon."

"I'd settle for that only in an emergency," Nager said. "How do you spend your time when you're not witnessing murders?"

"You think I made up this story, too?"

"If I did, I wouldn't have asked the question."

"I'm a stone sculptor."

"A stone sculptor?"

"Something wrong with that?"

"Stone sculpting is dead."

"Yes, it's dead."

"So you're a grave robber?"

"You might say that."

"Tombstones, or artier stuff?"

"When I need money, I carve copies of old ornaments that are in such bad shape they have to be replaced. Sometimes figures, too. And you?"

"I do plastic art. With different materials. Concepts, but not conceptual art in the strict sense. I look around, I imagine a piece, and I make it. Then I start over from the beginning until I get it right. Recently, I've become a professor. These are my students. A couple of the girls are missing. They're putting away their things, all the stuff women need for an eight-day trip: skirts, sweaters, pants, coats, shoes, and so forth. Otherwise their clothes will get wrinkled, and when they go out at night they won't look good."

"Ten years ago, I wanted to study art, too. I took one look at the academy in Düsseldorf and changed my mind."

"Art courses probably don't do any good. But they don't do any harm, either."

"Are you sure?"

"Have you ever thought about when the art of stone sculpture died and why? I mean, not so long ago, for whatever reason, a twenty-thousand-year-old tradition came to an end: carving stone with hammers and chisels, and then polishing it until it shines, even using wool in the end to make it smooth as glass. Brancusi polished his stones with wool for months, did you know that? In his day, stone sculpture was still alive, but it was in its death throes . . . or no, that's wrong. It was vigorous, but obviously on the way out. Why? My theory is that its demise was connected with technological progress. Technological progress has made a completely new plastic perfection possible, compared to which sculptures produced by hand in the traditional way look increasingly amateurish. Airplanes, tanks, even relatively simple devices like food processors—do you know these American food processors, KitchenAid? You throw a few ingredients in, turn a knob, and that's it. And the machines look fabulous. My wife's getting one for Christmas. Anyway, that's the sort of thing that brought down the curtain on classical sculpture. It began with the Industrial Revolution, and now you can take any object and record its measurements with a laser, right down to the exact millimeter. The data go into a computer, which is connected to a precision milling machine. You choose the material you want, and you get a one hundred percent identical duplicate of the original. There's nothing left for us to do by hand . . ."

Albin walked over to Nager.

Jan said to Livia, "Nager's a nice guy, but he talks confusing nonsense day and night."

He was blocking my view of her face. I figured he was doing it inadvertently. I didn't see that he wanted to talk to Livia alone and was shutting me out of the conversation on purpose.

"Albin thinks exactly the way your professor does," she said. "What's his name? Is he someone we should know?"

"Nager. Until four months ago, I'd never heard of him."

"Albin says he hates stone. At the moment, that is. Up until a few weeks ago, he still wanted to rescue stone sculpting from oblivion, and he described his plans for groups of figures, gestures, and surface structures in minute detail. He's constantly changing his position on this subject, sometimes in the course of a single day, depending on how much he's had to drink. When he actually carves something, it turns out fantastic. You wouldn't believe what delicate creations can be produced out of stone. Except as soon as it's finished, he finds it disgusting, and within a week he pounds the whole thing to smithereens. With a sledgehammer."

"You're a photographer?"

"At the moment, I don't know what direction I'm going in. Last year, I managed to do pretty well with reporting, but becoming a photojournalist wasn't what I originally had in mind. It's a compromise. I wanted . . . what did I want, actually? Expression. Intensity. Something High Romantic. On the other hand, I didn't spend five years studying so I could earn my living as a waitress. Besides, I don't absolutely have to do it. So that's the problem I'm wrestling with. One of the problems. At the moment, there's a lot of them, all coming at once. I have to make some decisions. In my private life, too, but that's a whole other topic . . ."

By this point, at the very latest, Jan and Livia had forgotten me.

I stopped listening to them, ordered another beer, and thought about why someone would make such personal revelations to a stranger she'd known for barely half an hour. Albin's tales had probably disturbed Livia's equilibrium so much that she had to talk to an outsider about them, and she especially had to talk, as much as possible, about her work as a photographer, about her years with Albin, about herself as a woman who wanted to change her life and had no idea how to go about it. She needed a third party, someone impartial, to form a judgment, and not necessarily an explicit one, either.

Swantje came in, sat down next to Fritz, and ordered apple juice. Nager and Albin laughed. By now, they had managed as well as Jan and Livia to insulate their conversation from the rest of us. I stood up to have a look at the décor in the Orient Lounge. The wooden ceiling, embellished with carving and inlay work, was designed to give the patrons the illusion that they were in a seraglio. The heavy carpets almost completely covering the parquet floor served the same purpose. Apart from the actual bar, the lounge was furnished with groups of brown leather armchairs. On the wall, there were reproductions of nineteenth-century paintings in the Orientalizing style: bazaar scenes, caravan scenes, a dancing dervish, veiled women with children, and a donkey, all in opulent frames. A mixture of designer furniture and kitsch. As I walked past Scherf, I heard him talking about his Iconoclastic Controversy installation. He wanted Hagen to tell him whether a painting-technique expert or a woodworker could teach him how to apply gold leaf. Hagen had no clue, but he did offer the suggestion that the use of gold was difficult on principle and could easily be misinterpreted. Corinna and Sabine came into the lounge with Adel. They didn't want to drink anything before dinner. "I'm dying of hunger," Sabine groaned, so loudly that Nager couldn't ignore it.

"There's a grill restaurant nearby," Albin said. "They have good appetizers, too."

"You show us the way, and you'll be my guests. Tomorrow, that is. If we all show up healthy at breakfast. Tonight you have to pay for yourselves. Let no one say that I don't take my professorial responsibilities seriously."

It was a quarter to eight when we stepped out of the hotel and into the street. The air was cool and refreshing. Nager and Albin went ahead. Nager was gesticulating. Livia and Jan were still talking, softly and with numerous pauses. She shook her head several times.

"I guess we've got these two around our necks now," Mona said.

"Maybe so."

"The guy gets on my nerves."

12.

I wanted the taxi driver to switch his meter on, but he hasn't laid a finger on it, it still reads zero. Apart from him, no one knows where I'm going. That fact is not sufficient for genuine reassurance. Not when you consider what's taken place in the past forty-eight hours.

When I told Poensgen we were flying to Istanbul, he said, "I saw a film on the cultural channel recently. It was about an old Istanbul coffeehouse, Café Lotte or something like that, where a French writer secretly met a very young Turkish harem girl. Later she died of a broken heart, because the writer didn't have the courage to take her away with him. Instead, he had her gravestone brought to France and cobbled together a novel from his journals. But the café is terrific. It's on a hill a little outside the city, and it's got a fantastic view. When the weather is good, you can see all the way to the Bosporus. At least, that's the way they showed it on television: countless minarets, cupolas, and towers, all spread out at your feet. You and Livia should go there and have a look. And send me a postcard."

If it hadn't been for Miller's death and these art students, who are just causing confusion, I would've gone up to that café by now, if only so I could tell the old man, "Master, you were right, that was the best place."

Mist is rising up from the road surface. The cloud cover is getting lower. It would be useless to go hunting for an elevated viewing spot in weather like this.

Maybe knowledge of the intervening distance makes a brief recovery possible. Or maybe the horizon can be pushed back by the mere idea of the panorama that will offer itself as soon as the wind opens up the sky.

Am I the hunter, or am I running away?

In any case: it's stopped raining. The last drops are running off the side windows. My clothes have been damp for days. The dampness has been sucked in through my pores to quench the larva's thirst. I'm completely hollow inside. The pupal stage is beginning. The metamorphosis would come next, if this huge mass of nerve poison hadn't accumulated. It's going to break off the transformation process and kill the half-formed insect. It had its last drink during the course of the past night, whose images I'm going to wash out of my memory without a trace. I'll flood my brain cells until they no longer contain any sort of information. If anyone asks where I was, what happened, I'll evoke ordinary places I've seen and inconsequential people I've met and spoken with: a melancholy bartender, dimmed lights, a band playing jazz tunes. After the last woman left the place, I'll say, I walked out, too, staggering—or not: ramrod straight—and maybe I got lost because the rain obscured the street signs and hid the fountains at important intersections. The streets became narrower and ended in an unlit area. Nobody knew I was wandering around there at that time of night. It got very late, because I never could find a taxi. Livia will believe this story. She's heard hundreds like it, many of which were even true. If I rave about the strong, illegally imported vodka from Novosibirsk, if I describe the red plush on the bar stools and the prominent cheekbones of the Turkish woman who sat next to me (but left without me, even though she would have preferred to take me home), and if I relate often enough how I watched one of the killing squads in action, the ones that go about shooting stray dogs—then I'll envision these scenes more and more clearly, and last night will gradually fade away. Sooner or later, it'll vanish for good.

I'm seizing the opportunity to take a few deep breaths before returning to the general craziness. They're just going to have to do their enjoying and getting bored and coupling and murdering without me.

No one knows me better than Livia. Livia barely knows me. Her love reached a limit and collapsed. There's no reason to tell her what I've seen. She wouldn't believe it.

It stinks in this cab. The animal skin the driver's sitting on is speckled. When he's not making staccato, evil-sounding grumbling noises, as if he blamed the people in the other cars for his miserable existence, he's chewing on his mustache, which has been turned yellow by cigarette smoke. Even his horn sounds bitter. Because the heat in the cab can't be regulated, he alternates between opening his window and closing his window. He's got his woolen cap pulled down low on his forehead. Either I'm suffocating or icy air is blowing hard in my face.

It's time to pause, gather my thoughts, consider the next steps.

It would have been better to stay close to Livia, even though that wouldn't do anything to change her resolve. She can't just creep away after five and a half years without saying that she's giving up on us, that we can't make it. Maybe she mistrusts her decision. Or she's persuading herself that I'm unpredictable and violent and therefore she has to plan her course of action carefully.

According to my reckoning, we should have turned right just then.

Livia makes me sick since we've been traipsing around the city with these students: the hypocritical way she pats my arm, the solicitous, nursely tone. When Jan looks at her, her face glows, as if she's fifteen and he's her first love.

We should have reached the waterfront long before this. Why is the bazaar on the right, and the entrance to the university behind it? So Tiyatro Caddesi has to be on the left, leading down to the Duke's Palace. We're going in exactly the opposite direction.

Gypsies with bears again.

*For weeks, Livia didn't know what she should photograph. I had to listen to her whining about her professional crisis. Now she's snapping pictures everywhere. Every sufficiently colorful shop display is captured on film, along with cats in garbage, bearded old men, and dirty children, who get a few liras for holding still. At breakfast, she talks about medi-*ated reality, *as opposed to* authentic experience. *Word containers she picked up in her student days as part of getting important pomposities to consider her an artist instead of what she really is, a craftsman who produces marketable work and makes good money.*

The Roman aqueduct? This is most definitely not the route he was supposed to take.

I specifically asked this thick-skulled, lice-ridden refugee from the mines to take the road that goes along the Golden Horn, because I felt like looking at water, even if it's a foul-smelling shithole. He nodded, only briefly, but as if he understood me. He said, "No problem," "Good price," and, "Close door tight."

I wanted to see the fog rising off the surface of the water in clouds, breaking up, floating away, disappearing in the white wall. I wanted to determine whether the people here perform the same routines that people carry out on a fall morning on the river Fries.

I've never been in this part of town. Young men in unwashed clothes lean on houses and have no idea what they should do. If the driver throws me out here, I'll find myself tonight on the bottom of the Bosporus with a stone hung around my neck. It's come to this: I get panicky when some random cabdriver takes a different route from the one I suggested.

It's not possible that they anticipated this. Even if they were shadowing me, they couldn't have guessed what my plan was. Without telling anyone what I was going to do, I picked the first taxi stand I came across and hopped into the first cab in line. Normally I would have walked. It was the sight of that filigree star decorating a lintel that

*made me think about Poensgen. Just for once, I wanted to make his wish
come true.*

"The Golden Horn isn't this way!"

"You wanted to go to the Café Piyer Loti. This is the right way."

"But this isn't the way I want to go."

"This way is better."

*He speaks into his microphone, a laughing female voice replies. I
hear "Piyer Loti" several times; apart from that, I can identify no syllable sequence. My name is not mentioned, nor Miller's, nor Messut
Yeter's.* "This way is fast and cheap," *he tells me. A man's voice comes
over the radio. He talks for a long time, interrupted by whistling
sounds. His voice sounds as though he's explaining a job that can be
performed correctly only if everyone follows his instructions to the letter. My driver nods. A couple of times, he says* "Tamam" *without
pressing the talk button.*

"Do you know the story of Piyer Loti?"

"You're going to tell it to me."

*He's made up his mind to play the tour guide in order to jack up
his tip.*

"Piyer Loti was a Frenchman, very famous, a navy officer. Dead
now, a long time, one or two hundred years."

*Or they told him to use diversionary tactics so as to distract me
from noticing where we're going.*

"He could speak perfect Turkish, and he wore our clothes, the way
they were back then, caftan, fez, he even carried a curved dagger in his
belt. You couldn't tell him from a Turk. He lived near the café where you
want to go. He would sit in there and talk to people about religion, pol-
itics, and so forth. But mostly he stared into space and thought about
the girl he loved. Her name was Aziyadeh, the youngest woman in an
old spice merchant's harem. A most beautiful girl. Of course, Piyer Loti
could only meet her in secret. Fortunately, he had a friend, Emre, who

really was his best friend. Piyer Loti was a high-ranking officer and Emre a simple fisherman, but with a good heart. As often as he could, Emre took Piyer Loti for a sail on the Bosporus at night. Even though he would have been killed if he'd been caught doing that. So that's how you can tell what a good friend he was."

I'm not going to get all worked up. I'm too tired, and I've had too much to drink.

"Then her master discovered that Aziyadeh had been cheating on him the whole time, and he had her executed. By the sword. Had she revealed Piyer Loti's name, her life would have been spared, but she was silent as the tomb. And now in Turkey some men and women admire and some hate her, depending on how their own lives are going."

All right, any minute now he's going to stop someplace where I can buy hand-carved marionettes of Piyer Loti, Aziyadeh, Emre, and the cruel spice merchant. The business belongs to his brother-in-law. Little inlaid wood boxes, camel saddles, and tea ware are on sale at special prices. Or I'll feel a pistol muzzle in the back of my neck.

"Piyer Loti sat up there for weeks at a time, silently staring at the Bosporus with tears in his eyes. He wanted to die. Sometimes his friend Emre came and tried to comfort him. He knew what the pain of love was like. Half a year later, the Russian War started. Because of his love for Aziyadeh, Piyer Loti fought on our side. He was a lion in battle, because he did not fear death. He died for our country. In the battle of Kars. With the caliph's banner in his hand."

We're at a red light. The ruins of the city wall built by Theodosius are in front of us. The driver looks at me expectantly. I don't know how I'm supposed to respond to his story. He looks friendlier now. He says, "Do you like Istanbul?"

"I'm here for business reasons."

"Business?"

"Yes."

"Import-export? Tourism? Or mechanical engineering?"

"Film business."

"Film business is good. Very good. You can make a film about Piyer Loti, that's a romantic story. It's like Gone with the Wind. Love, war, sailing ships, horses. People want that, believe me."

"We're shooting a thriller. And it's set in the present."

"If you want to know something, ask me. I know Istanbul like my living room."

"It's about precious stone smuggling, the Russian mafia, that sort of thing. With Marlon Brando in the leading role."

"I'm a great fan of Marlon Brando. I liked him best in Mutiny on the Bounty. Have you met him?"

"He's a friend of mine."

"Then you can get me his autograph? And one for my son, too, and two more for my two nephews?"

"If you give me your address, I'll send you a whole stack of them as soon as I get back to America."

"What's your name?"

"Al."

"I'm Aziz. Al, next time you come to Istanbul, come to my house for dinner. My wife's the best cook." Then he says, "Here we are."

I can't see any café anywhere around.

"You have to walk the rest of the way. Cars can't get to the Piyer Loti. Follow the cemetery straight uphill." He fishes paper and pencil out of the glove compartment and writes down his address. "Do you think Marlon Brando can write 'For Mustafa' on the card?" he asks, and he looks so shy it makes me feel ashamed. "Mustafa is my son."

"I'll ask Marlon. He can be a difficult guy."

"If not, no problem," he says, and extends his hand to me. "So long, Al. I wish you lots of luck on your movie."

As soon as Aziz's car is out of sight, I throw the paper away.

The road's heavily damaged. Moss is growing out of cracks in the asphalt, and in places whole sections are missing. The way goes past a graveyard where no one's visiting the dead. The graves are sunken. They haven't been filled in with earth since the bodies in them subsided. Apart from some wild bushes, the only thing growing here is grass. Even high columns and pillars were erected without foundations. Many of them are old pieces with writing in Arabic letters. They're standing crooked. Several have toppled over and broken on impact. There's a chest-high wall around the place, and inside it thousands of limestone grave markers are lined up on the slope of the hill like a defeated army. A few meters away, the color of the grass fades. Everything's dipped in the colors of stone and fog.

It makes no sense to climb a hill for the view in this kind of weather. Maybe I can buy a panoramic postcard from one of the street vendors. I must be north of Eyüp. My city map stops south of it. The water can't be far away. The streets are deserted. Oil floats on the puddles in the colors of the rainbow. The houses are falling down, but people are living in them. What do children and old people do at this time of day? Smoke comes out of sheet metal pipes. I hear recitations of the Qur'an, droning music from a cassette player, the shriek of a power saw some distance away. The curtains are drawn across every single window. A potted plant's leaves lie where they've fallen. The air deposits a greasy film on your skin. The road is now a sandy path leading downhill. A smell of rotten onions. My sense of direction is still reliable—I can see some wooden masts and rigging emerging from the haze. There aren't many boats tied up at the quay. Ferries, fishing boats. It's been a long time since they've been painted. One day they'll sink and no one will notice they're gone. From the highway bridge to the Duke's Palace must be six or seven kilometers. That'll take me about an hour and a half if I don't hurry and don't dawdle. I have to see Messut in the Sultan at six. I'll walk and think, think and walk.

Nobody knows I'm here. Not the people who know me, and not the strangers whose traces I'm trying to follow.

I'm going around in circles. Maybe I misinterpreted some detail or didn't classify a clue correctly, so now there are connections but no conclusions. The people I talk to in the bazaar would rather make up any sort of nonsense than admit they can't help me. When you ask one, the less he knows, the more hair-raising stories he tells, in hopes that you'll feel grateful and buy something from him. How can you tell the difference between deliberate attempts to mislead and lies told out of embarrassment? The Russian called Nicola admitted that Miller was in town a few days ago to inspect personally a delivery of emeralds from the Ural Mountains. He didn't want to exclude the possibility that the courier was stuck somewhere. Nothing to get excited about. Since Miller's death, I've seen Ireen at least once. She ran away from me, even though I'm the only witness to the murder. A new American has moved into the room next to the one where they were staying. Messut says he works for an insurance outfit that specializes in shipping companies. American tour operators require ferries to be insured according to American insurance standards so that appropriate damage claims can be met in case of emergency.

The sounds around me are getting indistinct. It's as though the heavy haze muffles them. In the midst of all this monstrous noise, the fog causes a disconcerting silence.

Why does Messut deny that Miller was staying in the Sultan? Then again, he drops hints that make me think my giving up the search isn't what he has in mind. He wants me to keep looking, but in another direction. He's organizing a kind of paper chase.

He knows things about me that he can't possibly know.

There's a hammer striking stone somewhere nearby. It doesn't sound like sculpting. Human shapes: men pounding pavement slabs into place. Planting young trees, putting up streetlights. They're laying down a promenade. *Ground torn up, mounds of sand and gravel between contractor's sheds and big trash receptacles. The blows become quieter and then die away. Even the traffic noise seems far off. The rhythm of my steps reminds me of a march that was on the one record that Father owned.* The Ceremonial Tattoo.

No sign of a kiosk that sells beer.

When I walk into the Otelo Sultan at five-thirty, Messut says, without looking up from his forms, "It's good that you've come, Albin. I've got news for you." He glances up at me and notices that I look dead tired. *"You had a terrible night."*

"How do you know that?"

"I've been working in this hotel for thirty years. Most of the men who come to Turkey for the first time have seen Hollywood movies about the Orient and want to experience something out of the ordinary. Bazaars and mosques are great, but there must be some opium dens or hot-blooded women hidden somewhere. Depending on where they wind up, the next morning they look as though they've ridden through the fires of hell or they need the telephone number of their embassy because their money and papers have disappeared."

"I'm not missing anything."

"Perhaps you were being protected."

"Nonsense."

"Listen. Someone called me, a man of my acquaintance. He knows a great deal, and he'll try to assist you in your efforts. Go to Düşünülen Yer with the others. Even if you've already told Livia you don't want to make the trip, go with them. It's safer there than it is here in the city center. Someone will meet you and take you to an informant. You'll find out where once you're over there—it will depend on the situation. You mustn't be too concerned, but there is, of course, some small risk."

"Why should I trust you?"

"I thought we had that sort of thing behind us."

"How will the middleman know who I am?"

"He knows you."

"That's good to hear."

"At the moment, I can't tell you anything else."

13.

During dinner, Nager and Albin continued their conversation about the state of art and the world. Nager talked nonstop, whereas Albin tossed in occasional remarks designed to get to the heart of whatever matter was under consideration. Both of them, glad to have met someone who wouldn't count the glasses in disgust if they drank to excess, indulged themselves in outlandish flights of rhetoric and reasoning. Later, when we were sitting in the Orient Lounge for the second time that night, they began saying *"Du"* to each other, like old friends. Nager declared that Albin, unlike us, understood what he meant when he explained connections and correlations; therefore, he concluded, the class's complaints that he expressed himself unclearly must spring from our difficulties with following his thoughts and not from the impenetrability of the said thoughts. He grinned, twirled a finger deep in his ear, and assured us that, despite this vindication, we needn't be fearful of his taking points off our grades—after all, his wife agreed with us. The important thing was that she put up with him. For his part, he didn't hold it against her when she needed a pocket calculator for arithmetic he could do in his head.

Albin seemed absolutely not to notice that Livia and Jan had been talking without interruption ever since we sat down on the stools next to them. It was so obvious that Hagen whispered to me, "She wants something from Jan. And Jan looks interested. Even though Mona's here." Mona also told me her view of the situation: "This sculptor and his photographer girlfriend—if you ask me, Olaf, they're through with each other. Let's hope Jan doesn't let himself get sucked into something. Besides, I have no idea what to think about this murder story."

Around twelve-thirty, Livia said good night. She stroked Albin's shoulders, kissed Jan on both cheeks, and waved. Shortly afterward, Jan asked me if I'd like to go upstairs and have a beer from the minibar. The conversation down here might never end, he said, and besides, there was something he had to tell me. Nager and Albin ordered vodka. Nager used the opportunity to ask the waitress some questions, such as whether she lived nearby and whether her boyfriend also worked at night, trying to elicit some personal information he could use to advantage later. He performed his pickup routine automatically, with no faith in the possibility of success. The girl, accustomed to keeping overfriendly men at a distance, laughed and brushed him off.

According to Livia, Albin came back to their room shortly after three, only slightly drunk and unusually pensive. For the first time since the beginning of the trip, he made no complaint about the moneygrubbing people in this stinking monstrosity of a city. He said, "I like this Nager. He's in hopeless despair, and he acts as though it's funny, because a mediocre artist's despair doesn't do anything for anybody."

Then he gazed at Livia with his soggy, boozy eyes and asked, "Do you or do you not believe that the gem dealer Jonathan Miller was shot? Give me an honest answer, or else keep your mouth shut."

"I can't tell you what I believe. It changes five times a minute."

"What do you suggest I do?"

"Drink water. Or Coke."

"Thanks. You're a great help."

Albin rolled over and fell asleep.

Livia lay awake most of the night, pondering the sequence of images that passed before her mind's eye and making decisions: She would mail the card to Thea; she would try to reach Thea by telephone; she would tell Albin she had decided to leave him once they returned home. She wouldn't do any of it.

The next morning, the weather was damp and cold. When Albin came into the breakfast room, he nodded in our direction. The greeting was meant for Nager. Mona sighed but, undaunted, continued reading aloud to us about how Hagia Sophia had gone from a church to a mosque to a museum. After choosing two sesame rings from the buffet, Albin took the last seat at our table and sat in silence. Mona embellished her reading of passages from her guidebook with half-digested facts about the heresies of early Christendom and enthusiastic praise for the different types of sheep's milk cheese on her plate. Nager chewed his bread and jam, made a pained face, and wished he were with his wife, who normally saw to it that he was able to ease into each day unmolested by alien voices. Mona might be beautiful, but he'd nearly grabbed her by the hair the previous evening, and her good mood this morning was practically intolerable. Before ten o'clock, he thought, silence should reign. Everything should be desolate and void, like before the creation, so that one's first thought might summon up the courage to creep out of the protective darkness and into the light.

"My dear Mona," Nager said. "Why don't you read us that passage when we're at the site? No one's going to remember anything he hears on an empty stomach. We're not ready to improve our minds."

"Professor Nager, I always like to have some preliminary information about what I'm going to look at. Otherwise, I stare at things like a cow."

Livia came in ten minutes after Albin, saw that there were no seats at our table, and without comment retreated to one nearby. I assume it was a relief to her not to have to discuss Albin's next move with him. She'd decided that the whole affair had nothing to do with her, and she didn't want to take part in any activity related to it. Her eyes were glued to the door. As Jan entered the room, I saw his reflection in them, even before he himself came into my field of vision. Just as naturally as Albin had joined us, Jan carried his tray to Livia's table.

Without looking up from her guidebook, Mona said, "Those two surely knew each other before. They're just not letting on."

"Who knows whom?" Nager wanted to know.

"Doesn't matter," I said.

"Can anyone explain to me what this is supposed to mean? *'In an impost capital, the individual forms of the capital and the impost block are fused into a single architectural element and defunctionalized. This is possible only through the dematerialization of the individual forms. Sculpted acanthus leaves have given way to a flat ornamentation detached from its background. In order to understand this transition from rounded forms to flat surfaces, consider the architectural sculpture of the Theodosian vestibule of Hagia Sophia, which can . . .'* "

"Nager, have you got a light?" Albin asked. "Or anyone else?"

" *'. . . which can be seen in the west forecourt. Here the acanthus leaves are already projected onto the surface.'* You could at least ask if I mind you smoking. I'm still eating."

"By the time you finish reading, my cigarette will be over. Besides, I'm going to smoke on the terrace."

Nager held out his lighter to Albin, stood up, and with one

hand waved away an objection that no one had made. "I'm going with you," he said. "So Mona can have her breakfast in peace. And because I want to see where this Miller person was shot."

"It's quiet outside," Albin said as they stepped through the door. He broke off pieces of a sesame ring and tossed them to the seagulls. The haze softened the contours of the surrounding buildings. The curtains in Miller's suite were closed. They moved, but not because of any wind. The room was occupied; someone was backing into the curtain or brushing it with an arm. There must have been more than one person, because the fabric was pressed against the glass in two different places simultaneously. The curtains parted a little, and you could see a light burning, brighter than the usual hotel room lamp. Shapes flitted in front of it, met, merged, separated. Albin wondered whether the people were careless or had simply decided to run the risk of being discovered. Surely, someone must have told them they could be seen. He tried to detect something that would help him figure out what was going on, but the glimpses he caught were too fleeting for him to discern anything but the presence of people. Whatever they might be doing there, they would have to know that it was a place where something terrible had happened. Either they were connected with the killer or someone had fed them a story about an accident or a suicide. They wouldn't necessarily have thought that the reddish brown spot on the carpet was the result of a violent crime, but there could have been no doubt that the stain was dried blood, and not even in Istanbul did people slaughter animals in hotel rooms.

"Well, in any case," Nager said, "this Sultan Hotel really is so close you can see what's going on in it."

"If the wind's blowing the right way, you can also hear what's being said. The buildings act like the bell of a horn. They amplify the sounds from that suite—oddly enough, only from that one suite—and carry them over here. He said, *Take care of you, baby.* Those were his last words."

"Not bad. Better, in any case, than *Would you please give me the butter, darling?* or *This dress is looking very cheap, honey!*" They laughed.

"Do you and Livia want to go to Hagia Sophia with us?"

"Why not? I have something to do later, though. I'll have to go away for a little while."

When Albin proposed this group excursion, Livia reacted guardedly. However, as he was pondering the alternatives, she made a quick decision to join us.

It took a while for everyone to gather on the street in front of the hotel. Tiyatro Caddesi ran in a steep climb from the Sea of Marmara to the western entrance of the Grand Bazaar. After a few steps, Albin started wheezing. In response to Jan's frown, Livia explained that Albin had been suffering from asthma recently. She'd asked him to see a doctor, she said, but he'd replied that he wasn't much attached to living, as she very well knew. He embarrassed her. She was afraid we'd draw conclusions about her condition from his. Nager was also panting for air. He undid the top buttons of his shirt and clutched his chest. After we'd gone half the distance, they stopped and leaned on a building, side by side, pale and sweating. After a while, they bent forward, pretending to be a pair of slavering old men supporting themselves on invisible walking sticks. Then they started giggling.

"Those two aren't going to make it much farther," Mona said as she passed by. She spoke in a low voice, unsure whether she wanted them to hear her.

Corinna was struggling with the fear of having stumbled into a situation from which there was no escape. Sabine had left her crutches in the hotel and was clinging to Adel's arm. Fritz was looking at the display window in a pastry shop. Immediately in front of me, Scherf was explaining to Swantje that the increasingly independent status of the icons in the course of the sixth and seventh centuries had been the source of the Iconoclastic Controversy. For people of simple faith, he continued, icons had clearly begun to take on the character of living beings, situated on the scale somewhere between talismans and angels, and far from existing merely as dried paint on wood. There were stories, Scherf said, in which icons drove out devils, predicted the future from dreams, and worked all sorts of miracles. Other icons bled or wept. They were also able to take revenge when they saw fit to do so. For example, people attributed the devastating earthquake that destroyed Trebizond in 682 to the anger of a precious icon of Saint Ephrem the Syrian that had been set afire three times during the Easter service because a drunken deacon kept dropping burning coals onto it from his censer.

All the while he was speaking, Scherf was making an effort to get rid of an eight- or nine-year-old street urchin who had taken it into his head to sell him a carton of fake Camel cigarettes.

As Jan passed us up, he called out, "There was no schism," because he knew that would tick off Scherf. Then Jan added, "Here's a tip: I'd use gold spray paint for the pedestals."

"You don't understand anything."

Jan whispered a few words to Livia and pushed her forward, his hand in her back.

I know that at least Mona, Swantje, and Fritz were as disappointed in Hagia Sophia as I was: a big old building that didn't know what it was good for anymore. The reasons why it was con-

quered and transformed had long since lost almost all validity, as
had the reasons why it was erected in the first place, a thousand
years ago. Now it was called a "museum," which meant that at
least one thing was certain: it was the responsibility of a certain
specific authority. Tourists went by, singly or in groups, and at different speeds. They moved here and there, snapping photographs
that would replace their memories in a few months.

"We could agree to meet back at the entrance in an hour and
a half," Nager said.

Maybe the light was wrong that Tuesday, or maybe we were
what was wrong, because we'd expected something else.

"This space is depressing," Mona said.

Most of us there in Hagia Sophia already felt that Albin and
Livia were exacerbating the generally bad feelings in the class. For
a month and a half, we'd been trying to get used to Nager, our new
professor. After six visiting professors in three years, hopeless confusion reigned among us. Under Nager's leadership, the class trip
was supposed to clear up quarrels based on differing artistic approaches, clarify the balance of power, and instill something like a
sense of community. Before this process could begin, Nager came
to the conclusion that he preferred talking to Albin. Jan, who'd
been at the academy the longest, except for me, was talking exclusively to a female photographer in the midst of a relationship crisis. And her partner was dragging us all into his own story without
our understanding what it meant.

As we stood before the mosaic of Christ in the south gallery of
Hagia Sophia, Mona said, "That's the saddest look any picture has
ever given me."

Mona had been the most determined promoter of a class trip.
She said she thought something had to happen; if not, she'd been

studying for nothing. Then, when it came to the choice of a destination, she got outvoted.

"I thought the weather here would be like southern Italy—mild temperatures in early November," I said.

"So did I."

Seraphs were painted on the wall under the cupola, angelic creatures that patrolled the skies with beating wings epochs ago. Under them were tablets with Islamic calligraphy, gold on black. Chests filled with junk stood in the corners.

When the group gathered again, Livia determined that Albin was missing. She didn't look surprised. Nager said Albin had gone off in search of a men's room and never returned. At breakfast, or maybe after breakfast, Nager said, Albin had indicated that he had something to take care of. Hagen had seen him heading for the exit half an hour before.

"He's probably investigating the Miller case," Livia said. "I'm staying out of it."

At first, Albin actually did go looking for a bathroom, because he suddenly needed to drink water, preferably cold. After taking a few steps, he saw one of the museum guards, who had been sitting on his chair as though never to stir again, rise to his feet with a start and begin following him. Albin got frightened and wanted to run away, but instead he decided to try an experiment to clarify once and for all whether or not he was suffering from a persecution complex. Just before the sultan's loge, he turned into the side aisle. For several minutes, he concentrated on the floor, which was made up of slabs of granite, porphyry, verde antico, and Prokonessos marble. He fished around inside his jacket for pencil and paper and wrote down the names of the different types of stone, the way Poensgen did. During all this time, the museum attendant from the main room kept an eye on him. When Albin walked on and disappeared into a blind corner, the guard accelerated. Albin could tell, because the man brought himself to a stop two steps too late. From that moment on, Albin was certain that the people who had Miller killed had been able within a few days to gather enough information to keep him, the witness to the crime, under surveillance. In the best case, they'd let it go at that until he left the country. Provided he didn't make any mistakes. Going to the police would be a mistake. Albin yielded to his flight reflex and directed his steps through the two vestibules to the exit. Once outside, he turned around and saw the guard's back disappearing into the darkness. Without haggling over the price, he bought a can of soda from a child, one of many children working as street vendors, and took a drink. Since these people were going to knock him off soon anyway, he thought, he might as well try to find out what really happened. Maybe doing so would provide him with a solution to his plight. At least he hadn't let himself get picked off like a sleeping dog. As Albin walked, he tried to recall the floor plan of the lobby in the Sultan so that he could decide in advance which way he would turn as soon as the revolving door spat him out. Twenty minutes later, he could see the entrance to the Sultan, fifty meters away, and all Albin knew was that he would need luck to get through the lobby without being seen by the clerk at the desk. The previous day, he hadn't noticed the two uniformed porters standing by the door. Albin put a relaxed expression on his face and nodded to them so they'd think he recognized them. They made no move to stop him as he walked up the red carpet and into the revolving glass cylinder. He tried to look over the layout of the room as fast as he could. Reception on the left. Young woman at the desk, using the telephone. Messut nowhere to be seen, though he could easily be hidden by a column.

Albin got the lucky break he wanted. At the very moment when the door opened into the lobby, two workers came from the side carrying a freshly painted partition wall. They gave him a few seconds' cover while he made a further effort to get his bearings. Two rows of pillars, three per row, supported the lobby ceiling. Across from him hung an enormous photograph of Hagia Sophia and the green park in front of it, gleaming in bright sunshine. The elevator was to the right of that. In any case, he couldn't use it. Next to the elevator a gallery with shops and display windows began. If he could reach that gallery, he'd be invisible to people at the reception desk. He slipped through groups of chairs and sofas. To his left, the workers with their wall cut off that segment of the lobby from the view of anyone at the desk; otherwise, he thought, Messut would certainly spot me. Shielded by the wall, Albin reached the last pillar unnoticed and glided from there into the gallery with the shops. At the other end, he turned into a wood-paneled corridor. He was sure that a hotel of this size must have several elevators and several sets of stairs, one of which had to be in this part of the building. Albin forced himself not to run. At the end of the corridor, he opened a door—despite the sign on it, which read, in English, *Staff Only*—and found himself standing in a bright stairwell. He closed his eyes for a moment and caught his breath. His first plan was to look around the seventh floor for whatever he could find. If a colossus of Miller's size had been shot and killed and his body carried off, traces must have been left behind. Once upstairs, he needed another break. He tried to figure out which way the intersection of the two streets was, which positions the hotels must therefore have in relation to each other, and how often he had changed direction. He reconstructed the hotel's floor plan in his mind until he knew which part of the building he was in and where to find Miller's

suite. As a sculptor, Albin had extraordinary powers of visual imagination, so he was sure he was going in the right direction. He
didn't come across anyone, not even a chambermaid. Just before
he reached the corridor where he was sure he'd find the door to
Miller's suite, he heard voices. He thought about Ireen's hair in
curlers, and her broken fingernails. Although he didn't understand
a word, it was clear to him that the voices belonged neither to
tourists nor to businessmen. He heard what sounded like curt instructions and oaths. On the floor, in a large roll, lay a new, wine-
colored velvet carpet, and above it two powerful-looking men,
gesticulating with rulers. One of them had his back to Albin; the
other had already seen him and shouted something into the room,
whereupon two more men, younger men, came running out into
the hall. He was surrounded. They bawled at him; one waved a carpet knife in front of his face. The one who was giving the orders
shouted something in the direction of the suite and received a
short answer. Albin was two heads taller than all four of them, but
he had no chance of running away. They were probably armed.

"So what happens now? *Wollt ihr mich einsperren?* You want to
lock me up?"

"*Deutsch,*" the boss said. Albin nodded.

"Thief," the man said in German. "You go prison."

Albin felt a sense of great calm. When he heard steps approaching, he hoped someone was coming who might clear up the
misunderstanding. Then Messut Yeter was standing in front of him.
After exchanging a few sentences with the boss, Messut turned to
Albin with an angry look on his face and said, "What are you doing here?"

"I decided to take you up on your offer to have a look from the
roof terrace and lost my way. Now I'm searching for an elevator."

"Don't lie to me."

"What else would I be doing here?"

"We'll discuss this in my office."

Messut jerked his wrist, and Albin followed. Even after the other men were out of earshot, Albin stayed with Messut, although he could easily have knocked him down and run off. They got into an elevator and stepped out into the main lobby. The flower beds on the great photograph of Hagia Sophia could have come from a German spa.

When they entered the room behind the hotel desk, Albin said, "I don't know what your purpose is. I think you're probably trying to get me out of the way. To tell you the truth, you'll be doing me a favor."

Messut ignored the melodramatic undertones of this statement. He said, "Albin, you're a guest in Turkey. As you've probably heard, hospitality is extremely important to us. A stranger receives special protection from his Turkish hosts. Whoever injures a guest is subject to severe penalties. But of course, the guest must behave like a friend. Otherwise he loses his protection."

"I'm not interested in protection. Yesterday, Jonathan Miller was shot to death in his suite on the seventh floor of your hotel."

"I can show you the reservations lists for the past month. You won't find anyone by that name."

"I saw it happen with my own eyes."

"Maybe you saw a djinn."

"A what?"

"Djinns are strange beings, shape changers. They're showing you things you need to see. You alone. And precisely at this point in time. They're a kind of reflection. Nevertheless, they really exist."

Albin tried to recall how much he'd had to drink the day before yesterday, wondering whether he'd been taken in by a dream figure's shadow play.

"I want to help you," Messut said. "Trust me."

Trusting him is another mistake, Albin thought. *But there's no other possibility.*

14.

Three young dogs are lying in front of the door. When my sickly smell wafts over to them, they get up and trot away.

Wooden models of the seraglio, the harem, in the shopwindows. Three-masted ships with paper sails stuck on toothpicks navigate a sea of dusty blue. The land is a felt surface, the kind used in billiard tables. The palace is a city made of building blocks with little gray domes. A city like a park, with the sea as a backdrop. Dungeons. A fairy wood. Mothers poison their children, brothers strangle one another. I must kill you, beloved, for my sake, for the sake of my firstborn son. For God.

I have no skin, I'm staggering, everyone can see I've lost my coordination, I can barely control my limbs. A look of contempt from Mona. I stick out my tongue at her and she waves me off. Corinna's afraid. Because of Nager and me, she won't be studying art very much longer. She'd imagined herself in front of an easel, painting with a marten-bristle paintbrush, her hair braided and coiled into plaits over her ears.

When was the last time I slept? When was the last dream I had that wasn't a nightmare of flesh and shrieking?

"Look at the wrought iron in these grilles," Nager says. "No one thinks about breaking in or out, because that would mean sawing through such beautiful bars."

I answer, "You stay stuck where you are, all your life, unmoving. Inside or out, it makes no difference."

"You can be my assistant, Albin. I'll request the academy board to make you my assistant. A full professor needs an assistant."

An assistant with trembling hands, who has trouble bringing a cigarette to his mouth, whose bronchia ache from the frigid air.

Tall cypresses, spreading plane trees. Withered leaves in the tops of the trees and on the lawns. Tubs with plants and shrubbery. Marbled flagstones. Stone disgusts me. A black cat enters from the left. I could never remember whether black cats from the left or black cats from the right are the dangerous ones. Livia photographs them, but they get no fee. A young woman's provocative laugh comes from behind a broken wooden shutter a bit farther up. It sounded like that when sultans lived here. The most unbelievable stories were told about the sultans, until finally they believed the stories themselves; then the buildings fell down, and their realms could not be saved. A helicopter's droning away above us. There's no connection between the sound and the things I'm seeing. Mona has hired a guide for the museum and the harem. He'll explain the exhibits, crack mediocre jokes, and get insulted when we don't laugh.

Livia's the woman I love, even though I've seldom let her see that. She'll go away with Jan.

The rays of the sun break through the cloud cover, bathing the sea and the mosques in pale light. Shouts come from the foot of the wall below. Who's being shouted at? Livia asks, "Do you know what kind of stone this is?"

I say, "Marble. One of a thousand different kinds of marble. Take some pictures of it. Poensgen will tell you where the slabs come from. As for me, I don't care. You can't imagine how much I don't care."

Her feelings are hurt. She stares, snaps a picture, and turns to Jan. I've got to have a drink. After the first swallow, I'll be able to think clearly again. Walk better, too. If not, I'll just lie down and go to sleep *in a spot where I won't disturb anyone.* "I'm interested to know what kind of sculptures you've made," Nager says. "You use the wrong material, my friend, but so what?"

"Forget about it. I chisel copies. I carve things others have imagined. It's a question of dexterity, of having a steady hand. In concrete terms, the real question is, has the sculptor had a drink yet today, or not?"

"Am I supposed to believe that?"

"Have you got any sort of alcohol on you?"

Nager reaches into the inner pocket of his jacket and takes out a silver hip flask in a leather case. He slips me the flask. Nobody notices it. In an entrance, I toss back a drink and focus on the sharp edge of the whiskey as it etches the walls of my stomach. I'll feel better in a few minutes. When I unobtrusively give the flask back to Nager, he says again, "You're my assistant." He's supposed to teach art to half-grown children. He's supposed to act like an authority figure. Authority figures don't hand around liquor flasks.

A tiled pavilion, the tiles ornamented with flowers, twenty different patterns, turquoise on white, a bit of green, red. No transition from one pattern to another—they clash like pieces of fabric cut with swords and stitched together by a bad tailor. I don't understand the importance of flowers and tendrils. There are too many of them for pure decoration, and they're too lavishly displayed. Jan asks Olaf. Olaf says, "There's a theory that floral ornamentation in Islamic art refers to the Gardens of Bliss, which are spoken of in the Qur'an. So the theme would be nature, tamed nature, shaped by man, who acts as God's deputy. Other researchers think this kind of decoration is an adaptation of Chinese floral patterns, which arrived in Istanbul with the first porcelain imports and were perfected here. I like the idea of the gardens."

Hagen says, "There are naked girls lying around everywhere."

"They're called houris."

"Were Mr. Miller and this Ireen person married?" Nager asks.

"As far as I know, they weren't."

"Was he married to someone else?"

"He never spoke about any other woman. And he didn't wear a wedding ring. Just a thick signet ring."

"That needs to be clarified. She might have had an interest in his death. If he was really as rich as you suggest."

"It was about something else."

"What was her last name?"

"He spoke of her only as Ireen."

"I went to Barcelona once for a group exhibit of new German art. I was there for a week, and I hung around with this Russian whore the whole time. I took her with me everywhere and paid for everything. I didn't much feel like being alone, and next door to my hotel there was the kind of brothel where you can go and have a nightcap, even if you don't want sex. She called herself Conchita. We never even fucked, but believe me, I had a good time with her . . . How did I get onto that? Oh, right, this Ireen, do you know how she earned her living? Are you feeling better?"

"Could I have another swallow?" He gives me the flask without comment.

Livia and Jan are walking so close together their shoulders touch. He's showing her things, suggesting viewing angles. She's taking pictures. In some of them, he becomes a model for her photographic feature on art students in Istanbul. Jan looks like a nineteenth-century painter, traveling the Orient with a camera obscura he built himself, painting portraits of officers and camel drivers. Three weeks ago, I would have beaten him to a pulp. Or snatched Livia out of here. Without hurting her. I never hit women. Even if one cheats on me, I don't hit her.

Oriental traveler Jan Kenzig lays his hand on the shoulder of photographer Livia Mendt and whispers something apparently funny into her ear. They both laugh, while her longtime companion, Albin Kranz, tries to drink himself sober.

I doubt that Mother was ever unfaithful to Father, not even after he disappeared.

"We have to go back toward the entrance or we'll miss the guided tour," Mona says.

"What's there to see in a harem besides bathrooms?" Scherf asks.

"No tits!" Hagen says.

"Then why should I go there?"

"To continue your education."

"You're the dumbest guy I know, Scherf," Jan says.

"Shut up."

The guide introduces herself as Hatidje. I've seen her before. Not here, in Hamburg. She's in her late twenties, stands five foot four at most. Long, dull black hair; thin lips; sharp, widely spaced teeth. She tells us she majored in art history and Middle Eastern studies at the university in Tübingen. Never been there.

"For the next two hours, I'm going to guide you through a world that Europeans as well as simple people in Istanbul imagined and reimagined continually over the course of the centuries. For some, it became an image of heaven on earth; for others, it was a stronghold of unimaginable cruelty. The starting point as well as the final goal of all those projections was right here. You will discover that the actual structures, the power relationships, and the realities of palace life under Ottoman rule, particularly the life of the harem, accord with the city's various images as much as they differ from them." She stresses the word harem on the last syllable. It sounds strange. It doesn't make you think about dusky slave girls, lolling about in warm water while the sinister character whom it is their task to satisfy is out of the house. "I'm going to say a few introductory words, and then we'll look at some of the collections on exhibit. If it's all right with you, however, the majority of our time will be taken up by our tour of the harem." My eyes and Hatidje's meet, and I notice the way her word flow slows down a little. She probably remembered me from somewhere at that very moment. Or recognized me. I was in Hamburg three months ago. I'd have to be mentally ill to assume she was already trailing me back then. And on whose account? "We have come through the Bab-üs-Selam, the Gate of Peace, and into the second courtyard. This is where the palace proper actually begins. Although we have comparatively few visitors on the grounds today, there's still some background noise—voices, and of course street traffic. To help you get an idea of the original atmosphere, you should try to imagine yourselves in a place of total silence, even though that's hard to do in Istanbul. We know from historical accounts that even in this outer, half-public area, talking was strictly forbidden when the sultan was present. And except for him, no one was allowed to ride a horse on the palace grounds. Gazelles, monkeys, peacocks, and exotic animals from everywhere in the world were kept in the parks, so that images of Paradise were inevitably conjured up in the minds of strangers, whether petitioners or envoys, Muslims or Christians. Moreover, at that time the enclosed grounds of the palace were considerably more extensive than they are now, although the city was by no means less noisy and hectic."

On the roof terrace of the Duke's Palace, the long thread of smoke from my cigarette, the morning haze over the city, the two seagulls hissing, from far off the whistle of a ship setting out to sea, nothing happens.

"I don't know if I can take two hours of this," I whisper to Nager.

"Without the girl, we can't enter the harem. And it's supposed to be really sensational. At least, that's what my friend Seppo says."

"Who?"

"Kurt Seppenberger. Know him?"

I nod.

"He was with me in Barcelona."

Nager stops walking and grabs my arm. "You're in bad shape," he says, and he gives me the flask again. "Drink it all. I've still got three quarters of a bottle up in my room. Duty-free."

I suppress a coughing fit, trying not to puke, and swallow some air. Then the warmth starts spreading. The warmth turns to heat and shoots up into my head. My temples are burning, my breath is fever-hot, a fire that could melt iron. I'm not imagining this. My joints feel tighter. "Seppo's the same way," Nager says. "He never leaves his apartment unless he's tossed down five or six shots." When I turn around, Livia's eyes are on me, sad, as if I were dead. She looks away reflexively, before my eyes can meet hers, and makes her face hard. Hatidje's gaze, on the other hand, follows me like a spotlight while her mouth forms sentences learned by heart in flawless German. She's observing me. I don't know why or for what. Her face hints at a smile, meant for me. Her thoughts are somewhere else: "We are now passing through the Bab-üs-Saadet, the Gate of Felicity, and into the third courtyard. In front of us is the audience chamber. This is where the sultan received special envoys. During the talks, water splashed out of a fountain built into the wall, so no subordinates could hear what was being discussed, because each of them was a potential traitor. The current furnishings of the room come from the nineteenth century, with the exception of numerous tiles, which were preserved from the demolition of some older buildings and put to a new use here."

How many façades have I shored up or reconstructed in Hamburg? If I add them all together, how many months, how many years have I spent there, living in cheap hotel rooms like so many little boxes? And during my various sojourns, how many women have I bought, picked up, or swept off their feet? How many of their faces would I recognize, or at most their moles or their tattoos, and how many would I fail to recognize at all? Was this Hatidje one of them? When you're drunk, outward appearances count for nothing. A woman's attractiveness increases in direct proportion to the percentage of alcohol in a man's blood. She's staring at me, even though she's noticed that I'm not listening to her, even though I'm sweating and swaying and leaning against walls and I have to watch out, otherwise I'll slip down inch by inch until I'm squatting on my heels, there to stay. She probably goes for hollow molds of the large, blond type. My eyelids are heavy. Don't get your hopes up, my girl. Ask Livia, she'll tell you: I'm hardly ever hungry anymore, and certainly not for you; I'm only ever thirsty. You don't own a bear, you're not even a well-meaning waitress filling my glass more generously than usual, you're an inhibited student who talks too much. Listen to me: I see lions in broad daylight, amber lions with diamonds for eyes and manes made of silver threads. I can look at the beam of a halogen spotlight and find your sultans, your viziers, your eunuchs, carved out of mother-of-pearl and lapis lazuli. Their turbans are set with rubies, and over them hovers the awe-inspiring Golden Elephant, a mutation out of the mythical past, a gift of the gods: "It was made in India in the seventeenth century," you say—it's good to know such things, they give you confidence—"and is one of the most splendid pieces in our collection. The chest holds a music machine in good working order, a masterpiece of precision engineering, set with pearls in a border of palms. The seascape in the central portion is probably of European origin; the sailing ships are mounted on metal rails. When the music plays, the ships pitch and toss in the waves. As you've probably noticed—please feel free to move closer—the elephant's trunk and tail each contain thirty individual segments, so fashioned that they can swing back and forth in time to the music as soon as the contraption is turned on. Unfortunately, I can't demonstrate that for you." Look at me: I'm the oscillation of the elephant; I'm the pitiless swinging of the pendulum between the beginning and the end of the present universe; time starts going the other way with me.

"Excuse me, madam, it's forbidden to take photographs in the exhibition rooms, even if you don't use a flash."

"I don't want to photograph the objects, just my friend. Strictly personal," Livia lies.

"I'm sorry, you're not allowed to take any sort of photographs here."

Thank you, little Hatidje. Straighten her out. Put a stop to this interminable picture snapping once and for all. If you take away her camera, maybe I'll go to bed with you. I'm thinking about it. You get the raki, I'll slap on a few discs, and we'll drink from ivory cups, gold-mounted ostrich eggs, nautilus shells. Then I'll mate with you on the gigantic, jewel-studded throne of Selim, Mahmut, and Mustafa, which is as wide as a bed, complete with canopy, around us a thousand glass splinters vying with diamonds to gleam the brightest. If you want, I'll make you a huge northern European baby, white as cheese, and we'll lay it on the costliest brocade cushion that the richest and most powerful of your forefathers possessed . . .

"Are you staying here, or do you want to come with us?" Livia asks, gently putting her hand on mine, looking as if she actually wants me around her.

"I didn't know you were still interested in me."

"Don't be like that."

"But that's the way I am."

She shrugs her shoulders under her thick leather motorcycle jacket, and then, when she's fifteen feet away, against the light, she shakes her head before stepping out into the open. I follow her anyway. Outside, Nager's sucking on an overheated cigarette. I light one up myself. The smoke makes my fingertips tingle; the smoke tastes like rotting marine creatures. "You were right," Nager says. "No one can take that for two hours. Hogwash designed for package tourists looking for a culture fix." I hear myself answer without moving my lips. My voice dies in my throat. I see humanlike beings in the branches of the cedars. They're agile, weightless, gliding up and down on long, soft fibers and jumping back and forth between copper roofs. Their transparent bodies show no boundaries . . . I run after Nager and reach another dark place. From far off, I hear the harmonious melody of Hatidje's sentences, decelerated. ". . . a traveler with hobnailed shoes is leaning on his packsaddle before an unlit fire and speaking to the half-naked figure across from him; two horses are grazing, and a couple of dogs are playing . . ." Spirits with burning beards and red, blue, and green robes made of human skin, dried and dyed, are attacking one another, reading the future, obliterating the past. Nager says, "My flask is empty." No problem, I'll do without. I fall into their burning eyes, they kill themselves laughing, and the cat from the right or the left is on the lookout for songbirds. She's runny at the edges. I see brush strokes; the clouds are brownish, smudged sepia. "It's painting," I say out loud. "Nothing but old painting."

"The older, the stronger," Nager says. "Astonishing."

"Djinns, evil spirits. By now they've almost all died out. Almost, not all."

"How about book painting for an art form? If you didn't have to earn money to feed your children, that is. Eight or nine hundred years ago, they sat down and did nothing for months except copy out one single book. And they came up with these insane images, knowing that no one would ever see them. Just imagine, you keep daubing away, better than anyone before you, better than anyone after you. How many pages in a folio like this one? Fifty, eighty? You paint the images, just because you want to get them out of your head and onto paper, just because you *want them to exist. No gallery owner pats you on the shoulder, no collector, either, and no woman wants to sleep with you."*

"Everything used to be better."

"And things were even worse before that. There's been progress since, but it's practically come to a standstill in the last two generations, so much so that now everything's headed straight downhill until the day when a better future will dawn on the horizon." He claps me on the shoulder. I stare into the semidarkness and concentrate. Jan's stroking Livia's back. No man strokes a woman's back that way unless they've already agreed to give love a try. I shouldn't have taken that Gypsy whore last night, but I was too drunk, long before her pimp, lover, brother, or whoever held his knife to my throat. The air smelled like fresh dog's blood, and the gigantic shadow of the enraged bear flickered in the topmost part of the tent. "She claims we're going to get to see some real relics now," Nager said.

"Do they have healing properties?"

"As soon as Selim the First had annexed Egypt to his realm, the caliphate passed from the Mamelukes to the Ottomans. Thus Istanbul became the fourth Islamic royal city, after Damascus, Baghdad, and Cairo." She talks about the Prophet's sword, his bow, his quiver, about the Sacred Cloak, the imprint of his right foot in gold, the hairs of his beard, a tooth, about the banner under which he led his troops to war, and she moistens her panties when she looks at me. After the tour of the harem is over, she says, we'll be free to investigate it further and visit whatever other sections we wish. She particularly recommends the Koranic manuscripts and the ceremonial robes. If anyone's interested, she'll be available to answer questions. If we would be so kind as to follow her.

"I can't do this," I say to Nager. "I didn't sleep a wink last night. I'm going to lie down on that bench over there and take a break. You can wake me when you're all ready to go. And make sure your painter

doesn't grope my photographer. If he gets pushy, nail him one, with my compliments. I'll pay your lawyer."

"See you later," Nager says. He runs after the others, calling out, "You go too fast! Isn't anyone weak in the knees from looking at those miniatures?"

15.

After eating lunch in different groups, we met again at the entrance to the underground cisterns.

Albin came on his own—Livia, Jan, Nager, Mona, and I had gone to a little restaurant without him. At lunch, Livia appeared confused and said little. When Nager ordered the third raki, her repulsion was written on her face. Nevertheless, she seemed glad that at least she didn't have to watch Albin drink while she sat there, condemned to silence and without hope that anything would change. Whenever she criticized him, he began a quarrel. Livia didn't want to quarrel anymore.

I have no idea where or how Albin had spent the intervening time. He probably followed suspicious trails that sooner or later led to a bar stool. Now, when we were standing in line for the cashier, he declared his opinion that the cisterns presented all the necessary requirements for the perfect crime, which was why they had been used as a setting in one of the James Bond films. If the victim doesn't fall into the water in the first place, all the killer has to do is give the body a shove and at least one problem is solved. "So don't be surprised if a neat hole suddenly appears in my temple and I topple over. Some people are interested in seeing me dead."

Nobody contradicted him, but I can hardly imagine a place less suited to disposing of someone. The ticket taker would only have to lock the entrance door and wait for the special forces to arrive. Apart from that, I did not and do not believe that anyone was interested in doing away with Albin. Maybe he was talking like that to scare Corinna and Sabine, or to conceal what the real purpose of his story was. This latter effort was successful. To this day, none of us, including Livia, knows where the whole thing was supposed to lead.

Nager said, "It seems that your criminal organization hires cultured sharpshooters. I presume that means none of the rest of us will be turned into a paraplegic or suffer brain damage by mistake."

After dinner, Nager and Albin separated from us. They must have done some fearsome drinking in the course of the night. The following day, the professor came to breakfast in pitiful shape. His eyes were swollen and bloodshot, and he complained about the roaring in his head: louder than low-flying fighter bombers, beyond nauseating. Albin had fewer complaints, but he smelled of fresh liquor from ten meters away against the wind.

"I need presents for my girls," Nager said. We had just crossed Yeni Çeriler Caddesi, a little before the Grand Bazaar. "That's the main reason I made the trip, to bring them back something amusing. They must laugh a lot so they'll become very pretty and I'll have a reason to chase their suitors out of the house. And my wife has to get something, too. Jewelry. Or silk. Silk's supposed to be cheap in Turkey. I wonder if they have anything in this funny old market that you can give somebody without embarrassing yourself."

"Antiques," Mona said.

"How am I supposed to transport them?" Nager answered. "Look, in my opinion, we don't all have to stay together. We'll get separated in the crowd in any case. Let's meet in the hotel lobby around seven and plan our evening. With or without alcohol, I haven't decided yet. Probably without."

There was a big crush in the bazaar, and bad air. The shops were filled with stuff all the way to the ceiling. Cheap blankets, towels, Oriental arts and crafts. Every guild had its own district. There were passages for stoneware, alleyways for inlaid works, engraved brassware, carved meerschaum pipes, entire streets full of gold.

Scherf was the first to break off from the rest of us. He said he wanted to visit the part of the bazaar where icons were sold. Maybe he'd find the two images he needed for his installation, he said; new originals would be better than old reproductions, and besides, what counts with icons isn't aesthetic quality but rather religious content; the images were conceived from the start as copies of a *Prototype,* not as independent works of art, and therefore painting wasn't called *painting* but *copying.*

Hagen followed him.

"All the same, you can distinguish between the good and the bad," Jan called out, but Scherf was out of earshot.

"Kitsch as far as the eye can see," Albin said. "If I were you, Professor, and one of my people bought any of this stuff, I'd throw him out immediately."

"In the past, I would've argued for the death penalty. These days, I'm always buying trash myself. Children are constantly asking for things that seem unacceptable to you. You give them what they want anyway, because disappointed children are unbearable."

"Children are unbearable in any case."

"Pointed shoes with embroidery and paste jewelry. Pretty, huh?"

Three shops farther on, Sabine was already trying on her fourth leather jacket. With outspread arms, she was trying to turn around on the heel of her walking cast so that Adel could examine her from all sides and in motion. The dealer was talking about the tanning process, employed in this form, he said, only in certain regions of eastern Anatolia to produce leather of the very finest quality: guaranteed nonallergenic, lasts forever, unbeatable price. Adel was familiar with this sort of sales pitch, having spent time in Lebanese markets, but he still couldn't make up his mind to warn Sabine about it. Instead, he rubbed the leather between his fingers, shook his head skeptically, and said, "Very thin for a German winter," and, "The color doesn't go with your hair."

"I want old carpets or fine calligraphy," Nager said. "Or china."

"Do you know a lot about that sort of thing?" Mona asked.

"I have eyes in my head."

"And you're confident you can distinguish real pieces from fakes?"

"What's the difference between a *real* rug and a *fake* rug? You can sit on both and drink tea, and neither of them can fly. I could buy a rug for my wife. Women appreciate that sort of thing, don't they, Livia?"

Before Livia could answer, Albin told her he had to go to the jewelry section of the bazaar and he absolutely did not want her to go with him. He refused to give her any reasons why.

"I've never paid much attention to carpets," Livia said after he left. "I like some, and others I find boring. As for what *women* appreciate, I don't know."

It took Albin ten minutes to find the jewelry district and another half hour to choose the shop where he wanted to begin his inquiries. He examined displays and watched dealers talking on the telephone, sorting their wares, speaking to customers, messengers, and assistants. He pondered his criteria, considered various rhetorical maneuvers and methods of proceeding, and came to the conclusion that in any case it would be sensible to feign an interest in making a purchase, ask to see some jewels, and discuss prices, rather than to begin with questions about Miller. Albin chose the first dealer because he thought the man had a wily-looking face, which Albin took as an indication of criminal energy. The gem dealer was in his mid-thirties, clean-shaven, with slicked-back hair and black eyes: the very picture of a crook, but also a student of human nature, who therefore quickly figured out that Albin wasn't really interested in buying an emerald. He excused himself—a pressing appointment—and left the shop to his assistant, not forgetting to suggest that this man, too, would give Albin a special price should he decide to buy something.

Albin let one of the polyglot touts lure him into the second shop, not out of submissiveness or weakness, but because he wanted to test whether anyone had followed him, whether anyone was reacting to his presence in the domain of Miller's colleagues and competitors. He quickly realized he'd be wasting his time if he talked about emeralds. The proprietor was as loquacious as his front man, and even Albin's inexpert eye could spot only semi-precious stones and costume jewelry. Nevertheless, it was some time before he could extricate himself from the man's endless sentences, long threads designed to wrap him up into a package, as a spider packages captured flies.

By the time he entered the third shop, Albin's state of mind had changed, though he couldn't explain why. He felt calmer somehow, despite the fact that all his alarm bells must have been going off. This is the way he told it to me: When he walked in, an older gentleman stepped out from behind his display table, greeted him in impeccable German, and shook his hand like an old acquaintance. And Albin thought: I'm safe with him.

Afterward, he tried to explain his reaction by citing the old fel-

low's restrained gestures, his pleasant voice. Albin spoke of his vi-
bration and his positive aura—expressions that he otherwise never
used. I suppose it was embarrassing for him to have been taken in
by an experienced bazaar hustler, and I imagine he needed to give
himself some explanation other than drunken euphoria for the way
the day fell in on him a little while later.

For the first time since arriving in Istanbul, Albin didn't turn
down the offer of tea. Calling through the door, the dealer spoke a
brief Turkish sentence, not excessively loud and addressed to no
one in particular.

"How may I be of service to you, my young friend?"

"I'm looking for a stone for my wife. Not just any stone—this
isn't a guilt offering—but something special. It has to be more than
a piece of jewelry. It has to heighten the expression of her person-
ality. It must reflect her, the way . . . let's say, the way the eyes reflect the soul."

"A difficult challenge. Not insurmountable. Provided, that is,
you know your wife well enough."

"I'm in a bit of a hurry."

"Let me tell you something. I lived in Germany for thirty years.
I was a dentist. In Bielefeld. Now my daughter has the practice. All
the people there are always in a hurry. Patients, language tutors,
dental hygienists, even the cleaning ladies. They would prefer to be
finished before they begin. Even the wait in the waiting room can't
last longer than thirty minutes; otherwise, the doctor can be sued
for damages, for lost time. Explain this to me. How do you lose
time? Does it fall out of your trousers pocket? Do you leave it in the
subway?"

"Do you have emeralds?"

"Of course I have emeralds. Do you have money? And are you
sure about an emerald for your wife . . ."

"Livia."

"Are you sure an emerald is the right stone for Livia? What sign was she born under?"

"I don't know. March fourteenth."

"Pisces. For a Pisces, opal is the best stone. It has the garnet's delicate fire, the amethyst's glistening purple, the emerald's sea green, and the sapphire's mysterious blue, so that all the colors shine together in a fabulous combination."

Albin noticed a table with the signs of the zodiac hanging on the wall behind the dealer's display case. The writing was Arabic, combined with numbers, letters, and pictograms whose origin and meaning Albin knew nothing about. They were arranged in concentric circles, which were divided into segments by lines radiating out from the center. Glazes of different colors distinguished the segments from one another. Albin couldn't discern a system in any of this. The table had been drawn up by hand.

"I want a Russian emerald. Do you have such a thing?"

"I have everything you can buy. And if I don't have it, I can get it for you. All the same, an emerald would be wrong for Livia. It would detract from her."

"Are there Russian opals?"

"Only in the Ukraine and Azerbaijan. Very small deposits."

"Show me some."

"For us in the Orient, the opal is the stone of undying hope. Because of the opal's combination of transparence and intensity, it is said to have originated in the waters of Paradise. I have white opals from Brazil, black opals from Australia, fire opals from Mexico. Have a look." He pulled out a drawer that contained perhaps thirty stones, distributed among little compartments lined with light gray felt. The jewels shimmered in every color, like oil patches on a summer lake, but Albin saw at first glance that his only possible choice would be one of five gleaming orange stones, all faceted, ground, and polished.

"Where do the orange ones come from?"

"Mexican fire opals. They are prized above all by young people, because the fire opal expresses pulsating life and increases vitality."

Albin plunged into a moment of forgetfulness that seemed very short and very long. Had anyone asked him about his present whereabouts, he would have shrugged his shoulders in reply. His eyes roamed around, settled on the table with the symbols, slipped off, and fell into an abyss, until a boy entered carrying a tray with a tin pot and two glasses, reverently, as though they were the queen of England's crown jewels. The boy bowed several times, but not the way Albin had done when he'd had to play the role of the servant as a child; to Albin's surprise, the boy bowed without any sign of fear. Then Albin remembered an American, a certain Miller, whom someone had shot dead before his eyes, and a German photographer named Livia, who was about to break up with him, a fact that he didn't even hold against her. He said, "I'll buy this orange stone. It's not what I imagined, but it suits my wife better than I would have thought possible. Jewelry bores me and I hate stones, but if you agree to answer some questions, I'll give her this fire opal, and that won't be a bad deal for you. There aren't many tourists in the city at the moment. So: How much for the stone? And do you know a Jonathan Miller from Chicago? Do you know where I can find him? We had an appointment the day before yesterday. I've set up some contacts for him, very valuable contacts, and he owes me money. Maybe he's cleared out, or maybe something's happened to him."

The old man poured two glasses of tea, held out the tray to Albin, and laid the stone on an electronic scale. "One-point-four carats. For you, two hundred and fifty dollars."

"An expensive gift for a woman who's going to leave me in the next few days and is already feeling good about it. Besides, who'll guarantee me that the stone is actually worth two hundred and fifty dollars? I've read that one should begin bargaining with half of the quoted price. We're in the off-season, so I'll say a hundred and twenty, *if* you tell me where I can get some information about Miller."

"This is an exceptionally fine specimen. A rarity. I've never had a fire opal of this quality before."

"A hundred and fifty."

"I buy my stones in Iran. I don't like Russians. They have different ideas about doing business. It's hard for me to read their faces."

"Will you help me, or not?"

"Two hundred and twenty is a reasonable price."

"I don't believe in astrology. Why does orange suit Livia? Green suits her, too. Are Russian emeralds exported to America through Turkey? If I want to buy precious stones from Russia, who is it I have to speak to?"

"I thought you had contacts."

"I was a witness to an incident. A hundred and eighty."

"Whatever people can get out of Russia is smuggled here. The stuff is provided with fake documents—certificates of origin, export permits—and cleaned up for the world market. Stay away from this business; you know nothing about it. These people are godless. Your life is worth less to them than their chickens. The stone will please Livia. She will rediscover her love. Opals reinforce the positive characteristics of those who wear them. The stone makes it easier to see the truth."

"I thought the idea was to compromise on a price in the middle."

"It's really a valuable object."

"Two hundred. Where can I find someone who knew Miller?"

"Go back to your hotel, drink some raki, and forget it."

"Two hundred."

"Everyone forges his own future. A German proverb. Both true and false."

"Two hundred and ten."

"There's a Russian market not far from here. Ask for Yevgeny Petrovitch or Parfyon, but don't tell them you got their names from me."

"How much does that come to in Turkish liras?"

"Dollars. I can't buy anything with liras. There's a bank with a foreign exchange window around the corner."

Five minutes later, Albin put the stone in the inner pocket of his jacket and left the bazaar.

"Albin's right," Nager grumbled. "Nothing but junk. Everything *Made in China.*"

At that same moment, a young man in his late twenties, pushing his way past us through the crowd, stopped and began to speak: "My uncle has exactly the carpets you're looking for. Most of the carpets in this bazaar aren't worth his money. They're mass-produced or fake. There are villages in the former Soviet republics whose sole business is to make freshly woven pieces look old. The carpets are spread out in kitchens or hung over fireplaces. Oil is sprinkled on them, burning coals are dropped on them, and in the end they're helped along with chemicals. Tourists are easy to fool. Speak a few scientific-sounding half-truths, and they lay their money down. My uncle specializes in really antique pieces, as did his father, my grandfather, before him. My grandfather supplied the last sultans, Mehmed the Fifth, Mehmed the Sixth, and Abdul

Mejid the Second. Our shop in the Bedestan, the oldest part of the
Grand Bazaar, built by the great Sinan himself, has been in the family's possession for more than a hundred and fifty years. From this
you can see that we're reliable partners. The carpet business is a
matter of trust, it's always been a matter of trust . . ."

"I'll look at his carpets," Nager said.

"A wise decision, Mister . . ."

"Nager. Professor Nager."

"A German professor. What an honor. My name is Yildiz. I
worked in Germany for many years, in the automobile industry—
Mercedes, BMW, Opel. I know all about your country: Oktoberfest,
Cologne cathedral, the Black Forest. At home I even have an original cuckoo clock. All my relatives have original cuckoo clocks."

Jan whispered, "Do these people behave like this in order to
correspond to our stereotypes, or do we have the stereotypes because they behave like this?"

Interrupting his flow of speech only to answer Nager's occasional questions, Yildiz led us into a shop that actually did look old
and venerable. The carpets we saw at first glance were clearly of
better quality than the ones we'd seen in other places. We would
never have found this place by ourselves. From the outside, it was
quite unprepossessing. Mona had read that serious carpet dealers,
who made their living from a regular clientele and long-standing
business relationships, characteristically operated out of inconspicuous shops. The room was at least ten feet high and lined with
shelves filled with folded carpets. Others were rolled up and leaning against the shelves, while some particularly bright pieces were
hanging behind a huge wooden desk. We discovered the little man
at the desk only after Yildiz called out something in Turkish three
times, the last time very loud. He received what sounded like a

pained answer, followed immediately by soft giggling, before the old man looked up, rose to his feet, and made us a solemn bow.

"Not bad," Nager said.

"What are you interested in?" Yildiz asked, aware that there was at most only one possible customer in our group, namely Nager.

"A rug, what else? Not too large, not too small. Old, but in good shape. Not something that will fall apart if you walk on it."

"Would you prefer a knotted carpet, or a kilim? Or perhaps a *sumakh*?"

"A standard rug with a warm red base color."

The uncle hid his face in his hands, rubbed his eyes, and shook his head incessantly. We couldn't tell if he was shaking it at us, his nephew, or himself, or for completely different reasons. He asked a question, which Yildiz translated: "What is your line of work?"

"Art."

"*Sanat cı.*"

For a few seconds, the uncle stared at a point outside the room. Then he moved the ladder, climbed up, and pulled out a bundle. After climbing back down, he threw the bundle outward with a single, long-practiced motion, so that the carpet unfolded in the air and fell flat at our feet. At the same time, he began to talk slowly, pausing whenever he had the impression that Yildiz's translation wasn't keeping up with him. "My uncle says he's been in the carpet business for more than forty years, and he's had some experience. He would never try to sell you a rug that he didn't believe would win your heart. A carpet, particularly an antique carpet that was not produced for export, deserves respect. It tells stories: of the girl, the woman, who wove it before her marriage, of the years that she and her husband and children lived with it. It tells of the roads it has traveled, of its passage through the Silk Route city of Samarkand. One must not walk on it while wearing shoes. For these reasons, my uncle asked about your profession. The carpet that he believes you will like is a special example of its kind. It would be difficult to place it with ordinary collectors, who demand classic, uncomplicated pieces; this one has too many peculiarities for them. But my uncle believes that an artist like yourself will understand this carpet."

Nager remained silent. He pinched his chin, looked alternately from Yildiz to the uncle to the carpet, and nodded. "This rug is completely crazy."

Yildiz flinched and said something to his uncle.

"You don't like it?"

"I think it's magnificent. Art has to be crazy."

"It's a Turkoman rug from the late nineteenth century. You see this repeated figure in the main field? It's called a gul. It's a kind of tribal emblem. This is the gul of the Tekke, a tribe that was renowned for the high knot count of its carpets."

"I'm interested in the mistakes," Nager said.

"It's a carpet in transition. Originally, the Tekke gul was almost square. The flatter it is, the later the date of the carpet. Here, in a single carpet, you can see the figure changing. The guls in the upper part are traditional. Then, row by row, they get more and more compressed, until in the lower part you see the degenerate form, as it has been knotted since the beginning of the twentieth century. The coloring documents the same development in parallel. You have surely noticed that there's a break in the color through the middle of the second row of guls. The upper part is cochineal violet—by which we know that the carpet was produced after 1860, because before that, there was no cochineal in Turkmenistan—and then suddenly the color is a dirty white. Right in the middle of the pattern. It makes no sense. But if you look closely, you can see, very faint, the original contours: the violet in this part is faded. Why? The weaver used magenta, a synthetic color of the first generation, one of the aniline dyes, as they are called. Well, as it later turned out, these were not nonfading colors. Within a few years, they had all faded away, which is why people stopped using them around 1890. So this rug no longer looks the way it was originally conceived."

"A failure," Nager said. "The man the woman wove the carpet for probably left her when he realized that her dowry wasn't any good. And his relatives laughed at him, because he'd married a woman who swindled him. How much does it cost?"

Maybe Yildiz translated what Nager said to his uncle, and he probably also gave him his estimate of what price they could ask; in any case, he spoke considerably longer than Nager.

"Do you see what kind of quality this is?" Nager asked us.

"My uncle says you should have the carpet. He believes it belongs to you, and therefore he has no wish to bargain with you. He makes you an offer, a fair offer. You can accept it or refuse it. Seven hundred dollars."

"Do you take credit cards?"

"You have to haggle," Mona whispered.

"Just be quiet."

"Visa, American Express, or Eurocard, no problem."

"He's out of his head. Everybody, absolutely everybody, knows you have to haggle about the price in Istanbul, otherwise they'll take you to the cleaners without mercy."

At first, I thought the same thing, but while the uncle was folding the carpet, putting paper over several layers, it was hard for me to consider him a cunning, hard-nosed merchant.

In the chaos of the following days and weeks, I forgot about the carpet, in spite of the complications it caused at the airport. Just about a month ago, it crossed my mind again. I asked Nager why he'd accepted the price without bargaining. We'd been sitting for hours in the dark little bar near the academy, and Nager was on his tenth beer. He said only, "I believed the dealer. He was no liar."

16.

Night is falling. The taxi's jolting along like a car on one of the country roads around Staudt before Father started to pave them. He got rich for a decade by doing that. Chickens run away from the beam of the head-lights. After forty-eight hours of rain, the potholes are full of filthy water, which splashes the walls of the buildings. An old Citroën comes toward us. We back up until there's enough room for it to pass. My driver honks at a donkey as a warning, as a greeting. When I pay him, he grins knowingly.

Who wants to hear my explanation: that I hardly sleep at night, that I can't bear the light of day? I want to get dead drunk, and I want a woman, in memory of my belief that as long as I had a companion, it could all be borne.

Mona read from her guidebook: "Sulukule, a run-down district near Edirnekapı and the old land wall, is where the Gypsies, who have immigrated to Istanbul from the Balkans, earn their money, in their own fashion: with music, games of chance, suggestive dancing, and maybe more. The men of Istanbul dream of Sulukule; tourists go there." Then she showed me the pictures. On one of them, the caption read, in German, "Wouldn't you like a hot-blooded Romanian girl? She'll make your most secret fantasies come true."

A promise nobody keeps. We pass hovels, shacks built of wooden planks and corrugated metal. It's the blue hour, the twilight hour of false emotions. The air smells of ashes, of garbage. Who's interested in *girls who unbutton their blouses in exchange for cigarettes and beer, whose teeth start falling out when they're sixteen? No one expects things to get better. The guard dogs sleep day and night; none of them has any territory to defend. This part of town looks like the remains of a city after the next big war in an apocalyptic film. The earth lies covered with nuclear fallout under a blackened sun. The rain has stopped. Handwritten notices announce, in English:* Fighting bear is back, come and see his pride, 10 Nov. 1994, 23:00. *Today's date, but no address or location. A fat woman, carrying plastic bags loaded with vegetables, fusses at her child. Where are the girls? Arm in arm, two drunks stagger out of a door. Some young men are standing under the nearest streetlight, exchanging banknotes. They pay no attention to me. I pass them and turn around. No one's following me. I ask them in English,* "Where are the dancing Gypsy girls?" *Four pairs of black eyes look me over. Am I worthy of buying their sister? Should they simply rob me? The decision is made in silence, inside their heads.* "No problem," *one says.* "We show you."

The oldest of them nods at me, indicating that I should follow him. I don't look like someone it would be worth the trouble of mugging. They speak some Balkan language. We walk along narrow streets, overhung by strings of colorful, flickering Chinese lanterns. No one's expecting any tourist business in this weather. We cross a square where bored young men are sitting on chattering mopeds older than their owners, mopeds that have fallen apart and been put back together umpteen times, passed on from father to son, from son to brother. Now and then, one of them does a few laps in the mud. I hear an accordion nearby, and also a lunatic tuba.

My guide says in English, "You must come to the fighting bears tonight!"

"What?"

"German? Or Russian?"

"Deutsch."

"Unser Bär kämpft mit Hunden. *Our bear fights with dogs.* Andere Bären, *too. Secret game. Dollars.* Viele *dollars.*"

I think, I'll get back the money I spent on the nonexistent photograph. He says, "I show you where. Später.*"

A few steps farther on, he knocks on a door and cries out a name: "Grigoriyan!" *A bald old man holding a cigarette in the corner of his mouth pokes his unshaven face out the door. The two men greet each other with handshakes and kisses. These are followed by a flood of friendly-sounding words. The old man says to me, "Come in." He reeks of rotgut booze as he laughs, grabs my arm, and pulls me inside. I'd like to push him away. I think about his daughters and granddaughters. The room is a dirty yellow color. Shiny wooden tables and wobbly chairs stand in front of a crudely built, lacquered brown counter. Blankets hang in front of the windows. Three men are leaning on the bar. They're wearing greasy hats with narrow brims and drinking a yellow liquid reminiscent of beer. In the spots where feet and knees rub against the front of the counter, the earlier coats of lacquer have all been worn away. The old man says, "Sit down, mister, sit down."*

The speaker in the portable radio seems to be having trouble handling Barry Manilow's voice. A shabby kitchen cupboard contains liquor bottles, glasses, and souvenirs from America, sent by an emigrated relative. There's also a rosary and a plastic statue of the Virgin Mary standing amid artificial flowers and holding her pierced heart in her hands. A gaunt, superugly woman tends the bar and the cupboard. Her hair is covered by a cap embroidered with mysterious signs. Her patched pink sweater is too small for her, revealing the contours of flaccid, low-hanging teats. In any case, she has a sufficient supply of alcohol. "Chief, explain to him, I want Mädchen, *girls, not* Mama.*"*

"Beautiful girls and original Gypsy music. Fünf Minuten. *What's your name?"*

"Al."

"I am Toppos. Ich. You buy whiskey from Seraphina, Al, ganze Flasche, OK? Whole bottles. Wir trinken zusammen, together, we have a lot of fun. Spaß, viel Spaß."

The owner of the bar sends away two of the four young men who brought me here. Toppos cries, "Whiskey, Seraphina, for Grigoriyan, Ziya, and me from our new friend, Al." I make no objection. Seraphina opens a door behind the bar, disappears into a dark corridor, and returns with a full Johnnie Walker bottle, which she sets on the table. Toppos says, "We are a big family. Brüder, Onkel, cousins." The bottle is full, but not new: the metal sealing ring hangs loose, the cap twists off easily. Who knows what she's put in there?

She says, "Twenty-five dollars," and stretches out her wizened hand in my direction. I've got $250 in my left pants pocket and Turkish liras in my right. How much do their girls cost? Better to keep the dollars out of sight at first. I hold out the right-hand wad to her. "How much in liras?" She rolls her eyes in unspeakable pain and extracts a few bills amid groans and lamentations. I don't care about the money, as long as I've got enough to pay for drinks and a woman.

I don't suppose Livia's going to come back to me. She'll leave with Jan. When was the last time she seemed as glowing, as happy as she's seemed in the last four days? She could easily figure out why I wanted to come here, but she made no attempt to stop me. Toppos opens the bottle and pours. "Good American whiskey!"

"Scotch."

"Johnnie Walker from Chicago."

"Johnnie Walker aus Schottland."

He waves his hand in dismissal and laughs; we clink glasses. The liquor is neither one thing nor the other. It's a homemade concoction, throat cancer guaranteed. "You have cigarettes, Al? Marlboro?" I offer unfiltered Camels. Someone knocks on the door. One of Toppos's brothers brings in four squealing young women in long coats. Ziya pushes tables out of the way. Seraphina gives the women plastic cups. "This is Inça," Toppos says. "Ayla, Ficiye, Slava. Friends of mine. Hot girls, very hot." Even before they take off their coats, they pour themselves some whiskey and drink my health, hoping to drive the cold out of their bones. "Cigarette, I need a cigarette!" I've read in the guidebook that cigarettes are used as currency, and accordingly my pockets are filled with them. There's another knock on the door, and in come a fiddler, a clarinetist, and a man with a banjo.

I gaze into the women's faces, the faces of girls who drink too much too often and don't know how to apply makeup. Two of them are beautiful and voluptuous; their heavy black hair has a bluish sheen. It won't be long before they look like Seraphina or the fat woman in the street. The fiddler stands before me, removes his hat, and holds it out. "Baksheesh!" he says.

"Don't understand."

"Tip. Money."

He's satisfied with what I put in the hat, sets it on the table, picks up his bow, and begins to play. Grigoriyan beats a drum. The girls throw their coats over the backs of chairs. They're wearing patterned cardigans, pullover sweaters, flowered skirts decorated with frills, and shawls tied around their waists. They stand there, then raise their arms and start turning in toddling little circles. Their sweaters are sheer, and you can see their tits spilling out of their cheap push-up bras. Inça is frightfully thin. The clarinetist can't decide whether he wants to go to Kiev, Delhi, or Baghdad. The music is ridiculous, a high-speed mishmash of styles. No diamond-patterned polyester in the world can spoil Ayla's grace as she lets her cardigan slip off her shoulders. If blackness can be compared, she has the blackest eyes. The men standing at the bar clap their hands. Cloths whirl through the air, dispersing the smoke. Wooden slippers stamp on the floorboards. The fiddle buzzes around the room like a fat fly, droning a single note that comes closer and then moves away. Eventually, its mindless flight from itself ends in total collapse. Now the room is quiet. Toppos holds up his hand: "You want more?"

"Much more."

"More baksheesh."

He lights up four of my cigarettes and gives them to the girls. Up to this point, I haven't seen so much as a naked elbow. The drummer plays a new rhythm, and out of it climbs a shimmering Arabian melody, holds its breath, glimpses its goal in the distance, rushes toward it, and gets lost somewhere in the Eastern steppes. Slava's the first to take her sweater off. She throws her head back; her white belly quivers rhythmically. Hoarse cries come from the men. Ayla kicks her slippers under the table and shakes out her hair. Inça, with castanets on her fingers, speaks to the drummer in rapid bursts. Her speech seems capricious, sharp as her hipbones. The fiddler goes down on his knees in front of her and tries to calm her down. She springs forward, snatching at him as he barely eludes her. Inça, fifteen at most, is the special offer for child fuckers. The clarinet imitates a bird copying a clarinet. Spring has sprung. Ayla's breasts bounce in a transparent brassiere. Hard, button-sized nipples. In the midst of her wild spinning, she smiles at me, and shortly afterward, on the verge of losing control, she comes to a stop. This whiskey has more than forty percent alcohol. I'm hot.

"Baksheesh, Al, baksheesh. And beer for the girls, Al. Say, 'Seraphina, beer for the beau-ti-ful dancing Gypsy girls.' "

"Beer and another bottle of this horrible whiskey."

The men whistle and applaud. I still haven't had to use any dollars. Toppos bellows in my ear, "You like our whiskey?"

"Man kann Tote damit auferwecken. It can raise the dead. Resurrection, you know."

Inça's childish legs end in ringed socks. Her underpants are printed with Mickey Mouse heads. *These guys are playing me dizzy, they're playing my brain into mush. If I don't watch out, they'll empty my pockets and throw me out on the street with the kitchen rubbish. But first I want Ayla. I have enough money to buy her for a whole night, even for two. When she dances, her arms move like branches in the wind. She's young, much younger than I am, but she's a woman. When she pulls her bra straps off her shoulders, her breasts don't sag; she turns down the twin cups and shows me, for a fraction of a second, two handfuls of firm flesh. Then she unhooks the clasp, pulls off the thin strip of material, and whirls it over her head like a sling. But instead of slinging a stone at me, she laughs and throws me the bra itself. I rub the cups between my fingers. They have a heavy scent, a mixture of sweat and fake ambergris. I drop one bill after another into the hat; I don't want this absurd music to end, I want Ayla's hips to rotate some more and her strong tight body to shape my field of vision. Meanwhile I administer high doses of various narcotizing substances to myself. The next time silence falls,* I say, "Toppos, mein Freund, I want it all."

"Other girls?"

"I want to make love."

"Welche gefällt dir?"

"Ayla. How much?"

"Ayla ist gut. Sehr gutes Mädchen."

"Wieviel?"

He calls her over and whispers something into her ear, as if I understood so much as a single word of their language. I don't even understand the gestures they make. Ayla's eyes attach themselves to mine. She locks on to them and hops away like a schoolgirl, leans against the wall, thrusts her hips out, walks toward me—slowly, very slowly, she takes an hour for the first ten feet—sits on my lap, speaks—what she says is of no importance—puts her arms around my neck, and presses my face against her breasts. "Einhundert. Dollar. Liebe kostet Dollar, Al. No *chance with lira."* For $100, I can get a first-class whore in Hamburg who'll do whatever I want. I say, *"Expensive. Very expensive. Gib mir noch einen Schluck Whisky." Ayla takes the glass out of my hand and drinks first, then holds the glass against my lips and pours, being careful not to spill any of the liquor. She digs her fingers into the back of my neck and talks and talks. She's probably saying, "You pitiful, drunken slash hound, what do you think? You think you can get me for a bargain price? I'm worth more than all the money you've ever earned in your whole shitty life. Come on, out with the dough, let's get this over with. I don't really have a lot of time." But her voice is deep and warm, and her words strike me as the friendliest I've heard in a long time. She should just tell stories, that's enough, I don't need any more.*

"OK, wo können wir hingehen?"

"Where can you go? You want a room? Kostet zwanzig."

I pay and try to hide how much money I still have. "Buy me champagne," *Ayla says. She stands up. Seraphina requires $10, for which I get a small bottle of Kupferberg Gold. Ayla opens the door leading to the rear part of the house.* "Come," *she says breathily. It's supposed to sound lascivious. I go back to the table, fill my glass to the brim, and follow her, staring at her solid round behind, her faded blue underpants, the rather too fleshy backs of her knees.*

She brings me into a tiny room. A red lightbulb hangs from the ceiling. Ayla places the champagne on top of a small night chest, takes a perfume bottle from the table, sprays herself with sweet scent. She's got gooseflesh, and she stoops to turn on an electric heater. The heater roars; the lights dim. The broken sections of a wall mirror held together by Scotch tape break the reflection of her back in two. A fuzz of fine, dark hairs runs along her spine. She turns away from me, toward a chair with laundry on it, and takes off her underpants, as if she were home and getting ready for a good night's sleep. She sits on the bed, which is nothing but a rusty steel frame and a mattress covered with

*stained sheets, pillows, and a woolen blanket. At the head of the bed,
two pictures torn from a magazine are stuck to the wall: Richard Gere
and the young John Travolta. She lies on her back with her thighs spread
halfway apart. Little wiry hairs grow thick on all sides, all the way up
to her navel. Her orifices are completely overgrown. Hasn't anyone ever
taught her that women shave themselves? How brown her skin is. I run
my hand over her belly. A shy, naked girl alone with a strange man from
a distant land. I sit down next to her and say, "Champagne." I sip my
whiskey. She smiles, takes a long swallow, breathes hard. I tell her in
German, "Honey, it looks as though you haven't sold yourself very often,
at least not completely. Mostly you dance, and either people's money
runs out or they're so drunk they can't get it up. Tonight you're out of
luck, but don't worry, it won't happen often. I don't know anyone who
can hold his liquor the way I can."*

"You have cigarette?"

"Right you are, let's have a smoke before we start."

*We flick our ashes onto the floor. She lies there, staring into space,
waiting for instructions or a groping hand. I pry her labia apart with
my thumb. In the red light, they look dark purple, as dry and wrinkled
as an old woman's hand. I press my face between her legs and give her
a wet kiss. Ayla's eyes are shut, her eyelids twitch, her muscles are
tensed. She just doesn't whimper, that's all. I straighten up and gaze at
her body. It's a while before she notices that nothing's happening.
"That's all right," I say. "Have a drink," and I cover her up.*

*This is a ghastly mistake. Worse than the worst of her fears. I've
wounded her honor, her awakening harlot's pride. She's staring, dumb-
founded, panicked, and when she speaks, her voice breaks. "You not like
me?" A cascade of Romanian or Bulgarian or Gypsy thieves' slang
breaks over my head. I say, "It's not that, Ayla, I do like you, du bist
wunderschön, you're a beautiful girl." She throws off the blanket,
kneels down in front of me, pulls off my leather jacket, kisses my throat,*

fumbles with my zipper. "Calm down," I say. "Es ist alles bezahlt, *everything's paid, dollars, no problem." She shakes her head and stammers something about Toppos.* "I can't understand you, Ayla. I don't know your language."

"Toppos angry."

"Toppos interessiert mich nicht."

"Toppos dangerous."

"Paß auf, hör mir zu. *Listen to me. There are two reasons for fucking.* Der erste ist, *because we feel lust for each other. Desire.* Der zweite: *We make a deal.* Ein Geschäft. *Business. Sooner or later, desire leads to* Schwierigkeiten. *Complications.* Das Geschäft *works like this: I give you money, I buy you a bottle of champagne. In return, for half an hour*—eine halbe Stunde—*you make a show, you pretend to be very hot for me. You do what I say, and you make no complaints. In fact, you do what I say so good, I forget your profession and your price. I come here* um mich zu amüsieren. *I come for having fun, not for watching a poor girl do her job.* Kapiert?"

My attempt at a smile may be successful, I'm not sure. In any case, she calms down a little, falls back onto the pillow, this time with her legs spread wide apart, and essays a look of longing, cribbed from the performance of some little pop star she's seen. I don't know what I should do with her. She's a sweet girl, she's got pretty breasts and a good ass, but I'm tired, I need illusions. In the real world, sex is no consolation for anything. She didn't figure on things turning out like this. Now she's afraid of Toppos, afraid I'll tell him I wasn't satisfied with her. I stand up, take off my shoes and my pants, and lie down next to her in my underwear and socks.

If we could understand each other, I'd suggest that we jump around on the mattress for a bit. After two minutes my groans could become louder, then there would be the final shout, I'd get dressed, and I'd leave.

We lie on our sides, heads in hands, and look at each other. Silent, amazed, and strangely curious. We keep staring until she lowers her eyes and starts to talk. Again I notice her uncommonly agreeable voice as she speaks quietly, slowly, in soft, fluent Slavic. Now and then she takes a swig from her little champagne bottle or asks me for a cigarette. I listen to her, observing the movement of her mouth, the way she exhales the tobacco smoke through her nostrils, the way the stream of air shakes the tiny hairs on her upper lip.

I stroke her heavy, dark-skinned body, I brush a strand of hair out of her face, and I think, If this keeps up, we're going to fuck after all, because she wants to, we want to, we desire each other. I lay my hand on her hip. She's going to like it, I think, she's going to make a lot of noise, and then there's a knock on the door. Ayla shrinks in terror and yanks the blanket up to her chin.

"It's time for the bear, Al."

According to my watch, it's twenty minutes to eleven. "No problem," I say. "Five minutes."

"I am waiting." He gives Ayla some instructions in a tone that bears no contradiction. She agrees to everything, gulping down the lump in her throat and shivering as she looks at me and lays her index finger on her lips. Her eyes implore me. I hear footsteps walking away and feel a pressing need to shove her pal Toppos's nose up into his brain. It would be suicide. Instead, I give her cheeks an avuncular pat. "Everything is OK, beautiful Ayla," I tell her, and climb into my pants. She watches me expressionlessly. I empty my glass and look back one last time before I open the door. She's turned her face to the wall. I push the door handle down quietly—there's nothing to say—step outside, and grope my way toward the streak of light at the end of the hall.

"Are you satisfied with Ayla?" Toppos asks.

"Great girl."

The other girls have vanished, and so have the musicians. Seraphina is speaking in single sentences to the men at the bar. She's cleared away my whiskey bottle. Business has been amazingly good this evening.

"Let us go." *The three old men with the hats slide off their stools. Seraphina remains behind, alone.*

The streets are soggy. Goats are bleating behind a wall. Enormous puddles reflect the light from illuminated windows. I don't know why I'm not afraid. Toppos says, "Bear fighting is old, tausend Jahre."

"Ich kenne nur tanzende Bären, *dancing bears. They were in Germany in the old days. My father told me stories about them.*"

"Tanzbären *are for children, women, and for European tourists.*"

The street is filling up. Other groups join us. The men greet one another with hugs and sing out battle cries. I hear barking in the distance. "Was sind das für Hunde?"

"Mutts. Köter. *There are many wild dogs in Istanbul. We have a solution to this problem.*"

We enter a brightly lit square. Diesel generators are powering searchlights. A blue-and-white striped tent has been put up in the center of the open space. More of this furious music, played at breakneck speed by a frenzied orchestra, is streaming out from inside the tent. We shove our way through the crowd. Toppos says, "Hier ist nicht wie in Pakistan. We love unsere Bären, they are very strong." *The expectant audience is made up exclusively of men, not only Gypsies, but also Russians and Turks. Improvised stands here and there sell grilled meat and vegetables or sweets dripping with honey. I bury my hands in my pants pockets.*

"Bier?"

"Always." *He leads me to one of his innumerable friends, who's standing behind a wall of beer: twenty cases of Stella Artois. I buy two bottles.*

"Hungry after love? You want shish kebab?"

"Yes."

Although Toppos isn't thirty yet, he stands high up in the Gypsy hierarchy. Everyone knows him, and many greet him obsequiously. He hands me a round flat bread, its pocket dripping with grease and sauce. The meat tastes stronger than what you get in the eating places in the city center. It's going to make me sick. But if I keep on drinking without eating, then I'll really be sick. A skeletal structure of reinforced concrete contains stacked bamboo cages with dogs inside. Groups of men stand around them, deep in debate, clutching pencils and writing pads.

"Can we look at them?"

"Natürlich."

We move closer to the cages. People step aside, making a passage for Toppos. He says, "You must remember the best ones."

They're mongrels, spotted, brown, black, all different sizes. Some are barking; others tuck their tails between their legs and whimper, hoping someone will take pity on them. I say, "Sie haben keine Chance."

"Of course not."

"Are they killed?"

"Die Bären sind unser Stolz, *our pride. These dogs are shit." Slips of paper with consecutive numbers dangle from the cages. The numbers correspond to those painted in red on each dog's flank.*

"You want to bet?"

"Mein Geld ist aus."

"You can win."

"Ich bin pleite. Broke."

"Think about it, before it is too late, Al."

Torches light up the inside of the tent. Bets are placed at a table near the entrance. Toppos writes numbers on a printed list and gives it to the bookmaker, together with a roll of banknotes. If I understand right, you bet on the dogs, not the bears. The stage is over on the left. A dozen musicians in tuxedos are playing so fast and so loud that lungs must be bursting in the horn section. In front of the orchestra is a microphone connected to an amplifier, which in turn is connected to some automobile batteries. The field of battle is surrounded by a wooden fence covered with barbed wire. In the center of the field, a metal pole sticks straight up out of the sand. A chain with a snap link at its other end is welded to the top of the pole. The bleachers start right at the top of the fence and climb five tiers high, ending against the tent wall. The first rows are already full. I'm taller than almost everybody, so I have a good view, even from behind. "Not much longer now," says Toppos. The burning torches heat the air, which stinks of pitch and damp cloth. The people next to me are speaking Russian: six men with Caucasian features and straggly black hair, each of them holding a hip flask. It doesn't look like they're here on my account, but who knows? Maybe they're supposed to gather information to help the supreme council of the organization reach its decision. Fear is a question of blood alcohol level. There's enough to drink; nothing can happen to me.

A drumroll announces the beginning of the program. Accompanied by a fanfare, the circus director steps onto the stage: a sharp-featured, slender man, wearing a top hat and tails. He lets the applause that greets his entrance go on for a long time before he raises his hand like a Roman emperor. The audience grows quiet. He takes the microphone and speaks. First he gives a sermon in Turkish, a long-winded discourse that never wants to end, followed by some heavily accented English: ". . . a few words for our friends from foreign countries. We welcome you to this evening with our brave bears. We are very happy that you are with us tonight and hope you enjoy the fights. Thank you."

"We can get closer, if you want," says Toppos.

"Ich sehe alles."

The first bear that's brought in is named Ushak. He belongs to the Kabakli family. Ushak's wearing an iron collar attached to a chain and a nose ring with a cord tied to it. He dawdles and looks around, hesitating between curiosity and fearfulness. When he sets himself to roll on

*the ground, his master gives the cord a violent jerk and strikes Ushak
with a club. The bear bellows. Why doesn't he defend himself, why
doesn't he bite the man's arm off or drag his claws across his face? "He's
young," Toppos says. "No experience." Finally the Gypsy hooks the end
of Ushak's chain to the snap link and leaves the ring. Ushak looks confused. He runs around a bit, dragging his nose cord behind him. The
torches, the howling, the strange smells. He turns around on his own
axis until two men open a gate and three emaciated dogs are kicked and
shouted out onto the sand. The dogs are as bewildered as the bear.
Gradually they grasp the seriousness of their situation, yap, and slowly
retreat to a point on the board fence as far away from the bear as possible. The orchestra is silent, except for the drummer, who's locked into
a muffled, monotonous rhythm, as though setting the rowing tempo for
galley slaves. Ushak disbelieves his eyes, stands to his full height, sniffs
the air. For a moment, he seems to be considering whether or not he
should dance, whether dancing would result in a beating or a reward.
He executes a few steps in place, drops onto his front paws, and hurls
himself with sudden violence at the dogs. His chain is long enough for
him to reach every part of the ring. The second his claws come into contact with the first dog, the wind instruments blow a brief heavy chord
and fade away, leaving behind only a kind of shawm. Its note rises and
swells, is chopped into a shrieking melody, breaks off. The dog with the
number two painted on its side lies motionless. Blood runs out of a gaping wound in its throat. Ushak growls, turns around, and trots away, as
though he's already forgotten what just happened. "Dogs no good," Toppos says. "It is training for Ushak. He must learn to fight." As soon as
Ushak moves, both the other dogs run away.*

*In vain. After ten minutes, Ushak's practice session comes to an
end. His master reaches for the cord and pulls on Ushak's nose ring in
case the bear has failed to grasp that his fight is over. He acts excited,
but completely subservient. Two men drag the dogs out of the arena by*

their hind legs. The orchestra produces so much noise that you can't hear the moans of the mutilated animals. I ask, "What happens to them?" The side of Toppos's hand draws a straight line across his Adam's apple.

"Hast du gewonnen?"

"Später."

A young man carrying a sales tray hung from a strap around his neck offers raki, vodka, and beer. I buy a small bottle of vodka. Toppos grins and takes it out of my hand, whereupon I buy another. The next bear and the one after that are also apprentices. Terrified street dogs are driven into the ring; the bears pounce on them and dispatch them without much ado. Audience response is measured. One injured cur goes into such wild convulsions that a handler has to slit its throat even before hauling it out of the ring.

Another fanfare sounds, and the director comes back onto the stage and seizes the microphone. He speaks in a melodramatic voice and makes sweeping gestures. The audience roars.

"Worüber redet er?"

"He tells Märchen, *fairytales. Stories about famous bears. Gypsy traditions.* Uninteressant für dich. *After this, the real fights start."*

Toppos seems very nervous now. He drank the contents of the vodka bottle in one long pull, and now he's drumming his fingernails on the glass. The Russians are staring at me. Is it because I'm staring at them, or the other way around? Supported by the orchestra, the circus director stirs up the crowd. The applause is continuous, and he leaves the stage amid shrill whistling and general jubilation.

"Mein Cousin Mikhail," *says Toppos,* "mit Vrobel, dem Bär von unserer Familie, *the best one we ever had." Vrobel is larger than the first three bears. He moves around fearlessly. It's a familiar situation for him, and he knows what he has to do. He stands there, looming above his master, inhaling the different smells, alert to the furious barking be-*

hind the curtain. Handlers agitate the dogs before the principal fights, but not even the fire irritates Vrobel. The violins, clarinets, and trombones rest; the percussion section plays on, falling back into the galley rhythm, with drums, bells, and two kinds of cymbals. Vrobel waits on all fours for his opponents. There are five of them, driven into the ring with whips. The dogs are muscular and aggressive, a mixture of fighting breeds. A bull terrier must have escaped from its owner and successfully reproduced its kind. Its descendants have been running in a pack since long before this night. They've conquered a broad territory in one of the most run-down sections of the city, far from the tourist centers, where they live off the rubbish in the streets. Maybe dummies are used to train them after they're captured; in any case, they're not undernourished. They stand close together, raising their hackles, growling, baring their teeth. Sometimes they bark briefly, not together, but serially. "He will kill them, he will make a good job," Toppos says.

Vrobel approaches the dogs. He shows respect, but no fear, bellowing into the sound of the drums. One after the other, the dogs lunge toward him and then fall back into their formation. Vrobel hesitates, looking attentively at the dogs; his nose quivers. Maybe he can identify something in the dogs' scents. Maybe he knows which one is most afraid, which one is the weakest. Now the barking sounds like shrieking. Vrobel is still about five feet away from them. He strikes at the empty air, then makes a sudden leap. His agility astonishes me. At the same moment, three of his opponents sink their teeth into his flank, while the other two spring to one side, run around him in a half circle, and attack him from behind. Vrobel rears straight up and rids himself of the first three dogs with a few mighty blows. The dogs whirl through the air and land hard, several feet away. Two of them are slightly hurt, on the shoulder, on the back of the neck, but the smell of their own blood whips them into frenzy, and they return to the attack at once, trying in vain to reach the bear's snout or chaps. Vrobel's paw catches the boldest of the three in midleap. For a fraction of a second, the dog seems to hover in the air; as it falls, it receives another blow. Toppos shouts, "You see, you see!" When the dog hits the ground, Vrobel breaks its neck with a single bite and then flings the lifeless body away. "Welche Kraft! What an animal! Unbelievable!"

The second dog falls into Vrobel's clutches almost inadvertently. The bear's claws slash its belly open so wide that the guts come spilling out. The orchestra is out of control; the drumbeats are like explosions, the brass instruments are wailing hysterically. Vrobel clamps the third dog in his teeth, just above the hindquarters, and shakes it like a rag. Its body rotates several times as it flies through the air. It lands in a heap on the sand and lies still. Although he's bleeding from numerous wounds, and although the strongest of the dogs has fastened its teeth in his throat, Vrobel seems to feel no pain. You can see the swollen veins standing out like blue lines. Vrobel tries unsuccessfully to get his snout around his attacker. The dog's chest and forepaws are covered with blood. It doesn't let go, it doesn't run away to save its life; the reflexes of its jaw muscles, bred into its forebears for generations, are stronger than the fear of death. Vrobel roars and lashes out, striking wildly until his paws find the right spot. A fountain of blood arcs onto the sand; the dog's movements grow visibly weaker, its strength ebbs, and it falls to the ground. Vrobel's final bite rips its throat open. Thunderous applause. Dance music. Mikhail gives Vrobel a sweet as a reward. I've had enough for tonight. I look at my watch, but it's not on my wrist anymore. It wasn't very expensive.

"You like it?"

"Yes, but I have to go now. My friends are waiting."

"Es kommen noch fünf Bären."

"Are there taxis anywhere?"

"I take you there."

When we step out of the tent, his brothers are already waiting to say good-bye. I doubt that this is going to be a friendly farewell.

"Do you think I was a good guide through Gypsy town, Al?"

"Ein sehr guter *guide*. Phantastisch."

"So what is about my pay?"

"Wieviel?"

I recognize the sound of a switchblade snapping open. I myself have one in my jacket. It's going to stay there. The four of them are standing so close to me—in front of me, behind me, beside me—that I can smell their breath.

"The dollars in your left Hosentasche."

"Fünfzig?"

"You said I was the best guide you could get." Immediately in front of my chin, I see the gleaming blade: long, narrow, sharpened on both sides. I hear another one snap open behind me, then two more, simultaneously, left and right.

"We have no time for discussions, Al. The next fight starts in a minute."

"Natürlich. Kein Problem. You earned it."

I sober up in a flash and hand him my remaining bills, even though I don't believe they would actually kill me. They don't want the police in their neighborhood, and the police would surely arrive. The others know I was on my way to Sulukule.

"Walk this way, always straight ahead, then you reach Beyazit. It was a nice evening with you, Al."

I have trouble lighting a cigarette and succeed only on the fourth try. The smoke and the fresh air clear my head and make me dizzy at the same time. The way back leads past Seraphina and Grigoriyan's house. My heartbeat gradually slows down, the sweat on my forehead dries, and soon I'm not staggering anymore. As I pass the house, I think *about Ayla, sleeping a deep, dreamless sleep in her shabby little room on the other side of the wooden wall. She'll forget me as quickly as I'll forget her and her purple cunt, covered with wiry black hairs. I should have stayed with her and fucked her. Why didn't I tell Toppos I preferred Ayla to bears? I try to remember where the taxi driver dropped me off, how many hours ago? Most of the streetlamps are out. Coiled intestines in the sand, the fountain of blood. Sometimes the moon shines out between clouds. I flinch when I spot a group of shadows, human shadows, heading toward me. I'm ready to turn out my pockets and hand over my last cigarettes without putting up any resistance. They're not interested in me. The bear's roars, the whimpering of the dying dogs. I know that soon I'll come to a wide, brightly lit, well-traveled street leading into the old part of the city. Maybe seven kilometers, maybe ten, two hours on foot. Not a pleasant prospect, but no grounds for despair. I'm warm, my legs are obeying me, I have the consolation of knowing I can't be robbed anymore, and there's a full minibar in the hotel room.*

17.

After Albin, contrary to his original intention, had bought an opal, he left the bazaar and found the Russian market by asking for directions along the way. It wasn't far. He inquired after Yevgeny Petrovitch and Parfyon, the names the jewel dealer had given him. He seems to have met one of the two. In addition, Albin spoke with a certain Nicola, who'd had business connections with Miller and declared himself prepared to reveal certain details if reimbursed for his expenses. Those details could scarcely have reached Albin before he vanished, unless he met Nicola on Saturday in Düşünülen Yer.

Right through to the end, there were big holes in parts of Albin's story. All efforts to fill in those holes sooner or later ran into a wall. Nonetheless, Nager believed him. When I asked Nager whether Albin had confided in him and told him things that went beyond what the rest of us had found out, he rejected the notion out of hand, but that doesn't have to mean anything; sometimes questions or topics disturb him and no one can understand why.

In the afternoon, Nager sat with Mona and me in the Orient Lounge, drinking coffee. He'd decided that this was going to be an alcohol-free evening. He pondered his carpet purchase and expatiated, in a fragmented way, on the idea that we must consider a new way of thinking about ornaments. When sequences of shapes and colors are used—without a center, purely as additions—what does that mean? It's probably about something more than decoration, display, and stultifying the masses, Nager thought. He had an idea of what might be behind all this: the principle of entropy, the inert, uniform distribution of temperature and energy in space, without differences, without dynamics. The end of all motion. That's what everything's headed for, he said. Millions of years from now.

Scherf came at six, without Hagen. Before he was through the door, he was shouting that he'd found his icons. At an insanely good price! Only two hundred marks, complete with certificate and stamp from a Russian monastery. These pieces would enormously enhance his Iconoclastic Controversy installation. No one wanted to listen to this now, but Scherf could not be stopped: instead of reproductions, originals were now available to him for his copies! The painters of these originals had worked under two constraints: they must attain the highest possible degree of similarity to the original images, and they must obliterate all traces of an individual hand. By using these icons, Scherf was going to be able to pose questions about reality, image, and individual and collective expression in a much more complex way. The craziest part was that he hadn't just found an icon of Christ Pantocrator, but a so-called *mandylion.* The *mandylion,* he explained, is not an image originally drawn by a human hand, but an image produced by a miraculous (in quotation marks) direct transfer, as for example Veronica's veil. This image went back to a cloth personally used by Christ, whose face left an imprint on the material. Moreover, Scherf continued, the Russian origin of the two icons would broaden the installation's significance by incorporating a reference to contemporary history; at least as much Greek Orthodox art was destroyed under Soviet rule as under the Byzantine emperor Leo III. According to Scherf, this demonstrates how much power rulers, even rulers of our own time, have always attributed to images, and it shows that iconoclasm is by no means a thing of the past.

Mona yawned. Nager was scratching his armpits with his eyes closed. "Let's see them," he said.

Scherf reached into a plastic bag and drew out two flat bubble-wrapped packages, each about eight inches by six inches. He said, "In Germany, these things cost two to three times as much."

Both the gold background and the painted images themselves were heavily crazed, the crackled surfaces either the result of technical errors or artificially produced in order to give the unsuspecting buyer the illusion of the objects' great age. The back side of both images was stained dark.

"Really pretty bad," Nager opined, and Mona said, "My grandma has something like that hanging over her house altar. In May and October, she lights candles in front of it."

It was a peaceful evening. The restaurant Mona picked was quite pleasant. Jan didn't start a quarrel with Scherf, nor Albin with Livia. No one drank too much, and no one had a hysterical fit.

After breakfast on Thursday, we went to the Museum of the Ancient Orient. At the end of our visit, Albin set off on his own. Livia, Jan, Mona, and I strolled around the city. After visiting some smaller mosques, we ended up back in the Orient Lounge, exhausted and thirsty, around a quarter after four. The conversation went clumping along. Nager said he was reminded of the Babylonian brick friezes in the museum in Berlin and offered a toast to Nebuchadnezzar. Jan asked Livia if Albin had always drunk so much. Livia nodded. He put his arm around her shoulders. For a moment, she leaned her head against his neck. Mona looked past them ostentatiously and grumbled about the weather.

At first, Albin didn't see us. He sat at the bar and ordered beer followed by vodka. He opened out a large city map and flipped nervously through the index. He was obviously looking for a specific place. His lips were moving, and he was hacking at the air with his left hand. Jan, Mona, and I watched him. Livia noticed our disdainful looks, got up, walked over to Albin, and gave him a kiss. He immediately started talking at her. He ran his hand through his hair again and again, like a man who could no longer see a pattern in the knotted threads of his life. When she asked him to come and sit with us, he said that first she had to go with him to the farthest corner of the lounge, where they would be undisturbed. Only for a few minutes, he said. He had something for her, a surprise, and he didn't want to give it to her in front of their new friends. Livia was afraid. As she walked behind him, she was preparing herself for hatred, shouting, even blows. Albin plopped onto a cushion; Livia kept her distance and took the chair across from him. He took a deep breath and said it was clear to him that they had gambled away their chance. Strictly speaking, he was the one who'd gambled the chance away. She should neither acknowledge that nor reject it now, he said; he understood her decision. He didn't want to ruin her life, too. He was surprised she'd stayed with him so long. More than five years, longer than all the others.

Livia says she tried several times to disagree with him, but she was aware of how halfhearted her efforts were. While he was giving a long speech about the end of their story together—an emotional speech, part of it loaded with self-pity—she imagined Jan's clear features, his decisiveness, and she knew that Albin was right. She was, however, not in a position to tell him so. At last, shivering and sweating, he rummaged around in the inner pocket of his jacket and brought out a little blue plastic box. He said, "The jewel dealer claimed that this was exactly the right stone for you. At first I thought that was just so much talk, but once he showed it to me, I had to buy it."

With a slight pressure from his thumb, the box sprang open. Albin leaned forward and handed it to Livia. Because his hand was shaking, the opal's sharp edges looked blurred, and its shining orange flickered like a faulty diode. Livia kept thinking, *This can't be true, this can't be true.* In the five years they'd been together, Albin had never given her jewelry. On the contrary, he'd even railed against men so lacking in imagination that they'd buy their wives some precious rock as a Christmas present or after enjoying a bit on the side; and the wives, who were stupid enough to be pleased by such gifts, were no better.

Livia would have known how to react to a tantrum. The stone struck her in an unprotected spot.

Albin smiled, as shyly as he'd done at their first meeting. Either accidentally or on purpose, she'd sat next to him in the middle of a crowded photographers' party. Without any clue as to what they might talk about, she'd offered him a cigarette. And now, for the last time, Livia saw the man she'd fallen in love with on the spot and gone home with twenty minutes later. Then his yellowish eyes moved into the foreground, along with the red spots on his nose. Livia was afraid that Albin could read her face, that he could see reflected equally there the images of the past, the present horror, and the future farewell. If he could, that made it even harder for her to understand what he wanted. He'd never apologized for anything, let alone tried to bribe her, even when she still wasn't earning any money and he was one of the best-paid stone sculptors in Europe. Contrary to her first impulse, which was to refuse the little box, her fingers closed around it. She held it in her hand, took out the stone, and turned it in the light.

"Do you like it?"

"Yes."

"It's a gift."

Livia searched for a suitable reply.

Once, in their first year, he came home one weekend from a job in Bamberg and brought her a long-stemmed flower with orange petals. It looked like a crane. He said, "This is the only kind that suits you."

"Why do you drink?"

Her question was a long time reaching him. His absent expression changed, very slowly, to contempt. Livia couldn't tell whether it was for her or for himself.

"You don't need a reason for that. You'd need a reason not to drink."

Albin stood up and stumbled one step. "We can go over to the others. At least, you can. I'm going to ask the bartender to call me a cab. I want to take a ride to the Gypsy quarter."

As he passed by, he waved and wished us a pleasant evening.

After a while, Jan said, "I'm going to see how she's doing."

It looked as though she was crying. As he got closer, he realized that her cut-glass water tumbler was reflecting the beam of a spotlight, focusing it into a shimmering spot on her cheek.

"What's that?"

"He gave it to me."

Jan leaned over the back of the chair and stroked her hair. She neither pushed his hand away nor drew back her head.

"He said he didn't want to destroy my life. He said if I left him, he'd understand. Then he pulled this little box out of his jacket. I didn't want to accept it, but suddenly I had it in my hand. I didn't even thank him. Now he's on his way to the Gypsy quarter, which is supposed to be pretty dangerous. Once he makes up his mind, ten horses couldn't hold him back. He'll probably buy a woman, and you know what? I'm not interested. I don't even care anymore, he can fuck ten Gypsy girls tonight, it's all the same to me. It's awful how little remains at the end. Do you think I'm cold?"

"No."

"Be honest. I've been lied to so much, I can't hear any more lies."

"I'll get you something to drink."

Jan went to the bar and ordered a double cognac.

"It looks serious," Mona said and bit her lip. Nager waved to the waitress and ordered another round. When she brought the cold beer, Nager asked her for a pencil and wrote something in his notebook. Mona's eyes followed her as she walked away. "On average, the women here have fatter behinds."

"You can get a good grip," Nager said.

Before we set out for dinner, Jan took me off to one side. "I need the room to myself tonight. At least for a couple of hours."

"Why don't you tell him?"

"That's Livia's decision."

It had stopped raining. We settled on a dilapidated joint where the only other customers were Turks. A cart full of fish stood in front of the entrance. The proprietor brought us each a raki and placed two more bottles on the table, along with some bread. A soccer game was being played on television. The score was one to nothing, an excited sportscaster said. The fact that no one else was eating should have made us suspicious, but neither the fish nor the dishes on display looked any different from those in other places. The neon lights and the shabby furnishings made us feel certain we hadn't fallen into a tourist trap. Nager sat between Mona and Corinna. He was mumbling a little, but with him that's no indication of the level of his drunkenness. He starts slurring his words after the second beer, but after that, his articulation hardly changes until the twentieth.

"I want fish," he said. "Fresh Mediterranean fish. Come on, Mona, let's order some fish. They looked good."

"I don't want fish."

"Grilled mackerel with olives. Mackerel is strong, not wimpy like cod filets or rosefish, the kind of stuff you eat in fish sticks. And don't look so cross. Drink some raki. It's quite tasty, in my opinion. When people eat and drink the same things, a personal relationship is automatically established between them."

"Not necessarily."

"Mona, my darling, you don't like me!"

"You're very nice, Professor Nager, but I'm not your darling."

Nager loosened his tie, crushed out his cigarette in the ashtray, and lit another one. Jan and Livia were sitting at one end of the table, whispering. Nobody dared disturb them. Adel was talking with Sabine. Corinna tried to take part in their conversation so as not to fall into Nager's hands. Swantje was explaining to Scherf, who naturally included Hagen, the background of her bondage objects. Fritz was drawing a bazaar cartoon in his drawing tablet. The appetizers were not poor enough to complain about. When the team in the red jerseys went ahead by two to one, the Turks breathed sighs of relief. Nager forgot that he and Mona weren't alone. He said, "I used to believe in ideals, too. Romance, eternal love. All rubbish, believe me. You're young. How old are you?"

"One doesn't ask a lady that."

"Makes no difference anyway. At your age, and until I was twenty-five, I was naïve, according to my mother. When you meet the right woman at the wrong time, it's totally useless. Great emotions—pure baloney. 'We were made for each other'—nonsense.

You're ruined when it's over, all the same. Your brain constructs a dramatic story so your trivial biography can gain some significance, a center it can revolve around, a black hole it can disappear into. You say to yourself: Failure is heroic! All is lost? It's happened before! There's no winner; nobody gets out alive. 'Drama, love, and insanity are the stuff of B-movies.' But no one kills himself for the fun of it, not even in installments . . . The woman was the hammer. The cunt. She stayed with her asshole, her rich old asshole. Rides around in convertibles instead of streetcars. Wouldn't we all? Villa. Yacht. Diamonds are a girl's best friends. She screwed around with me and married the lawyer. In the Steigenberger Hotel on the Königsallee in Düsseldorf, two hundred and fifty guests, including my humble self. I got so drunk you wouldn't believe it. I threw bottles at flowerpots in the entrance hall. Old Meissner china. Direct hit. Ship sinks. The drying-out cell where I woke up was in a district way over on the opposite end of the city. The damages had been paid by the honorable newlywed husband. She was able to buy my best work with his money. Every now and then she let me back between her legs, on the floor of my studio, in the park. The poor thing, I imagine she was starved for it. Her and her fancy Porsche. It's her own fault. She could have got a Volkswagen Golf from me anytime, even today . . ."

The general laughter at this disproportion interrupted Nager. He looked around confusedly until he realized why the rest of us were sitting there. "Listen up," he said. "Here's something for you to learn. This is the way things stand in the love department . . ."

But before he could go on, a pimple-faced girl brought the main course. Nager fanned the rising smell toward his nostrils and enthused over the aroma of the sea. He poured more raki, ate, drank, and tried more and more overtly to persuade "sweet Mona, lovely Mona" to go to bed with him.

After he'd eaten about three quarters of his mackerel, the expression on his face changed. "This fish tastes funny," he said, pushing his plate away. "Did anyone else order fish? Olaf, how's yours?"

"Nothing special."

"It's rotten! They're trying to palm off rotten fish on us!"

"Mine's all right. Just nothing special."

"I'm not going to put up with this. Is there a single business in this crappy city where they don't try to rip you off? I'm not paying for this. Who's the top Turk here? Hey, pal, get me the top Turk! On the double!"

Nager was red in the face and huffing like a sea elephant. To calm him down, Mona laid her hand on his arm, but he shoved it away. When the owner walked up to our table, the other guests forgot their soccer game for a minute. In a velvety voice, he asked if there was some problem, if he could help in any way.

"The fish tastes so bad I could puke. It's inedible. I've never been served anything like it. If I have food poisoning tomorrow, I'm calling the police on you. I'm a professor from Germany! They'll close you down, you can count on it. And don't even think I'm going to pay for this swill!"

Mona said, "Listen to what he offers first."

"I don't care what he offers. I'm not paying for this shitty fish!"

She was as pale as a corpse. Everyone was afraid that Nager would leap up and start hitting people and breaking furniture. At a word from the owner, the men from the neighboring tables would be standing around us with knives in their hands. It would be hard to get out of there in one piece. But Nager kept his seat, and the restaurant proprietor didn't want any trouble. Naturally, he said, Nager didn't have to pay for the fish, but might he not accept some substitute, on the house, of course? A dessert, perhaps? Coffee?

Nager swept his silverware off the table.

The owner offered to let us have the bottle of raki without charge, should we be so kind as to accept this small token of his apology.

Nager emptied his glass in one gulp and poured another. He said, "This is correct. This is proper. After all, that fish has been lying around for two weeks. But he apologizes. Good. Let's forget about the police."

Then he laughed and offered the owner a seat.

Five minutes later, Nager clapped him on the shoulder, passed him on to Corinna, and turned back to Mona. When it was time to leave, he had difficulty walking and took Mona's arm. "The moon's behind the clouds, Mona, so forget the clouds. We're going for a walk in the moonlight, except you can't actually see it. Seeing it's not the main thing. The visible isn't what's crucial. The important thing is the consciousness that something exists. There's definitely a full moon tonight. How do you like this? You and me on the boundary between Europe and Asia, a place where world history was made. Imagine the things that went on here. I'm thinking of the *Thousand and One Nights*. If only the cobblestones could speak! Emperors, sultans, viziers, metropolitans, whores. The stones' perspective wouldn't be bad. If you just think about the millions of shoes there've been since the Bronze Age, or the Ice Age, you have no idea: high, low, wide, pointy, leather, silk, brocade, wood, rubber: madness . . . Do you know the way back to the hotel? If not, let's take a cab. The others can walk. We'll have a nightcap in my room. I've got a bottle of Balvenie single malt scotch, the best there is, a golden brown color like your skin, and smooth, incomparably smooth. Do you know much about whiskey? That's OK, I can teach you. You're the only one I'd share my scotch with. The other blockheads I'm supposed to be teaching art to can drink whatever booze they want. Jim Beam, for all I care."

At intervals, Mona pushed his hands away from her breasts. When he stopped walking and tried to hug her, she pulled him along like a badly trained dog. He whined and then tried to remember a poem: " *'And my soul / Spread its wings out,'* or something like that."

In the distance, someone fired a gun. Jan and Livia walked ahead of us. When we reached the hotel, they were nowhere to be seen. Nager collapsed into an armchair, closed his eyes, and snored. We left him where he was; the hotel staff would take care of him.

Mona and I decided to have another drink in the Orient Lounge. This was, after all, my only choice. I'd promised Jan he could have the room and asked him to come down to the bar when they were finished. But I kept all that to myself.

Livia says she and Jan didn't sleep together that night. She says it was clear to both of them from the beginning that they weren't going to have an affair, not one of those brief flings you have when you travel. Mostly, according to her, they talked. For hours. They lay side by side on the bed and told stories, Livia more, Jan fewer. Shortly before two-thirty, he came into the lounge. He said, "Hello." He didn't like the fact that Mona was sitting with me. She didn't ask where he'd been. We ordered some more vodka.

Around four, Livia was awakened by the sound of the opening door, even though Albin was trying to enter the room as quietly as possible. He had glowing red cheeks and the look of a madman. At least he was able to move without reeling, but he talked arrant nonsense, while Livia came to terms with having been snatched out of a dream. She claims it took her a few minutes to wake up, so she was in no position to separate Albin's tales into true, possible, and made up. Among other things, he told her about fighting bears, and he said now he knew that all these *doners* and kebabs and *kuf-*

tas were made with dog meat, like in East Asia, and no wonder, the Turks came here from there, after all, they're dog eaters like the Chinese, and the Gypsies originally came from India, which is why their women have hair all over their bodies and why they're softer than European women. But shy, ridiculously shy, and so he'd spared a Gypsy girl, out of pity. He wasn't the monster she took him to be. In fact, she'd betrayed him as often as he'd deceived her.

At some point, this got to be too much for Livia, who could scarcely keep her eyes open. She told him he had to be quiet now, please, he should lie down and try to sleep. She was dead tired, she said, no longer capable of taking anything in, it had been a full, an overflowing day, tomorrow she'd listen to him as long as he wanted on the subject of his choice, but not anymore, not now.

Albin didn't complain, nor did he leave the room for more drinking. He nodded and said, "Forget what I just told you. Horror stories from my sick imagination." He took off his shoes and laid his clothes over the back of the chair. Then he fell onto the bed, turned over on his side with his back to her, and rolled himself into a ball like an abandoned young animal.

18.

Red flags with the crescent moon and star over the entrances to the shops.

The names he said sounded like "Parfyon" and "Yevgeny Pavlovitch."

Crowded. Screaming in about twenty-seven languages. The smell of human bodies. A busload of Japanese tourists, trying to follow their guide's open umbrella and blocking traffic. Lights sparkling and glimmering and flashing everywhere. Junk by the container load, Christmas twelve months a year. Livia's not a woman you give jewelry to. Even the vaults are painted in bright floral patterns. "Nein, no carpet. Hands off me." I have to get out of this throng before I jam my elbow into someone's face or smash a shopwindow.

EXIT.

The air is gray, polluted by exhaust gas. It looks like spray from an atomizer. The rattling of the tram. Any number of reasons to honk your horn. He said "Petrovitch," not "Pavlovitch."

Two names thousands of Russians answer to. And those names are why I bought a Mexican opal from a retired dentist, whose practice was supposedly in Bielefeld, where Livia went to school, where we met for the first time. Foolishness. Coincidence. He specializes in Western women searching for esoteric knowledge and talks about the signs of the zodiac and secret powers. All the same, he was right. It's the stone for her. I'll give it to her as a farewell gift. Just to be cruel. I want it to make her *lose control so badly she starts blubbering. Before she forgets me. Two hundred and ten dollars, without any guarantee that it's genuine, and without any proof that the two Russians really exist. The doctor's afraid of them. Or he pretended to be, quite convincingly. I assume they control the black market goods that come over the caravan routes from the Far East. They're not navigating by the stars anymore. Gangsters are mining minerals in the Russian provinces. Criminals are in the precious stone business, and the governments earn along with them. Diamonds, gold, uranium, and girls disappear without a trace. Better not to ask where they go. Istanbul is the sluice. This is where they wash stolen property and smuggled goods. Then they add a few stamps and signatures, and the stuff is off to Europe and America. Miller must have crossed paths with them. Maybe he was trying to set up his own network. Or maybe he had liquidity problems and turned a deaf ear to all warnings and showed up without money once too often.*

"No. Not English, not German, not French. Norwegian! Look—big and blond!" *Dirty adolescents carrying sales trays slung around their necks have divided the center of the city among themselves. Their obstinacy is incredible.*

The trading center the dentist talked about can't be far now. Why do I believe that it even exists? If it meant closing a deal, everyone in this town would swear that Paradise or hell begins just across the Bosporus, he's seen it with his own eyes. For $500, he'll take you there.

I think I'll have a drink before I start asking the way. A half-liter bottle of raki fits snugly into my jacket pocket. ". . . and a sesame ring." The salesgirl answers me in German and smiles. I say, "There's supposed to be a market somewhere near here with Russian dealers and shops. I want to buy myself a fur cap. Can you tell me how to get there?"

"Go in this direction, left at the second street, go straight ahead, bear right, and you'll run right into it. But all they have is cheap stuff."

The torso of an old Renault is burning in front of a mosque. No sign of an accident; someone parked the car and set it on fire. It's missing two tires. Black smoke. Smells like baking rubber. No one seems troubled by this. Crows roam over a little patch of grass. One of them tears apart a crumpled piece of aluminum foil with something edible inside. The bird interrupts its work and turns its head sideways. You can see it's thinking. I throw it a piece of bread. The others try to drive it off, but it escapes and flies away with the bread in its mouth.

Rows of trestle tables, their contents in total confusion. Men in camouflage clothing and quilted jackets rub their hands together because of the cold. They're wearing caps with plush earflaps. On offer: crystal, china, metal pots and pans, underwear, canned goods, vodka. The Eastern bloc's clearance sale. A fair number of customers. Women who look twice as old as they really are, haggling over household supplies. Children kicking a plastic ball from one puddle to the next. Stolen lamps, door fittings, incense burners, icons: stuff for tourists who don't know the customs regulations and for dealers who won't risk importing. Deals are concluded softly, prices are whispered, offers hissed through gaps in teeth. Real caviar—Beluga, Malossol—they're practically giving away the five-hundred-gram tins. No palaver; little gesticulation. The more military the goods on display, the fewer words employed. There are compasses, field glasses, orders of merit, rank insignia, and next to them night vision equipment, telescopic sights, Very pistols, brass knuckles. The real merchandise is in the aluminum cases under the tables. What's on display is decoration. Here goes. "I'm looking for Parfyon. Or Yevgeny Petrovitch."

"Parfyon's not here."

At least he seems to know who I mean. The doctor didn't cheat me.

"What do you want?"

"I'd rather tell him that myself."

"I can't help you."

"It's important."

"Ask the guy with the thick glasses. His name's Nicola."

"Where's his stall?"

"Beat it."

How many of the sellers here wear glasses? I can't find one in this section, but the market's large and chaotic. A swallow of raki for the pressure in my stomach.

"You want hashish?"

There's military clothing on the table in front of him. I'd gladly smoke a joint, but I don't want to wind up in a Turkish slammer. People are setting up and closing down at the same time. When someone gets rid of all his stuff, he drives off for fresh supplies. Others arrive and unload their wares from the trunks of their cars: electric samovars, amber.

If thick glasses is a sufficient description, then this must be Nicola with the woven things—pillows, bedspreads, purses. He's got lenses nearly half an inch thick set in huge horn-rims. They make his eyes look so big they completely fill the frames. I stop and look at some of his stuff and then at him. He says something in Russian. I have no clue, but when I shrug my shoulders, he switches to German: "From Siberia. Made by nomads. The best wool. You won't find this anywhere in Germany."

"Are you Nicola?"

"Who says so?"

"Where can I find Yevgeny Petrovitch? Or Parfyon?"

"Why?"

I take a high risk, bordering on lunacy: "I was a friend of Jon Miller."

"They're not here. They come on weekends."

I'll send up a trial balloon. Maybe he'll climb on. If not, too bad. "What's happened to his delivery?"

"That's not my line of work. I don't know what he was waiting for."

"Miller's been dead for two days."

"Чёрт возьми! What do you want?"

"I'm concluding his business for him."

"Shit."

"Cigarette?"

"Miller was all right."

"What can the holdup be?"

"Maybe there's war in the Crimea. The Black Sea is filled with Ukrainian and Russian navy ships."

"Can you help me? I'm new at this."

He shoves his glasses up on his forehead and rubs his eyes. They're totally normal-looking gray eyes. "Don't you guys get it yet? Istanbul isn't a children's playground."

"Nobody knows who Miller's contacts were. I'm starting from scratch."

"I can't promise anything. And it'll cost you—I have to feed my family. Buy a blanket for your mother. Or your girlfriend."

"When should I come back?"

"Sunday. Buy something. You can't tell who might be watching."

"What do the purses cost?"

"One and a half million. And don't run out of the market right away. Look at some furs. Or some binoculars. Bargain for something, anything at all. Better for you, better for me."

I'll be in Istanbul for another week. Just think, if I go about it right, I can get into the jewel-smuggling business. Earning money that way is easier than working on construction sites, and instead of dying from dust, you die from lead. I must be losing my mind. I must be nuts. A manic phase. Alcohol-induced megalomania. Uh-oh. Nesting dolls. "Nein, no matryoshka, thanks." They'll knock me off. If not the Russians, then Miller's side. A quick, clean death. That would be lovely. Not likely, though. There's a better chance they'll lure me into a trap, break my bones, and stub out cigarettes on my skin to make me tell them everything I know about clients and backers, none of whom exist, before they silence me forever. I can stand pain—I learned to do that as a child. No betrayal will do me any good. They'll check every one of my stories. They'll kick me in the balls. They'll cut me up and bleed me white, like a slaughtered calf . . . "Guns?"

"No guns."

"Where?"

"Nowhere."

It must be possible to get hold of a weapon. You don't forget how to shoot. Maybe that father of mine taught me something useful, after all.

Nicola's gone. I should have asked him. There's another vendor in his stall. The fewer people know my face, the better. All the same: "I want to buy a pistol."

"Piss off, man."

I need a story. Messut's the only one who can help me. From the start, he's given me free rein, even though I'm making trouble for him. He could have had me beaten to a pulp, just to show me how serious they are.

Cold sweat. Trembling knees. Not from fear; purely mechanical. Heart's fluttering. Coronaries are rare for people in their late twenties. I have to sit down, but not here in all this filth. That would attract attention. It would make Nicola furious. Focus. Concentrate. Stand still. Don't sway. Now, one foot in front of the other. Don't fall. Tongue feels powdered. Have a drink. Chew a bit of bread until it becomes sweet. Don't puke. Breathe regularly to stabilize circulation. Soon this will pass. Ten more meters. So far, no one's noticed anything. A clear bell sounds when the door opens. Empty table by the window, with a view of the square. I sit down. I'm tingling, as if thousands of beetles were swarming through my veins. When their carapaces rub together, it makes a sound like snow on a TV screen. Tom and Jerry. It's only one-

thirty, the sky shouldn't be so dark. The market's looking blurry. People's gestures seem slowed down. Their faces and hands are pale blue.
"Merhaba."

"*Coffee, please.*"

"*Turkish mocca or Nescafé?*"

"*Yes.*"

He brings Nescafé. I think about my grandmother. She believed in miracles and curses.

A woman comes from my right and walks past the window. Black leather coat, midlength. Chestnut brown hair pinned up with a golden needle set with pearls. I recognize the way she swings her hips. Too purposeful to be elegant. Ireen's exit Saturday night. I stared at her back as she moved away. She goes to the stall where the man who sent me to Nicola is. Speaks to him. I can't make out her face, but her profile is classic. I'm sure it's Ireen. I leap to my feet, but my body weight drags me back down onto the chair. I'm not going to be able to run after her and make her listen to me.

I must speak to Messut tonight. Let him tell his djinn stories to his children. I haven't lost my mind. Everybody in this market knows Miller. My brain isn't making things up. What I see is really happening. I drank whiskey with him. Two days later, he was shot and killed. Yesterday, they changed the carpet in his room. Ireen's talking to her contact. She's got her hands in her coat pockets, as though she's giving instructions. Messut's lying.

I don't have the strength to discuss the price of the coffee.

Drizzling rain, slippery sidewalks. The Sultan's a twenty-minute walk away. I've got an invisible bell jar around me, keeping noise and images at a distance.

Why am I turning for help to a hotel clerk who acts like some dignitary all the while he's lying to me?

The streetlights come on. A little old cemetery with faded grave-

stones right here on the main thoroughfare. That would be a good place to lie. The liveried porters are leaning on the façade of the hotel next to the revolving door and telling stories about ridiculous guests. They haven't been told to run me off—they lift their caps. Messut sees me. No reaction visible on his face.

"I want to know what game you're playing!"

"My friend, you are beside yourself."

"It was easier than I thought it would be to find people who knew Miller."

"Just a moment."

"I have—" A man who entered the hotel immediately after me stands beside me and without a word of apology interrupts me in the middle of a sentence and shoves me aside. Messut extends a hand to him. The man bows several times. He's wearing an expensive dark blue suit under his trench coat and a silver ring with a ruby. He kisses Messut's fingers. I understand only "ya sheikh, ya sheikh." Messut nods. Now and then he says "Inshallah" and "Hamidulillah." Everyone here says those words at every opportunity. To judge by his clothes and his whole bearing, this man belongs to the uppermost class, so why does he behave so obsequiously to an arrogant hotel clerk? Because the hotel clerk's job is a camouflage. Just like the Sicilian don who ran a newspaper kiosk for years, the godfather of Istanbul pulls the strings while working for an international hotel chain. Maybe his position is ideally suited to controlling and coordinating and making decisions about life and death. No one's surprised at the coming and going of businesspeople from various countries. The man next to me is speaking softly, furrowing his brow, like someone describing difficulties. Messut, not noticeably excited, listens before answering. What he says sounds solemn. Like he's reciting verses. The Italian mafiosi also like poetry and pious sayings. With a slight head movement, Messut signals to me to back away. I obey and drop into a chair with a view of the giant photograph of the Blue Mosque, which gleams behind rhododendron bushes in the evening light. Bands of violet clouds. The sea. Instead of pounding on the table and demanding to see the boss, I wait. He has a power to which others subordinate themselves. I wouldn't stand for it if anyone else put his hand on my shoulder and shoved me ahead of him like the accused in a courtroom.

"You're upset, Albin."

"I'm not going to listen to you going on to me about how I've lost my reason."

"Your reason is damaged." He insults me and I don't defend myself; he puts his hands on me and pays no price.

"Miller was in Istanbul to take delivery of some precious stones that were brought into the country illegally. It was easy to find that out. A source has promised to provide me with further information, but I'm not going to tell you from whom unless you show me you're willing to cooperate. No hotel likes having the police on the premises, and certainly not when they're investigating a murder."

"You don't have enough money."

"What does this have to do with money?"

"You can't distinguish true from false. You can't tell the difference between valuable clues and insignificant details. You've heard a few names. Some people are going to make an amusing pastime out of sending you here and there. For this privilege, you will run through stacks of dollars, more and more dollars, until you don't have a cent left, because you, my friend, are obsessed. You will pay without learning anything, and when you refuse, there are ways of compelling you. None of these dealers will be so stupid as to confide his secrets to you. As an opponent, you are predictable, and therefore you are useless as an ally. You're a cow that one milks because it's easy work and the milk costs nothing. You will leave Istanbul in a week. Until then, people will be lining up to earn some extra income from you. You'll follow false trails blindly. You'll go around in circles, around and around. And should anyone at all become worried that you have, contrary to expectations, seen something you should not have seen, then you're a dead man. Perhaps it will come to that; perhaps not. As Sa'di writes in The Gulistan, 'Two things are contrary to reason: to enjoy more than is decreed, and to die before the time appointed.' And he goes on: 'Fate will not change by a thousand laments and sighs, / By thanks or complaints, issuing from the mouth. / The angel appointed over the treasures of wind / Cares not if the lamp of a widow dies.' Maxim number seventy. You should be glad you happened to find Dr. Baış. At least you got something in return for your money: that stone in your pocket. It would have been a simple matter to hoodwink you entirely."

"I bargained and got a reasonable price."

"The Caucasians won't go easy on you. As far as they're concerned, your life isn't worth a piece of dried fish."

"I saw Jonathan Miller get shot. The forensic people will find evidence of his murder."

"I'm on your side, whether you believe it or not."

"The police will be able to find out who'd reserved that suite until Monday, where his permanent residence is, and whether anyone has reported him as missing."

"You're in big trouble, Albin."

"This is about organized crime. I'm the chief witness for the prosecution. The courts will protect me."

"This city is proliferating in all directions. Its shape changes every night—nobody has an up-to-date map. For someone with the right connections and inside information, it will be child's play to put you at the bottom of a site where a foundation is to be poured the following day."

"I'll defend myself."

"Look in the mirror. You're obviously sick."

"I'm healthy. I drink too much, that's all."

How does he break down all my resistance? This is the third time he's reaming me out. My temples ache. I can't bear to look him in the eye any longer. I'm fully conscious, and he's opening my skull. The pillars holding up the lobby ceiling become projection surfaces for organic structures. Threads leading to and from Messut shine in transparent, iridescent colors. His head has changed its appearance. His skin looks permeable, like a coat of wax, and under it run cords of exposed muscle through which something invisible flows. An exchange of peculiar substances is taking place between him and the outside world. His eyeballs hover freely in their sockets.

I clap my hands over my eyes until it grows dark and I feel his firm grip, grasping my shoulder with such force that I think he's going to press me down to the floor. "Come with me, Albin. I want to show you something."

He knows where I was and who I talked to. His reach is a thousand times longer than I feared. I don't have a chance of eluding his control here. It's not too late to get away. I could change my reservation and be on the next plane for Germany, with or without baggage, and with or without informing Livia. I discreetly withdraw—to their relief—accept the façade restoration job in Dresden, and disappear from the scene for three months. Then I settle down in a different city, maybe Frankfurt or Cologne. From the way he pushes me into the elevator, it's clear: I'm dead meat. He's humming. Or mumbling. Spoken words, following a melody. We go down to a basement under the basement. Yesterday he gave me a suspended sentence. I rejected his offer. Instead of playing it safe, I started poking around.

"You're standing before yourself like a man in front of a blind mirror, Albin. You can't even see your outline clearly." *He points to the left. I have to remember the way, in case he makes a mistake. The corridor smells damp. Neon lights tinge the walls a pale green. Messut's steps echo; my gym shoes squeak. Boilers and pumps rumble on the other side of the wall. Signs on steel doors refuse admittance with a threat:* No Entrance! Danger! *Lightning bolts, flames.* "I can help you clean the mirror." *He opens the door to a room full of dusty cabinets and various kinds of chairs, as well as brand-new furniture still in shrink-wrap, straight from the factory. It's waiting for someone to shatter his glass tabletop during breakfast. For example. Giant rolls of carpeting. Remarkably enough, I'm not afraid. Under the ceiling is a three-dimensional labyrinth of pipes, covered, painted, and shiny. The labyrinth gurgles. The hotel has flatulent innards. It's wrong to think of killing Messut. Although it would be easy. If he's not carrying a weapon. I could still find my way back. My thoughts get all tangled up before the idea of putting them into action becomes real.* "You've got the doctor confused with the poison maker." *No, it's different: on the way to the execution, I entrust my life to the executioner. The sound of pounding, iron on concrete. The lightbulbs are pretty dim—I can't see what's in the corners.* "But you're not yet completely lost." *He opens another door, the second in a row of four lined up like doors in a prison cellblock. And in fact, we enter a kind of cell. The trap snaps shut. That pounding. Water's flowing in the next room. There's a washbasin and toilet against the rear wall. High up, a grilled window at the end of a shaft, through which just enough daylight falls to let you recognize the various furniture items as soon as your eye adjusts. Not enough light to read by. A naked bulb hangs down from the ceiling. Why doesn't Messut switch it on? There's a bunk on the left with a thoroughly worn mattress. Next to it a narrow bookcase holding three books, so the prisoner won't go mad from boredom. After six months, he knows the first one by heart. If the guard shakes him out of sleep and quotes any passage in the book, the prisoner can go on from there. There are folded towels and washcloths on a stool and on the wall a poster with texts in tiny Arabic script. Messut says,* "Kneel down there." *He points to a threadbare carpet lying at an angle in front of the bed. I obey and wait for his accomplices* to arrive, wait for him to release the safety catch on his revolver. "You can drop out of sight and stay here. I'll hide you for a couple of weeks. After that, no one will be looking for you anymore. Then you fly home, and you start over again. And you don't give up." The carpet is a green lawn. A bronze oil lamp dangles above it. Box hedges stand roundabout, and there are beds of roses laid out according to geometrical laws. "No one except me has access to these rooms. I'll see that you receive food. Olives, dates, sometimes soup. You'll be on short rations, but they'll be good for you, and they won't cost you anything. If you need something, you can write it on a slip of paper and lay it in front of the door." The sound of a toilet flushing nearby is so loud it makes me flinch. He wants me to disappear. He wants to break my will so I won't be a danger to him anymore. "In the old days, we'd pick out a sheep together, and it would die in your place." I sit back on my heels and see them binding the body in a sack, weighing it down with boulders, loading it onto a speedboat, and heading out for the open sea. Messut or one of his men will drop the sack overboard before witnesses from the Russian organization, who will confirm that I've been done away with. "This carpet is a good place for you."

"How long?"

"Five and a half weeks."

"Why not four? Or six?"

"It's an ancient tradition. I'm going to give you a verse of poetry to learn by heart and repeat every day. The verse will protect you, and your soul will suffer no harm in your seclusion. Listen:

$$\text{فَإِنَّ مَعَ ٱلْعُسْرِ يُسْرًا / إِنَّ مَعَ ٱلْعُسْرِ يُسْرًا}$$

"The choice is yours."

"I don't understand a word. How am I supposed to remember something I can't understand?"

"Think about my offer. Talk it over with Livia. And make your decision. Soon. There's not much time left."

Instead of firing a weapon, he puts his hand on my shoulder again. I know he's not going to kill me. I know he's going to take me back to the lobby now and send me away. I stand up, even though I'd be glad to linger a while longer in the carpet garden. If you sat still there long enough, you'd hear birdsong and rustling leaves.

I walk in front of him as though in a daze. I see that I couldn't find the way back without him. When we're in the elevator, he says, "You know my offer is your only possibility."

"No."

When I walk through the revolving door and head for the Duke's Palace, a man on the other side of the street puts himself in motion, crosses over, and follows me. I walk faster. Although I'm considerably bigger than he is, he keeps up with me effortlessly. When I turn into Yeni Çeriler Caddesi, he passes me and turns to block my way. "You've been asking about me."

"Who are you?"

"So-and-so."

"It's about Miller."

"Miller's dead."

"His delivery."

He wrinkles his forehead. "You know, Miller wasn't a bad guy. He knew what he was doing—that is, for an American. In all the years he came here, he made fewer mistakes than you've made in three days. I have little interest in that, and you have nothing to fear from me. But if I were you, I wouldn't go poking my nose anywhere. And I'd give every police station a wide berth. There's nothing to divide. Since the breakup of the Soviet Union, the jewel trade is in the hands of the Caucasians. Three families split up the market among themselves. They were all satisfied with their portions. Miller's death was an accident. A short circuit *in the brain of a madman. What he did was damned stupid. Now a great many people are upset and doing their best to prevent a war. Nobody wants war. Sometimes it's unavoidable. But when you're between the two fronts, things can get distinctly uncomfortable, if you want my opinion. All the same, of course, I can help you."*

I have to get a night's sleep.

Did I say that, or did I only think it?

19.

I don't know how, but during the first forty-five minutes we spent on the grounds of the sultan's palace, Albin managed to get so plastered that he had to lie down for a nap on a bench outside in the cold while a young Turkish woman guided us through the harem. Livia assumed that his system was undergoing changes that would eventually result in his general disintegration. She said they'd spent the whole time together, from waking up that morning to the moment when he staggered through the gem collection and almost crashed into the glass cabinet with the music elephants, and she hadn't seen him drink anything except coffee.

Nager, Mona, and I hadn't slept much. Exhaustion disabled the defense mechanism that normally filtered our perceptions. We wandered with wide-open eyes through a jungle of extinct forms. Over three hundred rooms, from the storeroom to the reception hall, each decorated with ornaments made from plants, animals, writing, concrete, abstract, geometrical, as painting, tapestry, relief sculpture, tiled, carved, gilded, in stone, wood, terra-cotta. The ornamentation continued in the carpets on the floor, in the openwork blinds over the windows, in wrought-iron screens in front of the fireplaces, in the inlaid wood furniture. Our guide told us about the black and white eunuchs, the all-powerful mothers of certain sultans, the princes who were kept in cages and lost their minds. Ibrahim, Ahmed's brother, on the mere suspicion that one

of his concubines had betrayed him, gave the order to drown all of
the 280 women in the harem. Suleiman's son Selim never left the
guarded precincts and whiled away his days in drunkenness with
his mistresses, slave girls, and eunuchs. We were in a magical
world that did not exist and had never existed, but the magic
worked. Jan inhaled the scent of Livia's hair and whispered secrets
in her ear, Hagen pinched Swantje's side, Sabine revealed to Adel
something about love that bewildered him. Nager considered
the pros and cons of experimenting with ornamentation himself,
after all, even though it would stand in contradiction to his work
to date and cost him his gallery, and besides, he said, it was just a
lot of wretched handicraft, and you could never reach the quality
you see here. But on the other hand, he went on, no one has ever
done anything like this with brightly painted V2A steel; it would be
disconcertingly odd, and—detached from its original context—
completely pointless. What more could you want?

After the tour, Livia woke Albin up. He hadn't even been cold.
Obviously feeling better, he started talking about something he had
to get for Poensgen, a postcard from a famous café outside the city,
where a French poet had mourned for a Turkish girl. He assumed
that no one wanted to accompany him, so he'd see us back at the
hotel before dinner, he said. Then he stood up and went away without a word or a sign to Livia.

"What a piece of shit," Mona hissed. "He'd do that to me exactly once."

As we left the palace, Livia took the card to Thea out of her
handbag and dropped it in a postbox.

We had no other activity scheduled. Nager decided to retire for
a midday break. Jan, Livia, and I had the same idea. Mona had to
go back to the bazaar to buy a gift for her boyfriend. Scherf wanted
to go and see the Byzantine mosaics in the Chora Monastery. Ha-

gen put his arm around Swantje, and they turned into a side street. The air was damp and cold. Neglected children ran after us. A horse pulling an empty carriage trotted past.

"I'm not going to spend the night here," Jan informed me when we entered our room. "I'm just telling you so you won't be surprised when we're gone."

He picked up his toilet kit, called out, "See you later," and closed the door behind him. Twenty minutes later, the floor waiter brought a plate of mezes and a bottle of red wine that had been ordered for me.

Around seven o'clock, everyone met in the lobby and agreed, without debate, to go to the restaurant that Albin had proposed on the first evening.

The mood there was grim. The many reasons for this state of affairs formed a dark cloud over the table. Sabine was fighting back tears, and Corinna tried to comfort her. Adel had lost his appetite; he shook his head and didn't touch his skewered meat. Apparently, up until now Sabine had blocked out the fact that he wasn't interested in women. No one thought the trip would end well. In addition, we were afraid Nager might fly into another rage. He was drinking and talking. It was difficult to follow his train of thought. Only Albin understood him. Mona, laughing too often and too loudly, tried in vain to lighten the atmosphere by bringing up the *fascinating things* we'd seen in the past few days. Fritz drew intertwined patterns on blank, already stamped postcards. When Mona asked him if he intended to send off all his work, he answered, "I call it *mail art*. Of course, it's nothing new, but my drawings are better."

"How are you going to make a living?"

"I send most of them to a gallery owner."

———

After dinner, we ended up back in the Orient Lounge. Maybe it was hypocritical of me to sit next to Albin. I didn't want any trouble; I wanted Jan to be able to disappear with Livia. Mostly for her sake. Albin and I sat at the bar, while the others spread out to various groups of armchairs. For some reason, he decided to confide in me and started talking. His first sentence went like this: "I've never been happy to be alive."

"You're twenty-eight."

"My attitude has nothing to do with the fact that my father was a drunk and a failure. Even if he'd been an ideal parent, that would have changed nothing. I was three or four when something became clear to me one day, suddenly, all at once, and I thought, *I won't.* I won't. It was an unspectacular moment. There was no disappointment, no humiliation. A trivial thing: the man who was my father didn't come home from his construction site. It got to be eight o'clock, then nine, but he didn't come and he didn't call. My mother, who must still have loved him at the time, ran around the house, looking out of every window, opening the door, searching the horizon. She rushed over to his office but found no one there who had heard anything. She started whimpering: 'Something's happened to him. Something must have happened to him.' I felt disaster in the air, and I didn't leave her side. Father could have prevented the danger, but he was absent, and not only that: the catastrophe threatened him most of all. Mother was in despair, because she thought she wouldn't be able to save me and Claes and Xaver. She'd lost her protection, and ours, too. Mother stood in front of the house, combed her hair back with her fingers, and identified the neighbors' cars in the distance. She'd forgotten I was with her. I had little hands that couldn't fire a pistol, and no wallet with money I could give her for the things we needed from the stores. My father died around ten o'clock, when she threw herself on the sofa, crying. She was alone. I was alone. He'd abandoned us.

"The man one of his workers dropped off around midnight, roaring drunk, was a burned-out despot. He couldn't guarantee security, and so his power lost its legitimacy. For all dictators, security is the magic word. People will let themselves be spied on, locked up, or killed, they'll become traitors or murderers, for security. I declared his regime over; in fact, it lasted another ten years. But from that night, I refused obedience to him. He cleared off before I was big enough to trample him into the mud. He was a coward. I didn't want to be such a man. But I drink, and I'm like him. That's why I'm going to make sure it stops."

Albin talked for five hours without a break: about his father's flight, his mother's death, his first loves, his failure as a sculptor, his years with Livia.

Near dawn, he told me a horrible story, something that had supposedly happened between him, his mother, and his father in some woods near Staudt. He called this *the real beginning.* Livia told me she'd never heard this story. She suspected that Albin made it up that night. Either to justify himself or to impress me.

Shortly after one, she and Jan had disappeared. Neither Albin nor I saw them go. When he noticed they were gone, he asked me if I knew anything. I said, "No," and ordered two vodkas instead of telling him good night. I wanted him to think I was enjoying sitting there with him because he interested me, because I liked to have a good time. When I started slurring my words, I stopped talking, out of caution.

Jan and Livia had meticulously prepared their second night together. While Jan was telling me he was going to sleep somewhere else, Livia was booking another room, probably in the Duke's

Palace, but possibly in one of the other hotels. She's never revealed where. In the course of the afternoon, the two of them had planned how and where they would separate later and how and where they would meet again. They developed different scenarios for the evening. As luck would have it, the least complicated possibility turned out to be the case: Albin was on his fourth or fifth vodka and lemon, he was in conversation at the bar, and he seemed to have blocked out the fact that he had a girlfriend named Livia. He spoke of her in the past tense. Around ten to one, she said, "Good night," and left the lounge without telling Albin good-bye. Jan, with a clear view of Albin, observed him carefully when Livia left, and he was sure Albin didn't see her go. For the sake of prudence, Jan ordered another beer and drank it slowly. He didn't want to start the others' tongues wagging. At last, he said, "I need either coffee or sleep. I choose sleep."

Livia was pacing up and down in their room, trying to imagine what would happen and then rejecting the images her mind presented. She'd had three boyfriends before Albin, and she'd never cheated on him. But their time was up. He had acknowledged that himself. She wasn't going behind his back. She was equally afraid of two different possibilities: that being with Jan would be completely different, and that it would be exactly the same. Above the desk in the room, an art print depicted an odalisque dressed in gleaming white, standing on a rug with a red and gold pattern and lifting her veil. Before her stood a silver incense burner and behind her elements of Arabic architecture. Livia went into the bathroom and looked at herself in the mirror, uncertain whether Jan would prefer her face with or without makeup. Her mascara was old—it was forming little clumps between her eyelashes. There was nothing to be done about that, because she hadn't brought along any makeup remover. She put on some lipstick. She'd never met a man who objected to lipstick. If it got smeared, she'd look ridiculous, but if necessary she could turn out the light. She looked at herself with Albin's eyes and thought his words. Albin had never been interested in knowing what look she liked best for herself, and as a result it had nearly slipped her mind. She let her hair down, found it thin and stringy (different chemicals in the water here, she thought), pinned it back up, and hoped it wouldn't bother Jan that way. Albin had taken what he desired to take and released her from all responsibility. For the most part. She turned the radio on without knowing what kind of music she wanted to hear, looked in the minibar, and wondered whether it would be appropriate or corny to take out the two little bottles of champagne and put them on the table with two glasses. Middle Eastern pop music was trickling into the room from the ceiling. When they were planning the night, everything had seemed simple. Now she was afraid he wouldn't like her panties or her bra, afraid her behind was too wrinkly or her breasts too slack. Albin would have poured gin into himself and unbuttoned his trousers. "Don't compare. When you start comparing, love is lost." She would have liked to pour herself a glass of wine, and she would have liked to stay cold sober. She lit a cigarette and put it out after three drags, because it made her feel sick. She considered sitting on the side of the bed to untie her boots, whose laces had become knotted.

Although she'd been waiting for Jan, she jumped when he opened the door without knocking. Suddenly he was there, uncertain what he should say or do. He opened the minibar in his turn and asked her what she wanted to drink.

"White wine."

He uncorked a small bottle of Chablis, poured it out, and

dropped into a chair. She stood around indecisively and was glad when he handed her a glass and clinked his own against it. She took the other chair.

"It was easy," he said.

She pulled off her boots without averting her eyes from him.

"No one noticed anything, not even Olaf."

"I'm not going to talk about the way the room's furnished or discuss our impressions of the day. For me, this is no game. I can't have an affair. I'd rather be alone until I get used to being alone. It would have come down to that without you. Or maybe Albin would have managed to hold on to me. In the state he's in, you don't give up easily on someone you've loved."

Jan leaned forward and took her hand.

"How many women have you kissed? How many have you gone to bed with? And you've seen thousands of images, all the variations. I'm not asking out of curiosity, I don't care what your answer is. What I want to know is, could it be different? How could it be different? Can you do it without remembering other peoples' lips or bedroom skills, without thinking of how they tasted, what their sexual organs looked like, without imagining countless bodies from films, posters, newspapers? That's impossible, right? We're not young and innocent."

As she spoke, he pushed up her sweater sleeve and started stroking her forearm. Livia took her feet off the table and moved her chair closer, still afraid of crossing the line. She said, "I haven't come to you so I can free myself from Albin. I freed myself from Albin long ago. He was bad luck for me, so bad that I was becoming weaker as time went on. I didn't even have the strength to recognize the fact that it was over. I talked him into coming to Istanbul, to a place neither of us knew, because I thought we might rediscover the reason why we became a couple. From the moment we got to the airport until today, he's had one concern: absorbing enough liquor. He has no other thought except the next drink."

Jan laid a finger on her lips. Livia smiled apologetically, forgot that her hair looked ugly, and took it down. It fell over her shoulders with a reddish shimmer. "I'm not running away, Jan."

He nodded. His thumb circled a soft spot on the inside of her forearm. Rings formed around the spot, like water rippled by a stone.

"I have to learn everything all over."

The rings reached her collarbone and then encircled her neck. Her breath lost its independent status: every time she breathed, she had to give the order first. Jan rose to his feet, pulled her out of the chair, and put the bottle of wine on the night table. She sat on the bed. He held her hands tight, then threw her down on her back, laughing, and grabbed her hair—which felt as soft as baby goose down—ran his fingers over her ears, blew a narrow stream of air onto the most vulnerable spot on her throat, and watched the gooseflesh rise on the nape of her neck.

She lay on her back, staring into space, the way she used to lie next to Albin when he got drunk early and had to sleep.

"I often spoke to the wall while he was passing out. Who was I supposed to talk to? He was my sweetheart. I wanted him to know what moved me, what was on my mind. He wasn't interested in photography, but out of consideration for me he restrained his contempt. I didn't want to tell on him, so I never let anyone know that he preferred spiritual company—bottled spirits, that is."

Jan slid his hand under her sweater and stroked her stomach, which was flat and tense. He said, "A person like Albin leaves you doubly alone. He talks to you less and less, but because you love him, you don't talk to anyone else about him. You're ashamed for him, and you're ashamed of yourself for being ashamed."

She sat up, pulled off her sweater, and fell back onto the mattress with a sigh. "I know I'm saying the wrong thing at the wrong time."

Jan shook his head. The floral pattern in the lace of her brassiere showed through her light-colored silk shirt. She had a mole above her left breast. Jan took a large swig from the bottle, pressed his lips to hers, and let the cold wine run out of his mouth into her. Savoring the contrast between warm lips and cold liquid, Livia shut her eyes and slid down through a system of caves and onto a plain she thought should never end. Jan's hands slowly stroked her back, relaxing her tenseness and undoing her bra in the process. The boundaries of his face grew blurred, his eyes became her eyes, and they reflected a landscape of sand dunes, grass, and footprints, through which a brook meandered, drawing closer to the sea without seeking it, following the gravitational pull of the earth. She wanted to spend the rest of her days in this place, where her most arduous task would be to brush away grains of sand. Her shirt, her panties slipped off, her legs were drawn up, and between them his hand began a game she'd almost forgotten. There was no winner and no loser. She said, "I'd like some more wine." Jan reached for the bottle, rested it against his throat, and gave her a drink. She'd never drunk such cool wine; it was like springwater that had flowed through mosses and upland meadows and taken on unfamiliar flavors: slate, loam, clover. She allowed her pelvis and her hips to follow their own rhythm. Jan didn't refuse it; he moved in her tempo and took her hand away from her mouth when she was frightened by the loudness of her own outcry. Water mixed with salt flowed into her navel and ran down her ribs. She had trouble saying, "It's never been like that," and she didn't know whether he'd heard her, didn't even know whether she'd spoken or thought the words.

Later, they lay quietly dozing, side by side, pressed against each other like a pair of young dogs, drowsily aware of the ticking alarm clock. By the time Albin and I staggered out of the lounge, it was at least a theoretical possibility that Livia could have gotten up early and left their room to go shoot some photographs: the unloading of a newly arrived ship, perhaps, or the movements of the awakening city. Or she might have sought refuge in a café because she feared—no, she knew—that Albin would come back to the room drunk and his reactions would be unpredictable.

In spite of all the precautions they'd taken, Albin assumed that Jan and Livia were in bed together. He also had deep suspicions about the previous night, even though he'd found Livia in the room when he came back from Sulukule. Maybe this is an explanation for Albin's sudden disappearance: he was proud. He absolutely did not want to take on the role of the abandoned lover for all to see. The opal he bought Livia, not to mention the melodramatic gesture of its presentation, fits this theory, too. He removed himself from the scene so he wouldn't have to hear Livia's words of farewell. This seems more probable than the assumption that he was killed or carried off by jewel smugglers, whether Caucasians, Turks, or Americans. Not even Messut made any mention of a crime.

20.

Nager springs for a round of raki, but paying for it makes him forget he owes Livia and me a dinner.

As soon as a sufficient amount of ethanol passes through your stomach wall and into your bloodstream, your altered blood causes changes in your entire physical state: your skin shimmers as though it's being brushed and scrubbed from inside. The cold air outdoors is pleasant. I'm not shivering anymore today. The larva's painful movements have become twitches in my arms and chest. Islands of silence are forming on Istanbul's main thoroughfare.

Livia's talking with Jan. She doesn't want to know what I plan to do.

While we're waiting for Corinna and Sabine and trying to decide what to do with the rest of the evening, Nager asks me, "Do you know a quiet bar where we can talk? The kids will have to amuse themselves without us. You can measure the distance between them and art in light-years. If I had to listen to their eager-beaver culture-babble for seven days nonstop, I'd have a nervous breakdown."

"I'm a craftsman, not an artist."

"You're a special case."

He's nuts. They despise and fear him. We're scouts on the same frontier.

"Let's go over to the Sultan. They've got this Irish Pub. Messut sent me there so I could get used to the idea of Miller's nonexistence. I'll

show you the hotel—maybe Messut's on duty tonight. Maybe you could talk to him and form your own judgment. I won't deny there's a chance he'll throw us both out. In any case, the bartender knew what was up. When I asked him about a fat American with an attractive girlfriend, he started talking about Marlon Brando. It seems Brando's a Turkish favorite, especially as the godfather. Either this guy had seen too many movies, or he was trying to warn me. I told him that Brando had been in town, shooting a film about gem smugglers, but that he'd been shot and killed in the Sultan that morning. The bartender stopped talking, rinsed a couple of glasses, and stared at his television screen. If you want to go to the Sultan, we have to turn left."

"It's been a long day, and you're all tired. You go back to the hotel; Albin and I are going somewhere else." No one asks to be taken along. Livia doesn't care to join us. She knows we're going to wind up drinking ourselves stupid, and her mouth contorts in a grimace of disgust. Scherf looks insulted and starts whispering with Hagen. Nager prefers my company to his students'. The ethanol has reached my brain and docked at the Control Center for Well-Being, providing the uplift there's no other reason for. "Have fun, kids. Sleep well and sweet dreams."

All the guests have got out of a tour bus that's blocking the street in front of the Sultan. Pubescent boys in uniform are loading the guests' baggage onto carts. Under the spotlights, the red carpet gleams like a lake of blood. The lobby is filled with British pensioners, waiting at the reception desk or sitting on the sofas, leafing through travel brochures. As soon as one guest heads for the elevator, another takes his place at the desk. Nager says, "Is that Messut?"

"No. Maybe he's in his office. You see that door that's not closed all the way? There's a light on in there."

Nager walks up past the queue and leans on the counter as though he's about to order a beer. In atrocious English, he says, "I vant to shpeak viss Messut." I keep my distance. The assistant clerk stares at

Nager in amazement. His face shows no sign of suspicion. Apparently, not all of them are in on it. An eye, not Messut's, peers through the crack in the door. Someone wants to know who's asking for him.

The clerk says, "Mr. Yeter doesn't work tonight. May I help you?"

"It vas for private reasons," Nager says, then grins and adds, "Too bad."

The bar is neither empty nor crowded. We choose the sectional sofa to the right of the entrance, because from there we have a clear view of both the oval-shaped bar and the door. "That's him, the one that's mixing a drink." Along with the bartender, the staff includes an inconspicuous girl and a man in his late twenties who apparently spends all his free time in the gym.

When the girl comes to serve us, we order a Guinness and a Tullamore Dew. Nager says, "He recognizes you. He's not thrilled at the sight."

"What did you expect?"

The bartender says something to the waitress, who turns around and looks at us. I don't imagine they're talking about our order. Nager says, "He pours a generous drink."

"Maybe he wants to get us drunk."

Making a show of not paying any attention to me, the bartender goes on with his work, stirring tall drinks, cracking ice, drawing beer. After fifteen minutes have gone by, he ambles over to the farther end of the bar and makes a telephone call. "Pretty damn unobtrusive," Nager says.

"A mediocre piece of acting."

"Incidentally, do you know what you're going to do?"

"I'm going to keep on investigating. This morning I saw something instructive. The situation was a bit tricky—ask me about it in a few days. And then I spent two hours walking up and down this street. There's no café where you can sit and get a good look at the Sultan's re-

ception area. I was trying to find out what kind of people frequent the hotel. This doesn't seem like the right season for tourists or business travelers, but the Sultan's quite busy, all the same. Most of the visitors I saw were Turkish men. Some of them came on foot; others arrived in automobiles. All of them stayed inside for a short time only—fifteen minutes at most—before they were gone again. So they weren't hotel guests. And take a look around—do you see a single Turk? That doesn't prove anything, but it's another bit of circumstantial evidence." The bartender's keeping an eye on us, but he looks over here at such widely spaced intervals that there's no reason to give him any trouble.

"Something funny happened to me and Seppo in Düsseldorf once. It was late at night, around one-thirty. We'd been to an opening, and we wanted to eat some bratwurst in the old part of town. So we were swaying through the Hofgarten, completely loaded, when we saw two men ahead of us, about a hundred yards away, screaming at each other. One of them had a knife in his hand. As we came closer, he stabbed the other man in the ribs, twice, quick as a flash, and ran away. We went up to the wounded guy and asked if we could help him. He didn't say anything, didn't show any emotion. He just kept his hands pressed to his chest. Then, all at once, he started yelling: 'Fuck off! It's none of your business! If you jerk-offs don't beat it, I'll call the cops and tell them you tried to mug me!' Two days later, I read in the newspaper that the body of a stabbing victim had washed up on the banks of the Rhine south of Meerbusch. The victim's identity was unclear, and the police were looking for possible witnesses. When we reported to the police station, they gave us some information about how the law works and told us what the penalties for perjury were; we admitted we'd been stinking drunk. Then we had to go to the forensic medicine department, where a doctor pulled a drawer with a dead body in it out of the wall, the way they do on television. We identified him as the man in the Hofgarten, signed the statement, and went on a binge for three days, out of pure paranoia. To this

day, there's no trace of the killer. They don't even know the victim's name. Why didn't he want us to help him? Later, Seppo made a picture of a yellow and white foot. A ticket with a number on it was hanging down from one big toe, and goldfish were swimming in the background. He wrote some words on the picture: 'Nonsense Wards Off Lunacy.' "

A few gentlemen from the British tour group have taken seats at the next table. Even before ordering his favorite whiskey, one of them says, "Excuse me, madam, Cornwall may not be Irish, but it is one of the most beautiful regions in England." The others nod. Nager shakes his head and buries his face in his hands, shaking with laughter, then stops and says, "I've got a question . . ."

I know what question he wants to ask, and I don't want to hear it. He goes on. "I know a few hundred artists. You're one of them. It's not something you can choose. Why don't you make any art?"

I could say, "Shut the fuck up, that's none of your goddamn business." He wouldn't be insulted. I say, "I don't think about reasons much. I had to spend a few years living with my uncle on his chicken farm. He had a neighbor, a stone sculptor named Poensgen. I must have been fifteen or sixteen. During the lunch break, I'd drink schnapps with the workers, and I often used to watch him. He had incredible command of his material. Without a moment of uncertainty, he'd carve letters, patterns, or profiles in relief. Rich farmers would pay him to turn stone into Madonnas or Christs for their family vaults. I'd hang on the fence, amazed, thinking, How can he do that? Nobody has those skills anymore, they've all died out. I found one book about Michelangelo and another about Rodin in my mother's little library. And I observed the gestures—some lovely, some terrifying—my parents and my brothers and their girlfriends made. I memorized their faces, the expressions that couldn't be described, only shown. Life in Staudt was pretty dull. Worse than dull. One Tuesday in the summer of 'eighty-two, I asked Poensgen, 'Jupp, can you lend me a stone and some tools?' He looked skeptical and hesitated, but then he went with me to the pile of old gravestones he kept, things he'd removed from cemeteries. Different shapes and sizes, moss-covered, damaged at the corners, some broken into pieces. 'Find your stone,' he said. The way he put it was new to me, but I understood that he was talking about a particular stone I'd recognize as mine, and I realized that stones weren't chosen at random. Poensgen left me alone and went back to his black marble candelabrum.

"I stared at the blocks without a clue. I knew nothing about the different kinds of stone, nor did I know that each one reacts differently to the chisel. But I had an image of my statue in my mind. There was an arm and an outstretched hand, thrusting out of a block of stone, and the fingertips of the hand were touching another block of stone. The arm and hand were life-size. They were supposed to form a kind of spark, leaping between two electrodes. After an hour and a half, I found a stone that had served as a pedestal for something. It had two relief profiles, one above and one below, but no inscription. The side that used to face the west was green. I went to Poensgen and said, 'I've got it.' He raised his eyebrows, but he believed me. He looked at the stone, gave me a hammer and chisel, and showed me the basic stroke. For the first few days, he corrected the sequence of my movements, but nothing else. I had to hack away a lot of material, so I knew the stone by the time things got complicated. The hand was extremely difficult for a beginner, especially since I wanted the thumb and the little finger spread wide apart. They didn't break off, but you couldn't feel any tension in them. Poensgen said, 'You could be good. Better than me,' and he let me pick out another stone. At the end of eighteen months, my grades were so bad I had to repeat a year. And so I started studying at Poensgen's. I swept out his workshop, dragged stuff from here to there, sawed slabs, put in new windowsills, laid floors, built stairs. A boring, strenuous waste of time. All the same, I liked working with Poensgen.

"Everything he does, he does with great concentration. He prefers *not to accept many jobs. Since he's the best around, he always manages to get by, mostly by doing restoration work and replicas. Already in my second year, I was allowed to finish the decorations of some Gothic altarpieces and copy Baroque lintels. After hours, I worked on my own sculptures. I carved mostly gestures, moments of physical contact, and portraits, one after another. I didn't want to wind up as a tombstone cutter, so I submitted portfolios to three different art academies. During the admission interview, one of your colleagues asked me how I came up with the outlandish idea that I could get into an arts curriculum with such kitsch, with such totally unoriginal, low-quality knockoffs of the nineteenth century. He advised me to get a job on some cathedral worksite. It would be ideal for me: I wouldn't need to develop any formal language of my own, I could just imitate to my heart's content. Luckily for this guy, I was paralyzed; otherwise, he would've needed a plastic surgeon. None of the academies wanted me, not in Düsseldorf, not in Hamburg, and not in Berlin. Nevertheless, I kept on carving, at night and on the weekends. I traveled to Florence and Rome to look at Michelangelo's statues. They're the standard. Rodin's stuff is sloppy. I spent a week in the stone quarries in Carrara, looking for the right blocks. I had them send me some of the whitest marble. If you polish it right, you can make it look more alive than living skin.*

"I made busts from those stones, busts of Poensgen and Claes and my mother. Their arms were free, held away from their upper body, and their hands were folded or resting on each other. In Mother's portrait bust, her fingertips were touching, like the framework of a hemisphere in front of her chest. Although her eyes had no color, you could tell the woman was spent. Her hands were fragile, but also extremely flexible. She could bend back her index finger until it touched the back of her hand, and she could perform all sorts of contortions. In part, I went beyond the limits of the material, and then when I was almost finished an ear popped off. I dropped the chisel, and a moment later all that was left

of my attempt at a portrait bust was a heap of shards. Your professorial colleague was right: my statues looked old, they belonged in the past. It wasn't just my statues—even the impulse behind them came from yesterday, not today. My belief that they were possible was too weak. When night falls and you've got a bottle of vodka in your hand and you stand in front of a portrait that's no better than the ones others have already made, a portrait that looks as though it came out of a time capsule, then it can happen that you put aside your precision chisel and pick up a sledgehammer. And since it takes many nights and many bottles of vodka to produce a new image, you don't wind up with very much. When I met Livia, I thought, Now I'm landing in the present; now I'm going to accomplish something. I'm going to make one more try, with a real woman this time, a woman who wants to be with me, a woman who won't leave, a woman I won't leave.

"Livia also has unusual hands—have you ever noticed that? Different from my mother's hands; stronger. Hands that can clasp something and lift it up without squeezing it and hold on to it without letting it fall. My mother dropped everything. Even if she was concentrating on holding a glass or a knife, her fingers would open. She had to sweep up shards of glass or crockery almost daily. That's what I wanted to portray: hands that couldn't hold anything, and a terrified face. And then hands holding something, but not crushing it. My bust of Livia would have been almost a success. Her upper body ended just above the navel. She looked straight at you and yet past you. It made no difference where you stood when you looked at her, you had no chance of meeting her eye, but you kept thinking that all you had to do was change your position. Her right hand was pushing some strands of hair behind her ear. In her left hand, more or less at the level of her nipples, she was holding a small camera, which was aimed like a weapon at the observer. Instead of her eyes on you, there was a lens. I worked on that bust for nine months, night after night. The hair looked just like hair. Livia thought it resembled her more than her reflection in a mirror. As I worked, I imagined that the result would be something new.

"Then a process was set in motion that I don't understand to this day: I wanted to make the wrists thinner, so I took off a few millimeters, but then the arms looked too plump and the hands too strong. After I corrected those, she had shoulders like a boxer, her tits were huge, and she looked like she had hydrocephalus, with a swollen head perched on top of a long neck like a giraffe's. Then her arms were anorexic, she had fingers like little twigs, she was holding an outsized camera, she had a horse's face, and her breasts were withered. I spent three months trying to bring the different parts into a proper relationship with one another, drinking a bottle of liquor per night. Then one night—it was shortly after eleven—while I was polishing the vertebrae in the back of her neck, the hand with the camera broke off at the wrist. I hadn't touched it—it still had a diameter of a centimeter and a half. The sound of the chunks of stone hitting the floor awakened me from the sculptor's dream. The fingers were as thin as marble can be. Two of them were lying a whole meter away from the hand and the camera. I took a few steps back. The look had long since vanished from her eyes, even the look that seemed to focus somewhere beyond the observer. It was a moment of clarity, despite half a bottle of brandy: I grabbed the sledgehammer and pounded away at that stone until there was nothing left of it but splinters and shards the size of pebbles.

"Then I took all the other busts and torsos and studies off the shelves and brought the rest in from outside—there weren't many pieces, eight or nine altogether—and smashed them into smithereens. It took hours. Really exhausting work. The other pieces weren't as fragile as Livia's portrait. By three-thirty or so, none of my sculptures existed any longer. That was five years ago. Since then, I do façade restorations, I put the finishing touches on tracery, I add details to arrangements of folds. That sort of work pays pretty well. I do as little *of it as possible. If I get an idea, I stop working. Once in a blue moon, something comes over me and I try my hand at a sculpture. I think I've seen something that hasn't yet been shown. But that one night has stayed with me, and what it left behind always leads to the same automatic sequence: at a certain point, not long before a sculpture's finished, I know it won't get better, and I know it isn't good. Sometimes I leave the thing standing there for a few days. I show it to Livia, and she tries to convince me that it's fabulous, but I have eyes in my head. After a week at the longest, I take up the sledgehammer or the compressed air pistol. There was one bust I reduced to marble scrap with my hands and a pointed chisel, just for the pure pleasure of it. I carved the thing up as precisely as if I were making a sculpture instead of destroying one."*

"You should have documented all that. Your girlfriend's a photographer. Tell her to get herself a glass plate camera. You work on a bust or some other sculpture until you can't go any farther. Then you let Livia light it perfectly and take photographs of it. The prints should match the original size of the sculpture so every detail can be seen. Then you destroy the thing. Brutally, if you want, or according to some strict system. You dash it to the ground somewhere or demolish it piece by piece. At the end, all that's left is gravel, some of it coarse, some of it fine, except that here and there you can recognize a part, finely carved and still perfectly intact, a nose, say, or a finger joint. You sweep everything up and dump it into a bucket. If you're as good as I suppose you are, people will be shocked. They'll see photographs of reactionary, technically perfect stone statues, and then they'll see them turned into rubble. You can film the action and show it as a video. The artist denies his work, becomes his own iconoclast. That would be a radical rejection . . . Have you ever been to Egypt? In Luxor and Karnak, there are thousands of carved figures and reliefs with missing noses, knocked off by the devout, either because then the soul escapes, or, conversely, because then evil spirits can't

enter the graven image and dwell in it. With one blow they split faces and gouged out eyes. You look at these things and weep. You'd like to mutilate those assholes the way they mutilated these sculptures. The re-action to the stone fragments in your photographs will be similar. Rage, pain. No one can conceive what has led you to this lunacy. That's what art collectors like to see: things no one can conceive. Intelligent people who earn a lot of money will take pleasure in the offspring of your dis-eased imagination. They'll talk about them over their champagne. Just do it. I'll introduce you to my gallery owner."

"Why?"

"Why not, if it doesn't matter either way?"

"I hate stone."

21.

What did Albin do in Düşünülen Yer? Something must have happened there. On the way back, he exchanged a few sentences with Nager but didn't say anything about his reconnaissance. And after the trip was over, we never succeeded in finding out either exactly where he'd been or whether he'd met an informant.

The morning voyage on the silvery Bosporus past country houses and palaces was a moment of relief, a promise of better days. For the first time since our arrival, Istanbul lay bathed in sunlight under a blue sky, cloudless except for a few high, white wisps. The air smelled fresh, not like fouled seawater. There were some Turkish girls on board, students, but none of us spoke to them.

Soon after we left the ship, Albin said to Livia, "Stay with the others. You can't help me." He spoke so loud that all of us heard him. Then he hurried off in the opposite direction. Livia took this rude behavior well, more relieved than hurt, and smiled at Jan.

I don't think Albin was heading off to some designated meeting place. If he'd had an appointment, he would have needed a separate map. On the Istanbul maps we had, Düşünülen Yer showed up only as a brown spot on the northern part of the Asian side of the city. Albin didn't look at the street names and didn't ask any of the people he passed to show him the way. He ran away from us, looking back several times to make sure no one was following him.

Düşünülen Yer lies on rising ground, surrounded by restricted military areas. The only way to reach it is by water. The land around the bay has been inhabited since prehistoric times. There's a table displaying an archaeological dig in cross section, indicating the various buried settlement levels. Over the centuries, Düşünülen Yer has grown from a fishing village to a small town with wooden houses, souvenir shops, dealers in carpets and ceramics, restaurants, and on the edges, a dreary residential area. The cutters are economically meaningless; they set sail so we can find it picturesque.

Despite its small size, the layout of the town is inscrutable. You come to a mosque or a fountain, and you believe you've already seen it, but you don't remember the nearby buildings. The town's growth has been uncontrolled, but some neighborhoods contain streets laid out on a strict right-angle grid. You get the feeling you're going in circles. Somewhere, there must be a town center that will clarify the overall architectonic context, but every time you think you've found it, the street leads you out of it again. Sooner or later, you end up in a little seafood restaurant, where you eat, drink, and come to terms with the local riddles. To this day, Nager sings the praise of the grilled John Dory he had. The sardines and squid rings tasted fresher than the ones at the Greek restaurant in S. The greatest sensation of the day was a grotesquely stuffed she-goat and kid in the display window of a butcher's shop.

During the five hours we spent on land, no one saw Albin, not even from a distance, even though the place was so small it seemed we would almost have to run into one another.

When we all met on the quay before the return voyage, Albin was yet more taciturn than before, even with Nager. Both of them were a little drunk. An ominous calm radiated from Albin, but I couldn't see any difference between that and his dark mood of the previous days. It's possible that he had said a final good-bye to Livia while wandering around Düşünülen Yer. She stood on the quay and snapped pictures of a half-decomposed dog that was floating in the water. There was something alive about that dog, despite its gaping wounds. Livia was disappointed later when the pictures didn't come out. Albin watched Jan and Livia with a balanced mixture of attentiveness and indifference. He wasn't doing this because he was looking for proof; it was rather that he wanted them to notice his eyes on them and to acknowledge that the game was over. Jan and Livia gave off such an aura of intimacy that even Hagen noticed it. Scherf, vacillating between envy and scorn, said, "An unhappy woman: either a good fuck or talking therapy."

He was visibly proud of this formulation. Jan overheard him.

Had Nager not used such fervor in addressing the sailor responsible for hauling in the gangway, had he not slipped the man some money, had he not gone so far as to invoke his professorial status, the ship would have sailed without Mona. At the last moment, she came running down the street to the quay, out of breath, and excused her tardiness with the drawings she'd absolutely had to make. Nager said we all belonged in a kindergarten. When the ship cast off, the suction of its propeller pulled the dog's carcass down into the water.

From that distance, Istanbul looked like the fabulous oriental metropolis we'd wanted to visit. Minarets, cupolas, and towers shimmered in the late afternoon sun as though covered with molten gold. Albin hung over the dangerously low railing and stared into the water. From time to time, his knees buckled.

When I asked him whether he was suffering any ill effects from the previous night, he said, "Barroom babble. I can hardly remember it."

He looked toward the sun, which was setting behind a mountain range like a cardboard cutout, but his eyes weren't fastened on anything in particular. Behind his back, Livia's hair was ablaze in the evening light. She was leaning on Jan's shoulder as both of them smoked. Nager was sitting on the wooden bench next to Mona, trying to explain to her why art and picture painting weren't the same. "Art is the result of a disease," he said. "You don't make art because you want to bring Mama a Christmas present."

"If I see something special, I draw it. There's nothing wrong with doing that."

"How? My dear, that's the only question: how?"

He was sweating, even though it was cold now, in the wind and the twilight. He called out, "Albin, my assistant. Can you translate me?"

But Albin must have left shortly before, probably heading for the bar, without our noticing. Nager waved, saying, "I need beer," and staggered in his turn toward the swinging doors. Mona shifted back and forth in her seat, shivering and rubbing her thighs for warmth. She pondered Nager as he left and then said, "Why is he so discouraging?"

"I have no idea. Ask his assistant."

"His assistant can't even move his limbs in any coordinated way. How's he supposed to think clearly?"

When Albin and Nager returned, they were talking about George Foreman, who had won the world heavyweight boxing championship at the age of forty-five the previous week. Albin went back to staring at the horizon. Nager fell down on the bench like a sack. First the sky turned orange, then a dark turquoise, studded with the light of some isolated stars whose names none of us knew. Corinna, Swantje, Sabine, and Adel took their leave and went into the inner rooms. Shortly after that, Mona left, too, on account of the cold, though she would have preferred to stay. She was followed by Fritz and Hagen, whose relationship to Swantje was un-known. When Hagen didn't come back, Scherf left as well. Nager draped his head, faceup, across the back of the bench. His mouth opened, but the roar of the engines drowned out the gurgling sound coming from his throat.

I would have been glad to talk to somebody about the build-ings in Düşünülen Yer, about the mixture of orderly and chaotic structures, in which I had never managed to get my bearings. I wondered whether it would be possible to develop such composi-tions for pictures: forms in which construction and improvisation balanced each other out. And I wanted to talk to Albin again—I couldn't stop thinking about our long conversation the previous night—but he'd barricaded himself behind an invisible wall in which there was no door to be found. From time to time, he turned around and took in the fact that everyone had gone, including Livia, except for Nager and me. He couldn't have cared less. A hint of mockery crept into his features. He smoked one cigarette after another, panting, and his fingers drew figures in the air, as though he was holding forth in sign language. Nager was snoring loudly, explosively, and in the pauses between snores he stopped breath-ing. I told Albin I wanted to draw and went below, too.

That was probably a mistake, leaving him alone like that. The first person I saw was Adel, who was kneeling in front of Sabine, holding her hand and declaiming on the subject of friendship. I sat down with Livia and Jan and said, "He knows. You have to talk to him."

"Tomorrow."

"Why not now?"

"Because he's drunk and he's flipping out. When he's sober, he's not strong enough for violence."

"Where are you sleeping tonight?"

"Together."

The sky shone violet through the windows. Inside, the light was a dim green. In the semidarkness, the roar of the engines was louder than during the day. Although Albin might have come in at any time, Livia pressed herself against Jan. A Turkish father clutched his son while the boy's mother stared mutely out the window. I didn't know what was weighing on them, but I could see they were no solace to each other.

"Actually, we could have spared ourselves this particular excursion," Livia said. "I don't care for Düşünülen Yer. It's like all places where people live for the sake of spectators—there's something depressing about it."

She was speaking so softly it was sometimes hard to understand her. "The women play fishermen's wives. The fishermen play fishermen, and we're supposed to believe that the mackerel and the calamari we eat in their father's or brother's restaurant were caught with their own hands and not bought at the central market. The men scratch their arms to make it look as though they've been cut by ropes while hauling up nets or setting sails. The only good thing about it is this nighttime voyage. The gentle rocking, the blurring contours. I love to be on ships. I never get seasick, not even when there's a storm . . ."

Livia was talking to herself. She didn't even turn toward Jan, and she didn't care that the wrong people were listening to her. ". . . my father's sister, Tante Gisa, got married on a steamboat on the Mosel River. I was allowed to carry the candle and scatter flowers. I envied Tante Gisa. I thought, Now she'll have a wonderful life. It was summer. The ship sailed past vineyards. They'd hired a pop group who did Abba and Boney M. songs as well as their own material. Everybody danced. Early in the afternoon, we cast anchor between Ediger and Bremm. Right where the steepest vineyard in the world is. A little motorboat came from the other side. Robert, Gisa's husband, went down the ladder first, followed by Gisa in her enormous white dress. The skipper of the small boat held out his hand to her. Everybody laughed. If she had fallen into the water, she wouldn't have had a chance of drowning—everyone would have screamed and thrown her lines and lifesavers. I wept and begged to be allowed to go on land, too. 'I'm the bridesmaid,' I said. 'I belong there.' I carried on so long that Gisa said to my mother, 'It's all right with me if she comes. But it's going to take at least an hour. She'll get bored.' The boat coasted along the opposite bank until we came to the ruins of a convent church. Nothing was left but the foundation walls and a semicircle of pointed arches, flooded with light, standing right where the Mosel makes one of its great loops. The photographer was waiting for us there. It was sunny and cloudy by turns, and there was such a strong wind that Gisa had to hold on to her veil and Robert's top hat flew into the river. They looked like an eloping couple on the run from vengeful relatives. I was the lady's maid, who had secretly arranged for horses and lodging. Later I would marry Robert's servant, Georg, whom I had loved for a long time and who was, in reality, Robert's cousin.

"We climbed out of the boat. I carried Gisa's train so it wouldn't get tangled up in bushes. The photographer told us what he had in mind for positions and backgrounds and picture formats. He raved about the weather conditions, which he thought were perfect, except for the wind. At first, he told jokes to loosen everyone up. When we entered the ruins, where the official pictures would be taken, he grew solemn and spoke about the momentous decision they had made that day, a decision for better or worse. Gisa and Robert were scared for a minute, but soon they started acting silly again. The photographer shouted, 'This is serious!

Think of it: you're man and wife, until death do you part.' Robert frowned; Gisa gave her face the expression of someone about to be interviewed. The photographer went on: 'The ruins are the optimum framework for a representative picture. Afterward, you can send it off or throw it away if you want to. A little more relaxed. Just like that. Don't panic, we'll do something funny in a minute. Wonderful. Hold the flowers in front of your chest. Put your arm around her. Look at her. A bit more fervently. Take her hand. Tenderly. She's the light of your eyes. Hello, look at the camera. Not quite so sternly. Fantastic. And now for the entertaining part. Pretend I'm not here.'

"Although the photographer never stopped talking, he seemed completely relaxed, unlike the old jerk who came to the school and took the photos for our passes, which were made in his studio. This photographer, a childhood friend of Robert's, flew all over the world to take pictures for travel magazines. Sometimes he photographed television stars. He operated two cameras at the same time, one color and one black-and-white. As he intended, his ceaseless chatter led Robert and Gisa smoothly from one mood to another, according to what kind of expression he wanted to see on their faces. They forgot they were posing for wedding pictures. A while later, when we were shooting down on the riverbank, on a patch of sandy beach, he made them scream and circle around each other. Robert threw Gisa up in the air and caught her. Gisa protested and giggled. Robert was playing Cary Grant at the end of a comedy with Grace Kelly or Doris Day.

"The longer the shoot lasted, the less I envied Gisa. I envied the photographer, who was making them into something they had never been and never would be, and yet in the future they would see themselves this way, because there would be these pictures, more precise and more beautiful than anything their memory could conjure up. From that day on, I wanted to be behind the camera. Later, when we were back on the boat, I declared to my mother, 'I'm going to be a photographer.' "

"An *awakening*!" Scherf said. "She was called to become a photographer while still a child! What a privilege. We bow before you, Livia."

Livia blushed, and Jan stood up. He walked over to Scherf and asked, "Don't you want to apologize?"

"For what?"

As Scherf spoke, Jan grabbed him by the throat, directly under the chin, and lifted him off the bench. Scherf, a whole head shorter than Jan, choked and wheezed. Corinna, Sabine, and Adel jumped up and started talking to both of them, telling them to let it go and not cause trouble. Jan didn't release his grip. Fritz joined the group and told Scherf he should apologize, as that was the best thing for all concerned. Since Swantje was on Jan's side, Hagen didn't dare speak up for Scherf, whose face was now as red as a crab. He was standing on tiptoe and pressing his hands against Jan's chest with no visible result.

Jan said, "Repeat after me: I'm an idiot, and I'm sorry."

Finally, Mona went up to them and said, "Jan, let him go. No matter what he said. Do me this favor."

Jan complied, but just when Scherf felt the floor beneath his feet, Jan put all his weight behind a violent blow to the unprotected spot just above Scherf's stomach. Scherf doubled over and sank to his knees, gasping for breath, and then spewed half the beer he'd just drunk onto the planks. By that time, Jan was already sitting in his former seat, next to Livia. He had his arm around her shoulder and was talking with her as though nothing had happened. Scherf recovered and dragged himself back to his place, saying between clenched teeth: "You'll be sorry you did that."

Hagen was ashamed of not having helped his friend, but he couldn't think of anything he could do to erase his failure. Mona buried her face in her hands, shaking her head. Our trip abroad had turned conclusively into tragedy. She went to the bar and said in English, "Somebody threw up over there."

The barmaid gave her a questioning look, pointed to the sweets in the display case and then to the drinks menu, and shrugged her shoulders.

The howling of the engines during the docking maneuver woke Nager up. The steward was making his rounds, and maybe he woke Nager up, too. In any case, Nager felt wasted. He had a splitting headache, as he always did when he went to sleep instead of continuing to drink. He kicked open the swinging door, hurtled through, and brought himself to a full stop one step before reaching the puddle of vomited beer.

"Did someone puke in here?"

Scherf nodded, but Nager didn't see him. Everyone was silent. Nobody wanted to start the scene again: Scherf's knockdown was an embarrassment to him; Jan felt that he was in the right but could see no reason to parade the fact; and the rest of us hoped to prevent things from getting worse by simulating normalcy.

"Man, man, man. If you can't get drunk and remain decent, you ought to skip it altogether . . ."

At this moment, a woman's voice came over the loudspeaker, telling us in Turkish and English that the voyage from Düşünülen Yer would be over in a few minutes. The shipping company hoped we'd enjoyed our trip, looked forward to welcoming us on board again soon, and wished us a pleasant evening.

We all climbed up the stairs to the deck and gathered in a pack around the spot where the gangway would be let down.

By this time, it was dark. Spotlights illuminated the quay. Mer-

chants on the shore were warmly recommending the almonds, wal-
nuts, and pistachio nuts that stood before them in pyramids a meter high. Mona looked at me and said, "If I could, I'd fly home
tomorrow."

Jan and Livia were standing together like very close friends.
Nager was sucking his cigarette hot. Although we hadn't spoken of
a meeting place, we all gathered in front of the postcard display. After five minutes, Nager asked, "Is everyone here?"

"Albin's missing," Livia said.

22.

At the end of the corridor, there's a picture of a black coppersmith decorating a lampshade with a pattern of holes. At his feet, his Arab assistant is bending up the edges of a punched metal tray and shaping them into waves.

Livia's in high spirits and hungry. She practically runs to the elevators and presses the buttons for all three of them.

Restoran—Dining Room: 12th Floor. I won't come near her. I'll keep quiet and hold my breath. When the door makes the whistling sound that signals its closing, I flinch, even though I've heard it twenty times. Not much room in here. Where are you supposed to look when you don't know each other? Rosewood and pink granite. Tinkling background music. I stare at my feet, as though I were standing across from a stranger. The door opens and sets us free.

She looks beautiful in the glaring autumn light, lucid and lost.

"Which table?"

"On the left in the back, because of the sea view. You can sit with your back to the wall."

It's so blithe, so casual, the way she loads her plate and then starts shoveling down mold cheese, scrambled eggs, and smoked fish. She works her jaws like a cow chewing her cud. The smell turns my stomach. And she talks the whole time. "What do you want to do today?" She smiles like someone in love. "Shall we visit a museum? Or maybe just stroll about? Would you like to go for a walk on the Golden Horn?"

She knows I can't talk to anyone in the morning, yet she looks as though she thinks I'm capable of making decisions. "There's so much to see, it's incredible. And we don't know anything about any of it. Let's look at something together. Everywhere we go, it's for the first time." She's disappointed because I don't answer. She thinks I've been drinking on the sly. I drink to make the shaking stop. I drink so she won't be afraid of me. I call to the waiter, "Hello, another cup of coffee, please."

She says, "Have you noticed that all the waiters have pimples? How do you explain that? Harmful chemicals in the air? Greasy food?" I want to scream: Shut up! Shut up!

Who's leaving whom? Is she leaving me, or am I leaving her? I'm not capable of living with someone who thinks well-ordered thoughts, takes serious photographs, and assumes that two people in love have no secrets from each other. "Do you have to eat garlic sausage?"

"Sorry."

This city is our—my—grave. I don't know why she dragged me here. It was too late. She says, "I'd really like to go to a Turkish bath. They're supposed to be wonderful." Suddenly she straightens up in her chair and stares at a point in the distance, like she's trying to ward something off. She seems confused. Then her concentration snaps. She lets her shoulders slump, as if she's missed her chance and the game has turned against her. Her face is empty. I'm glad she's finally stopped talking.

The look she gives me might be more than I'd hoped for. I don't withstand it. I say, "The minarets stick up into the sky like acupuncture needles, diverting energy into the right channels." She makes no reply.

The gulls are sitting there, waiting. Except for me, no one has fed them anything in the past few days, but they're still hoping that somebody will show up and toss them some scraps. "It stinks in here. I need some fresh air. Enjoy your breakfast."

"You've hardly eaten anything."

"Shall I call you Mama?"

"I'm almost finished. Then I'm going to take a shower."

It's practically quiet. No voices, no droning. From far below, the echo of the street noise. Ship's sirens.

I can tell the two seagulls apart. One has darker wings than the other. It perches on the railing, watching the sea with its left eye and the breakfast room with its right. The other one's lighter, with a red spot on its beak, and it walks up and down in front of the big glass windows. When I step out onto the terrace, it hops away. I throw a piece of sesame ring in their direction so I can watch them fight over it. I don't care who wins. They're the same size—if they weren't, one of them would give up. It's a question of strategic decisions, of planning for the consequences of every movement. Livia looks over at me, then eats some more. The birds circle the piece of bread, two duelists chained in the center of the arena. They hiss at each other, attack with outspread wings, parry, and retreat, flicking out their thin, hard tongues like knives. I make a lunging step, and they both fly up onto the parapet. When I move away, they hop down and head for their preferred positions again, taking sidelong steps.

I go around the corner of the terrace and light a cigarette. No one in the breakfast room can see me. The vodka from the minibar shoots into your veins like heroin. The cleaning woman will mark the bottles on the ticket, which Livia will find. She'll ask when I drank all that and get an evasive answer. Within seconds, icy fingertips, but at the same time a feeling of great warmth flooding through all my organs: the narcotic for the larva inside me. Its movements grow calmer, less painful. For hours, I can forget its existence.

Pleasant light.

My view into strangers' rooms is obscured by the smoke I exhale, which the cold thickens. Inside those windows, other people are living or

*staying as guests. And what do other people do? Work, eat, fuck, sleep.
It must be possible to be satisfied with that. A young Turkish woman
brings her husband and children tea and cakes and pastries. On the
floor below them, a man in pajamas is training his biceps with dumb-
bells. An airplane comes out of the west, heading for the center of the
city and losing altitude. I think it's going to crash. When I lose sight of
it, I wait for smoke or the echo of an explosion, but nothing happens.*

*Nobody's spared. It's a matter of postponement, of reaching the
end a few years later. Not now.*

Now would be better.

*Fifty meters away from me, Ireen, wearing a purple silk nightgown,
opens the curtains in her suite. She acts as though she lives there,
straightening up the flowers on the chest of drawers and emptying the
ashtray. Then she disappears into the bathroom. Pigeons chase one another in the canyons between buildings. An older woman hooks her bra.
As a businessman on a business trip, Miller's an early riser. He's on the
telephone, fully dressed. He hangs up. He's got greasy leather patches
on the elbows of his mustard-colored tweed sports jacket. It's amazing
how dancelike his movements are, all three hundred pounds of him. He
takes an apple, throws it up in the air, catches it, bites it, makes a face,
throws the apple away. I should have either drunk less coffee or ordered
beer. He opens the balcony door, sits down at the table, opens an American newspaper, flips through the first pages, takes a notebook out of his
jacket, and writes something down: share prices, prognoses for development in the regions where his supplies come from. Yeltsin's threatening
the Chechens with war. Ireen flits half naked through the semidarkness
with her hair wrapped in a bath towel like a turban. Flawless figure. She
bends over and picks up a little top she flung clear across the suite last
night, to Miller's amusement. Hardly paying attention to her, he negli-
gently strokes her behind and says something to which she responds by*

kissing the crown of his head, more affectionately than I would have thought. Then she turns around and disappears into the next room. She's not holding his lack of interest against him.

Miller could play Marlon Brando in the film version of his autobiography, they look so much alike: Miller's got Vito Corleone's air of resignation and omnipotence, with something of Colonel Kurtz's depressive craving for pleasure. He clutches his head, stands up, and fetches an attaché case from a nearby chair. After unlocking a padlock, he turns the combination lock to the proper numbers and presses two buttons on the side, and the lid of the case springs open. He takes out two small white envelopes and shakes their contents onto the table. He's too far away for me to see what he's got there, but it's probably jewels, a preview of the delivery he's expecting or some samples from a new exploration prospect. He reaches for a big magnifying glass, picks up tiny objects from the damask tablecloth, and turns them carefully in his fingers. When Ireen comes back—in a checked miniskirt and a top with spaghetti straps, in spite of the cold outside—Miller points to the invisible things in front of him, puts his plump hand on her shoulder, and says: "Maybe something went wrong. Maybe we've got a problem." I was right to be fearful the night before last. I'm amazed that whole sentences can be heard over such a distance. The wind blows away her answer. He says the word "trouble," but I can't understand the context. Both of them look up. Miller sticks his wares back in their little envelopes and snaps the case shut. Ireen waits until the lid is closed before she goes to the door. A waiter with a long apron pushes a stainless steel cart to the table, uncorks a bottle of champagne, and pours. Miller and Ireen clink glasses and drink. The waiter serves a basket of European bread and plates with cheese, cold cuts, and marinated vegetables. He presents dishes with silver covers, which he lifts as though on command to reveal ham and eggs, sausages, baked beans, and potato wedges, *freshly prepared, appetizingly arranged; then he bows and silently with-draws.*

Miller eats like an animal. He looks up only to help himself to more food. Ireen talks. In the chasm between our two hotels, every gust of wind spins in a different direction, bearing sounds along or swallowing them at once. Maybe Ireen's voice doesn't have the proper frequency, be-cause I hear only scattered words, never a complete sentence. Something must have gone wrong; they've been tricked, maybe, or they've been sent a shipment of inferior quality. I'm a good judge of marble and basalt, but not precious stones. Maybe their emeralds are just a front for other activities. Now she's calming down. She takes a packet of tissue from her purse and blows her nose. I can't tell from here whether she's got a cold or she's crying. Miller's still shoveling it in, one mouthful after an-other. He speaks briefly from time to time, calls out names. Switches be-tween coffee and champagne. He pours his third glass, while Ireen hasn't touched hers since the toast. She wipes a tear from her eye, takes deep breaths, and smiles like a little girl apologizing to her father.

He's had enough; he pushes his plate away and has her bring him his cigarillos. She gets a cigarette for herself. He holds out his lighter. I can see him suck the smoke deep into his lungs and exhale it through his nose. He lets the next puff waft out between his lips. He says, "What we're doing is very risky. I don't know what will happen." She nods. A cloud of smoke hangs solemnly over the remains of the meal. Miller waves his hand and says, "Take care of you, baby," whatever that might mean. You have to be American, fat, and rich to call your girlfriend "baby." She doesn't react. I think: He's about to get shot. Taking refuge in film scenes in order to make the world less unwieldy. A short, crisp sound sizzles past. Where's its source? Miller jerks, his head falls back-ward, and a second later his chin sags down onto his chest. His forehead strikes the glass tabletop heavily, just missing his plate. Ireen jumps away from the splintering glass and the spattering champagne. She stands there, thinking he's had a heart attack or a stroke, and then she sees the blood flowing out of his back, or maybe out of his chest, at the level of his heart. On the immaculate velour rug, a red pool forms, sinks into the fabric, coagulates.

The shooter must have been posted to the right; otherwise, he couldn't possibly have hit Miller under the shoulder blade through the open door. He was hiding behind a chimney on one of the surrounding roofs or behind some drapery in a room. There are twenty windows with closed curtains, a couple where the curtains are parted, and three, four, five wide open. The lengths of fabric sway slightly in the draft. No abrupt movement anywhere, nothing that looks like someone escaping. The rifle barrel will have stuck out for only a few seconds, if at all. From how far away can a paid murderer with a precision weapon and a telescopic sight hit his target? Both of the roofs I'm looking at are empty; there's no hint of anything unusual. Maybe the shooter didn't fire on Miller from one of the adjacent buildings. There are at least two vacant lots he could have shot across from buildings on the next street over.

Ireen staggers and falls or collapses. Her upper body trembles. She sits on the floor next to Miller's chair and pushes him, moving his corpse a centimeter to the side. Should a second shot come, his bulk might cover her, and she knows it. She assumes that she's in danger, too. She lies flat on the floor, rolls carefully away from him, and crawls to the door. Now she must be out of the line of fire and invisible. With her back against the doorjamb, she slowly pushes herself upright. She grasps the handle, pulls the bolt, yanks the door open, and stumbles into the hall. She turns on a light. A mistake—like that, she's a good target even at a distance. Why doesn't she call for help? The shock paralyzes her voice. If I start running now, it'll take me ten minutes to reach the Sultan. In less time than that, she'll find someone, a chambermaid or guests returning from breakfast. In any case, she'll surely make it to the *elevator. The elevator can't be far. She should get down to the lobby and call the police and an emergency doctor. Maybe Miller's still alive, and Ireen's got fifteen minutes to save him from bleeding to death. I don't see anyone disappearing into a shaft or climbing down a fire escape anywhere. Over on the right, a woman at a window beats some pillows and then shuts the window. Is she an accomplice? In the next few minutes, anybody who steps out of a nearby building and hastens away could have done it. The same goes for those who haven't left their apartment. Nothing's stirring behind me. Miller's suite can't be seen from the breakfast room. The silencer made the shot almost inaudible. Ireen's gone. She was smart enough to close the door.*

I've seen only one other person die. It's a sight that forces you to take responsibility. You don't even consider the possibility that someone will be killed before your eyes. That happens to other people. I'll talk to Livia. Livia's a woman who's sober in her dealings. You think something awful's going to happen, and at that very moment, it happens. Did it happen because I thought it? Did I have a premonition, or am I the victim of a coincidence? I won't drink so much tomorrow. Get out of here, you little shits, you're getting on my nerves! Livia's gone. No sign that anyone in here broke off his breakfast because something just didn't seem right. Soft-voiced conversations, tourists planning their day. The waiters ask, "Coffee or tea?" The older of them looks tranquil, as though nothing could disturb his serenity, not even "Excuse me, sir, a man has been . . ." No, it's pointless. He won't believe me. If he sees Miller, gravely wounded, with his head on the table next to the empty bottles, he still won't believe me. Miller's drunk whiskey in the Orient Lounge for years. The waiter will say, "He had too much champagne in the morning, now he's tired, needs a little sleep," and, "Sorry, I have a lot of work." As soon as Livia's ready, she's got to go up to the terrace and check on whether anyone's changing or stealing anything; meanwhile, I'll walk over to the Sultan. Two double vodkas aren't enough to make my hands stop shaking. Computerized music everywhere: in the restaurant, in the corridors, on the elevators.

Turn the key. Livia's still in the shower. She'll assume the story I'm handing her is a string of lies, designed to accomplish some end she can't conceive. I've told her a lot of nonsense in all these years. She turns off the water. Early in the morning, after endless sex and two hours' sleep, kneeling down in front of her in the shower and licking her until she lost her balance. The police have probably cordoned off the area by now. I'll go over there and make a statement. Livia dries herself off thoroughly before she gets out of the tub and massages a rinse into her hair. Her body leaves nothing to be desired. When did I lose interest in it?

I just say the words: "Miller's been shot."

23.

We waited on the quay for twenty minutes. No one was surprised when Albin didn't join us. During the past few days, he'd continually taken off on his own, without revealing to us where he was going. Hours later, he would turn up again, shrouded in mystery, and leave most of our questions unanswered. "He likes playing his detective game," Mona said. Nager speculated that Albin had been given some leads in Düşünülen Yer and wanted to check them out. He seemed disappointed that Albin had neither included him in his plans nor reported to him on the progress of his search.

That evening, Livia wasn't worried about Albin. His absence made it easier for her and Jan to be together. After two sleepless nights, she was totally exhausted, but in high spirits all the same. On the street, with her camera bag over her shoulder, she stretched out her arms and did a pirouette, singing, "There's a moon over Bourbon Street tonight." Her past had come to an end.

No one was really angry at Jan for punching out Scherf, but the open enmity between the two of them poisoned the atmosphere for good. Everyone assumed that Scherf would try to get even. Corinna looked scared, and Mona still seemed paralyzed. Hagen's bad conscience was gnawing at him. Fritz saw himself surrounded by overexcited comic-book characters. Nobody knew how we were going to make it through the rest of the trip without further escalations.

"Can anyone explain to me what's wrong?" Nager asked on the way to the hotel. "Are you all ready for bed? It's eight-thirty, and we've got only two nights left in Istanbul."

"I've had enough for today," Scherf said.

"The city looks fantastic, all lit up under a clear, starry sky. Before, you did nothing but bellyache about the rain; now the weather's better and you're all completely depressed. Today's Saturday. Party time. Oriental night life, belly dancers, opium dens, music clubs. What does the guidebook recommend, Mona?"

"I'm dead tired."

"How do you people expect to make art when you don't see anything?"

No one answered him.

Jan and Livia were walking hand in hand. They were the only ones who didn't think the day had been ruined. Jan was talking to her about his paintings, which was something he never did. He went on to complain about most contemporary art, whose tendency, he thought, was to replace the visible with jabbering, and about the deliberate dilettantism of video and computer installations. Livia listened to him, laughing. Albin had often sounded like that.

They kissed each other right before our eyes.

"That's all we need," Nager said.

The next morning, Albin didn't appear at breakfast. Livia checked her watch at shorter and shorter intervals. Around ten o'clock, she gathered her courage, left her half-full plate on the table, said, "He probably overslept," and went down to their—now his—room, determined to tell him that she was leaving him for Jan. Immediately. I don't know whether she looked forward to their meeting with hope or fear. Jan couldn't rest until he followed her. He waited by the door, ready to intervene if necessary.

There was no hint that Albin had been in the room since the trip to Düşünülen Yer. His things lay scattered on the floor, just as they had done two days previously. The bed looked untouched; the minibar was full; there was no note anywhere. Livia went through his suitcase, in the hope that he'd written down the names, addresses, and telephone numbers of supposed contacts, and found two empty flasks of corn schnapps, which she threw into the wastebasket. She hadn't cheated on him, she'd left him. It was a decision, not a slipup. His flight made everything simpler; nevertheless, she felt bad. She believed neither in Miller's murder nor in a conspiracy of secret organizations; nevertheless, she feared for Albin's life. She wanted him to stay in the world for a long time, just not as the person she loved. Guiltily, she picked up two rolls of film he had shot and put them in her bag. Maybe, she thought, there's a frame in here that will provide some kind of clue. Then she packed up her remaining things and left the room. She almost ran over Jan, who was leaning on the wall beside the door, wondering where he could stub out his cigarette. She excused herself in English before she recognized him. Jan dropped the butt, ground it into the carpet, and stroked Livia's hair. She swallowed the lump in her throat, forbade herself tears, and threw her arms around his neck. "He hasn't been here, at least not last night. I'm sure something's happened to him. They've kidnapped him because he absolutely had to keep sticking his nose in things that weren't his business. Once he's decided on something, he never lets it go, no matter how absurd it is. He probably became too dangerous for someone. That doesn't mean his Miller story has to be true. All he had to do to get in somebody's way was to ask the right people the wrong questions . . . I can imagine him . . . I mean, probably he just decided to clear out."

Jan held her in his arm. He didn't know how he should react, and so he remained silent.

"What shall I do? We're supposed to fly back the day after to-morrow. If we miss the flight, the tickets aren't refundable. I can't leave him here without knowing how he is, but then I've got a shoot next Thursday, a commission for four thousand marks, with more to follow. To think he would just up and leave like that, with-out saying anything . . . Where can we look? And how can we find someone in this huge city, especially someone who never tells you what he's doing?"

"I'm sure he's going to turn up again. He probably drank un-til he passed out and spent the night lying in dog shit, so he'll be hungover and filthy."

Jan and Livia decided to wait in Albin's room until noon. If he showed up, they'd face him together. If he didn't, they'd go to Mes-sut or the police. Jan went back to the breakfast room and in-formed Nager that he was going to skip the visit to the Sinan Mosques. Then he sat down beside me and asked about my long conversation with Albin two nights before. Had he said anything that might give us some clues about his later activities? I told him what I knew. On Tuesday, Albin had been shooed off while he was allegedly watching some workers in the Otelo Sultan changing the carpet in Miller's suite. On Wednesday, an elderly gem dealer who had formerly been a dentist in Germany gave him the names of two Russian black marketeers, Parfyon and Yevgeny Petrovitch, who in their turn put him onto a certain Nicola, who wore enormous glasses. On Thursday, Albin had gone to the Gypsy quarter. On Fri-day, Messut had urgently recommended that he take the boat trip to Düşünülen Yer. Albin probably had an appointment to meet somebody there yesterday, I said.

"That's not much," Jan said. "But thanks all the same."

They lay close together in Livia's half of the bed, smoking and watching television. Jan drank beer; Livia had room service bring up some tea. They had imagined the beginning of their love affair differently: a final confrontation with Albin, the two of them on one side, Albin on the other, shouts, slammed doors, and after that everything would become easy. They'd forget him, like a nightmare you don't write down after it wakes you up. But instead, they were taking turns staring at the hands of the clock, flinching whenever they heard footsteps approaching in the corridor, prepared to do battle, but thinking in different directions.

Albin didn't come.

Around one o'clock, Jan asked, "What do you want to do?"

"The stone," Livia said. "He didn't buy this fire opal because he wanted to please me. He needed an excuse to sound out the jewel dealer in the bazaar. We could try the same thing."

"Have you seen how many of them there are?"

"I owe it to him."

Jan considered it a mistake for them to follow Albin's trail on their own. Of course, he didn't believe in a conspiracy any more than Livia did, but he was afraid they were in a place where any-one who asked too many questions would soon find himself in trouble. He knew that two foreigners with no knowledge of the lo-cal language or the local customs would have no chance of gaug-ing the truthfulness of any given statement; but Livia pleaded with him so urgently that he couldn't refuse her, and besides, he cer-tainly didn't want her to go to the bazaar alone.

Jan didn't ask her whether she still loved Albin or, if not, why she felt so responsible for him that she was prepared to put herself in danger pointlessly.

Right after they left the hotel, he dragged her into a bakery to be sure she ate at least a little something. She chose a baklava, carried it out into the street, took one bite, said, "Delicious," and threw the rest away.

The golden inscription over the university's Moorish main gate reflected the light of the afternoon sun.

There was an even greater throng in the bazaar than there had been four days ago. This time, both Jan and Livia found the dealers and touts almost unbearable. Jan kept hissing, "No!"

Livia was worked up. Her eyes darted up and down the aisles, and she was breathing like someone about to have an asthma attack. Jan was determined to prevent her from being sucked into Albin's mad fantasies on the basis of a misunderstood sense of responsibility. When they found the part of the bazaar where the gem dealers were, Livia stood still in the middle of the walkway, her lips moving, whispering, "This idiot, this goddamned idiot, why can't he leave me in peace, why won't he get out of my life? I never want to see him again."

Jan placed himself behind her, covering her back, and put his hands on her belly. The passage was narrow, and they were jostled and shoved about; a few men turned around and stared at them angrily. Jan tried to shift Livia gently to one side, but she didn't budge. After a while, her arms started twitching as though from a series of electric shocks, and then she had a shivering fit. With a look of despair, she said to Jan, "Maybe he needs my help. For the last time. And I'll never be rid of him unless I tell him to his face that it's over . . . Will you light me a cigarette?"

She calmed down a little and made a plan to track Albin down, without the faintest notion of how this plan could be translated into action. Jan was considering how he might go about convincing her that Albin had simply cleared out. So they both just stood there, helplessly staring at gold jewelry, thousands of armlets in varying thicknesses, different sorts of chains, rings with and without stones. Jan said, "I'd buy you something, but I'm broke."

"We should find out who deals in opals."

"What do you want to ask these people? 'Do you know a Russian gem smuggler? Can you give me his address?' It makes no sense, Livia. Let's go to the police and report him as a missing person, and then let them take care of it."

"Let's ask at one shop, anyway. Then at least we can say we tried. How about that old guy? He looks nice. He could have been a dentist."

"Albin probably wants to start a new life and just doesn't feel like discussing it with you. There was no better moment for him to make his getaway."

At this point, Jan felt Livia's strength giving way. After a long silence, she said, "But let's have a look at this guy Nicola. And Messut, too. All right?"

Jan took Livia by the hand and steered her in the direction of the exit. He was glad when they stepped out into the open, with the bright sky overhead. It got so warm in the sun that they sat down on a patch of lawn and watched the passersby, who were mostly students. Livia fell over backwards onto the grass and shut her eyes so her thoughts could come over her undisturbed. Suddenly a pack of raggedy Gypsy children—the youngest six years old at most, the oldest perhaps twelve—began running in circles around them. They uttered loud, guttural sounds, cried out, "Money, money," made faces, chanted a counting-out rhyme, and bumped into Jan's shoulder. Seeing that the situation was too much for Livia, he said only, "Come on, let's go."

The children followed them a little way and then fell upon a Scandinavian tour group that had just come out of the bazaar with shopping bags filled to bursting.

Jan asked several passersby for the nearest police station. Unusually, they spoke neither German nor English and shrugged their shoulders, even though the Turkish word *polis* scarcely differs from "police." After twenty minutes, Jan and Livia came across a station by chance.

The room was broad but low, the air thick and dank. An infant was bawling. Its mother was speaking very fast and hammering on the counter with her fists. Several telephones rang at the same time. The typewriters, all products of the 1960s, set up a barrage of sound. Voices came over loudspeakers, calling out the names of witnesses and suspects, who passed through a glass door and disappeared into offices.

Jan and Livia got into the third of the six lines, because they thought the officer who was serving that line looked agreeable. The tables buckled under piles of unprocessed files, to which new files were constantly being added. Livia seemed apathetic. She squinted in an attempt to fend off at least the optical impressions of their surroundings. It took them forty-five minutes to reach the counter.

"Can I help you?" the policeman asked in English.

"We have a problem," Jan said. "Does anyone here speak German?"

Without answering, the man turned around, shuffled over to the other end of the room, and bent over a seated colleague with a bald head and a bushy mustache, pointing several times toward Livia and Jan. The colleague wrinkled his forehead, distinctly unenthusiastic about taking over their case, but in the end he got up and approached them. He was still some distance away when he called out, "Whatever they stole from you, you can forget it. Just write it off."

"We haven't been robbed."

"What, then? Someone whacked you on the head? You paid hundreds of dollars for a piece of junk? Or was it Gypsies? People on the street forced you to pay some exorbitant amount of money for a couple of snapshots? It's all the same, it happens every minute. You'll never see a single lira of your money again."

"A friend of ours is missing. He disappeared a day and a half ago . . ."

While Jan was speaking, the detective dropped out of sight behind the counter. They could hear him opening a series of doors and drawers. He hit his head and cursed. At last he reappeared, a crumpled official form in his hand. "The name of the missing person?"

"Albin Kranz."

"Nationality?"

"German."

"Date of birth?"

"Just a second, I'd like to tell you a few things about the circumstances. You see, Albin claimed that he'd witnessed the murder of an American businessman last Monday, a man named Jonathan Miller, in the Otelo Sultan . . ."

At this moment, Jan asserts, the look on the detective's face grew dark for a fraction of a second, and then, immediately afterward, he clasped his head in both hands and sighed: "Did he report this to the police?"

"The clerk in the Sultan told him that the hotel had no guest by the name of Miller. So Albin tried to clear the matter up on his own. Supposedly, he was able to contact some informants . . ."

The detective's eyes flashed threateningly. "He didn't go to the police? Do you realize he made himself liable to prosecution by failing to do that?"

He stooped to the cabinets under the counter again, found a second form at once, and copied onto it the data that Jan had given him thus far. Then he continued his questioning: "When and where was he born?"

"June 21, 1966, in Staudt," Livia said.

"Albin thought Miller was eliminated by Russian gem smugglers . . ."

"If someone witnesses a murder and doesn't go to the police, he commits a serious crime—more specifically, he commits several crimes at once: obstruction of justice, failure to render assistance, homicide by omission, impeding a police investigation. If he used binoculars, he might even be guilty of an offense against public morals. It would be better for your friend not to turn up; if he does, he's in a world of trouble."

"We're afraid something's happened to him."

"How many men do you think come here and drop out of sight for a few days while they're having a bit of fun in Sulukule or the Russian quarter? If I wanted to find all of them, half of Istanbul would have to go to work for the police."

Livia would have liked to be able to protest that Albin wasn't the type for that sort of thing; she would have liked almost as much to believe that the detective was right.

"Personal description: what does Mr. Kranz look like?"

"Tall, over six foot three. Blue eyes, midlength blond hair, slender . . ."

"Distinguishing features?"

"Scarred hands."

"Is he your brother, husband, brother-in-law?"

Livia blushed. "My fiancé, actually my ex-fiancé, but—"

"You're neither related nor married? In that case, I can give you no further information about this matter. If we find him—him or his body—we'll notify the embassy, and they'll contact his family."

Jan realized that any additional word would be superfluous, if not dangerous. He said, "Forget it."

The detective said, "I wish it were that simple, but the law obliges us to look into the accusations you've made against Mr. Kranz." He tore up the missing persons report. "The matter is now out of your hands. Turkish justice will take it from here. Rest assured that the public prosecutor will be brought into the case. I've taken down your statements. Please check them to make sure they're accurate, and then sign at the bottom on the left. I'll also need your addresses in Istanbul and Germany."

Jan asked, "Will there be anything else?"

"Enjoy the rest of your stay."

On the way out, Livia whispered, "I'm starting to understand Albin. The people here behave very strangely. Something's not right."

Jan turned around one last time and saw the detective engaged in a lively discussion with several colleagues, two of whom watched them leave.

24.

The barometer's low, and a heavy depression lies over the city. The potholes in the street are filled with water. Garbage floats in the gutters. I'm freezing, and my head's about to explode. Drinking American whiskey does nothing to alleviate the consequences of drinking American whiskey. Miller's business must be doing all right if he can afford a trophy girlfriend like Ireen. She's the woman at his side. In return, he fulfills her every wish, provided it can be bought. They have a mutually beneficial arrangement.

Despite the mercilessly gray sky, Livia photographs everything she finds in front of her lens: donkey carts, people waiting at bus stops, a mangy bitch with puppies, Hagia Sophia. Sometimes, when people come walking toward her, she tries to steal the expressions on their faces without their noticing it. How many million negatives identical to hers are there between Tokyo and New York? She says, "Naturally, these pictures won't be very good. I'm just running through a couple of rolls. Getting used to unfamiliar light and unfamiliar proportions. And breaking down my inhibitions. Some places have an invisible shield that protects them against being carried off in photographs."

When she started talking about going on this trip three months ago, I swallowed my impulse to scream "No!" and for half an hour I let myself be infected by her hope that we could do it.

The woman I'd be capable of sharing a single room with for a week and a half does not exist on this earth. At home, we keep a safe distance *and sleep in separate beds as soon as we start feeling cramped, with no resulting hard feelings.*

"Are you getting bored? I don't have to spend the whole time taking photographs."

"It's going to rain."

"That lowers the kitsch danger level."

Taking an original photograph in the center of the old part of Istanbul is about as likely as discovering a painting in the Louvre that no one has ever seen.

"Are you hungry? Do you want something to eat?"

"Yes."

Three veiled women scold and turn away when Livia points her camera at them. She says, "People here don't move the way people do in Germany. Have you noticed that?"

We're going to bore ourselves rigid for ten long days and fall to quarreling over trifles. At some point, she'll have a crying fit—in a restaurant, perhaps, or out on the street—and then I'll stand up and leave her for the rest of the day and the night. When I come back, she'll already have forgiven me.

"I think you're snapping photos for a guidebook called Istanbul for Suicides."

She laughs. You can see her gold crowns. She says, "At Meydanı. This is where the Hippodrome was, where they had the chariot races. It could seat a hundred thousand. And that's the Egyptian obelisk. The Byzantines themselves built the other one. And between them, the famous Serpentine Column. Do you like it?"

"I don't want to hear about stone."

She's a dedicated tourist.

Her face repels me. It's a beautiful face. Men stare at it as though it's an apparition. "Can we have a drink, or do you want to finish the book first?"

"*This place looks nice. Café Gautier.*"

She heads for a tourist joint with French-Oriental furnishings, bistro chairs, and cast-iron tables with white tops. The apricot-colored lamp shades end in veils made of strings of glass beads. On the wall, browning nineteenth-century photographs of the Orient: desert nomads at an oasis, the pyramids, a ragged whirling dervish. I feel sick. I'm glad to sit down. The drinks list looks European: Marc de Champagne, Jenever. "*For me, Fernet-Branca and a large Amstel beer.*"

"*Tea, please.*"

She looks out the window and puts two fingers on her lips, as though she's deep in thought. About what? Her skin is translucent, glistening. A nerve twitches under her right eye. Absentmindedly, she stirs a spoon of sugar into her cup. Her features relax. Only a vague sadness remains as a reminder of her affair with me. Now she looks defenseless, like someone who's been stood up. I successfully bring the schnapps glass to my mouth without spilling a drop. Sharp stomach pain, but it goes away fast. There are newspapers on racks, Turkish and European newspapers, side by side. Has anything important happened? Torrential Rains and Floods in Southern Egypt Claim over 500 Victims.

"*Shall we go to a museum?*"

"*You choose, it's your trip.*"

"*I thought we . . .*"

"*May I have another Fernet, a double one, please?*"

Disappointment becomes her. Livia looks for ways to blame herself. The cigarette smoke in here smells like roasted nuts. It's getting brighter outside; the cloud cover must have sprung a few leaks. Mysteries of brain chemistry: no one can predict how different types of booze will react together, whether they'll form syntheses or remain separate or explode. Don't worry, Livia, the worst is over; after this double, my mood will be positively festive. The day can be a success even if the clouds open up, even if we get drenched. I say, "We could go into the Blue Mosque. I've never been in a mosque. Have you?"

She hesitates. "When I was twelve or thirteen, I visited the Alhambra."

A bearded old man wearing a white lace cap growls, "Shoes off," and sends us to an outer room off to the right. And suppose somebody steals our shoes here in the capital city of thievery? The shelves are nearly empty—the mosque has hardly any visitors. Livia takes a dark blue silk shawl out of her bag and throws it over her head, because she's read that you can avoid problems with pious Muslims by doing this. Strange, the feeling of embarrassment you get when you walk around in your socks in public, even when they don't have any holes in them. Livia pushes the last few strands of hair under the cloth and smiles at the doorman, who maintains his somber demeanor and grants her not so much as a glance. We're intruders. He doesn't like having to let us in.

I think of the Karl May story. "A giaour! A giaour!" screamed the Bedouin warriors in Mecca after exposing Kara Ben Nemsi as an unbeliever, and they would have killed him, had there not come into his hands the robber Abu Seïf's camel, which sped through the desert as if it could fly.

I've lost the desire to go into this place, but I can't make up my mind to turn around, either. Livia opens the door and steps over the threshold on tiptoe. I follow her. The floor is covered by several layers of carpets. We've stepped into the largest covered space I've ever been in. It's unbelievable. The main cupola rests on four pillars that look strong enough to bear the universe. In the center there's a golden point that reflects itself and contains everything. The first Arabic words turn around that point. Quivering rays grow out of the words and flow into a band of writing. Their number triples when they enter the stream of letters. They end in smaller cupolas with smaller centers, spread out in all directions. *Planets and satellites of calligraphy travel in calm orbits. It's a giant stone book, with no beginning and no end. The words flower into a bewildering variety of forms, becoming lilies, tulips, and roses, cypresses and vine leaves. A bright blue, overlaid by veils of white and shades of green and brown: the colors of the earth as seen from the moon. The weight of the space forces you to the floor. Livia's sitting down against a pillar, her head bent all the way back, her mouth open, trying to understand what she's seeing. The god to whom this house belongs must be a mighty god. It's just stone, tiles, plaster, paint, and glass, I say aloud. Four men are kneeling off to one side, three of them in a row and the fourth, the oldest, immediately in front of them. They throw themselves down, press their foreheads into the carpet, hold that position, and then raise themselves up. Their performance means nothing to me. I'm a tourist; I want to look at the capitals in this part of the mosque. They must expect that. The prayer leader recites a kind of poem. His voice moves between song and speech. The sounds coil around one another like the curving letters on the wall:*

$$\text{"... أَلَمْ نَشْرَحْ لَكَ صَدْرَكَ}$$

$$\text{وَوَضَعْنَا عَنكَ وِزْرَكَ}$$

$$\text{ٱلَّذِيٓ أَنقَضَ ظَهْرَكَ}$$

$$\text{وَرَفَعْنَا لَكَ ذِكْرَكَ ..."}$$

The absurd thought that anything would change if only I knew what those verses meant.

The men pay no attention to me. It's possible that they carry daggers in their belts in this part of the world. I move away backward, ready to fend off an attack if I have to. I say, "I can't stay here any longer."

Livia nods. She's pallid. She creeps along behind me as though she's hiding some stolen object in her jacket.

When we get outside, I'm not going to ask for her impressions, and I'm not going to answer her questions about mine. She says, "Incredible," and then she stays quiet for a long time.

The starry sky's tipping over to the left. The glowing embers of the last cigarette are dying out on the wooden planks in a quivering line of smoke, blistered boat varnish, scattered ashes, and burn marks.

Behind my back, Nager's shifting about restlessly on his bench. A welter of images resolves into a dream: his older daughter's playing with crab claws, detached from the crab but still capable of pinching, and razor-sharp. He recognizes the danger too late. The mother picks up the amputated finger and screams.

The Orient Lounge, eight days ago, opens before my mind's eye. I hear my own voice:

"Marlon Brando's here, too. With his daughter."

"Where?"

"In a corner in the back. The fat slob with the whiskey bottle."

She taps her forehead at me, saying, "And how many vodkas have you had?"

I finish my drink, say, "We're on vacation," and wave my glass at the waitress. Livia presses her lips together and starts flipping through some postcards of Byzantine mosaics. It's been an hour since she touched her wine, but she's on her third glass of water. She wanted to come to Istanbul, and here we are. We've had a good meal, and now we're sitting in a tastefully furnished hotel bar that's neither crowded nor empty. We're smoking duty-free cigarettes. The drinks list offers every kind of alcoholic beverage you can imagine.

Livia yawns, even though we slept for ten hours last night. A voice, speaking English, rises and cracks: "I don't want that, Jon!" It belongs to the woman sitting with Brando. "I can't live like that any longer!" Everyone in the bar stares in their direction. Jon grabs her wrist with one hand and clamps her mouth shut with the other. Furious, she shakes her head and tears herself away from him, then says in a hiss, "No, no, no, Mr. Miller! That's enough!" His face remains impassive. He empties his glass of whiskey and pours himself another one. "Listen, darling," he says. Then, thinking better of it, he waves her off. The woman leaps to her feet, throws her jacket and her bag over her shoulder, says, "Have a good night." Although she's running to the door, she moves her behind like a model on a runway.

"Right out of the movies," I say.

Livia, not interested, shrugs her shoulders. "What time is it?"

"A little before one."

"I'm going to bed. Are you coming?"

"I'm going to have one more nightcap."

"Can't you try to stop before you start staggering?"

"Why should I?"

I see that Miller's observing us now. He grins as he lights a cigarillo and then laughs softly. When he blows the smoke into the lamp, his laugh turns into a hacking cough, which he washes away with a great gulp of whiskey. Livia says, "Have it your way," and leaves. Miller lifts his hand in greeting. We've formed a bond, though nothing has to come of it. The bar gradually empties out. Two French salesmen are sitting at the bar and drinking cognac. A few feet away from them, there's a group of three Russians. They're wearing Rolex watches and heavy gold bracelets, and their fur coats are draped over their stools. Love has so distracted the young Scandinavian couple sitting near the door that they've forgotten their cocktails. Miller's still working. He's reading various dossiers, underlining parts of them, and making notes on a calendar. I order another vodka with lemon and ice and lift my glass to him. A slightly sloshed Englishwoman in her mid-forties sits down next to the

Frenchmen and starts talking with them. This long after midnight, the state of suspension that the whole day's been headed for finally sets in. Why doesn't it last forever? The waitress brings a new bottle of bourbon to Miller's table. He looks over at me, points to the whiskey, and waves to me to join him. I take the seat next to him instead of the one across from him, because I want to be able to look out into the room.

"What's your name?" he asks in English.

"Albin."

"What?"

"Al."

"OK, Al, I'm Jonathan, but you can call me Jon." He asks the waitress for a second glass.

"Your girl is angry and so is mine. Cheers." Maker's Mark tastes surprisingly good.

"Do you like Istanbul?"

"My girlfriend wanted to come here."

"I hate it."

It's a quarter to two. All at once, the Swedes are in a hurry. As they're walking out, he shoves his hand down her pants.

"Are you here for business?"

"Yes."

"What kind?"

"Precious stones from Russia."

"I did not know that Russia exports precious stones."

"Smaragds and diamonds from Yakutsia."

He's obviously not interested in talking to me about his business. As a matter of fact, Miller feels no need to converse at all; he just doesn't want to drink alone. His eyes follow the girl who's rinsing glasses behind the bar while the bartender wipes off bottles. They're not allowed to close until the last guest leaves. The Frenchman on the left is stroking the drunken Englishwoman's thigh. He'll take her up to his room.

"Shitty weather."

"Bad day."

Here we have a rich boozer who invites a stranger to his table without subjecting him to hateful tirades or heroic reminiscences.

"Cigar?"

"Yes, thank you."

"Whenever I travel outside of the United States, the first thing I buy is a box of Havana cigars." He holds out a large, burning match. Neither of us finds the long pauses in our conversation unpleasant.

"You have a beautiful girlfriend."

"Ireen. Yes, she's nice. But she's no good under pressure."

If I hadn't seen it myself, I'd never guess that he's drunk at least one entire bottle of whiskey in the course of the evening. Only the pearls of sweat on his forehead hint at his intake. This cigar's keeping me awake.

"Do you see the Russian guys over there, Al?"

"Of course."

"I wouldn't trust them."

"Why?"

"Instinct. And experience."

Why would an American gem dealer come to Istanbul to do business with Russians? The Cold War is over. There are guaranteed loans for investments in the former Eastern bloc countries. Governmental subsidies, too. He must know what he's doing. If I stand up now, I'm going to wobble. This place has the most comfortable chairs. A fellow could fall into a dreamless sleep right here in his seat. I could wake up once an hour and have another swallow. I could do that for ten consecutive days, while Livia runs through the items on her sightseeing program.

"It's very dangerous to deal with them, but I don't care."

For some reason, he's confiding in me. The Englishwoman pulls her Frenchman away. Miller says, "I'm sure everything will be fine." He pours himself a final drink. "Cheers!" he says.

It's been a long time since someone has drunk me to the verge of surrender. I'll prop my eyes open with matchsticks and keep my eye on the Slavic mafia. Miller pays with a gold credit card. "It was a pleasure to meet you."

"Thank you, Jon."

He takes a pair of handcuffs out of his leather briefcase and attaches it to his wrist, as though that were the most normal thing in the world. He stands straight and walks steadily to the door. Now the Russians are paying, too. It's close to four. The waitress is not going to ask me to come home with her. Since when do I hide more things from Livia than I tell her about?

The direction of time is reversible. But our ship is definitely not going backward. In fact, it's picked up speed. All the same, if we don't go any faster, it'll be almost daybreak before we reach the mooring dock.

Inside, Livia's telling about how she became a photographer. I've heard the story. Scherf's imagining her breasts.

25.

Jan and Livia wandered around Cağaloğlu for a while without speaking. They were both mentally reconstructing the conversation that had just taken place in the police station. The starting point had been their desire to report Albin as missing. In the exchange of questions and answers, the detective had discovered some hints that led to a gradual reinterpretation of the entire situation; a second form had replaced the first form, which was consigned to insignificance and oblivion; and in the end, the detective suspected Albin of several crimes. Now his name was on some low-priority wanted list and no one would look for him.

Livia broke their silence: "Let's assume that Miller really was shot," she said. "So, a week later, we're the first people who go to the police about this, but nobody asks us when and where the crime took place? Or with what weapon? Or whether we knew the victim? On top of that, the only witness, a German tourist, has disappeared. But they're not interested in that, either. Instead, we get this farce . . ."

"That detective probably deals with such cases all the time."

"A person who conceals a murder can only be guilty of homicide by omission if the murder has really been committed."

"You sound almost like Albin."

"If he had gone to the police and made a statement about what he witnessed, he would have been charged with an offense against

public morals, just because he stood on the roof terrace of his hotel and looked into someone's room."

"Albin wanted to avoid further awkwardness because of your
breakup. Moreover, he couldn't bear the fact that you're with
me now. So he bought himself a new ticket and caught the next
flight out."

"But why would he leave his things behind?"

"Out of pure malice. He knew we had guilty consciences and
so we'd panic and get ourselves into all sorts of difficulties. Which
is exactly what's happening."

"But the police detective . . ."

"You yourself have told me about how Albin likes to play jokes,
how he leaves fake trails and false clues."

"In that case, can you please tell me why the detective tore up
the missing persons report?"

"Once you start believing conspiracy theories, the most harm-
less coincidences suddenly turn into evidence. Paranoia seeps into
your brain and shuts off critical thinking. General suspicion infil-
trates your thought structures and reproduces itself uncontrollably,
until finally the men in white coats come for you and you know
that all your fears were justified."

Jan considered it inexcusable to deceive the woman he loved,
and yet here he was, doing it already, before they had been together
for four days. Even as he tried to convince Livia that there was an
innocent explanation for everything, he was remembering how
he'd seen the detective's face darken at the mention of Miller's
name and the rhetorical precision with which the vanished witness
had been transformed into a fugitive from justice.

As far as Jan was concerned, it made no difference which parts
of Albin's story had really happened, which were due to his talent
for invention, and which were pure delusion. If a person took Al-

bin's hallucinations as the truth, they could drive him to perform certain actions, and those actions could have consequences in which the figments of Albin's imagination might appear as actual causes. Jan didn't know the reasons for the police detective's maneuvers, but one thing was clear: he and Livia had been urgently requested to butt out.

"I'd like to go to the Russian market," Livia said.

Jan was silent. Any further attempt to change her mind would increase her mistrust. He felt guilty. He offered her one of his cigarettes, held out the lighter, and avoided her eyes.

She said, "You don't believe what you just said any more than I do."

He didn't deny it.

By now it was a quarter to four. The shadows of the buildings ended on the other side of the horizon. It was getting cooler. Someone screamed. The screaming began in a side street and came closer in a hurry. Immediately after that, a man dashed around the corner, thrashed the air with a stick, and came to a stop directly in front of them. He could as well have been thirty as sixty. He wore a jacket, a parka, and an overcoat, one on top of the other, along with several sweaters and two pairs of pants. The pupil of his right eye was turned inward, and he gawked with the good one like a berserker liable to attack them at any moment. Foam was gathering in the corners of his mouth. While he dried his lips on his sleeve, his good eyeball rotated wildly. "Halt!" he screamed. "Not one step farther! Infidels! You spawn of devils and rutting bitches! You blood-sucking eaters of pigs' flesh! I know your country, where mothers sell their sons, where fathers violate their daughters! Be gone! Run for your lives! Hide in crevices and holes before you're swept away! The day of reckoning is near! The storms of the desert have ended their assembly and pronounced judgment upon you!

Run, before they send seas as high as mountains! Take flight, before floods of water wash you away and falling rocks crush you . . ." He spoke German without an accent. Saliva was running down his chin. His stick whipped the air dangerously close to their faces. Although he was crazy, his single eye had the power to hold Jan and Livia in check. ". . . out of here! Vermin shall devour your stinking carcasses!" He sent a last scream to heaven and ran off as suddenly as he had appeared.

Livia was trembling. Jan was skeptical about the authenticity of the madman, but he had sufficient presence of mind to take advantage of Livia's shock. "Let's go to the hotel," he said. "It's late. The market's going to be dismantled in a little while. We can try it early tomorrow morning."

"Maybe I should postpone my return flight."

When they entered the lobby of the Duke's Palace, Livia hoped in vain that Albin's key wouldn't be behind the reception desk. Nevertheless, they went up to the room to see whether he'd been there in the meantime. There was nothing to suggest that he had.

"Good painting," Jan said, gesturing toward the wall where the Janissary warrior shouldered his musket. Livia picked up the telephone, listened to the dial tone for a few seconds, and hung up. "Who could I call?"

"If the others are back already, they're probably in the lounge. Let's go make Nager try to remember whether Albin dropped some kind of hint about his plans while they were out getting smashed."

After the visit to the Suleyman Mosque, the class had separated. Most of them had no interest in Sinan's architecture. Fritz took off at once. Hagen wanted to walk with Swantje, just the two of them, and he got rid of Scherf. Adel felt obligated to console Sabine.

Corinna joined them. Mona and I stayed back with Nager, who started moaning about the art students of today. When they travel, he said, they want the same things touring pensioners want: souvenir shops, coffee and cakes, and enough sleep! But then he asked us, "Is it my fault that the general mood is so awful?"

"You've done your part," Mona said.

"We'd been hoping it would get better here instead of worse," I said.

"I probably should have made it clear beforehand that group dynamics isn't my specialty."

We set off together and visited the Sokollu Mehmet Paşa Camii, behind the Hippodrome, and then the Rüstem Paşa Camii, by the ferry station, not far from the place where we'd lost Albin. The increasingly dense thicket of blue faience induced Nager to give up his ornamentation project before even beginning it. Mona and I were amazed by the exactness of his perceptions. Sometimes we felt like nearsighted people without eyeglasses. Since he wasn't drinking, Mona was able to remain unmolested, except for when he told her she had a fabulous ass and he'd take her from behind.

I don't know where the others went. Swantje and Hagen seem to have reached an agreement in the course of the afternoon; in any case, after they got back to the hotel, they tried to organize a bed exchange, and the result was that Scherf slept with me.

Nager, Mona, and I walked into the Orient Lounge a few minutes before Jan and Livia. Nager was also worried by Albin's disappearance and thinking about going to the police. When Jan and Livia came in, he yelled clear across the room to ask them if there was any news. While they took turns telling their story, the expression on Nager's face grew somber, he started smoking even more avidly, and he chugged down his second beer without a pause. He said, "Does any one of you believe in the incorruptibility of the Turkish police? Up until recently, Turkey was a military dictatorship, and these guys were sitting at the same desks back then." He ordered five double Moskovskaya vodkas, "To give us strength," he said. "We have to go and grill Messut."

"You know, I can watch James Bond at the movies," Mona said. "That way, I get to see the original."

Livia was grateful for the support. "I'm thinking about postponing my return trip. At least until I'm certain that it's pointless to keep on looking for him."

"Then I'll leave later, too," said Jan.

It was dark when we stepped out of the hotel. Nager rushed down the street, leading our little group. He was obstinately staring straight ahead with his hands in his overcoat pockets and his shoulders up around his ears. Livia played through different scenarios for our meeting with Messut. To give herself courage, she practiced a resolute tone of voice.

"The bar here isn't bad at all," Nager informed us as he stepped onto the Otelo Sultan's red carpet and the doormen tipped their hats to him. Once in the lobby, he hesitated, as though he had to drive away his last doubt that Albin's story justified the risk we would be exposed to, all of us, including him, the moment we changed our status from observers to participants. He turned around like a field marshal eager to arouse his troops' enthusiasm for the imminent battle, but inflammatory words failed him, and so he settled for stretching out his arm and pointing toward the reception desk, which was hidden behind some pillars.

Although Albin hadn't described his appearance in any detail, we all knew that the man filing papers behind the counter was

Messut Yeter. He inspired respect. Moreover, *Messut* was on the little nameplate attached to his breast pocket. Nevertheless, Nager said, "Good evening. Excuse me. We're looking for Messut Yeter."

"You have found him."

"Good."

There was a pause. Messut inspected us, one after the other. His look was benevolent, but he saw no reason to continue the conversation. Nager scratched the back of his head and then his nose. "May I smoke?"

"Of course," Messut said, placing an ashtray in front of him.

"Here's the problem. As you may know. A friend of ours. I'm a professor at the Art Academy in S. These are my students. Jan and Olaf. Except for Livia. We're on a class trip. Tomorrow we fly back to Germany. The name of our friend, Livia's boyfriend, or rather her ex-boyfriend, is, or perhaps was, Albin. We don't know. He mentioned you."

"Albin Kranz. I tried to help him. He's staying in the Duke's Palace."

"Albin has disappeared. He's been missing since yesterday afternoon . . ."

"Why did you tell him to go to Düşünülen Yer?" Livia interrupted. "What did you say to him? Why did he listen to you?"

"One at a time," Nager said. "This isn't an interrogation. We're asking Mr. Messut to give us some help." Turning to the clerk, he said, "Albin was on the trail of something. A delicate situation. Also very puzzling. He spoke of an American named Miller. I'm sure he mentioned that name to you, too. Last Monday morning, we were still in Frankfurt."

"That's when Albin came to me for the first time."

"Of course, there's the possibility that Miller was using a false name," Jan said. "Still, we should be able to find out who reserved that suite for last Sunday night and Monday morning . . ."

Livia was too wrought up to listen. She said, "We could beat around the bush for an hour, but my time is getting short. So I'm in favor of clear questions and clear answers. What do you know about this man Miller?"

"No more than what I told Albin: there was no one named Jonathan Miller registered in this hotel."

I was standing behind Nager to his left, and I could see his brain working. He was concentrating hard, intent on separating the different threads of the conversation and identifying the various interests and emotional states, while at the same time trying to interpret Messut's gestures and facial expressions in the hope of finding an opening or a starting point.

Livia was determined not to be put off a second time. "That's not an answer to my question."

Nager asked, "Do you rule out the possibility that a man was shot in your hotel, whether or not his name was Miller?"

"To do that, I would have to have been in all the rooms simultaneously, and even then I could not be absolutely certain."

"Therefore, Albin could have *objectively* witnessed a murder?"

Messut laughed. "No. That's an *impossible possibility*. Let me give you an example: You call a movement from left to right around a center *clockwise*. But should you observe such a movement from the clock's point of view, you would see the hands moving in the opposite direction. Consequently, what one should really say is this: The movement of the hands of a clock, if one observes them in reverse, that is, from *in front* of the dial, is called *clockwise* . . ."

"Look," said Livia. "As far as I'm concerned, you can discuss this problem with Professor Nager later. Right now, I want to know why you told Albin to go to Düşünülen Yer!"

Jan put his hand on her forearm.

"Because of the beauty of the place and the possibility of thinking clearly in the fresh sea air, and because Albin was going around in circles, searching for a direction without knowing where he was. In Düşünülen Yer, as anywhere else, he might have met someone in a position to help him sort things out."

"If you're trying to make fun of me, I'm going to the police."

"As you already know, the police are hopelessly overburdened."

Livia flinched. She concluded from Messut's reply that he'd been informed of the steps she'd taken. She felt horrified and at the same time, incomprehensibly, relieved. All the same, she tried one last threat: "I'm a journalist," she said. "I can cause you trouble. I'll put this case in headlines. Everything, including your name and the name of the hotel. The investigating authorities will be interested in that . . ."

Her voice broke. Messut's face looked sad. He leaned forward and spoke so softly that only Livia understood him: "Take the lesson of this story to heart. *An enormous fish swam into an inexperienced fisherman's net. The fisherman was afraid that his hands alone would not be strong enough to hold the net, so he looped it tight around his hips. With the next blow of its fins, the fish caused the boat to capsize, and the young man was dragged down into the deep.*"

Livia nodded. Tears stood in her eyes.

Later, more than once, we tried to figure out what exactly the nature of Messut's power was. How did he get us to do what he considered correct, even though he answered none of our questions? Even Nager bowed to him: "You're right about the hands of the clock, Mr. Messut. We'll go now."

Nobody objected.

Livia says that something in Messut's gaze—she can't pin it down—rendered her incapable of grasping the meaning of his story. On the way back to the hotel, she kept repeating the words again and again so she wouldn't forget a single one. But even though she took a piece of paper and wrote the story down less than an hour after she heard it, she says some crucial detail must have escaped her along the way, a nuance that made her departure from Istanbul seem urgently necessary. To this day, she can find that nuance crystal-clear in her memory, but not on the paper.

Because of this exceedingly banal little tale, Livia says, she ran away without Albin—or from him.

26.

A shooting star plunges out of sight behind the mountain crests. Scherf's wishing he and Livia were on the ship alone. The ship turns into a steamboat on the Mosel; a small boat brings them to the bank, and they lie on the sand. He's putting his hand between her legs—it's wet there—when he feels Jan's eyes on him. He thinks: Why's he looking at me like that?

The sound of the engines has moved far away. While my hips strike the deck rail, again and again, so hard that it should hurt, a cushion-like object, strangely alive, seems to float above the surface of the water and swell to the size of the swinging doors. Although its edges are clearly outlined, it looks porous. There's a constant exchange going on between it and its surroundings. Its glow illuminates the ship's hull. In spite of the night, I can distinguish colors: rust red, a streak of white.

Portrait of Livia asleep as a relief bust. Her head on rumpled pillows. Different surfaces: cotton fabric, skin, long hair falling in waves over folds of material and lying on her temples and the back of her neck. Pressed flat; matted. And behind her forehead, scenes neither remembered nor forgotten.

The birds here are so loud I wouldn't need an alarm clock from April to October. Livia's drawn her knees up to her chest. The spring sun comes in through the window and throws the shadow of the mullion and transom onto the parquet floor. Half an hour ago, the shadow was touching her hand, which hung over the edge of the bed. Now, slowly, the shadow's moving away. The sheet has slipped off her shoulder, but she's not cold. There's a smile in the corners of her mouth. No evil enemy is following her through the last minutes of her dream. The Japanese cherry tree is in bloom. For the first time this year, the air isn't wintry anymore. Today will be warm. A dove coos. I've always hated Sundays. Either we'd get bored or things would turn catastrophic. It's up to Livia to decide what we're going to do today. Her last semester starts tomorrow. I have to drive to Hamburg early in the morning and start three weeks of polishing tracery; we won't see each other again until after that. The day will be exuberant and wistful. We'll console each other reciprocally with the promise of future delights. Livia turns over onto her back. The tops of her breasts are exposed; her left hand rests on her thigh. She sighs softly. I sit up and observe by turns her motionlessness and the movement of the branches of the trees in the wind. The dark blue satin sheets give her hair an orange sheen. I stroke a thick tress with the back of my hand. We could go to the Wunderbar for breakfast and discuss the subject of her degree dissertation. If you ask me, she should do the report on the Delphinarium at the Duisburg Zoo: outdated swimming-pool architecture, screaming children, dolphins that giggle even when they're terminally ill, and a marine biologist ready to defend his domain.

Livia's eyelids flutter as though she's just about to wake up, but she opts for sleeping on. As long as she doesn't notice, I could draw her. The tension in her neck muscles, the curve of eyebrows. Her eyes must be turned inward behind her lids. If you manage to capture that in stone, it comes out as kitsch. Thea or Ralph gets up in the room above us, comes downstairs, enters the kitchen, opens cabinets, turns on the water faucet, fiddles with various objects, and goes away again. Livia rolls onto her belly before my drawing's finished. I flip to the next page.

To lie propped up on the bed next to her, paper and drawing pencil in hand, to watch over her sleep, to follow the lines of her cheeks and her torso in silence, on a day off after winter's end—this might be the beginning of happiness, an open landscape where we'd sit under an ancient tree, her head in my lap, watching the peaceful animals, eating fruit, drinking the water from a nearby stream. Time would pass at a steady speed, undisturbed by events.

Livia opens her eyes and stares at the wall. Numerous pictures are fastened onto the wallpaper, including some proofs and reproductions of famous photographs. She regains consciousness gradually, inserts this new day into the series of days that have passed since her memory began. I've been there, in her consciousness, for the last two and a half years. For a moment she looks surprised, but then she remembers.

I'd like to tell you something now, something to erase all the disappointments. I'd like to offer a simple solution for difficulties that never existed. I'd do it with the firm voice of a man to whom lying is unknown and whose words, therefore, contain not so much as a hint of falsehood, but I'm not that man, and the words have been used too often. She looks at me as though she might trust a side of me I know nothing about and says, "How are you?"

"Good."

The bells of Saint Nicolai's Church ring out from the old part of the city. The shadow of the mullion and transom cross the shadow of the chair where her clothes are hanging. "You made a drawing of me." I nod. "While I was asleep," she goes on. "That's forbidden."

"Call it a study. I might do a relief."

"Then it's allowed." She sits up, wraps the blanket around her breasts, and takes my hand. "Yesterday was lovely."

I pluck a cigarette from the pack and stretch for the lighter. Masses formed of smoke and sunbeams hover over the desk.

"I'm thirsty."

"What would you like?"

"Orange juice."

"I'll get some."

"Don't go yet." She's looking at someone else. He looks very much like me. I hope she's telling him the truth.

We could sit under the tree in the happy garden, surrounded by silence except for the rustling of grass, the buzz of insects, and the occasional lark. But the sun would shine mercilessly hot in the early afternoon, the light would hurt our eyes, I'd get pains in my back. We'd get sticky with sweat and intolerably bored, and neither of us would know what to do about it. An insane reflex shoots through my head like a bullet, impossible to dodge, and I dig my teeth into Livia's neck until I draw blood.

I need a few minutes alone. I say, "Today, you don't have to do anything."

"All right, but don't go yet."

The kitchen smells like coffee and toasted bread. Fifteen minutes without her looking at me. I'll bring her breakfast in bed, for the first time since we've known each other. I turn on the radio. Sunday preaching. Turn the dial. Sunday pop music.

"What are you doing?"

"It's a surprise."

All possibilities still lie open to us. We'll let ourselves be carried along. For the first time in six months, we can sit outside. Later, we'll go to a movie or drive through the woods, and after that we'll end up in bed. Sex. Television. Pizza delivery. "Today, after a construction period of four years and at a cost equivalent to nine billion marks, the Euro Disney theme park in Marne-la-Vallée, France, thirty-two kilometers east of Paris, will open to the public." The refrigerator is full. Put salt in the water, otherwise the eggs will crack. Fix the toast. She likes hers with half marmalade, half cheese. Black bread, too, with salami. Disgusting, but I fight down the nausea. What else? An apple, yogurt, her vitamin *pills. How will she react when she sees me standing in the doorway with a full tray in my hands? The news announcer is so loud she can't hear me open the freezer and pull out the vodka bottle. One, two, three swallows. To warm my heart and make me laugh in anticipation of a great day with Livia, who declares she loves me, although—but she loves me without any "although."*

The coffee's too strong for her. A bit more milk makes it right. And one more swallow of vodka.

"Are you having the oranges flown in from Morocco?"

"Almost there."

Put on the right cassette: John Coltrane.

"Good morning, madame. Room service."

She wasn't expecting this. She wrinkles her forehead and wonders what the catch is. There's no catch. "Didn't we say we were going to have breakfast at the Wunderbar?"

She tears herself away and shoves me against the tree. Blood runs down her neck and gathers in the hollow above her collarbone, drawing wasps. Walk off and leave everything behind.

I say, "I thought you'd be pleased."

"Of course I'm pleased."

Scherf thinks: Sentimental hogwash. And: A woman, any woman at all. Jan loathes him; his loathing overlies Livia's story; he loses the thread.

Instead of engines, I hear voices running, side by side, no mingling. Sentences, beginnings of sentences: the colors of brain waves. The floating cushion below me swells and bulges. Although the openings in it have grown, too, they won't let me see what's inside.

Open Studios Night in Bielefeld. Seventy-two addresses, scattered throughout the city. Artists can live here. On the telephone, Maria said, "It'll be the best party you ever went to." The voice on the intercom yells,

"Third floor!" I'm not the first guest to arrive. Maria and Vincent are showing their stuff together in his apartment. She and Vincent are in the same class. There was a time, a few weeks or so, when they were an item. They've even put pictures along the stairs, postage-stamp-sized pictures in disproportionately large double-glass frames: hotel rooms, palm trees in the rain, a desiccated sandwich; black girls selling themselves; black men with nothing to do. The images are crowded against the edges of the frame and deliberately out of focus. "And don't start criticizing right away," Maria told me on the phone. "We happen to be in the process of repealing the dogmas of traditional photography."

The apartment door's open. A student with a ponytail is chopping onions. He says, "I'm Vincent."

"Albin."

"Ah, you went to school with Maria."

The woman cleaning the salad greens is pushing forty. The place smells like grass, cooking fat, and human bodies. I take a beer from the case. Candles and strings of lights in the living room. In the middle of the room, a long table, set for guests with cloth napkins and silverware. Maria has raided the drawers in her mother's kitchen. On the main wall, a display of giant photographs, in which grainy, gray surfaces collide with one another. If you look more closely, they're details of Gothic arches. House music. A sixteen-year-old girl with dreadlocks rolling a joint for her best friend. The friend has the face of an Indian girl. Judging from the mattresses and sleeping bags, several people have been staying here for days. Maria's deep in conversation with a blasé type in a suit, as though there were some chance he'd give her a show in his gallery. About twenty people here altogether, but it's only nine-fifteen, and dinner's not till ten. Surplus of women. I don't know anyone except Maria. A dancer in skintight orange-colored clothing is showing a shy southern European girl hand movements from the repertoire of Indian temple dancing. Her boyfriend looks at them jealously and gets a glass of fizzy wine from the kitchen. He's got a limp. Maria has told me about Ben—he lost his leg when he was seventeen, he studies fashion design. His prosthesis is covered with imitation leopard skin. I sit down on an old sea trunk. Maria sees me and calls out, "Be right there." We haven't seen each other for a year and a half. Of all the women I've been with, she's the only one who doesn't hate me.

"So what have you been doing, besides drinking?"

"Hammering on stone."

"Successfully?"

"Not very."

"And your love life?"

"Frequently changing sexual partners. How about you?"

"We're going through a crisis of purpose. The photojournalists have realized that the truth can't be caught in a camera, and the art photographers are struggling with a decision: poverty or compromise?"

"And what are you?"

"Well, strictly speaking . . ."

A narrow silhouette in the door. The outline of a woman. Her hair is pinned up behind. She's waiting. She waits until her eyes grow accustomed to the dim light. Then she steps in, distinguishes between friends, acquaintances, and strangers, kisses Ben and the dancer on the cheeks, puts her arm around an anorexic girl. Maria waves to her and asks, "How many people did you all have?"

"More than we expected."

This is not her first time in this apartment. She notices changes, locates herself in the mirror over the sideboard, checks to see if the wind has mussed her hairdo, turns toward the gray surfaces, shakes her head, and switches on the fluorescent lights. All conversations stop and back up: "As I was saying . . ." She looks observant, playing with a lock of hair escaped from its clip. Unusual hands. Vincent's explaining his concept to her. He speaks quickly and softly. I understand some words:

"... *extreme reduction ... final point ... one simply has to stop taking postmodernism ...*" *Someone turns the music louder. Those two are surely not a couple. He likes her, but she doesn't attract him. The older woman puts her arms around his stomach from behind. I would've thought she was a teacher.*

"... *you're not listening to me, Albin,*" *Maria says, laughing.*

"*Who's the girl Vincent's explaining his pictures to?*"

"*Livia. She's our age. She's nice.*"

"*Her waist and hips are in perfect proportion.*"

"*She'll be glad to hear it.*"

The crowd's close to thirty strong by now. The table's big enough for about half that many, at most. Vincent starts bringing in a tabletop, some trestles, and some folding chairs from the next room. Maria says, "I've got to help Vincent. Shall I introduce you to Livia?"

"*Maybe later.*"

Livia turns around. She's beautiful. Our eyes meet. The Indian girl switches off the fluorescent lights. Vincent whacks a wineglass with a spoon until everyone's quiet and then says, "I'm sorry, we don't have enough places to sit, but there's plenty of food. Serve yourselves."

I'm in no mood to eat. A French girl sits down next to me and says with a strong accent, "I'm Héloïse. I'm studying graphic design. And you?"

"*I'm a plumber.*"

"*Comment?*"

"*Water pipes. Toilet installations. That sort of thing.*"

She considers for a moment how a French graphic designer ought to talk to a German skilled laborer. Looking for help, she stares around the room until she discovers an acquaintance: "Oh, there's someone I have to talk to."

Livia leaves the kitchen with her plate filled to the rim. All the chairs are taken. Is it a coincidence, or has she noticed that the trunk's big enough for two people to sit on? In any case, she's noticed that I can't take my eyes off her. This fact doesn't make her the least bit uncomfortable. She heads straight for me. "Is this place taken?"

"No."

"Lucky for me."

"Enjoy your meal."

"You're not eating anything?"

"No."

"It's really good."

"I'm not hungry."

"What's your name?"

"Albin."

"I'm Livia."

"I'm told you're nice."

"I wouldn't believe Maria."

"Why not?"

"Just wouldn't."

"But she's usually right."

She puts her plate on a windowsill and digs a pack of Camels out of her handbag. "Cigarette?"

"I was just about to offer you one."

"Too late."

"Light?"

"Thanks."

"You're welcome."

After drawing the smoke down to the bottom of her lungs, she slowly blows it out through her lips in a thin stream. I say, "What'll we talk about now?"

"I'm having a little trouble understanding you."

"Would you rather we keep quiet?"

"That's not what I meant."

"Then let's go somewhere else."

"Have you got an idea?"

"I live around the corner."

"Doesn't one generally save that for the end of the party?"

"Whenever you want."

"Do you always do this?"

"Never."

No one's surprised when we throw our jackets over our arms and head for the door. We don't tell anyone good-bye. Maria will assume I found a better place to sleep than her couch. For the sake of the couple we meet on the stairs, we look at two of the photographs on display: the window of an English coffee shop; the Sun on a bright blue laminated tabletop. In the darkness outside, Livia shakes with laughter. Gusts of icy wind blow in our faces. There's no moon—the sky is clear and filled with stars.

"I'm studying to be a photographer," she says. She's started something on a whim, and now she doesn't know how to make it stop, but nothing could be easier; all we have to do is go back to the party. Nobody noticed us leaving. Then, with just a little effort, we could avoid each other for the rest of the night. As though she's read my thoughts, she stops laughing, stands straight, and grabs my arm: "I don't know anything about you, but I've seen you. And I'm quite serious."

"An awakening!" Scherf jeers.

I believe her and ponder what she means. Despite the cold, I feel warm. She asks, "Can you pick out the zodiac constellations?"

"I just know the Big Dipper."

"That's the only one I know, too."

"What a privilege. We bow before you, Livia."

Another woman, one who very much resembles you, blushes, resents her blushing, and keeps silent. Back then, though, a proper response would have occurred to you before Scherf finished his sentence, and maybe you would've spat on his shoes.

I'm too far away to defend you. And where am I supposed to get the strength for that? I can't even lose my temper anymore. The muscles around my loins are giving way. I cast my eyes out over the water to the north, south, east, and west, but I'm detached from these ocular movements. The Bosporus sparkles.

27.

After we left the Otelo Sultan, Nager said, "Now be quiet and listen to me. As the professor, I bear the responsibility. For you, too, Livia. You're indisposed at the moment. Albin will either turn up or remain missing. Whatever he does, we won't have any influence on it. I have no idea what role Messut Yeter plays in this whole affair; in any case, he's no ordinary hotel clerk. I don't think there's any chance he belongs to a criminal organization, but he's familiar with operations and activities we don't have the first clue about. There must be reasons why he's keeping his secrets to himself. I'm sure about one thing, though, and that's that he wanted to help Albin or protect him. He probably wasn't successful. We won't learn anything else about this, because we're all going back to Germany tomorrow."

Actually, Nager's speech was superfluous—Messut had broken Livia's resistance, Jan had refused to participate in any further private investigating, I was neutral—but at the time we were relieved to hear him make a clean break and glad he brooked no opposition.

For the rest of the walk to the Duke's Palace, no one said a word. A cloud of apprehension settled down between the buildings and covered us. It seemed to emanate from Messut. He wanted to chase us out of the city. When I saw shadows in doorways, I jumped. I looked around, but no one was following us. The darkness transformed figments into possibilities, the possibilities became probable, and the probabilities formed an immediate threat.

Livia and Jan told us good night in the lobby and went up to their room. Throughout the rest of the evening, they tried to reconstruct the events of the foregoing week, step by step, but the result of their efforts contained too many gaps to be definitive. Livia eventually accepted the idea that Albin had withdrawn from the scene before she could leave him, just as his father had set his workplace on fire and disappeared before his business could be taken away from him. Jan was sympathetic about how difficult it was for her to bid Albin a final farewell, and Livia was grateful to him for that. When she asked him for his opinion of Messut, he evaded the question. "I've spent a lot of time in Africa," he said. "I've seen voodoo magic and Sufi ceremonies. That sort of thing makes you stop believing that there's a reasonable explanation for everything."

Nager and I were standing in the entrance hall. After a while, he asked me if I'd like to join him for dinner. We could call up Mona, he said; the meal would be on him. He thought it would be too dreary to spend the last evening in Istanbul alone, lounging in front of the television set and emptying the minibar. Mona came down at once. She was bursting with curiosity, but she kept herself under control. Nager suggested we go to the restaurant in the hotel; he thought we'd earned a bit of luxury after such a muddle. As soon as we were seated, before Mona could ask a question, he said that if she wanted to know how the conversation with Messut had gone, she should think about the meaning of the term "clockwise." As soon as she grasped why this word, taken in its strictest sense, described motion in the opposite direction, she'd know the most important thing. As for the rest, he went on, she could figure it out by deduction. Otherwise, she was to erase the whole matter from her memory and address herself to deciding between fillet of sole and saddle of lamb.

She looked at me uncomprehendingly.

"He means our inquiries didn't lead anywhere at all, but now we realize we must learn to live with our ignorance."

"Something like that."

"Doesn't sound as though I missed anything."

After dinner, we met Swantje, Hagen, Scherf, and Fritz in the lounge. We sat in a group in the enormous leather chairs, drank raki and water, and looked at images of the Orient produced by nineteenth-century European painters. Scherf was unable to keep his eyes off the waitress's behind. An outsider would have taken us for members of an ordinary tour group on the eve of their departure, exhausted by the sightseeing marathon and filled with new impressions. Nager talked in his customary way about gallery owners, collectors, and friends of the arts. Nobody listened to him. At intervals, Mona removed his fingers from her arm and returned them to the back of her chair. Hagen and Swantje vied to see which of them could grab the other's wrist first. Hagen won and pulled her onto his lap. When Mona said good night, he sat down beside me and said that as far as he could judge, Jan's bed was free, and so he wondered if I'd have anything against letting Scherf sleep there tonight. I could hardly refuse him. Ten minutes later, I was on my way to the room with Scherf in tow. Before the silence became intolerable, and before the name Jan was dropped, he asked me whether this Albin fellow had turned up or not. I had no interest in having a conversation with him, and so I merely answered, "No."

Then we turned out the lights.

During the night, new rainstorms came rolling in. In the morning, the air was so gray that you couldn't glimpse the sea from the breakfast room. The sky shrouded the minarets.

Since Nager's cocompetitor in endurance drinking was no longer around, the professor arrived at the breakfast table looking well rested. Fritz announced that Adel, who shared a room with him, apparently had picked up a case of salmonellosis or some other kind of food poisoning. He told us that Adel, Corinna, and Sabine had decided to have their final Istanbul meal at a restaurant expressly recommended in Sabine's guidebook; they ate some spoiled meat at this place and had been puking ever since. Corinna could scarcely stand up. Sabine was clutching a plastic bag out of fear that her bad ankle would prevent her from reaching the toilet in time. Scherf snapped at Hagen about a missing half packet of peanuts.

Jan and Livia gulped down a couple of cups of coffee. They had various things to take care of. After several false starts, and with the help of a friendly hotel employee, they succeeded in getting Livia a seat on our flight, because she didn't want to be alone. Livia then tried in vain to reach Thea and instead recited the most important points into her friend's answering machine. After all that, she packed her things. She decided to take Albin's bags with her back to Germany, wrote him a short note, and left it at the hotel reception:

Dear Albin,

Since I've heard nothing from you, I'm interpreting your disappearance as the final break between us. You anticipated my decision to separate from you by half a day. The hotel wasn't prepared to store your luggage gratis, so I'm taking it with me. As soon as possible, I'll put it in the apartment, together with anything else I've got that belongs to you.

Good-bye.

Livia

There were four hours left before we had to board the bus for the airport. Jan, Livia, Mona, and I sat in the hotel lobby. We were too tired to be bored, we'd had our fill of the city, and the rain was coming down in torrents. The weather was unfit for man or beast, but Nager went back to the bazaar one last time. With all the excitement, he'd forgotten to get a gift for his wife. Since nothing better occurred to him, he took an example from Turkish husbands and bought her a gold armband. For his older daughter, he found an Arab inlaid casket with a musical clock from Taiwan built into it. When you opened the casket, a twittering bird flew around in a circle.

We got to the airport shortly before three. Sabine and Corinna felt so weak that we put them on baggage carts and pushed them through the halls. Perspiration beaded Corinna's forehead; Sabine gagged and vomited into her bag. Adel was feeling somewhat better. Fortunately, we were the only people in the check-in line. The customs officials only glanced at our passports and waved us through—until it was Nager's turn. Maybe he had annoyed them by ostentatiously taking no notice of them and turning his head toward Jan while they were trying to compare his face with his passport photograph. They waved him over to the side and had him open his suitcase. He had to shake out all his clothes to show that no smuggled objects were hidden in them.

They rummaged through his shaving kit and sniffed his toothpaste. When all his things were spread out on the table, they pointed to the tightly bound package at his feet and asked in English, "What's this?"

"Carpet."

"Open."

While Nager was swearing, one of the customs men cut the twine, tore off the paper, rubbed the carpet between his fingers, and ordered, "Unpack! Completely!"

Nager turned red but obeyed.

"Very old carpet. Show us documents."

"I have no documents."

"So you are smuggler!"

"I knew that fucking thing would cause trouble, I knew it," Mona whispered.

We were afraid that Nager would fall into a mad rage in the next seconds, but strangely enough he found the situation comic. "My friend Seppo would say, 'Self-administered justice through faulty shopping,' " Nager said. "But in this case he'd be wrong!"

The officials used a radio to call in reinforcements. Nager walked up and down in front of the table. After twenty minutes, the expert on duty appeared, a thin-lipped officer of about forty who spoke remarkably good German. "A Tekke, I see," he said. "Around 1870. Lovely piece. An interesting break in the coloring. And you have no export authorization? This is bad. Very bad. In addition, for the export of any antique, a certificate from the Office of Antiquities is required. You didn't know about that either, did you? I presume you're hearing it for the first time, and—let me guess— you can't remember the name of the dealer who sold you the carpet. Am I right?"

Nager kept silent.

In the meantime, two heavily armed border policemen had taken up a position behind us. The carpet specialist leafed through Nager's passport.

"Have you no wish to speak, Mr. Schaub-Scheffelbock?"

"It is exactly as you say."

"Year after year, thousands of Turkish art objects disappear into private collections in Europe and America. Our cultural heritage is being carried off like war booty. We manage to catch only a small fraction of the perpetrators: between two and four percent. At the most. And of this two to four percent, one hundred percent have absolutely no clue that they've done anything wrong!"

"I'd like to keep the carpet. Is there a possibility of redeeming it, or will it be confiscated?"

"According to a principle of international law, ignorance does not excuse from punishment."

Nager rubbed his thumb and forefinger together by way of indicating that he was prepared to pay.

"Naturally, not all antique carpets are excluded from export. Much depends on the quality of the individual piece, on whether it represents a particularly significant example of a certain group or period; and that's why you need those documents. Obtaining them after the fact is complicated. And expensive. An abundance of formalities must be carried out. Now, your piece came originally from Turkmenistan, which simplifies the process considerably. I must try to reach the appropriate colleague in the Office of Antiquities. You should figure on a wait of at least three quarters of an hour. In addition, there will be a fine to pay, along with administrative costs. A considerable sum. Have you got cash?"

Nager nodded and followed him.

"I will not get anxious," Mona said. "I couldn't care less whether he makes the plane or not. As far as I'm concerned, he can rot in an Istanbul slammer."

"What can happen to him? He's got three different credit cards."

Livia said, "A little while ago, there was a call for a Mr. Miller and a woman named Irina Koklova to report to the gate for the flight to Washington."

"The announcements in here are pretty hard to understand, don't you think?" Jan replied. "And there's a million people named Miller. It's over. We're already outside of Turkish national territory. I'm going to the duty-free shop to buy cigarettes. And a bottle of bourbon. You come, too!"

Nager got back to us with time to spare. He was in a good mood, even though the customs officer had relieved him of five hundred dollars. "I would have paid twice as much," he said. "This isn't just any carpet, it's mine. Woven especially for me."

There was such heavy turbulence over the Mediterranean that Corinna burst into tears from sheer nausea. The sun went down. Jan decided to travel to Berlin with Livia. The chicken was cold and tasted like fish. It was only just before we landed that we were able to distinguish buildings, streets, and parts of the city. The airplane touched down almost imperceptibly. The pilot thanked us and announced the weather in Frankfurt: rain, gusty winds, five degrees Celsius. The plane came to a stop at the edge of the runway, and a bus brought us to the terminal. No one was missing any luggage. Nager ran off to catch the train for Cologne. Jan and Livia went to get tickets for Berlin. The rest of us had to wait half an hour to board the InterCity train Wilhelm Conrad Röntgen for S. Mona and I sought out a bench at the end of the platform.

"Who was it had the stupid idea of flying to Istanbul?" she asked.

"I have no idea."

"It was probably one of Messut Yeter's mysterious emanations."

"He appeared to Nager one night in a dream."

"On a flying carpet."

28.

Why do they wait until half the trip is over and then turn on the string lights? Except for Nager and me, there's not a soul on the foredeck. Livia's afraid Jan will beat Scherf black and blue, but not because she's worried about Scherf. She's thinking, I hope Jan doesn't react the way Albin would. The shining points form a parallel universe and mingle with the stars in the northern sky. These altered constellations permit no conclusions about personal characteristics or future events.

"Repeat after me: I'm an idiot, and I'm sorry."

Jan's not going to put up with anyone who tries to make the woman he loves look ridiculous. It's a calm decision, not an uncontrolled outburst. I would have defended my own pride instead of Livia's. She'll stay with him.

All the days are the same. The place stinks. It stinks of chicken shit, chicken feathers, and chicken blood. If you don't leave the grounds, your nose adapts to it. I leave the grounds daily and go off to cut stone slabs for the kitchens, bathrooms, and staircases of wealthy former swine fatteners and poultry barons, their attorneys, and their accountants. I carve the names of the dead into black basalt. The air is chickens' breath; it vibrates with heat and covers over fodder silos and cage batteries. Uncle Gerald pulls off his boots, loosens the knot in his tie, and calls through the house: "Gertrude!" He throws his sport coat over a chair, takes a bottle of fruit brandy out of the refrigerator, and pours a round: "Cheers, Heinz, Rudi, Franz." His workers get a shot of schnapps every two hours; otherwise, they wouldn't be able to endure their jobs. "Cheers, Albin." Gertrude comes home from shopping, laden with heavy bags. He asks her, "Why isn't the coffee ready?"

She apologizes: "The supermarket was so crowded." In her Chanel dress, she serves out plates of cake: the wife as maid with limitless budget. "Homemade cake tastes better." Her husband has hardly any hair, sweat stains under his armpits, and a belly hanging down over his belt. He owns a big house with a swimming pool, a Mercedes 400, and an appropriate sport coupe, as well as valuable jumping horses.

"So how old are you now?" It's the third time this month he's asked me that.

"I'll be twenty-one tomorrow."

"Legal age."

"Eighteen is legal age."

"Nonsense. Come into my office."

"I'm not asking for a gift."

His fleshy neck, covered with thick hair, spills out over his shirt collar. "He was a tough nut, your father, my brother."

I make no reply. He reaches into his desk and pulls out a bottle of cognac, Remy Martin, as befits a self-important farmer. "To your birthday."

"It's tomorrow."

"Look, I can tell you're dying to know why you're here. Sit down and prepare yourself for a surprise." His look expresses, in turn, shiftiness, pathos, and childish anticipation. Gerald straightens his spine and assumes a pose. "As you know, after your father was taken from us so early and so tragically, his mortal remains were interred in the New World. In Argentina. He was a pioneer. A battler. He fell often, and he always got back up . . ." He's touched by his own solemnity; his voice breaks, his eyes grow moist. He goes to the closet where the wall safe is, opens the safe with a flourish, and takes out a framed photograph. He says, "What do you see?"

"A grave."

"Your father's last resting place. In the cemetery in Bahía Blanca. A worthy spot." The grave is a mausoleum of pink granite with a porch supported by two columns. Between them, two angels are praying with someone who represents Father. The stonework is ghastly. Who paid for it? They assured us that he owned nothing. But then, no one ever knew the details of Gerald's business trips. He disappeared for several days on a regular basis. If one of us asked, "Where?" he would dodge the question and Gertrude would remain silent.

Now he says, "Tomorrow, you're flying with me to Zurich. I've got the tickets here. You won't have to start from nothing like Walter and me. He provided for you."

He disappeared without a trace. Every now and then he'd send us silly pictures: Buenos Aires, primeval forest, rocky desert. He posed in colonial khakis, with a wide-brimmed hat on his bald head. Sometimes a young mulatto girl stood by his side, looking on him with devotion. His housekeeper, allegedly. The pictures would be accompanied by threadbare explanations of why he couldn't let us in on what he was doing. Nothing made sense; we were surprised, and we were glad he was gone. I say, "You knew the whole time? Gertrude knew, and Mother, and Claes and Xaver . . ."

"They received their share on their twenty-first birthdays. That was his last will, and I'm bound to respect it."

"Where does the money come from?"

"It's in my account. The rest is unimportant."

"I want to know how he earned it."

Gerald shakes his head.

"How much?"

"About four hundred thousand."

"You lied to me for five years. You and my shit-ass brothers and my—"

"Watch what you say. Walter and Ina are dead. Don't disturb their rest."

He stands up, steps over to me, and claps me on the shoulder. "You can be independent. You can set up something really big. 'Kranz Natural Stoneworks, Staudt,' for example. You can get your master craftsman's diploma."

The cognac scratches my throat. My hands are trembling. "I have to think about it."

The few steps to the door seem endless. He calls after me: "Departure time is eleven-twenty A.M."

Finally outside in the burning sun. Not the slightest breeze. The dog's sleeping in the shadow of the tractor. I'm rich. Scorched weeds wither beside the pathway. There's not much water in the Fries. Rich, thanks to the father I heartily wished in hell. A cloud of midges dances above the reeds. I could buy a house, and the most expensive whiskey. It's dirty money—it comes wrapped in a web of lies. Gerald won't reveal anything, and even if he does, he may just as well have made it up. He presents himself as our benefactor; people bow before the selflessness with which he supports his brother's widow and sons. I could order marble blocks from Carrara. Gerald's upright brother, my father, wanted us to be mutually deceived after his death. Our mistrust was to be preserved. If we had begun to talk about how it was when he was alive, his power over our memories, a power built on treachery and helplessness, would have been destroyed. Everything adds up. I'll take the money. I won't mention it to Claes and Xaver. It's all paid out now; everyone knows what's going on. There are no documents certifying anything at all and no comprehensible transactions. A heron's lurking on the opposite bank. I'll keep my mouth shut and spare everyone the shame and the excuse making. I could cross the Atlantic on a steamer. The deceased *asshole, my father, would spring for the trip. I could spit on his grave, the most hideous grave in the world. It would be a fitting farewell. He's not worth the expense.*

Clambering among the stones in Carrara, choosing the whitest block, finding for every statue the stone that contains it, like Michelangelo . . . I could bring a truckload of marble into Germany and carve gestures, carve people touching—not striking—each other. Compensation for what I owe. Claes says Gerald's enterprises are doing well. His business grows by four percent every year, and now he's added a turkey-breeding operation, giant hothouses where the birds wade in their own shit. The river smells moldy.

Not the smallest detail has been lost.

Beyond the speed of light, time changes direction. The archive of events is stored there, in spaces without height or breadth or depth. Everything happens at this moment: Scherf doubles over around a center of pain located above the pit of his stomach. Jan regrets that the blow was necessary. Gerald and I get out of a taxi in front of the main office of the Credit Suisse bank. We sit in the office of a customer adviser. I open my own account. I have to make several tries before I can sign. "Claes and Xaver were trembling, too," Gerald says. Nager's dream capsizes; his daughter is so pale she blends into the background. Mona despairs, but not definitively.

Their voices get farther away, become whispers, barely audible. They're drowned out by strange noises from my innards, a rustling sound like someone crumpling thick silk: the larva has become an insect. It's moving. The segments of its carapace haven't thoroughly hardened yet. It's breaking me open.

Night after night, the same unrest drives away sleep. I cower before deformed faces, wide-open mouths. They whisper or scream. Their speech is no human language. When I open my eyes and switch on the lamp, they withdraw. I creep past Claes's room, then Xaver's, and slink down the stairs in the dark. The kitchen clock says one-thirty. The television set's on in the next room. I'm not worried about getting caught. American policemen shoot down a gangster who's holding someone hostage. She's nodded off in her chair with the remote control on her lap. I steal a glass of her wine. Even if she notices me, she won't react. She's given up on herself and us. Her days are arranged around the taking of medication. Her hair's greasy. She's stopped wearing her pearls. We used to be proud of her when we walked through town at her side. We had the most beautiful mother of all. Gertrude forces her to eat; otherwise, she would've starved to death long ago. She surrendered us to him in an effort to save herself. Her attempt failed. When's the last time she put makeup on because she wanted to please someone? Herself, if no one else? I say, "Go to bed. You're going to get a crick in your back." I don't know how many pills of what kind she's supposed to take in the evening. She's allowed a glass of wine, but no hard liquor. "It's almost two. You'll catch a cold." If she's exceeded her prescribed limits, I'll have to carry her upstairs, which is child's play, as she weighs about 105 pounds. The combination of alcohol and tranquilizers extinguishes consciousness. "Mama, wake up." She doesn't react when I shake her and doesn't notice when I stroke her forehead. Her forehead's cool. My slaps don't hurt her. Her hand is colder than the hand of a person chilled in her sleep but not as cold as the hand of a dead person. Her chest isn't moving. There's no sound of breathing. I see myself turn on the light, clear away the liquor bottle, and pick up the telephone: "This is Albin Kranz in Staudt. We need emergency medical help, right away! My mother's very sick!" I run up the stairs, yank open Claes's and Xaver's doors, and hear myself shouting, "She's dying!"

"She's been looking like she's dying for weeks."

"She's really dying."

We stand around her, talking to her, talking nonsense. We've always shaken her hard when she's fallen too deeply asleep and stopped moving, but now we don't dare lay a hand on her. Always before, her chest would rise and fall, sometimes she'd even snore, and then she'd open her eyes. Minutes would pass before she recognized us. I can hear the ambulance siren. It's getting closer. They ought to drive faster. Xaver calls up Gerald. Claes cries. Gerald and Gertrude ring the doorbell. The emergency doctor rings the doorbell: "Where is she?" He looks businesslike; as far as he's concerned, she could be anybody. They lay her flat on the floor. He feels her pulse, pries her eyes open, shines a light into her pupils, unbuttons her blouse, and removes her bra. She has withered, ugly breasts. I want to cover her up. He shouldn't see that; we shouldn't see that. An EMT pulls a rubber mask over her face and pumps up her lungs. The doctor lays both hands on her thorax and presses down with all his strength. She jerks mechanically. Her ribs crack. Gertrude turns off the television and sobs. He presses and presses, but he doesn't believe he'll succeed. At last he says, "It's pointless."

We stand there, unmoving. None of us knows a suitable gesture or any appropriate words. We all look past one another, past her. Our movements and thoughts are peculiarly slow. We see our reflections in the windowpanes. If it were light outside, our eyes would have an escape, but as it is, they're trapped in here, wherever they turn. I try to touch Mother once again and feel a kind of disgust at the strangeness of her dead flesh. That's not her anymore. What's left has no similarity to a human being. The doctor sits down at the table and definitively confirms her death: "Heart failure. My condolences." He produces a pen and begins filling out the certificate. The pen scratches over the paper so loudly I wonder why it doesn't tear. The EMTs strap her to a stretcher, cover her with a white sheet, and carry her out. Gertrude says a Hail Mary out loud, but no one joins in. Gerald goes to the refrigerator, takes a swig from the bottle of schnapps, and holds it out to me: "You have a swallow, too." He's wearing a pair of dirty athletic socks and plastic sandals. We sit down together, even though we don't like each other, and empty that bottle and then another until the sun comes up.

A pain that doesn't hurt creeps down my back. The skin along my backbone swells up and rips apart; layers come off and bulge sideways. There's a tugging on my inner thighs, as though hooks were tearing the flesh from the bones. They aren't my muscles. They're not my bones. There's water below me and the starry sky above me. I can see them both at once, and between them the floating cushion, coming closer to my face. In the central opening, Mother's standing in front of the door to our house, which belongs to the bank, and holding a light blue air-mail letter in her hand, postmarked five days ago in Buenos Aires. She recognizes the handwriting and says, "It can't be," and then tears open the envelope: "Oh, God, he's alive." She turns white as chalk and gnaws her fingernails. "He's well. It's impossible for him to return at this time. We shouldn't worry about him, he says."

"Give it here."

"No."

I snatch the letter out of her hand and throw it on the ground without reading it. She slaps me, even though she's a head shorter than I am. A ridiculous gesture. She doesn't dare look me in the eye. I despise her: not for the slap, but because she's always loyal to him instead of us.

29.

The Academy of Art in S. is located on the edge of the city center, not far from the castle grounds. It's an old building. In the beginning of the nineteenth century, encouraged by the support of the grand duke, artists came together in this place to revitalize and reconstitute the medieval painters' and sculptors' guilds. The secrets of chalk-based paint, color mixing, and stoneworking were to be passed on from one generation to the next, with pupils serving their masters first as assistants and then working with them on projects, gradually gaining the experience that would allow them to develop independence and find their own expression. During the 1960s, the idea that artistic working methods could be taught through a craft apprenticeship disappeared. Today, the building accommodates eight classes of students (the sculptors are housed in a converted mansion, formerly an industrialist's villa, behind the train station). The classes are led by well-known artists, who because of their different aesthetic positions are sometimes enemies and propagate this enmity among their students. Some of them take their teaching activity seriously, others don't. In the inner courtyard, there's a little park with an artificial lake. During the summer semester, professors and students, divided into camps, sit at tables around the lake and drink beer. The academy is surrounded by grand buildings that were hardly damaged in the war; there are restaurants, little boutiques, an art supply store.

Since we got back from the trip, Nager's class has lost half its students.

Jan and Livia went to Berlin together. They had the photographs that Albin took in Istanbul developed and received pictures of different kinds of stone and hastily snapped café scenes with people staring out of a window or holding a glass or reading a newspaper. There was no indication that he'd taken these photos in connection with Miller's alleged murder. After two weeks had passed without word from Albin, Livia called up Claes, who works as a veterinarian not far from Hamburg, because she didn't know what she should do. At first, Claes wasn't at all worried about his brother. He considered Albin a nutcase perfectly capable of disappearing without a trace and just as suddenly showing up again: "He's probably in Uzbekistan, Tanzania, or Uruguay, looking for treasure or women, like his father."

All the same, after three months, when the rent on Albin's apartment was in serious arrears, none of his bills had been paid, and his mailbox was overflowing, Claes flew to Istanbul so he'd have nothing to reproach himself for later. However, he was unable to find any clue whatsoever to Albin's whereabouts. According to what Claes was told in the Otelo Sultan, Messut had taken a holiday to go to the Dervish Festival in Konya; in the villages of the region, where he was born and still had relatives, there were, for the most part, no telephones. Claes didn't have the feeling that anything was being concealed from him. The Russian market had emigrated to a part of town north of the Golden Horn; no one there knew Parfyon or Nicola. Because of the lurid warnings in his guidebook, seconded by the tourism office in the Istanbul Hilton, Claes didn't visit the Gypsy quarter in Sulukule. From the start, Xaver, who worked as a television journalist, had felt no responsibility in the matter. Probably, with the help of the German embassy or the Foreign Office, it would have been possible to get the Turkish authorities to initiate an investigation, but neither Claes nor Xaver had had much contact with Albin in the past several years, and both of them accepted his disappearance: it was just his style. In the meantime, his apartment was given up—Jan and Livia helped clear it out. In the wardrobe, they found a small sculpture about a palm's breadth in diameter, a study of Livia's face in yellowish wax, apparently the only piece Albin didn't destroy.

Immediately after the trip, Jan gave up his studies at the academy. It had become clear to him that he couldn't learn anything from Nager, and none of the other professors interested him, either. Above all, ever since his sojourn in Africa, he'd found life in a provincial town like S. increasingly unbearable. He and Livia live together now. He earns his living in the construction business and continues to do portraits on the side. We speak regularly on the telephone, and we've gotten together several times since his departure. Livia seems glad that her time with Albin is over. She takes photographs for important magazines and also does advertising shoots for cars, hotel chains, and insurance companies. Nevertheless, she still finds it difficult to accept Albin's disappearing like that, without a trace. After all, they were a couple for five years, in the beginning she'd believed he was the love of her life, and later she hadn't had the strength to separate from him. Sometimes she breaks off in the middle of a sentence and falls mute. Then she says she regrets never having had that concluding talk with Albin, and she blames herself for the cowardice or weakness that led her simply to give up the search for him in Istanbul. She finds it hard to bear when Jan gets drunk.

These days, Scherf spends most of his time in workshops—painting techniques and lithography—trying out gilding methods and photomechanical reproduction processes for his Iconoclastic Controversy installation. He has allegedly found a gallery owner willing to give him financial support. His relationship with Hagen has never been the same again.

Hagen waits tables more than he paints, but when he paints, he considers his work brilliant and acts like the self-proclaimed "Prince of Painters," Marcus Lümmels, who taught in the academy in S. before being appointed rector of the Städelschule in Frankfurt, and who liked to have his students polish his shoes so they could learn the right way to use a cloth. Hagen and Swantje didn't stay together.

Even before Christmas, Corinna came to the conclusion that it would be better for her to keep her German major but change her minor from art to history.

Fritz is drawing as much as usual, but he doesn't come to the academy very much. His exhibit with the Istanbul postcards was successful. Among other people, the art director of the town magazine has taken notice of him, and now Fritz publishes a regular cartoon series there.

At the end of the semester, Sabine and Swantje transferred out of the class. Adel's stipend ran out, so in the middle of February he had to go back to Beirut.

For a long time, Mona thought about leaving, too, but now she's grown so used to Nager that his talk amuses her instead of irritating her.

Since Nager's given up his apartment as well as his studio in Cologne and comes to S. only every three weeks for two days, the classrooms are mostly empty. New applicants won't be admitted until next winter. He's decided to give me an appointment as a master-class student so that I can stay at the academy another year and he won't have to deal exclusively with beginners. All the same, he's happy at the prospect of meeting new students who don't know anything about his unfortunate start as a professor. Mona and I try to avoid talking about the Istanbul trip, but Nager often feels the need to discuss it. He still believes that Albin was on the trail of some dark secret and asks if I've heard anything more of him through Jan and Livia. He always speaks of Albin with great respect, and after the third beer he often sounds sad, as though he lost a friend when Albin disappeared. As for the carpet, he had it appraised by an expert with Sotheby's. Apparently it's worth more or less exactly the price he paid for it, not including what he spent in fines and bribes for the Turkish customs officials.

30.

In the pale green shimmer framed by the waves, the night, and the reddish hull, flames blaze up, sixty feet high. There's the boom of oil tanks
exploding, followed by fireballs. Cardboard, wood, and plastic objects
fly through the air. The roof of the main shed gives way with a tremen-
dous roar. Hot dust whirls around. "Go back! Get away from here! This
is no place for you!" A side wall collapses and buries the office wing.
Steel beams, excavator arms, and parts of cranes jut up out of red-hot
metal plates. Flashing blue lights everywhere; shouting, helmeted men
with hoses and useless axes in their hands. A fountain of sparks rises
from the assembly pit. Fiery embers rain down on King's kennel. The
dog runs around in demented circles, burning alive. I see him yapping
and whimpering, but I can't hear his bark. The sky glows orange. Fresh
firefighting equipment continues to arrive. Mother steps behind me and
lays a jacket over my shoulders; maybe she says something. On the horizon, dawn begins to break over Staudt. The tires on the trucks in the
forecourt are melting; blisters appear in the paint on the drivers' cabs
and the yellow Caterpillars. We hear thunderclaps, as though a storm
were raging above our heads, and the fire pelts down like thick drops
from a cloudburst. Blazing tarpaulins rise into the air, blow away in the
wind, and plunge down into open fields or the Fries. Cows in the
meadow panic and break through the fence. Mother pulls me away.
Claes and Xaver are sitting on the garden wall, pressing handkerchiefs

*against their faces to protect themselves from the acrid smoke. "We have
to be strong now," she says. "We have to stick close together."*

I nod. I know that the company has filed for bankruptcy.

"Where's Daddy?" Claes asks.

"When I woke up, he was gone."

*The red ball of the sun climbs above the buildings of the town.
Mother says, "We have to be prepared for the worst." Banks of fog lie
on the Fries. He set the fire with his own hands so he wouldn't have to
watch them take his business away from him. He said, "I'd sooner burn
the whole operation to the ground." The tanker was here last week, and
since then not a single forklift truck has moved. I'm cold, so I go back
to the house. Soon we'll move out of it and into what used to be a dairy-
man's cottage on Gerald's farm, where the freshly starched bed linen
smells like chicken droppings. Gertrude says, "You mustn't be afraid,"
and gives me a glass of water. The air smells toxic. I hear Mother
screaming in the hall. Someone's trying to calm her down. She alternates for a while between short shrieks and endlessly drawn-out howls.
Then they break off. She walks into the kitchen, smiling the way she
smiled when he called her a "brainless slut" in public. Maybe he died in
the fire.*

*Darkness above and below me. Although the ship's still moving at a
very slow crawl, the insect's several yards away from me now. It resembles me from head to toe; it's wearing the same pants, the same jacket,
the same shoes. A manlike figure, bent slightly to one side and doubled
up, topples over the railing. As I draw near the floating cushion, it
surges up and opens out into an endless room, and I slip into it. Its walls
are backlit. They're a shimmering, flawless gray, as if they consisted of
gauze stretched taut or frosted glass.*

*Strings of images flicker around me, faster and faster. I'm tearing
along forest paths on Xaver's moped. He has no idea. He'll beat me up*

when he finds out. Ruth's hands are clasping my hips from behind. She screams. Blackberry brambles have scratched her legs. We push the moped into a clump of bushes, sit down in a clearing, and share a can of Coke and some stolen cigarettes. Our naked upper arms touch. She runs away when I try to kiss her . . . If I steal one of Gerald's horses and ride south at the rate of forty kilometers a day, I can reach Italy before winter. Once I'm there, I'll join a troupe of traveling showmen. I'll help them put up their tent and take care of their animals, and I'll live free. I'll do it next spring . . . The dining room window is open. Crows are building a nest in the acorn tree opposite the window. Father gives me his air rifle. He says I'm to try my luck, if I have the nerve. I line up the sights in the center of the circle set just above the mouth of the barrel. The trigger sticks, the rifle shifts, the circle blurs. I take aim again. I feel a slight pain in my shoulder, feathers are suddenly whirling through the air, and the bird describes an arc as it falls to the ground with fluttering wings. I run out of the house. I can't find the bird anywhere around the tree . . . Every night before falling asleep, I'm afraid we're going to be the Baader-Meinhof gang's next victims . . . I get a good report card and receive a reward, fifteen marks, which I secretly use to buy a lottery ticket so I can make Father a loan with part of my winnings . . . Someone smashed the living room window, stole vases, pictures, and all the electrical appliances, knocked over shelves, and devastated cabinets, but failed to find the treasure. Father declares his intention to strangle the guy if he gets his hands on him . . . Grandmother's head on a pillow, her stuffed face, in the cemetery chapel after the funeral. Constant flashes of light, because Uncle Gerald's taking pictures of her . . . I fall off the merry-go-round and split my chin open. A friendly young lady doctor sews it up with three stitches . . . Germany wins the World Cup; the sun shines . . . We're flying our paper kite, higher and higher. No one else's kite is so magnificent. It climbs so high that it's just a small dot in the sky, and the cord breaks. The kite flies off in the direction of the woods . . . I drive excavators on Father's lap. I drive Porsches on Father's lap . . . He pulls a pike almost as big as I am out of the Fries. Mother refuses to cook it. The fish is lying on the kitchen floor. Then it gets kicked under the bench and disappears . . . Muhammad Ali beats Joe Frazier in the middle of the night, in hazy black-and-white . . . The reed-covered gable of our house sticks up over the top of the dike. A flock of sheep. I shovel sand onto Father's stomach. He growls in a friendly way, until I throw some in his face. He grabs my arm so hard it hurts, lifts me onto his shoulders, and runs down to the beach. The tide is at its highest point. He flings me into the sea. I cry. He laughs . . . A woman has died. When you die, if you were a good person, you go to heaven, where it's beautiful for ever and ever. The woman was a good person. Why is everyone crying? . . . Mother sets me on a pony that tramps through sawdust in a circle, with sunken head and blinkers on its eyes. It smells good. She walks beside us and holds me tight . . . Songs that sound friendly. Menacing songs . . . Someone bends down and hands me something colorful. It feels soft and makes new sounds . . . Two blue eyes . . . A dark room; a sweetish smell; the familiar voices sound strange. Cold shivers . . . Sudden brightness . . . Distress . . . The drumming of my heartbeat in clouds of red . . . A first sensation . . .

The walls of the room are gray again. Behind me, a changed body consisting entirely of myself plunges past the ship's hull, turns on its own axis, doing a forward one-and-a-half somersault with a simple twist, and strikes the surface of the water on its belly, sending spray in all directions. It goes under briefly. Its leather jacket has trapped some air, and so it doesn't sink at once; it stays afloat, not far from the ship. When the ship leaves it behind, it gets caught in its wake, is tossed here and there, disappears.

Now the grayness has enveloped me entirely. There's no possibility of looking back. Nor do I feel the need to look back. I stare calmly, *straight ahead, into the wide room, which is neither threatening nor enticing. I'm dry and warm. I'm not sweating. I feel as though my hair's standing on end, but my hair's not connected to me. My skin presents no boundary. I should be afraid one last time. I'm not afraid. My feet, knees, pelvis, shoulders, neck, and head are freed from the connections of anatomy. They grow entangled with one another and form a transparent bubble with skeleton and organs inside. The bubble contracts and expands as though breathing. I'm not standing, not sitting, not lying. The bubble moves forward, uniformly, incessantly, its acceleration barely noticeable. Its surfaces touch the walls without being squeezed or distorted. A soft undertow, a gradual convergence of the lines of perspective. Farther ahead, they bend a few degrees to the left. Beyond the bend, a second room, clearly set apart, though the passageway is open. The second room's not as big as the one I'm floating in; it's like a small chamber, but very high. I can't see into it completely, but I know that the tunnel ends there, in front of a very narrow wall, and I'm surprised. Immediately before I slip into the chamber, all movement comes to a momentary stop. The floor glows a bit more brightly, and a hairline crack appears in it. There's no strength I could set against the power of this attraction. Nor do I have any desire to resist. The bubble lengthens and becomes an elongated, hollow mold. While it inclines itself inexorably, the crack branches out in all directions, opening to a slender, sharp-edged crevice. The blackness inside it is beautiful. There's nothing else.*

A NOTE ABOUT THE AUTHOR

CHRISTOPH PETERS was born in 1966 in Kalkar, Germany. He studied painting from 1988 to 1994 at the National Academy of Arts in Karlsruhe. His debut novel, *Stadt Land Fluß* (1999), was awarded the Aspekte Prize for Literature. In 2001 he published a highly acclaimed collection of short stories called *Kommen und gehen, manchmal bleiben*. Christoph Peters lives in Berlin.